Oaths & Vengeance

Susan Illene

Some people thank God for their inspiration, but I'm reasonably sure he doesn't want credit for this novel.

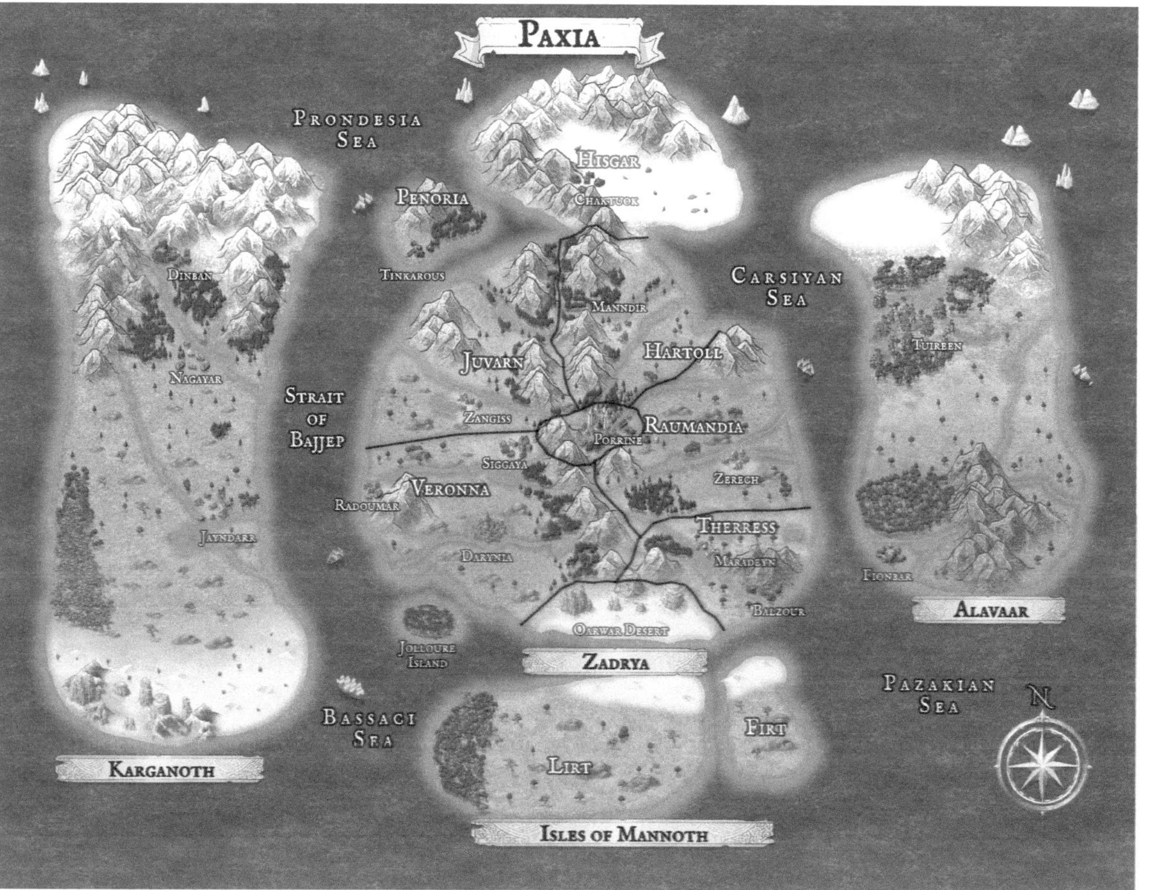

Paxia
Prondesia Sea
Hisgar
Chaktuok
Penoria
Tinkarous
Carsiyan Sea
Manndir
Juvarn
Hartoll
Tuireen
Dinban
Nagayar
Strait of Bajjep
Zangiss
Raumandia
Porrine
Zerech
Veronna
Siggaya
Radoumar
Therress
Jayndarr
Darynia
Maradeyn
Fionbar
Alavaar
Balzour
Oarwar Desert
Jolloure Island
Zadrya
Pazakian Sea
Bassaci Sea
Firt
Karganoth
Lirt
Isles of Mannoth
N

ZADRYA
PRONDESIA SEA
HISGAR
CHAKTUOK
PENORIA
CARSIYAN SEA
TINKAROUS
ANDALAGAR TRIBE
MANNDIR
STRAIT OF BAJJEP
JUVARN
HARTOLL
ANDALAGAR TRIBE
ZANGISS
RAUMANDIA
SIGGAYA
PORRINE
ZERECH
VERONNA
RADOUMAR
THERRESS
MARADEYN
ANDALAGAR TRIBE
IVORY CASTLE
DARYNIA
BALZOUR
ANDALAGAR TRIBE
OARWAR DESERT
JOLLOURE ISLAND

Chapter 1

Aella

Tending my garden took a lot of time and patience, considering half my plants were sentient and temperamental. They couldn't speak, but they expressed their feelings in other ways. The spittlestalk I focused on now was thankfully in a good mood. It rubbed its soft pink petals against my cheeks as I pulled weeds around it. A full flower was larger than a person's head and contained toxic elements inside, so it was a little intimidating when it became affectionate—like being kissed by a venomous snake.

This particular species sprouted a few weeks ago at the start of spring and had grown to two feet tall already. While they usually died at the approach of summer, I could make the blooms last through early fall by strategically placing them in the shadier areas of the garden and keeping the soil moist. Also, they didn't like competition with each other. I had to space each plant about ten feet apart to ensure they didn't vie for the specific nutrients they required from the soil. They could get quite temperamental otherwise and cause trouble in the garden.

If anyone they didn't know or like came close to the spittlestalks, they would spray a thick cloud of poisonous yellow pollen. For elves, they ended up with extreme stomach cramps and severe migraines for several days. A large dose could even kill them. For druids, they would suffer from blurred vision and vertigo. I had no idea why each race reacted differently, but since I was half of both, I got a milder form of all the side effects at once.

It only took an incident when I was seventeen—fifteen years ago—to learn my lesson. Over time, I'd become more adept at tending beautiful yet dangerous plants. There were many safer species that other fae preferred to cultivate, but I liked the challenge, and the garden was my sanctuary.

Creating an inhospitable environment kept visitors from entering my space uninvited. The twelve-foot-high ivory-colored stone walls surrounding it also helped. It was mostly peaceful at the rear end of the castle, aside from occasionally overhearing the kitchen servants on the north side if they were handling outdoor food preparation or grilling.

"Ow!" a male voice said.

I jerked my gaze toward the garden entryway with its high arch and fought a grin. My cousin, Tadeus, had only made it one step inside before two of my crunchertraps—one on each side of the stone path—began snapping at him. One had left a small cut on his hand because he had not retreated quickly. They could extend their stalks just enough to reach the entrance and frighten people away.

Under normal conditions, they only bloomed in the fall. Since it was mid-spring, they shouldn't have been growing at all, but I'd worked out a regimen for the carnivorous plants to keep them thriving year-round. They were among the smartest species in all of *Paxia*, our planet, and made excellent guards. If one earned their loyalty, they wouldn't hesitate to defend them. I tended mine like they were my children.

Tadeus looked nervously at my sentries. He knew better than to come into the garden, but he must have had something important on his mind to make him forget. I noted his coppery-red hair, which he always kept a few inches long, wasn't perfectly groomed like usual and appeared as if he'd raked his fingers through it many times. His ivory skin was flushed with a light sheen of sweat, and his pointed ears were tinged red. He was upset or nervous since either of those emotions would affect him that way.

Tension filled me when I noticed that my cousin wore his forest-green and brown battle garb, a black armor chest plate with a yellow hippogriff emblazoned on its surface, and a full complement of weapons strapped to his body. He was a tall, fit man who appeared even larger now. There was only one reason he'd have dressed that way and rushed to see me.

I rose stiffly to face him. "Is there an attack?"

"Yes." He lifted his ocean blue eyes to mine, gaze softening. "Father demanded that I bring you immediately. We have little time to intercept if we hope to save Palbour."

I exhaled a breath. For the last six months, peace had reigned. Not because the leaders worked out a treaty or because the king intervened. The conflict between *Therress* and *Veronna*—rival lands within our kingdom—had been ongoing for nearly five centuries since Therress rebelled and claimed independence from Veronna. We'd grown tired of either paying higher taxes or sending our soldiers to die in a war with the dark elves that didn't affect us.

We had breaks now and then, such as recently, to recover and rebuild from losses, but this one hadn't lasted as long as I'd hoped. The previous truce endured for almost two years. I should have known we wouldn't make it that long before the greedy Veronnians came after us again. Why couldn't they understand we wanted to be left alone?

"Okay, I'll hurry and change."

He shook his head. "No time. I've already ordered your mount readied, and I know you can protect yourself with your magic. That will be enough since Father always keeps you guarded and away from the fighting anyway."

I supposed it didn't matter if I showed up for a battle with dirt-encrusted fingernails and a loose brown tunic and pants—my standard gardening attire. Everyone else would be filthy soon enough. I only wished I could have had time to change into something with a bit more protection. The clashes had only reached me a couple of times over the years, but I'd thankfully worn the right wardrobe in those instances, or else I would have been severely injured.

Giving the spittlestalk's pink petals a last caress, I rushed from the garden. We moved away from Ivory Castle toward the portal ring near the western wall. The castle received its name more than a thousand years ago when my ancestors built it, along with the rest of the keep, using stones of that light, creamy color from a nearby quarry. Tadeus led me past the training area and barracks at a near run. He was the only male cousin I liked, and he was always kind to me. His older brother was vicious, much like his father, and he enjoyed finding ways to demean me.

Finally, we arrived at a large, open field used for public events and mustering troops. Armed fae and war horses filled most of the trampled space where grass didn't stand a chance to grow. Shock filled me since we only had two hundred stationed here full-time, which meant my uncle must have requisitioned more from Tradain, where we housed the main army.

Tadeus and I worked our way toward the portal gate—also known as a faery ring by outsiders—past rows and rows of elves on their mounts, along with fae of various races on foot. The centaurs in the middle, with their long spears and swishing tails, stood out the most. Everyone wore matching green and black uniforms, dark plate armor with the hippogriff crest, and a complement of weapons and shields strapped to their bodies. All eyes were on me as I passed by them with anxious anticipation filling the air, along with an eye-watering amount of sweat and fresh horse dung.

I hated being the center of attention, but it couldn't be helped. It seemed they'd waited until the last moment to call for me. Why was I not surprised? I was always an afterthought until it was time to leave, and no one else in the keep could channel a portal to a border village and maintain it long enough for several hundred troops to pass.

Tadeus led me to the side of the gate where my bay mare, Astra, waited. He handed me a small pouch of the holmium I needed to work my magic, and I clutched the precious mineral tightly. Through the thin, black cloth, I could feel its hum of energy. Few fae could use the finely ground ore for their magic, but it was a necessity for opening portals.

I mounted my horse, wanting to be ready to leave directly after the regiment. Carefully, I poured a third of the powder onto my palm before pocketing the bag. Drawing a deep breath, I began chanting and extended my hand toward the dark silver ring that stood twice as high as me on my mare. Ivory-colored support stones held it upright. Seventeen dark gray algodonite stones about the size of my palm were evenly spaced around the circle, each displaying a different symbol carved into their flat surface.

Directing my magic with a stream of golden light, the soft beam touched the five relevant ones in a sequence that would initiate a link to Palbour. Within my palm, the powder dissolved as I began to channel and form a connection. If I measured it right, only a few grains would remain to brush away once I finished.

When I started using my gift as an adolescent, it took me several minutes to open a portal to border villages two hundred or more miles away. Now, it only took me ten seconds. My power had grown considerably since it first developed nearly twenty years ago. It also helped that I had a lot of practice and had become the best in the realm at doing it. Only a few people I trusted knew exactly how good I'd become. I kept that a secret, or else my family would use me in ways that would stain my soul.

The air popped as the massive ring filled with a shimmering blue light. The width was twenty feet at the center, allowing four to five mounted soldiers to pass through at a time. My uncle Morgunn, the Lord of Therress, sat atop his smoky black stallion and began shouting orders for the lead troops to depart. His eldest son, Ulmar, sat mounted next to him with a calculating look on his face. That was his most common expression and didn't necessarily mean anything.

As soon as the first riders—all elves—entered the ring, they disappeared. The next group went through a few seconds later. Everyone else followed, departing in a steady progression with satyrs and then foot soldiers at the end. The last section consisted of multiple races, so there were quite a few height variances and different musculatures among them. The shortest ones—dwarves—formed the rear line, primarily used for defense and evacuating the wounded.

The spell drained me but at a slow trickle. For this one, at the distance I bridged, I could keep it open far longer than it would take for three hundred and twenty soldiers and horses to pass.

As the line of fae troops came near the end, Lord Therress gave me a brief scowl. What had I done to annoy him this time? Ulmar had a pleased glint in his eyes that said he knew and couldn't wait for me to find out. That didn't bode well.

"Why are they looking at me like that?" I asked Tadeus in a whisper, no longer needing to chant now that my magic held steady.

He looked at me apologetically. "From what I heard this morning, Father is arranging a betrothal for you. I don't know who he's chosen, but my brother bragged that you'll hate him and likely protest."

Several available men were within my uncle's close circle of allies and friends, but none were remotely appealing. He tended to affiliate with cruel, greedy types who enjoyed inflicting pain on others. A shudder ran through me. "I'll find a way out of it."

"You know he won't give you a choice." Tadeus gripped his reins tightly. "If I knew how to help, I would, but he never listens to me."

True, since he barely tolerated his youngest son. "It's okay. Thanks for the thought."

"Of course."

My younger cousin and I were the last to go behind my uncle and Ulmar, so the portal closed behind us. Transport wasn't quite instant, but since the distance wasn't too far, it only took a few seconds to appear on the other side. Despite the dizzying colors as we moved lightning fast, it didn't affect us or our mounts. It was only on the first few occasions that people and animals experienced a bit of vertigo, but the transition was so smooth that everyone quickly grew accustomed to it.

Tadeus and I guided our mounts from the ring. My uncle, his eldest son, and his three captains shouted orders at the troops ahead of us. They'd moved out of the way of the ring to allow us room. We were at the top of a hill covered in trampled blue-green grass, and below in the valley, less than a mile away, lay the village of Palbour.

It wasn't large and only had five hundred residents, but we had to protect those people. Just because I didn't have any love for my uncle didn't mean I wouldn't do anything for our people, which he knew very well.

Veronna's army wouldn't hesitate to burn everything to the ground. They had done it in the past when our Therressian troops didn't intercept them in time, but that problem had stopped since my uncle began using me to move his soldiers quickly. Our other four portal channelers could only funnel their magic for five to fifteen minutes to reach this distance, depending on their power level, which didn't allow as many soldiers to get through. I couldn't remember the last time I'd hit my limit, but it had been a few years.

I became a valuable asset when I developed my abilities and proved stronger than average. Lord Morgunn had pushed me hard to develop my talent even before I lost my father and subsequently moved into Ivory Castle with his family.

Tadeus gave me a nod. "See you when this is over."

"Take care," I said, forcing myself to give him an encouraging smile. He was an excellent fighter, no matter what his father said. The real trouble was that he killed cleanly and not cruelly like his older brother. I couldn't figure out how they came from the same parents.

He nudged his horse into a gallop and joined the rest of the forces ahead.

In the distance, I scanned the Sobaryan Mountain range that cut directly through most of the *Realm of Zadrya*, our kingdom, and defined some of the land borders. The violet peaks were so high that hazy clouds obscured them. Veronna lay on the other side, but they didn't have a strong portal opener like me. Whenever they wanted to attack us, they had to use one of three passes between us and make it past the border sentries that we kept stationed in camps up top.

Our people could see them long before they reached the top of the trails, and they usually sent a warning to us through *sebeskas*—birds that had cerulean feathers tipped in black with white underbellies. Then, we could deploy forces quickly to intercept them before they reached the base of the mountains. Something stopped those sentries this time. Veronnian forces must have used a new magic spell on them, and we didn't have a counter for it yet since I couldn't think of any other reason for the lack of early warning.

Each border town close to a pass also maintained an observation point near the foot of the mountains to watch for adversary troop movement and receive alerts from those above. I assumed the ground tower was the one to contact my uncle's top military commander. Their later warning meant we couldn't intercept in time, and they'd already begun attacking the village when we arrived. Smoke rose from where several buildings burned, and faint screams reached our distant position, filling me with dread.

My vision was good, but I had to squint to catch sight of the Veronnian forces. They were almost as numerous as ours. Therressian captains led their soldiers, racing to meet the enemy on the outskirts of town. They needed to move quickly if they hoped to keep the battle from going deeper into the village and burning more homes. I could no longer make out my uncle in the throng, but I spotted each of my cousins on opposite flanks.

One soldier stayed behind with me. While I had some training, I was too valuable to risk sending into the fight. Still, I nudged Astra toward a closer hill rise for a better look. It was too difficult to observe much near the portal ring.

Off to the north, I noted a sizeable section of dry, withered land that stood out from the surrounding blue-green grass. I hadn't visited Palbour in nearly five years, but there had been flourishing crops in that area before. It appeared the ever-spreading blight had also made its way to this part of Therress. The farms to the south of the village continued to thrive, but for how long? The amount of food we produced declined with each passing year, which worried me deeply. We had no way to stop it.

I forced my attention back to the immediate threat. My guard and I had reached the most ideal point to observe the battle, and my uncle's forces had just clashed with our enemy. Swords rang as soldiers attacked each other, and flashes of magic in various forms and colors flew across the ranks. Some would blind opponents, others would cause pain, and still more would cause various injuries or afflictions. Fae battles were merciless and gruesome. We were on higher ground, which gave us a clear view of the terrible things they did to each other.

Normally, our army would have used offensive range magic first, but there was no time to prepare. Instead, it came down to a close-quarter battle in which our enemy excelled.

One man stood out on a large dapple-gray mount. His hair was a brindled mixture of brown and onyx black, sunlight glinting from the strands hanging over the sides of his face. His shoulders were broad. I knew that for certain because, unlike everyone else on the battlefield, he only wore light armor without the heavy metal plates most preferred for protection. His olive and black Veronnian army uniform was snug, molding around his muscular build. I wished I could see the details of his face, but the distance was too great for that.

He raised his arms toward the Therressian frontline, fingers outstretched. I watched in horror as six of our foot soldiers lifted into the air, kicking their feet but finding no purchase. With a twist of his hands, their heads spun clockwise until their necks cracked. They fell to the ground in a heap, dead before impact.

I gasped, realizing who he must be. "Is that Lord Gannon's second son, Darrow?"

"It is." My guard's lips thinned. "It's been years since we last faced him, and it's bad news for us that he's here today."

"He'll decimate us at the rate he can kill," I whispered, a chill running down my spine.

The soldier's eyes reflected the same anxiety I felt. "It appears that way."

Darrow was his father's second son from a subsequent marriage after his first wife died in childbirth. He was known to be powerful and ruthless on the battlefield. The fact that he was half dark elf made him especially dangerous because they weren't known for compassion or mercy. He and his twin sister had been the products of a failed peace treaty agreement between our realm, Zadrya, and *Karganoth*—the realm of the dark elves that lay across the sea to the west.

I recalled that he had fought in battles against us during the first few years I'd begun opening portals. The last time I could remember seeing him was over a decade ago, when I was in my early twenties. He'd been a ruthless killer even back then, but couldn't break that many men simultaneously before. Like most fae, he would continue growing stronger for a few more years until he reached fifty and peaked.

I had family and friends out there who would die if this elf targeted them. No one on our side had magic that could counteract Darrow's without getting too close, but of course, he was surrounded by elite soldiers so that he could do his dirty work without interference.

A risky idea occurred to me. There was something I could do if I were brave enough, and right now, I needed to push past my usually passive role. Too many people would die if I didn't.

When a high fae's magic first appeared as an adolescent, they could only perform lesser spells that were a prelude to something bigger that would develop over the coming year. I started with wind and light power, which later combined to form portal channeling. Although I rarely had cause to use those, I did practice them since they worked well as a defense when I needed them, especially wind.

Darrow was lifting another handful of our soldiers into the air. If I didn't hit him immediately, they'd die in the next few moments. I let go of Astra's reins and raised my hands, focusing on the half-light/half-dark elf, and pulled the air around me. In a streamlined burst, I sent it straight at him.

Just as he began to twist his hands to kill the soldiers, it struck him full in the chest. He went flying backward off his horse. The Therressian soldiers he'd targeted next dropped to the ground at the same time—shaken but alive. Darrow landed on his butt ten feet behind his mount and skidded to a stop in a plume of dust.

I grinned, pleased that years of weekly practice with my wind power had finally paid off. That was far more satisfying than directing it at leaves and other inanimate objects. I had used it in self-defense a time or two, but never at such a distance.

"Well done, my lady," my guard said, giving me a respectful nod. "That certainly distracted him and gave our people a chance."

"Thank you."

We watched with rapt attention as Darrow slowly rose to his feet and dusted off his uniform. I still couldn't make out his features, but his rigid body language told me he was not pleased with what I'd done. He ran his gaze around his surroundings until it eventually fell on me. I waved and blew him a kiss.

Darrow lifted one arm toward me, and a moment later, I rose off my horse to hover a few feet above my mount. Shock filled me. I'd never dreamed he could extend his magic so far, but I couldn't do anything to stop him. My heart raced as he slowly brought me forward like he had strings pulling me.

My guard's voice sounded panicked as I floated away from Astra and him. "Lady Aella? Are you alright? What can I do?"

"I...uh," I began.

My braid lifted and wrapped around my head, gagging my mouth. The floral taste of my cleanser coated my tongue. My locks stretched taut, pulling at my scalp enough to cause discomfort but not quite pain. With all my limbs immobilized, I couldn't free myself. Did he seriously muzzle me with my own hair? Lord Gannon's son was playing with me in the middle of a battle like I was a toy, but I couldn't let him get away with it without a response.

I forced myself to calm down and think. Darrow hadn't gripped my body so tightly that I couldn't breathe or make minute movements. Slowly spreading my fingers, I gathered the surrounding air once more. After I gained enough, I hit him with a burst of wind again. It didn't slam into him as hard as the first time, but it did send him stumbling back. The hold on me evaporated. I dropped to the ground, knees buckling, and my breath nearly knocked from me. At least nothing was broken.

"It's okay," I said, hands trembling as I straightened. "He had me for a moment there."

"Perhaps you shouldn't draw his attention again," my guard advised.

I cleared my throat, hoping no one else saw what happened. "Yeah. I think that was more than enough distraction."

I got back onto my horse and looked for my nemesis. Darrow also sat on his mount again and stared in my direction. It was hard to tell his expression, but I couldn't miss the kiss he blew toward me, especially since I felt the lightest touch on my cheek. Our displays of power had definitely been an amusing game to him. I worried he'd try something else as he continued to stare at me, but just then, my uncle's forces broke through his ranks. My diversion had worked.

Darrow had to shift his focus to defending himself and forgetting about me. He sent the first few Therressian soldiers flying away, but after that, he drew his sword and slashed at his opponents. I watched with rapt attention at how brutally efficient he was, even without magic. It would have been awe-inspiring if he hadn't been wounding and killing our forces.

A half-hour passed, with numerous soldiers on both sides dead and dozens more wounded. Veronna's regiment finally called for a retreat. They rushed toward the mountain pass half a mile behind them, using the horses who'd lost their riders to carry their dead and wounded. We'd have to deliver any remaining bodies they hadn't quickly grabbed to our mutual border later—a strict law enforced by Zadrya's king.

Lord Morgunn finally reappeared on the right side of the battlefield. I always lost track of him during the fighting, but now he glared at our enemies' backs, likely considering whether to follow. Then, he took in the state of his troops. If he saw things the way I did, he had to realize this was one of the deadliest battles we'd faced in years. He needed to take care of his injured soldiers so they could live to fight another day. Attempting to continue the fight in the mountain pass would be lunacy, especially with Darrow present.

My uncle shouted an order I couldn't make out from my position. When I noticed everyone sheathing their weapons, I breathed a sigh of relief. He'd chosen not to pursue the enemy. I prayed to the nameless ones that I didn't have to see the half-dark elf across a battlefield ever again—once had been enough.

A short while later, Lord Morgunn rode his horse up to mine. "What were you thinking, Aella? Darrow could have killed you and left us without a strong portal opener. He's well aware you are an asset to us."

Of course, I didn't matter personally, but losing the use of my abilities would be tragic.

"He didn't kill me, and I kept him distracted long enough for you to break his ranks," I said, meeting his gaze. It was a rare moment of defiance since I tried not to draw my uncle's wrath too often. He always made me regret it.

"That's the only reason I won't punish you this time." He pulled his horse alongside Astra. "But if you do it again, you'll find your magic bound for the next month."

I was thirty-two years old, but under fae law, he could still treat me like a child. Highborn females had few rights. It didn't matter to Lord Morgunn that if I hadn't interfered, he and all his troops would likely be dead right now.

He refused to acknowledge that I had been the one to take on the most powerful elf on the battlefield and lived to tell the tale. Of course, I couldn't imagine why Darrow didn't kill me unless perhaps I was too far away, or maybe he'd intended to draw out my death but became distracted when the fighting drew too close to him. It was impossible to say. I was only glad that my rare show of overt courage helped and didn't end in my death.

"Of course, my lord." I lowered my gaze, playing the game I'd been forced to learn from an early age. "It won't happen again."

His stern gaze burned into me. "See that it doesn't. Now, get the portal open. We have dead and wounded to transport."

Chapter 2

Aella

I sat in my chambers in comfortable silence, reading. My room was small compared to most, with ivory-colored stone walls typical of the entire castle and a single burgundy and gold rug to take the chill from the floor and add a little color. There was just enough space for a small bed, wardrobe, chest, and nightstand.

One side had a fireplace, so nothing could be put in front of it except a footstool. I was grateful the window caught the evening light perfectly, so at least I could curl up and read romantic tales without needing a fae lantern. It also afforded a perfect view of my garden below. I was the only one with a direct line of sight to it, and it was one of the few kindnesses my uncle had ever done for me since I moved here at fourteen years old.

I'd spent well over half my life here now. My father, who was the general of the Therressian army at the time, had died nineteen years ago in one of the many battles against the Veronnians. Lord Gannon had killed him with fire magic that burned most of his body so severely that I'd only been able to identify him by a birthmark on his ankle where the flames had missed. I'd had nightmares for months after seeing him that way.

My mother—the one who'd given me my druid half—had passed a year and a half before him. One of her greatest passions was searching for the *Naforya Fountain*, a vital artifact our world lost more than six centuries ago. We desperately needed it before circumstances became even worse on our planet as the land slowly died. While on a trip to the Oarwar desert in the south, looking for answers, one of the powerful sand worms living there attacked her and her five traveling companions. They weren't like the ones we might find in gardens, but rather, their bodies were nearly as wide as a small cottage, and they could grow to a hundred feet long.

She'd known it was dangerous, but she'd been desperate to find the fountain. My mother and three of her companions died battling the creature, with only two others surviving. They were the ones to bring us news of her demise.

With my brother falling in battle when I was only eight—killed by Lord Gannon's firstborn son and heir, Hagon—I only had my older sister, Priyya, remaining. She'd fled for Alavaar—the druid continent to the east—right after our mother passed because she'd wanted nothing to do with the conflicts here and had a passion for dragons. Her healing magic for the beasts complemented being a caretaker for them. That was the only continent they lived on these days after too many died assisting fae in the early wars after we arrived two millennia ago. I usually visited Priyya once a month when my uncle allowed it, and I loved seeing them.

A knock sounded at my door.

I set my book down and moved to answer it, finding the castle healer on the other side. Briauna was an older elf who'd seen nearly two centuries. It was difficult to say how much longer she might live since our kind could survive anywhere between a hundred and fifty and two hundred fifty years old. Her long, white hair was pulled back into a bun, wrinkles lined her features, and she stooped a little in her blue muslin dress. I noted she was wringing her hands.

"What is it?" I asked.

She drew in a deep breath, sorrow in her blue gaze. "Rynn has not improved from the faebor fever. In fact, she's looking worse tonight. I'd hoped she'd have improved by now, but this makes the third full day."

My throat tightened. Every fae got the faebor fever sometime between the ages of eleven and thirteen when their magic first emerged within their body. The illness was a process that changed us so we could handle our new power, but unfortunately, a third of adolescents didn't survive. Anyone who didn't begin to improve by the end of the third day was guaranteed to die within two weeks in a painful, brutal fashion.

Like me, Rynn was an orphan. Her parents had died while on a sea voyage five years ago by one of the large serpents that live within the waters, so she had also been placed under our uncle's guardianship. Her mother was his younger sister.

Though Lord Morgunn did his duty by taking us into his home as young, unwedded female relatives, he hardly paid attention to Rynn, and he only cared about me because of what I could do with my magic. We were bound to him until we got married and became the property of our husbands, per fae law concerning highborn ladies.

"I want to see her now," I said, smoothing my skirt.

I wore one of my nicer ankle-length gowns with bell sleeves, a cinched waist, and a scooped neck top that revealed a hint of cleavage. I'd planned to wear it to dinner that would be ready in an hour, but it didn't matter now. I needed to visit my cousin. She'd already suffered so much in the twelve years of her life, and now this?

Briauna led me down the corridor to the central stairs. We took them up to the third floor and headed straight for Rynn's room down the hall on the right. Like me, she had small chambers that gave her just enough space to meet her basic needs. Unlike me, she had brought more of her personal belongings when she came here, so her room was full of dolls, figurines, and toys.

Her parents had been merchants who exchanged goods with other realms across the world and had acquired gifts for her from many places before they passed away. She'd kept everything, whereas I'd only brought what could fit in a chest and held some importance because so much served as painful reminders of happier times. My parents had been strict, but they had loved their children and each other.

I moved closer to her bed and sucked in a breath. Her ivory skin was flushed bright red, and her blue eyes were glassy with fever. Even Rynn's beautiful, wavy auburn hair had lost its luster and was plastered to her head and pillow from sweat.

"Hey, sweet girl," I said, attempting a gentle smile.

While I'd seen her a couple of times a year when her parents brought her to visit, we'd become especially close after she moved into the castle. In a way, she felt more like a younger sister, and I'd grown to love her deeply. It was all I could do not to cry at seeing her this way.

Briauna had told me Rynn came down with the fever when I returned from the battle at Palbour a few days ago, but I'd thought she would make it just fine. She had always been so energetic and full of life. How could she not? I'd even sat with her that night to speculate what kind of magic she'd develop. Sometimes, it was hereditary, but at other times, gifts appeared that no one in that line had seen in centuries. My portal channeling was an example of that.

"Aella," she whispered my name. "Sorry, I'm not going to make it."

I shook my head and drew strands of hair from her face. "Don't say that. Maybe you'll be better tomorrow, and we're only off on the timing."

It was a faint hope, but it had been known to happen a time or two—only never with Briauna attending the afflicted. She was the best healer in all Therress. If she said Rynn wouldn't make it, she wouldn't.

"Can I get some water?" my cousin asked, glancing at her nightstand where a full cup sat.

"Of course."

I helped her sit up and brought the drink to her lips. From the scent, Briauna had added a few herbs. Likely things that would reduce Rynn's discomfort and help her sleep more easily. There was little to be done aside from that.

As I laid her back down after finishing, I noticed her fingertips were beginning to darken, which was also a sign she wouldn't survive. That blackness would slowly spread from her extremities to the rest of her body. When it reached her heart, that would be the end. Fae were generally healthy, and we healed fast, but nothing could stop the faebor fever.

During times like these, I dearly wished my mother had succeeded in finding the Naforya Fountain. Then, children like Rynn would have access to a cure and wouldn't be forced to suffer like this. In some families, they would even poison the children before they reached the final, most painful stages to spare them the agony. I'd heard my uncle did that with his third son. That happened when I was only three years old, so I didn't remember it.

What if he killed Rynn once he heard the news? He might not wait until she was truly in bad shape and finish her early. My gaze shot to Briauna. "You can't tell Lord Morgunn."

"I haven't said anything yet." She heaved a sigh. "But I can't keep it from him for much longer, or you know he'll be angry. Not unless..."

I frowned. "Unless what?"

"We'll speak of it later," she said in a curt tone.

I wondered what she meant, but knew I'd have to wait. Instead, I continued talking to my cousin until her eyelids drooped, and she fell into a deep sleep. Only twenty minutes had passed since I entered her room, so she hadn't lasted long. Despair filled me as Briauna followed me out the door.

"Your room," she whispered, gesturing for me to take the lead.

I couldn't imagine what she planned to tell me, but I did as she requested. Once we were inside my chambers, she gingerly sat on the window seat, and I took the stool in front of the fire. It still blazed with heat from when I'd stoked it earlier while reading. Springtime brought warm temperatures during the day, but in the evenings, it cooled quickly.

"So, what did you mean by *unless*?" I asked.

Briauna smoothed her skirt. "You know there is no cure for the fever, and there's nothing I can do to make it much easier on Rynn. But...there is one person who might be able to help her."

"What?" I sat up straighter. "Why have I never heard of this before?"

"Because that person is my sister, and her abilities are a closely guarded secret."

Everyone knew she had an older sibling who left Therress more than a century and a half ago to marry an elf she fell for while visiting the king's court. Unfortunately, he was Lord Gannon's uncle in Veronna. Since our lands were mortal enemies, the two sisters rarely found a chance to see each other.

"Do you even know where she lives now?" I asked.

She shook her head. "We lost touch a few decades ago. I visited her when her husband passed, but she was grieving and wanted to be alone, so I didn't stay long.

There is one person she was clearly close to then, and rumor has it he still looks after her when he's able."

I frowned. "Who?"

"Her great nephew, Darrow."

I cursed under my breath. "Even under the best circumstances, he'll never agree to speak to me peacefully, certainly not after our encounter a few days ago."

"I thought you said you blew kisses at each other. It can't be that bad if you managed such a thing on a battlefield," she said with amusement in her eyes.

When I returned after the battle, I'd told her and Rynn all about our exchanging magical attacks. Since I was unharmed, we'd had a good laugh.

"We were toying with each other, not exchanging love letters."

She nodded. "True, but if you could talk him into cooperating somehow, he could take you to my sister. Her greatest talent is healing incurable ailments, including faebor fever. I saw her do it several times myself before she left with her husband."

"How have I never heard of this before?" It seemed like something everyone would know.

She rubbed her face. "Doing such work exacts a terrible price. It's very hard on her body and requires rest for a week afterward. Her husband was protective and only allowed her to heal those who were truly deserving and would keep the secret. My family handled it the same way before that."

My mind raced. There was a real way to cure Rynn out there, but how could I even take advantage of it? In what world would Darrow ever listen to me, much less agree to help? The very thought of facing the half-dark elf with his telekinetic powers was daunting. The chances of him going along with the plan were nearly as impossible as curing my cousin in some other way. He was a cold-blooded killer who'd snapped six soldiers' necks so easily that he must lack a soul.

"He'll never cooperate," I said, a tear falling down my cheek. There were very few things I could count as good in my life, but Rynn was one of them.

Briauna stood and came over to me. "Maybe, maybe not. He is my sister's favorite relative and the only person she tolerates, so there must be something redeemable about him. It's up to you if you want to take the chance for your cousin."

Hopelessness filled me. I skirted rules now and then, but I avoided doing anything that might border on treason. During my first few years at the castle, I'd learned the hard way what would happen if I made my uncle angry. Sneaking off to meet Darrow would definitely earn me severe punishment if I were caught.

The healer patted my head. "It's a lot to consider. I'll give you two days to decide what to do before I must inform Lord Morgunn."

I understood she didn't want to anger him, either. "Thank you. I'll let you know by then."

Chapter 3

Aella

I'd barely started working on my garden the following day when a servant in a crisp black uniform appeared at the archway entrance. Parzival cleared his throat, unwilling to risk the ire of my plants. Ten years ago, a new groundskeeper from a distant village had made the mistake of entering my sanctuary without knowing the dangers. He'd brushed against one of the crunchertraps and lost a chunk of his thigh.

As he'd howled in pain, the other one snapped at his rear end. I'd heard the screams from my room above and looked out my window to find several species of my flora had de-rooted to chase the poor man. It'd taken me an hour to wrestle them back into their places. Once blood spilled within the garden walls, some of my plants became opportunistic and vicious.

I'd worried my uncle would be angry about his new groundskeeper getting maimed, but I should have known better. He found it amusing. It was one of the rare times he'd even seemed pleased with me, which nearly made me want to do away with the whole garden, but I loved it too much and couldn't do that. I'd brought Briauna to heal the injured man.

Feeling horrible about the incident, we found him safer employment in a location far from here. Ever since, though, no one had dared enter the walled enclosure without my permission. That was exactly the way I wanted it.

"Yes?" I asked, setting my trimming shears down.

The tractvine I was tending primarily grew underground as it should, but the coiled top with a single yellow bloom could take over the garden if I didn't keep it under control. If anyone upset it, the vines under the soil would shoot out and wrap around a person's body, squeezing them to death and then slowly consuming them like a snake. All the while, it secreted toxins to break down the body faster.

It was a gruesome way to go. The plant typically grew in the thickest forests to the north and wasn't easy to acquire. Thankfully, I had a natural affinity for flora, so I could coax the seedlings to leave their home. I also offered mice to keep them busy and content during transport.

"Lord Morgunn has requested your presence in his office." The stuffy butler looked me up and down scornfully. "I advise you to wash and change into something presentable first, but do hurry. He does not wish to be kept waiting long."

This was one elf I wouldn't have minded tossing into my garden to feed my plants. Parzival wasn't only a butler but also a close confidant to my uncle. More than once over the years, he'd caught me doing something "questionable" and snitched on me. Lord Morgunn was especially cruel in his punishment if his favorite servant told him about the offense.

One time, when I was fifteen, Parzival caught me sneaking out of my room at night. He had my ankle chained to a tree in the northeast orchard. The whole night, I had to fend off vicious night creatures by throwing stones and using my wind magic, which I wasn't very adept at using then. While most fae parents used creative punishments to keep their offspring in line, my uncle was brutal.

"I'll hurry," I said, taking the trimmers to a lock box at the far end of the garden.

If I left them out, some of the plants couldn't be trusted, and bad things might happen to my passive varieties that couldn't move or fight back. I didn't need another massacre to clean up after leaving out the shears last time.

Parzival was already gone when I exited the garden and rushed to my chambers. I had exactly three dinner gowns, four day dresses, and two plain ones for horseback riding and other outdoor activities. All my ball gowns and garments for special events were stored elsewhere and tailored specifically for each affair since my uncle wouldn't want to appear cheap beyond our household. Everything else I owned was pants and tunics for gardening or battle attire.

Most high-born elf ladies had a lot more formal wear, but my uncle hated spending any more funds on me than necessary. He'd taken most of my parents' estate for himself, so my sister and I only received a thousand gold coins each, a few of their belongings, and none of the property. Most of that inheritance was gone, supplementing my wardrobe and purchasing plant supplies and seeds for my garden. I'd negotiated a small stipend for my portal opening services, but it barely covered any basic needs that my uncle wouldn't handle, so I couldn't save much.

I chose a pear-green day gown and quickly donned it after washing my face and hands. Uncle Morgunn tended to treat me kinder when I wore it since he liked the color. The style was the latest fashion, hugging my slim figure, and had intricate lace across the bodice and sleeve cuffs. It was one of the few regular dresses he'd ever commissioned. I initially wore it when a few highborn guests came to visit from Raumandia, which was why he'd been willing to finance it. The fabric matched my eyes, which was the part I liked the most.

After putting on matching slippers, I hurried downstairs to the lord's office near the castle entrance. He answered at the first knock, beckoning me inside.

My uncle stood behind his desk, wearing a dark blue doublet and pants with a white undershirt. The outfit would have looked good on some men, but he had a large oval torso that made his attire less flattering than he realized. He also kept his dark red hair cut short, making it less evident that it was thinning. As for his facial features, they could only be described as stern and uncompromising. Today, his ice-blue eyes reflected an especially malicious glint.

I took two steps into the room before freezing at the sight of a hawk-nosed elf with oily brown hair he kept slicked back. He leaned against a bookshelf next to the window. His gaze was cold and devoid of humanity, but as he studied me, a lecherous expression took over his pale features.

Something about him sent my internal alarm bells ringing and turned my stomach. I'd seen him around a few times in recent years—he was hard to forget—but I'd never done more than exchange stilted pleasantries.

"I believe you've met Baron Elgord," my uncle said.

"Yes." I forced myself to take a few steps forward and tried very hard not to show my disgust. "He oversees the Balzour mines, I believe."

The ones that produced the holmium mineral I needed to open portals. I'd never been allowed near the place because my uncle didn't want me tempted to steal the ore and be able to "traipse across the continent" without his knowledge or consent—his words, not mine. That was exactly why he didn't know I saved some of the dust he allotted me for opening portals each time, and my sister acquired some secretly for me as well. I'd been *traipsing* across the continent for over a decade since I grew powerful enough.

Lord Morgunn nodded, pleased. "Yes, that is right. I have been negotiating a betrothal contract between Baron Elgord and you. All that is left is to request permission from the king."

Shock and horror twisted my gut. I managed to keep my face blank thanks to years of practice, but inside, I was screaming at the top of my lungs. He couldn't do this to me! This elf was a weasel and known for harassing female servants in vulgar ways. I could never consider him a suitable husband. Technically, my uncle was my guardian and could pressure me to marry anyone he wanted, but how could he have possibly chosen this man? Did he have any concern for my well-being at all?

Drawing a deep breath, I formulated my argument. "That is kind of you, my lord, but I had hoped to choose a husband myself."

In fact, that had always been my dream. Find a nice, decent-looking man who truly loved me. We would have a beautiful wedding with me in the most gorgeous gown, and we'd be devoted to making each other happy for the rest of our lives. I especially looked forward to having children with my dream husband.

We would have a lovely home where there was a lot of love and laughter. Sure, my fantasies might be a little unrealistic, but that dream got me through some dark days in my life so far. Since I'd reached adulthood, I'd searched for that elusive man but had yet to find him. Even if it was unlikely, I wasn't ready to give up.

My uncle laughed. "Oh, Aella, you were never going to choose for yourself. If not for your useful portal abilities, I would have married you off years ago rather than continue with your upkeep here."

"What changed your mind now?" I asked, keeping my tone neutral.

He gestured at Barron Elgord. "By my estimation, you should be strong enough at this point to open more than one portal back-to-back if the distance isn't too great, so no need for you to remain here any longer. The baron has also assured me he'll keep a firm hand on you, and your services will still be available whenever Therress needs you."

Firm hand? What was that supposed to mean other than he might be more abusive than Lord Morgunn? Elves lived long lives, and I was only thirty-two years old. As I recalled, he was twenty years older. That was an awfully long time to tolerate someone in marriage when there was no hope of divorce. The king could grant annulments under a few rare circumstances, but those involved certain health conditions, great acts of betrayal, or the discovery of a true mate. Barron Elgord would take care to avoid such issues. Never mind that my uncle had apparently figured out I was somewhat stronger than I let on, so that was a problem I'd have to worry about as well. At least he didn't know the full depth of my powers.

My hands began to tremble, and I clasped them behind my back. "I have no say at all?"

"No," he said firmly, then stood. "I will leave to let you two get to know each other better for a few minutes. Lord Elgord and I must spend the next week traveling on official business, but when we return, we'll petition the king for his approval. Our plan is to hold the wedding in early summer. Won't that be lovely?"

That was less than two months away.

I barely managed to nod my head. In reality, I wanted to scream at him that this was wrong, but if I did, the punishment would be severe. I also knew nothing I said or did would change his mind. He'd wed me to this sick man to break what spirit I had left.

Even running away wasn't an option with the curse mark my uncle had placed on the back of my neck. It was what kept me from escaping this place beyond brief visits elsewhere, such as seeing my sister or exploring a distant village. If I intended to leave Therress permanently, my uncle would know as soon as I acted on it, and I'd fall into an instant deep sleep while he collected my comatose body and placed me in confinement.

I knew since I'd tried once about six years before Rynn came to us. It was all I could do to block the memories of the horrible weeks that followed. How my uncle had used solitary confinement, lack of food, days of darkness, and a whip to punish me.

The iron cuff I'd worn during that time ensured there was no way to fight back or escape. By the end, I was crying and begging for mercy—anything to end the punishment. He gloated about it for months. How pathetic I'd been, but the gods help me if I showed more than a hint of backbone at any other time. He wanted me strong, but never against him.

Every time I left now, sometimes without his permission, I had to keep it in the forefront of my mind that I would return soon so he wouldn't discover I'd gone. For all that I wanted to avoid a punishment that extreme again, I tried to defy him in small ways.

Visiting distant places for a few hours was my little rebellion. He had no idea of the remote portals I'd accessed or how I'd found a book in the Royal Court of Porrine library that gave me the rune sequences for dozens of locations all over Zadrya and some to the other three realms on Paxia. My uncle would use that knowledge to further his quest for power and dominance over his adversaries. The only portals I opened for him were the ones where he knew the sequence.

My heart rate picked up as Lord Morgunn left, closing his office door firmly behind him. Elgord gave me a salacious smile that made me ill. I forced myself to stand my ground as he moved closer, stopping two feet before me.

"I've been watching you for some time now, you know," he said.

I stayed silent as he picked up my blonde braid and twisted it in his hand. "Such beautiful, golden hair with so many shades. I can imagine what it will look like when it's loose and spread across my pillows."

"What if that's not what I want?" I asked, managing to keep my voice even and steady by some miracle. My stomach threatened to revolt at his close proximity.

Elgord laughed. "My lady, the first lesson I will teach you is that your wants matter little. Those of us in power are the ones who always win."

I couldn't help it. The way he spoke infuriated me, and I couldn't hide my disgust for him. "Maybe my uncle will force me to marry you, but I'll never submit."

The baron grabbed me, wrapping his fingers tightly around my upper arms, and pulled me close. He was stronger than expected, considering his lean physique. I tried to wriggle out of his hold, but his grip was too tight. His face was inches from mine so I could smell his sour breath.

"Go ahead and fight me. I'll enjoy every moment of it, but you will end up in my bed with your naked thighs splayed wide open, and you'll take me inside you however many times a day I want. Your belly will swell time and time again with my children until you have forgotten what it was ever like to be free of me." He shook me. "Understand?"

I ground my teeth, fighting tears. "No."

He leaned down and forced his lips upon mine, attempting to open my mouth. I kept them firmly shut, so I ended up with his slobber on me. No matter how much I tried to pull away, it was impossible, and using my magic to force him away would land me in all kinds of trouble. Only when he got tired of the kiss did he let go.

There was rage in his eyes. "You'll learn, Aella, soon enough. Enjoy your freedom while you can because there will be no escape once I've got you. That curse mark on you...your uncle will transfer that to me as well."

My eyes rounded in horror that he knew about it.

"No," I whispered.

He sneered. "Oh, yes."

Fear like nothing I'd ever known filled my gut. The worst, darkest, bleakest future lay before me, and I could do nothing to stop it. I grew light-headed. With Elgord's hawkish face swimming before me, I spun around and ran from the room. He didn't stop me, but his terrible laugh carried down the hall as I made my escape.

Chapter 4

Aella

The next morning, I stood outside in the front courtyard and saw my uncle and Baron Elgord off for their journey. My future betrothed forced a kiss on my cheek before mounting his horse. I couldn't wait until he left so I could scrub my face. They would be going on a journey to inspect villages and manors throughout Therress, so they didn't require a portal. Surveying the roads and bridges along the way was part of their agenda.

Lord Morgunn was horrible in many ways, but he ensured his people had little reason to turn against him. Maintaining travel paths, ensuring everyone had enough to eat, and keeping them safe were his top three priorities. He might bully some of us, but he appeared benevolent and kind to most others.

The people of Therress often sang his praises. Considering that more crops were failing and food was becoming less plentiful across Zadrya, they knew how much worse it could be. I wasn't even certain how he pulled it off since perhaps half of our harvests managed to survive the blights spreading through Therress' lands. We should have had shortfalls.

It was a relief when he and Elgord disappeared through the gates. After the meeting in his office the day before, I'd gone straight to my room. I'd sobbed and thrown up my breakfast, then thoroughly washed out my mouth. Once I felt calm enough, I spent some time with my cousin, whose condition hadn't improved like I'd hoped.

My uncle hosted a formal dinner in the Great Hall last night, where I nibbled at my food while having to sit across from my "intended" at the table with my entire family in attendance. Baron Elgord kept running his foot up my leg, making me shift in my seat. My cousin Ulmar must have figured it out because he smiled knowingly each time, enjoying my torture. Tadeus had the decency to give me a sympathetic look.

It was a good thing children weren't allowed to eat with the adults until after their magic ascended, or we would have had to make excuses for Rynn not being there. Even my Aunt Kailin had attended, though she hardly ever left her room.

She managed to mumble a few words to please Lord Morgunn since it was a rare moment he remembered his wife's existence.

I hurried back inside Ivory Castle, maneuvering past the numerous servants who worked tirelessly to keep the huge place clean and well-maintained. They had to toil hard, but at least they had a choice about their marriages. Only the high-born could be forced into one.

Along the way, I spotted my aunt wandering the corridor listlessly. After last night, I'd figured I wouldn't see her again so soon, but she often came out of hiding when my uncle left for a journey. I heard she used to be vivacious and cheerful when they first married, but he'd slowly broken her over the years. All I'd ever seen was the quiet shell who never said a word unless someone spoke to her first.

Lady Kailin didn't meet my gaze, and it was like seeing a ghost. Her strawberry blonde hair was dull in a loose braid down her back with numerous wisps hanging free. Her gray dress was clean but worn with no frills or anything to indicate she was the lady of the castle. During my early childhood, when I visited with my parents, she was quiet but still made some effort to dress nicely and speak to others. There was color in her cheeks then as well. Now, her skin was so pale I didn't think she'd seen the sun in years, and her voice never came out above a whisper.

My uncle didn't prohibit Kailin from looking nice or going out, but she'd given up on life since her youngest son died of faebor fever. While her husband's verbal and physical abuse wore her down steadily over the years they'd been together, that loss was the last blow. With her being a little over a century old, she could live for many more decades as only a shell of her former self.

Would I become like her after being married to Baron Elgord for a while? The thought horrified me as I passed my aunt. I gave her a small smile, but she didn't see it with her gaze locked on some point ahead of her. We passed like silent ships in the night.

Before I knew it, I was at Rynn's door. Briauna opened it and gestured me inside. My cousin was asleep on her bed, making low keening sounds. The sight of her broke my heart. I sat on the edge of the mattress and picked up her left hand, noting that the black now covered all her fingers. A quick check of her feet proved they were also almost entirely darkened. Two days ago, only her fingertips and toes had shown any signs.

"I give her no more than a week," Briauna said quietly.

My world was falling apart in more ways than one. Rynn lay there, deathly ill with all the life and vitality taken from her, and my only option to save her was to turn to my enemy. "Do you really think there is a chance Darrow will help us?"

The healer sighed. "Yes, though he'll want something in return."

"Of course," I agreed. The Veronnian wouldn't do it out of the goodness of his black, murderous heart. "But what? I don't have nearly enough gold to bribe him or much of anything valuable that I can give." I refused to consider some of the precious items of my mother's that I'd inherited after her death, since I didn't dare allow those to get into the wrong hands.

"You have your gift," Briauna said, coming to stand by me and rubbing my shoulders.

She already knew about my engagement and was sorry for me, though she couldn't do anything about it, either. We were both so powerless when it came to our stations in life. She was a distant cousin with one highborn parent and one lowborn, leaving her somewhere in the middle regarding fae ranking.

I gave her a questioning look. "You mean offer to open portals for Darrow?"

"Why not?" She shrugged. "Just stipulate your conditions on when and where, but I'm certain he has no one half as powerful as you in his land. It'll be a generous offer."

I let out a hysterical laugh. "If he doesn't kill me before I can propose the idea."

"He won't," she said confidently.

"How would you know?" I asked.

"I only saw him once briefly when he was a very young man, and I can't say I could judge him from that meeting alone, but I know my sister. He wouldn't be her favorite if he were all bad. There must be some decency in him, and he didn't kill you the other day—that's a good sign."

Oh, yes. If a man doesn't kill you at first sight, they must have a good heart.

I lifted my brows. "We were too far apart from each other for him to kill me."

"From the stories I've heard, he can kill anyone he sees clearly, using his power."

"But he lifted me high into the air." I tugged on my braid. "And manipulated my hair around me like it was child's play, but he didn't hurt me, so I assumed he couldn't."

"You're alive because he chose to keep you so," Briauna said, shaking her head.

Could she be right? I'd been so certain that he wanted me dead and simply couldn't do the deed from a distance. Then again, how hard would it have been to break one neck from half a mile if he could pick up six men at once from fifty feet away? I still wasn't sure.

"I suppose I have nothing to lose by trying." It wasn't the worst-case scenario if Darrow killed me, considering I wouldn't have to marry the baron. He'd be saving me from a horrible fate.

She patted my back. "Exactly."

I mulled the idea over. "How will I even find him in time?"

Briauna smiled. "I checked into that today, and if you go to Siggaya tonight at nine o'clock, he'll be in the back room of this tavern." She handed me a paper with the name of the place. "It is well known that this is his favorite place to visit when he's in town."

I had the rune sequence for the trading city. It was in the northeast corner of Veronna, close to the Sobaryan Mountains that divided our continent and just across the border from Raumandia, Juvarn, and the royal court of Porrine.

They'd placed it near as many other lands as possible so that it was easier to access, and they allowed sales of items in the city that most others would prohibit. As a result, it attracted all sorts of seedy types and had a rougher edge to it. While I'd never dared go there, I'd heard many rumors. On a bright note, the city was neutral. Technically, a citizen from Therress could visit, but that didn't mean it wouldn't be dangerous or I'd be welcome.

What did I care at this point, though? I was about to be married to the worst possible man, and my cousin would die if I didn't go.

"I'll do it," I said, rising to my feet. "That will be late enough that no one will notice me missing, and I can easily return in a few hours."

She nodded, grim-faced. "Find me before you go, and I'll show you a map to guide your way."

"Thank you. That would be helpful."

Chapter 5

Aella

I checked myself over, making certain I wasn't missing anything. For this excursion, I'd chosen my outfit carefully. I wore form-fitting black pants with a belt that had two sheathed daggers, one on either side of my waist. My midnight blue tunic had tight sleeves, buttoned at the front, and flared at the hips to cover my butt and conceal my weapons. The top had four-inch slits on the sides, though, so I could easily reach my blades.

I probably wouldn't need them. My wind magic usually did the trick when I needed to repel attackers, which I'd done a few times during my travels when it turned out my destination wasn't as welcoming as I'd hoped.

Satisfied I'd prepared as best I could, I moved to the side of the fireplace and stretched upward to push an ivory brick about a foot above my head. A slight grating noise sounded as a small opening appeared on the bottom right. It was only two feet high and two feet wide, leaving just enough space for a person to fit.

When I moved into this room eighteen years ago, the secret opening hadn't been there, but the tunnels behind the walls had been in place. I'd only learned about them because my cousin Tadeus had shown me how to sneak from the second-floor library to the downstairs kitchen if I wanted a late-night snack. That was after I'd gotten caught sneaking around the main corridors of the castle by Parzival and punished severely. It took me the better part of four months, working at night, to create the secret openings I wanted.

Most of the tunnel pathways had fallen into disuse, but my uncle and his family regularly used a couple of sections. Thankfully, they never strayed near my end of the castle. I'd mapped the whole place out and crafted a way to enter my garden through the system. Since my room overlooked it, I only had to follow a very narrow set of stairs down, take a hard turn around, and walk ten steps. It took about one minute.

My only light source came from a glow stone I'd activated when I entered. I found a little handle near the floor and pulled. Another opening appeared about the same size as the one to my room. I quickly crawled through it to get outside and shut the stone door behind me.

One of the most significant advantages of my garden being so closed off was that no one could see it except when standing at the archway or my bedroom window. I maintained an open section in the back, obscured by a strategically placed trellis and creeping vines.

The ground in that part was covered in plain, flat stones, but a small zaphiri-am-metal circle with the necessary algodonite stones embedded within it was also part of the pattern, creating a perfect loop. Acquiring all I'd needed to install that had taken most of the earnings from a side job in Alavaar I did long ago, but it was my greatest investment. I made the addition a few years after the tunnel alterations, once I'd had a chance to research how to design it.

I could technically channel a portal from anywhere if I had the right supplies and space, but the endpoint had to be at one of the permanent circles, so returning without being caught would have been impossible. Temporary setups couldn't be receiving points.

My uncle had the ring inside the Ivory Castle keep constantly guarded. It made it hard to return without his lackeys instantly reporting me. Also, my room was too small to channel one from there, so I learned to get creative if I wanted to come and go without anyone knowing.

Almost fifteen years ago, I began researching how to make my own. It meant sacrificing time with my sister so I could travel to the Court of Porrine while my uncle believed I was in Alavaar, but it was the only way. The king's court and territory encompassed a large city surrounded by farmland and forests, teeming with animals to feed the two hundred thousand fae who lived there.

It also boasted an extensive library on one end of the palace. I researched everything I could on how to build a portal and became romantically involved for a while with one of the young apprentices who worked there. He surprised me one day by letting me look at a tome from the private section, where I had no access. I was able to copy all the rune sequences of the realm listed on the pages, which were considerable.

He'd been a nice man of lowborn status who at least knew how to please me, but we eventually got bored with each other. As soon as fae reached maturity, we craved carnal pleasure. It was part of our nature. Going more than a couple of months without it was like torture, so most of us kept at least one regular partner until marriage.

After that, it was up to the husband and wife if they wanted exclusiveness or to be open once they produced the necessary heirs. Some fae could be extremely possessive of their partners, while others didn't mind sharing at all. The rare true mates never strayed once they were intimate together, and a link formed. My parents had been like that.

My copied list from the library came in handy now as I pulled out my secret stash of holmium. I held out my hand and began pulling power into me. My fingers trembled as I sent a soft golden beam toward the appropriate runes, using the sequence I'd memorized from my cheat sheet.

They'd warded the receiving circle against anyone from Therress despite the trading city being open to almost everyone else. I pushed more magic, bypassing some of their spells and unraveling others. By the time I finished, I'd nearly drained myself. It would take almost two hours before I could regenerate enough to return home. Hopefully, I could survive that long in enemy territory.

Grateful channeling hardly made any noise to draw attention, I stepped into the swimming blue circle. This trip was much farther than when we'd gone to battle, so it took about ten seconds of traversing the whirling tunnel of light before I reached my endpoint.

Darkness enveloped me as I stepped onto solid ground. An upright receiving ring didn't affect anything, and the portal adjusted a traveler's body position accordingly. No one was standing around the courtyard encircled by trees and benches where I'd landed, which didn't surprise me.

Professional portal channelers only opened them at set times of day and seldom this late at night. They wouldn't be expecting anyone now. I'd waited until nearly ten o'clock to leave my chambers so Darrow could imbibe a few drinks before I arrived. Hopefully, that would make him more amenable and less likely to murder me at first sight. I was trying hard to be optimistic.

After dinner, Briauna provided me with a map of the city, helping me plot my route to the tavern. It wasn't too far. I only had to travel about six blocks in a zigzag pattern. Checking my surroundings one last time and finding no one, I began my trek onto the dark streets.

Part of me wished I'd brought a cloak, but it would have hindered my movements if I needed to fight. Thankfully, my tunic had a hood, which I pulled over my head to hide my golden blonde hair. It would have drawn attention with the moonlight shining on my locks otherwise.

All the buildings were one to two stories high in this area and consisted primarily of closed shops and private homes. Considering Siggaya had been established nearly eight hundred years ago, it was no surprise the buildings had a worn and dated appearance with their gray or beige stone walls covered in vines and moss. The windows were wide, but the doorways were narrow. All the gabled roofs boasted chimneys to heat the inside when winter brought its chill. The place felt familiar, with a design reminiscent of the larger towns in Therress, and yet, I knew I was an outsider here.

Walking through the empty cobbled streets, my soft footsteps sounded loud to my ears. After the second block, I spotted other fae ahead as I moved into a busier area with taverns, inns, and gambling dens. Sounds of laughter and shouting filled the air. My nose wrinkled at the stench of sour ale and urine.

A few large male faeries walked in a group together ahead of me, with their luminescent wings drawing my attention. They had enchanting personalities but rarely interacted with anyone other than their own kind. Those three likely visited Siggaya for trading purposes from the Isle of Penoria, where most of their kind lived. It was one of many lands belonging to the Kingdom of Zadrya.

I passed others going in the opposite direction. There were sylphs, sprites, nymphs, and many elves since we were the most numerous in this area of the realm. None of them seemed interested in me, for which I was grateful.

It wasn't until I was two blocks from the tavern that two large ogres stepped out of an alley and blocked my path. Each had clubs in their hands. I stopped about six feet from them and put my hands on my hips. One thing I'd learned in my travels was to project confidence and never hesitate when force was needed.

"Move," I said, lifting my chin.

The two of them grinned. "Give us all your coins, and we might not harm you...much."

Their kind were total brutes and couldn't be trusted. I had a few coins in my pocket, but even if I handed them over, it wouldn't satisfy the ogres. Most of them reveled in violence and any opportunity to start it.

I laughed and began gathering my power. "No."

The moment they moved, I thrust my hands out and shoved a torrential force of wind straight at them, angling it so they swung down the alley into a pair of large rubbish bins. They hit them so hard that their bodies smashed the wooden containers and splintered them into pieces. I didn't bother waiting to see how they fared and hurried toward my destination.

The stupid ogres had likely assumed they were dealing with a lesser fae since elves came at all power levels, and most were nowhere near my strength. Highborn ladies didn't usually travel alone at night, especially in a city like this.

I'd like to say that relief filled me when I finally reached the tavern after more than twenty minutes of crossing the city, but my journey to this point was the easy part. The next step could end with me dead. I took a deep breath and opened the door. Inside, I found the dimly lit place teaming with fae. Some sat at scarred wooden tables chatting, others stood at a wide bar to the left, and still more were doing interesting things in the back booths that would have made me blush when I was younger. The mood was a mix of joviality and lust inside.

When I entered, no one paid attention to me, so I headed straight to the back. There were several doors. One was marked as a privy, while another was half open, revealing a bustling kitchen. That meant the door on the far right was my best bet for where to find Darrow.

A dryad bumped into me near my destination. She was covered in foliage, and soft twigs made up her hair. Her arms and legs appeared stumpy compared to humans, but her eyes were dark green and almost normal. She inclined her head, countless little leaves rustling with the movement, and wandered away. They tended not to speak unless it was something important.

I finally made it to the door, turning the handle easily. Fear clutched at my throat, but I shoved it down in that place that helped me deal with my uncle during one of his tirades. I had to do this for Rynn. If this were the only chance she had to live, I must take it.

The room was bigger than I expected. To my right, about ten elves sat at a large oak table littered with bronze mugs. The booth had custom seats on three sides attached to the hunter-green walls, plus a few chairs at the fourth end. They drank and chatted, not even noticing me for the first minute I stood watching them after shutting the door. I took a few steps closer, debating what to do. This was going to be awkward with such a large audience.

"Darrow!" I said just loud enough to reach over all the other voices.

It quieted to a murmur, and nearly everyone turned to look at me.

A man with familiar brown and black hair tied at the nape of his neck had his face buried in a female elf's ample chest. He lifted his head without turning, keeping his eyes on the woman.

"Who is asking?"

Here goes nothing, I thought, and lowered my hood to reveal my blonde hair. "Aella from Therress."

The room went from quiet to deathly still.

He stiffened and turned to face me. It was all I could do to keep from gasping. He was unlike any other man I'd seen before, with startlingly good looks that should have been criminal. His slate-gray eyes stared at me as if he could penetrate my soul. He had firm, high cheekbones and a strong jaw that might as well have been carved from stone.

His skin was a light, sandy color, indicating that he had seen a decent amount of sun, but I couldn't recognize the shade as being common anywhere. At best guess, that was because he was half-light elf and half dark elf. He had a muscular build with broad shoulders. I was certain that even without his powers, he could knock down almost any opponent with a hard punch. The man was even larger than I'd estimated on the battlefield. I'd never seen a more stunningly lethal elf, which made me wish to the nameless ones he wasn't my enemy. Recalling the memory of my father's fire-scorched body, burned by Darrow's sire, helped me put the dangerous killer into perspective.

"Aella?" he asked, lifting an arched brow. "The same half-elf who sent me flying off my horse last week?"

Oh, good. I left an impression on him. "Yes."

Darrow lifted a hand, and the next thing I knew, my back slammed against the wall behind me. The air *whooshed* from my lungs. I had expected a less-than-welcome response, but not exactly this. It was all I could do to keep from trembling.

"Hmm, you're prettier than I expected. It was difficult to tell from a distance."

I narrowed my eyes. "What does that have to do with anything?"

"It's the only reason I haven't broken your slender neck already. What are you doing here?" Darrow asked, arching a dark brow.

I swallowed. He had me plastered against the wall so I couldn't move, but he'd applied just the right amount of pressure so I could still breathe and speak. It wasn't as bad as him gagging me with my hair the other day. That was at least something. Maybe he was going to do me the courtesy of asking questions first, as I'd hoped.

"I need to request a favor from you," I said, keeping my gaze on his.

Laughter burst from everyone at the table.

Darrow's eyes danced with merriment. "Did I rattle your brain a little too much?"

Wonderful. The half-dark elf had a sense of humor.

"Would I come into your territory alone at night and announce myself to a room full of enemies if I didn't have an extremely good reason?" I asked, surprising myself with my courage to speak to him in such a way. Why couldn't I be that bold with anyone else?

He appeared to mull that over momentarily and then gestured at several elves across the table. "Go outside and make sure she didn't bring company. Considering her special talent, it's possible. If there's no one suspicious out there, stay on guard for now."

Four elves rushed from the room, each glaring at me as they passed. I'd ruined their fun night. Darrow ordered the others to leave, except one female sitting at the table's far end. Based on her matching hair, skin, and eyes, I assumed the woman was his twin sister, Faina. She was rumored to be a formidable warrior and close to her brother, but that was all I knew about her.

"I didn't come here to fight you," I said, annoyed by my awkward position. "Or become a wall ornament."

Darrow rose from the table and sauntered toward me with lethal grace. I was tall at five feet, ten inches, but he had to be half a foot taller. He stopped just before me. It was all I could do to keep my breath steady as his close presence threatened to overwhelm my senses. I had to remind myself of all my family members that his side had killed—their faces swimming before my mind's eyes. We were enemies, and that would never change.

He brushed a stray hair from my face, almost like a lover would do, but I knew he was playing with me. "Imagine the notoriety I could claim if I made you a permanent fixture on this wall. Your head would look lovely here."

"Don't touch me," I warned.

He grinned but took a step back. "Your uncle often uses you to transport his army, but never this far. Did you have to portal hop?"

That was what most people with my gift did if they needed to travel far. It required channeling to a nearby ring, waiting a few hours for one's powers to recharge, and then opening another in a series until finally reaching their ultimate destination. It was a giant pain and something I only did in those first few years while training and expanding my powers.

"No." I rolled my eyes. "Getting here was easy and direct."

Sure, I'd struggled a little to get past his wards, but I refused to tell him that.

Darrow crossed his arms. "*Easy?* Where else can you go?"

It was a valid question. The only other fae who could open a portal at this distance through wards was in the king's court. She used to be stronger than me, but I was reasonably certain I'd surpassed her in power by the time I reached my mid-twenties. Since she was well over a hundred, she wouldn't be getting any stronger.

"Hear me out for why I came here, and I'll tell you."

Faina shook her head. "Why bother? Go ahead and kill her, and we will have far fewer problems. Her uncle won't be able to sneak into our territory and raze our villages as easily anymore."

I stiffened. Lord Morgunn had sworn he'd never do that again, and as far as I knew, he hadn't.

Darrow narrowed his eyes, studying me. "How do you get through our wards? Every time you come here, we strengthen them more, yet you still make it through."

Of course, I was well aware of that. "It just takes more power and concentration."

Irritation twisted his features, and the pressure on me tightened until I could barely breathe. I needed to speak fast if I wanted to live. "I came here...to ask for help...but I'm offering my...portal services in return. You know...you don't have anyone...as strong as me."

His hold eased a fraction as he gave me an incredulous look. "What could you want so badly that you'd offer a deal like that? And does your uncle know you're here?"

"Lord Morgunn...doesn't know...and will punish me...if he ever finds out," I admitted, hoping they wouldn't use that as blackmail against me as I sucked in shallow breaths. "The reason I came...is for my cousin, Rynn. She's had the faebor fever...for five days now. Our healer...Briauna...told me her sister could save her...but you're the only one...who knows how to...contact Durelle."

Darrow turned toward his sister. The expressions on their faces changed over the next couple of minutes, but they didn't speak aloud. Some fae twins could communicate telepathically, and I guessed that was the case here. My discomfort at being pinned against the wall and barely able to breathe grew. They took their time arguing whatever points they made to each other while I had an itch on my arm that I couldn't scratch and grew lightheaded.

"Um...hello? Still here," I said, drawing their attention back to me.

Darrow studied me for a moment and then shook his head. "The answer is no. I'm not risking my aunt's health and safety for your cousin."

Faina moved from the table and stopped a few feet from him. "*Dare*, come on, brother. Think of the possibilities."

He eased his hold a little more so I could fully breathe again.

"There's no way we can trust her," he said, shooting me a dark look. "Anyone that lovely and powerful must be treacherous, especially from Therress. She'll turn on us."

I wanted to shout at him that he didn't know me at all. It was infuriating to listen to his insinuations when he had no idea of the abuse I took from my uncle. I would never do more than absolutely necessary for that man, and even then, my motives lent more toward helping my people and keeping them safe.

"So you want to kill her now?" his sister asked, gray eyes lighting up. Despite her taking my side a moment before, she suddenly seemed to relish the idea of my death.

I'd had enough. Pulling my power tight into my body, I twitched one finger and sent a rush of air at Darrow. He slammed into the opposite wall with a shout. I kept the wind going, amused as his hair came loose and swirled across his face. Maybe I couldn't break his hold, but he wouldn't be able to break mine, either.

"I've kept portals open for an hour using twice as much power as I am now," I said, staring hard at him. "If I wanted to hurt you, I could have done it already. That's only my wind magic. If I draw light, you'll start losing pieces of yourself."

That was always a weapon of last resort because it was deadly, and the risk of hurting anyone nearby—friend or foe—was high. I still hadn't quite mastered the art of pinpointing it the way I could with wind or keeping it from cutting through things beyond my target.

Faina pulled a dagger and moved toward me. "Let my brother go!"

According to everything I'd heard, she didn't make idle threats. It wasn't a good idea to let her get too close. I sent her flying against the wall beside Darrow, barely breaking a sweat to hold them both. All the loose objects in the room flew in a swirl now. Even the table rattled as if it might launch into the air soon.

While Darrow watched the maelstrom with narrow-eyed curiosity, his sister glared at me.

"Can we please discuss this without the theatrics?" I asked, shouting to be heard over the wind.

Faina struggled against the wall as her waist-length hair swirled everywhere. "How about you stop first? Show us you didn't come here to cause trouble, and maybe we'll believe you."

I debated it and decided to make a goodwill gesture, as I was the one who had sought their assistance. It wasn't as if I couldn't start the wind back up again if necessary. I reeled in my powers slowly, and all the loose objects dropped to the floor with *thumps* and *clangs*. The pressure I had against the twins was the last to ease.

A moment later, Darrow released my body. Relief filled me as I regained control of my limbs and scratched that annoying itch on my arm. His lips twitched as he watched. Oh, good, I could amuse him.

"Tell me." He stalked closer. "What makes your cousin so special that you'd come here asking *me* to help save her life?"

That was a fair question and one I'd prepared myself to answer. "Rynn is only twelve and became an orphan five years ago when her parents died after a sea creature attacked their ship. They worked in trade and were never soldiers, so your side never faced them on the battlefield. She's sweet, innocent, and the kind of person you'd want to keep in this world. Maybe some of us are bad, but not her."

Faina rolled her eyes. "Plenty of us were innocent at that age. We don't know what magic she might gain if she lives, and with our luck, it would be used against us a few years from now."

"My sister has a point," Darrow said, rubbing his chin. "The smart move would be to kill you and let her die. Two fewer Therressians to cause us trouble."

Faina played with the dagger still in her hand, a gleam in her eyes. "I'd be happy to take care of her."

They looked ready to reject my offer. I thought of Rynn, lying on that bed and becoming weaker by the day while in so much pain. Soon, I'd be tied to a monster, but I wanted to do one good thing before I became a prisoner to a horrible, demented man. It could very well come down to proving to them how important this was to me. Was there anything I wouldn't do for my cousin?

Letting go of my pride, I dropped to my knees. Hopelessness and despair filled me until I didn't care what they thought anymore. Saving Rynn was everything. If they had a scrap of decency, I had to appeal to that part of them. "Please. Just save my cousin, and I'll do what you want if it's within my power. Don't let her die because you hate me and my family."

The twins exchanged looks that told me they'd begun another silent conversation. I hung my head and prayed to the nameless ones that this trip wasn't in vain. Briauna had assured me there must be some good in Darrow. Could she have been wrong?

"How far can you open a portal?" he asked in an even tone.

I stared at the floor so he couldn't see my despair. "In the last few years, I haven't found one in Paxia that I couldn't open. The only exception is Darynia because I don't know its rune sequence."

That was their capital and most protected location. No outsiders were allowed inside except the king and queen when they came on official visits. Rumor had it that the city was beautiful and unique. I'd been disappointed that I couldn't find a way to get there despite searching every book in the royal libraries and pulling favors from those who worked there. I couldn't say why I wanted to visit Darynia so much, other than to see it for myself—and the challenge of reaching it.

Footsteps sounded against the wood floor. Black boots came into view, and then Faina kneeled next to me, pressing her dagger under my chin and forcing my head up. "You can access all our cities except that one?"

"Yes," I admitted, blinking as I met her gaze.

She frowned. "Then why have you only attacked our border towns?"

"Because my uncle thinks that's as far as I can go."

Faina gave me an incredulous look. "You kept the extent of your powers a secret from *him*? Why?"

"I'm well aware that if he knew the full extent of my powers, he would escalate the war. I only do enough to stay on his good side," I admitted.

She pressed the dagger deeper, nicking my skin. "You're a greater threat than we even imagined."

"Don't be hasty, sister." Darrow dropped into a crouch next to Faina, a sly grin spreading across his face as he looked at me. "You said you'd do anything?"

I gulped. "If it's within my power and won't cause innocent people to die."

Probably should have included that before, but I was upset.

He cocked his head. "What about marriage?"

"What?" I frowned. "My uncle plans to petition the king in a week to betroth me to Baron Elgord. I don't have a choice in the matter."

Darrow forced his sister's blade from my throat. "I'm aware of Lord Morgunn's plans, but how do you feel about them?"

I didn't understand this change of topic, but I'd play along to see where it led. "Elgord kissed me yesterday, so I spent the morning throwing up and washing my mouth out."

The twins fell back on their heels and laughed.

"So it's safe to say you'd do almost anything to get out of that marriage?" Darrow asked, amusement in his gaze.

I knitted my brows, confused by the direction of this conversation. "Probably."

"Then you'll marry me instead."

Chapter 6

Aella

My jaw dropped. "What? You can't be serious? My uncle would never allow it, and the king..."

"...will officiate it," he interrupted as a calculated expression crossed his face. "In secret, of course. My father likely won't approve of the idea any more than your uncle, but thankfully, His Majesty owes me a favor or two. The news of our nuptials doesn't have to come out right away."

"But..." I shook my head. "How will that stop my betrothal to Elgord if no one knows?"

"The king won't approve it if you're already married to me, and he doesn't have to explain his reasoning to your uncle. He can say the baron is a bad match, which isn't stretching the truth. That man doesn't deserve a swine for a bride."

I rose to my feet and stepped back, unable to comprehend his proposal. It was unthinkable. "Why would *you* want to marry *me*?"

"Let's just say I have my reasons, and they're worth the sacrifice." Darrow and his sister stood, but he took a step closer with an intense look in his gray eyes. "You're far too powerful to leave available to anyone else. Opening portals for me will remain your price if I convince Durelle to heal your cousin."

I sucked in a breath. "You'll ask her?"

"Yes. If you agree to my terms."

"Okay," I said slowly, mind racing at the implications. "What exactly are your terms?"

"You will open portals for me to wherever I want, except Therressian lands. The exception to that is if I need to retaliate because your uncle attacks another of our villages and kills more innocent civilians." He gave me a dark look. "If you aid him with that, then you don't get to argue about helping me return the gesture."

I shook my head. "He wouldn't do that."

Faina snorted. "He's done it several times with your help."

"But..." I tried to think back on our trips over there. "He said he wouldn't do that again after I caught him ten years ago. He swore it."

That was the first time I brought him and his soldiers inside Veronna when my powers developed strongly enough. I'd wandered closer to see what his soldiers were doing. The village had been defenseless, with most civilians holding gardening tools for weapons, and those with swords ran through the roads, screaming with their bodies ablaze. When I saw what Lord Morgunn's army was doing, I used my wind power to stop it. They were slaughtering everyone, no matter their age, status, or gender. I couldn't stand by and do nothing.

My uncle had been furious with me for interfering and punished me harshly, but I didn't care. I told him that if I caught him doing it again, I wouldn't open another portal for him, even if it meant him killing me. He saw the truth in my eyes and relented. I'd watched closely for the next few years to ensure he kept his word, but after that, I'd assumed it wasn't a problem. Had that been a mistake?

"He's done it twice in the last year," Darrow said, gray eyes darkening.

"But until last week, there were six months of peace, and I didn't open any portals to your lands," I argued.

Faina began playing with her dagger again. "Both times were before that, and we retaliated just enough to make him think twice about doing it again—hence the months of peace. Maybe you should keep a better eye on the destruction you help cause."

"Why did you attack the other day?" I asked, because I knew I hadn't brought my uncle's forces over there in over half a year. "You started the fighting back up again this time, not us."

Darrow's gaze darkened. "He sent saboteurs to destroy several of our grain silos. Too many crops have been struggling and failing in recent years, making it difficult to afford the loss of even one. We know you had nothing to do with that one since we traced their route, but you'd better make damn sure you don't help with others."

Targeting food stores—even an enemy's—was heartless and cruel. It wouldn't be the lord and his family who starved, but instead, the poorest people and children who had nothing to do with the conflict. Only the worst kind of monsters forced vulnerable people to starve, even in enemy territory. I despised such methods.

Of course, I'd learned long ago my uncle was evil in that regard, and I was permanently trapped to be his tool of destruction. Maybe, though, I had a chance of undermining him without his knowledge.

"I promise I'll pay closer attention." I glanced between them, hating that I couldn't disprove their claims when I knew it was possible based on his past behavior. "But you can't really think I'll let you come to my lands and do the same to Therress."

I wasn't about to let my people starve or die, either.

Darrow worked his jaw. "We aren't interested in hurting innocents or destroying crops, but we will burn their homes and businesses as a message to your uncle. That method has worked in the past to stop him for a while."

It would do the job because Lord Morgunn worked hard to stay on his people's good side. Losing their homes and livelihoods would weaken their loyalty. They'd blame him for not protecting them better. He'd help rebuild, but that would cost him funds he didn't like sacrificing. I hated that I may have abetted my uncle in such atrocities, but maybe if I made certain he didn't hurt innocents again, it wouldn't be a problem anyway.

"Fine," I said, squaring my shoulders. "I can agree to that."

He gave me a serious look. "Would you swear to it?"

A lump formed in my throat, but I didn't have much choice if I wanted to save Rynn. Darrow had me backed into a corner. Not to mention, his argument made sense from his perspective, even if I hated what it would force me to do if I didn't contain my uncle. "Yes. Help my cousin, and I will open portals under those terms—I swear."

"And the marriage?" Darrow asked, amusement lighting in his eyes.

I clenched and unclenched my fists. "How exactly is a secret marriage supposed to work?"

"You will tell no one about it except your cousin and Briauna for obvious reasons, and I will limit who knows on my side." He ran his gaze up and down my body with a critical look. "But despite your beauty, we won't be consummating it on our wedding night or likely any night thereafter. We're still enemies, and I don't trust you. Making you my wife is purely to keep you out of enemy hands and grant me easier access to you."

I tried not to take offense, though it was hard not to be insulted by his insinuations. "Not that I'm arguing the point because I'm not interested in sex with you, either, but why?"

"Your father killed my grandfather. Your uncle and cousins have killed many of my other relatives. Unless you prove yourself trustworthy or maybe if you beg prettily enough—both cases doubtful—I have no intention of bedding you," he said coldly.

I crossed my arms, trying to contain my rage. As if Darrow and his people were so innocent, or I'd ever want him, either. "My father is dead because your father killed him. Your brother killed my brother, and the list goes on. Don't act like this is all one-sided."

"True," he agreed. "All the more reason we keep the marriage as a business arrangement and nothing more."

"But this will be forever unless one of us dies or finds our true mate," I pointed out, shifting from foot to foot. "You're not planning on killing me once you don't need me anymore, are you?"

His lips quirked. "No. Luckily for you, I will always find your portal-channeling skills useful, but if it makes you feel better, I'll ask the king to include vows of protection in the ceremony so neither of us can turn on the other." Darrow shrugged as if that was no big deal, though I felt a wave of relief at the suggestion. "As for true mates, less than one percent of us ever find those anymore, so I'm not too worried about it."

He was right. With the Naforya Fountain gone for so long, far fewer fae found their mates in recent centuries. Many of us still tried searching because such relationships were the most intense and powerful, with many benefits, but it was mostly a hopeless search. In the rare instances where it did happen, it was one of the only ways a couple could dissolve a marriage, allowing one of them to be free to marry their true mate.

Other points ran across my mind. "What about children? And I assume you're not going to go without sex and be faithful to me."

Darrow shrugged. "I'm a second son, so I don't need heirs, and my father would never pass me the title even if something happened to my brother."

Oh, right. The twins' mother was a dark elf from Karganoth. The marriage had been intended to build peace between our realm and theirs, but it only lasted a little under thirty years before it tragically went wrong. Darrow and Faina's mom had betrayed them and secretly worked with my uncle to plan a large-scale attack. That was how the former lord of Veronna, the twins' grandfather, ended up getting killed, as well as hundreds of his soldiers.

I was only fourteen at the time and still honing my abilities, so I hadn't been involved in the conflict, but it was a defining period in my life. When Veronna retaliated, I lost my father, and all my hopes and dreams died with him. He never would have allowed my uncle to do all the terrible things he'd done in the years that followed or treat me so horribly.

"Okay," I said, looking away. "So, no sex together and no children."

"Do you have a problem with that or are you already finding me irresistible?" he asked, wry amusement in his tone.

"Uh, no." I cleared my throat as a wave of embarrassment came over me. "The no sex part is most certainly fine. It's just that I already have a lover, and I'm wondering what I'm supposed to do about that."

I forced myself to look at him again.

"You can keep sleeping with Camden," Darrow said, waving a hand. "And I will continue seeing other women the same as before. Don't tell him about our marriage, and it won't be a problem."

I blanched. "How do you know about Cam?"

Sure, we'd been lovers for years, but I didn't flaunt the relationship, and neither did he. Few people outside Tradain were even aware of it, though my uncle certainly knew I had visited one of his captains, since I often stayed overnight at the training village. Camden and I weren't *in love*, but we were comfortable together, and he was very good at meeting my sexual needs.

Darrow gave me a sly look. "I have spies in your land and know much more about you than you'd think. Even the little things like your garden and vicious plants."

A chill ran down my spine because that meant he'd studied me before tonight.

From now on, I'd pay closer attention so I could try to pick out his people. "How very resourceful of you."

"And you're fine not having children? Because I won't allow it with Camden or anyone else. Even I have my limits. I won't let another elf's child be passed off as mine," he said, warning in his voice.

My gaze dipped, realizing in the past few days that I'd lost any chance at a happy marriage with babies. There were no good options, but at least Darrow wouldn't touch me, whereas Elgord would have every chance he got. "That's fine."

He took my chin and forced me to look at him. "What are you thinking?"

His touch was almost gentle. "It's nothing."

"That look in her eyes is not *nothing*," Faina said, cocking her head curiously.

Darrow arched a brow. "You want children, don't you?"

I brushed his hand away. "It was a stupid dream—the idea I'd have a happy marriage and babies. It was already gone the moment my uncle announced he wanted me to marry Baron Elgord. I probably would have thrown myself from a cliff before getting pregnant with one of his children, anyway."

"You aren't going to regret marrying me and fling yourself from a cliff, are you?" he asked, arching a brow.

I let out a harsh laugh. "Don't be ridiculous. As long as you don't force yourself on me, it won't be a problem."

"Good. Then it's settled." Darrow glanced at his sister for a moment before turning back to me. "I'll need three days to make arrangements with the king and ensure my aunt will help your cousin. If all parties are agreeable, I'll send word on where to meet. Considering the urgency, we'll have Rynn healed first, and as soon as your powers have regenerated enough after returning her home, we'll head to Porrine. How long does it take to regain your strength?"

"It depends on the level of wards on the nearest portal ring to your aunt," I said.

He frowned in thought for a moment. "Aunt Durelle lives at the edge of the Sobaryan Mountains, northwest of our mutual border. The nearest portal gate is a thirty-minute ride from her cabin. I can temporarily drop the wards on that one if it will decrease the time you need to regain power."

"That would be helpful. By the time your aunt heals my cousin, I'll be strong enough to send her back with Briauna. After that, I'll need about an hour and a half to regain enough strength to open a portal to Porrine."

Darrow and Faina exchanged disbelieving looks.

"That's it?" he asked dubiously. "No channeler can regenerate power that fast."

I shrugged. "Haven't you noticed how quickly I get my uncle's soldiers home after an attack? I need a little more time to regenerate because I have to hold it open longer for that many troops, but your gates are rarely close to the villages, so the time they spend riding to and from their destinations is usually enough to help me regain my strength."

Maybe they'd never put that together before or assumed we used more than one person. Most portal channelers couldn't open more than two or three a day, with at least five or six hours between each. On the other hand, I noticed that it got even easier for me with each passing year.

"That explains a lot," Faina said, assessing me.

Darrow nodded. "And will open many opportunities for us we have yet to explore."

"Pleased to make you two so happy," I said drolly.

"Indeed." Darrow took my hood and pulled it up. "Now, I'm going to escort you out of here, hopefully without anyone recognizing you."

"I can walk back to the portal by myself," I argued.

He grasped my upper arm. "Allow me the illusion that you can't run around my land without an escort, would you? I'd like to make certain you don't kill anyone on your way back."

"I may have done some damage to two ogres and a rubbish bin on the way here," I admitted.

Amusement danced in his gray eyes. "That was likely a favor to us all, except the rubbish bin. Point that out on the way back so I can see it repaired."

"Replaced."

Darrow shot me an amused look. "Fine. Replaced."

He rushed me through the tavern's main room, moving so quickly people would hardly have a chance to see me, especially with the hood and my head ducked low. Only once we entered the darkness outside did I lift my gaze a little, and he let go of my arm.

We walked side by side at a swift pace. The streets weren't as crowded as before since it was getting even later, but there were still fae milling around and some stumbling drunkenly. Everyone recognized Darrow. They swiftly moved out of his way as we headed toward the portal ring.

Partway there, I spotted the alley I'd passed before, though the ogres were long gone. I pointed at them. "There are the destroyed rubbish bins."

"Hmm." Darrow frowned at the debris. "I don't suppose you'd be willing to switch sides in the conflict between our lands, would you?"

I snorted. "No."

He sighed. "It was worth a try. I suppose I should be grateful your uncle doesn't allow you to participate in most battles, or else our side would face real trouble."

Did he just compliment me? "He wasn't happy I attacked you last week despite how it helped our side. I got a stern lecture for it."

"That is one more difference between him and me because I wouldn't hold you back in a battle," Darrow said, completely serious.

I averted my gaze, unsure of what to say to that. We walked the rest of the way in silence. Once the ring's shiny metal and glinting stones came into view, I found the area was as empty as before. He guided me to a post office outside the courtyard and pressed me against the side wall. The mixed scent of sandalwood and leather coming from him nearly overwhelmed me.

"What are you doing?" I asked, glancing between his hands that laid flat against the bricks on either side of my head.

His gaze was intense. "My sister isn't here, so I can speak more freely."

"Okay, but does it have to be this close?"

Darrow kept his face inches from mine, breath fanning my cheeks. "You might be my enemy, but if you think there's a chance you can get out of the marriage to Elgord, I won't push for our wedding. That isn't part of the deal to help your cousin."

Maybe Briauna was right, and there was a good side to him. "I spent the last two days trying to think of a way out, but there isn't one."

"You can't run away?" he asked.

I sighed, deciding he should know the truth. "No. Look at the back of my neck."

He hesitated a moment, then spun me around, lowering my hood and lifting my hair. "A curse mark?"

It was a simple red circle with a black dot in the middle—my uncle's signature design. "It's Lord Morgunn's specialty." I turned around to face him. "He put it on me a few days after my father died, making sure I'd never be able to escape him. If I'm careful, I can make brief trips wherever I want, but if I ever think of getting away from him permanently, he'll know right away, and I'll fall unconscious. Trust me when I say I tested it once. It works."

Darrow swore. "The only way to break that is with your death or his."

"Elgord said my uncle plans to transfer the curse mark to him, but I haven't had a chance to confirm it," I said.

There was almost pity in the elf's eyes. "That explains the cliff comment earlier."

"I'm not sure if I could jump, but it gives me some consolation to think there is a way out—even a bad one," I admitted.

Darrow stared deeply into my eyes with such intensity I had to fight squirming. My breath stuck in my throat as he lowered his head and pressed his lips to mine gently. I didn't move for a moment, but then he began kissing me in earnest.

To my shock, it felt good, and I opened my mouth. His tongue danced with mine. I softened against him, unable to help myself. It was the most incredible kiss I'd ever had, and without thinking, I lost myself as I clutched at him. The passion between us was so unexpected. Sure, he was easy to look at, but I understood who he was and that I should never feel anything besides hatred for him. Except right now, I forgot all about any of that.

He pulled back, and a sardonic smile formed on his lips. "Feeling any nausea?"

"No," I said, confused.

"Good. I wanted to be certain that when we kiss during the wedding ceremony, neither of us throws up in front of the king." Darrow dropped his arms, no longer caging me. "That would be awkward."

"What?" It took me a moment to understand. "Oh, because of what I said about Elgord. That's not the same thing as…"

His gaze turned cold and hard as ice. "Whatever you do, remember we aren't friends. We're enemies with centuries of blood and death between our families. While I don't want you repulsed by me if we are to be married for the rest of our lives, I also don't want you to develop feelings for me. Do you understand?"

"Yes," I said, nodding jerkily. Horror filled me that, for a moment, I'd thought becoming his wife wouldn't be so bad. He'd certainly cleared up those delusions.

He expelled a harsh breath. "If you want comfort or soft touches, go to Camden. There will never be anything between us except business."

"Don't fool yourself, Darrow. No man has ever made me fall in love, and it certainly won't be you," I said, lifting my chin. He wouldn't get the best of me now or ever.

"Does that mean you aren't the clingy type?" he asked, skeptical.

"You kissed me first, remember?" I gave him my coldest expression. "I went along with it out of curiosity, nothing more."

If I'd lost my head for a moment, it likely had to do with a bad week and attempting to wipe away the memories of Elgord's hands on me. No one could blame me for that.

"Excellent. Glad we understand each other."

"Now let me go home," I said, pushing him away.

Darrow gestured at my hair. "You might cover yourself first before you step out of the shadows."

Begrudgingly, I did as he suggested. As I tucked in my hair and pulled my hood back up, I kept a watchful gaze in case anyone came our way. Thankfully, no one did. I didn't bother telling him goodbye before sweeping past him. He didn't move from his spot while I set up the portal, and he remained there when I stepped into the blue shimmer.

Chapter 7

Darrow

She'd said opening portals to my land was easy, but I'd still had difficulty believing it until I watched her. Over the years, we'd spent considerable time and resources warding Veronna's rings so that no channeler could use them except our own and the king's. Not only could Aella do it anyway, but faster than our people. Generations could pass without someone like her appearing. I knew because I'd investigated those with her gifts in regard to another matter.

After the blue light disappeared behind her, I headed back to the tavern. There were still fae on the streets—mostly drunks or criminals—but none dared come near me. They knew better. I was Lord Gannon's dark elf son with enough power to crush any of them in seconds if the mood struck me. Over the years, I'd even done it a few times before they'd learned not to cross my path. Only those who deserved it, of course, but I'd made a spectacle of their deaths as an example. Many believed I had no soul.

That wasn't quite accurate. I rubbed at the back of my neck where I had my own curse mark, though, unlike Aella, I came into the world with mine. My father's entire male line had inherited it for more than six centuries. It dimmed most of our emotions as soon as we gained magic at adolescence and rendered us incapable of love.

It was one more reason why Aella was my perfect match. Who else besides an enemy should be bound to someone who could never feel more than slight concern for them? I'd make certain she never forgot the bad blood between us and remind her whenever she appeared to soften toward me. She would because that kiss proved it, giving in to me too easily.

Though she was Therressian, even she didn't deserve to fall for a man who couldn't love her back. I'd seen the damage it did to my father and grandfather with their marriages and, more recently, with my older brother and his wife. On the other hand, she could also be the one to help break our damn curse. Wouldn't that be ironic?

My sister waited for me outside the tavern, standing next to one of my closest friends, Loden. He had a strong, medium build, short brown hair, and lightly tanned skin. Though he was as good a fighter as anyone in my inner circle, he was the least obtrusive. I appreciated that he was a thinker and often poked holes in my plans so I had a better chance at success.

"Any problem seeing your intended off?" Faina asked with a smirk.

I shook my head. "She opened the portal like it was hers rather than ours."

"Aella is one of the puzzle pieces we need then," Loden surmised. "I heard about the deal you made with her, and I think it was the right call, though I'm surprised you two came up with that plan without me."

I gave him an exasperated look. "We occasionally get something right."

He snorted. "I'm even more surprised you convinced a Therressian to go along with it. Marriage...to you?"

"Her other choice was to abide by her uncle's plan to betroth her to Baron Elgord," I said, then informed them about Aella's curse mark. "At least she'll have more freedom with me."

Faina shuddered. "I think I'd rather marry a troll than that baron."

"I could have that arranged."

She punched me hard in the shoulder. "Don't even think about it."

We paused our conversation momentarily when a pair of pixies exited the tavern, giggling and holding onto each other as they passed us. This wasn't the best place to discuss sensitive matters.

"Let's go to my loft," I suggested.

It took up the entire second floor of a building and included three bedrooms, a spacious kitchen, and a large living room. It had several shops below that closed by early evening so we could be as loud as we wanted at night.

"Yes, let's do that," Faina said, taking mine and Loden's arms.

We didn't speak again until we'd poured drinks and settled onto my comfortable couches. This place was an escape from the drama of court life. The curse muted my emotions, but they weren't gone. I seemed to be able to feel stress, anger, and annoyance at near-normal levels, but since they rarely had to do with love, that made sense.

I gulped down my drink and set the glass on the side table. "We've got three days to organize matters before I summon Aella, and there's much to do."

"You need to speak with the king first thing in the morning with that timeline," Loden said, leaning forward to rest his elbows on his knees. "And someday, you'll have to tell me how he owes you favors."

There were some secrets even my best friends didn't know—not yet, anyway.

I sat back in my seat. "Siggaya's channeler opens a portal to Porrine every morning at eight, so that won't be a problem. It might take me a full day to get back, though, so I'll need you all to run interference with everyone else while I'm gone. Only you two can know about this for now. I don't want to risk the wedding getting blocked before it happens."

After that, there would be some explaining once my father discovered what I'd done, but he couldn't undo it without the king's blessing. I preferred my marriage to stay a secret until certain elements came together. None would be easy, but Aella would make their chances of success much higher. She had no idea she'd handed me a precious gift, and all I had to do was ask my aunt to heal her cousin. I'd gotten the better end of that deal, even if she had no idea.

Faina started laughing to herself.

I lifted a brow at her. "What?"

"She really thought we'd kill her." My sister rubbed mirthful tears from her eyes. "Threatening her was almost worth it just to see how she reacted, and wow, I've never seen anyone channel that kind of wind in a closed space."

Neither had I, and it had stunned me when she forced us both against the wall. I was used to being the one who flexed power like that, but my future wife would be a true challenge. At least she had some spirit. She'd need it in the coming months because some of my plans would be dangerous, and she had to be able to protect herself.

Loden stared into his drink. "How long will you wait for her to take us to Jolloure?"

I mulled it over. "Perhaps a week or two after we're married. I'll have to work around her schedule and mine if we want to avoid notice. My father doesn't make that easy with his endless tasks, which he claims are to keep me out of trouble."

More like he didn't trust Faina and me since our mother's betrayal, so we were forced to prove ourselves constantly. It was why I rarely fought against Therress, and instead, he usually kept me on our western coast, pushing back any dark elves who tried to infiltrate our land. My mother, Zareen, also made demands of me. The two of them were exhausting when I had my own plots to hatch on top of theirs.

"Do you think Durelle will heal that girl?" Faina asked.

I nodded. "Our aunt said she could do one more before she lost all her strength, but it has to be someone especially worthy. Aella wouldn't have gone to her knees and begged us for help unless she truly believed her cousin was worth it—never mind offering her power up for trade."

My sister took a long drink before meeting my gaze. "Agreed. That's what sold me, too."

Of course, we still needed to play the game because it would have been suspicious if we'd acted too eager at the tavern. It came in handy that Faina and I could communicate mind to mind so no one would know what we discussed.

"Check in with the spies when you get a chance," I told her, mind racing ahead to everything I needed to accomplish in the next few days. "Find out all you can on Aella that we don't already know and let the ones living at Ivory Castle keep and Tradain know to maintain a close watch on her, though not so obvious she'll suspect them."

She grinned. "I was already thinking the same thing."

"Good." I stood and stretched. "I'm going to bed, but you two may feel free to keep plotting without me."

"As if you expect anything less," Loden said, shaking his head.

Chapter 8

Aella

The temple where we worshiped the nameless gods was at the rear corner of the keep. It sat in a secluded area surrounded by tall frost trees with creamy white leaves and mysteria bushes with their delicate pale-blue flowers that bloomed all year except in winter. I had to pass the rear stables, blacksmith shops, and servants' quarters to reach the place. Most of my family rarely visited, but they were wise enough to maintain it. Angering the gods was a bad idea because they could be rather vindictive.

As I entered the serene garden before the temple, I stepped past an altar where one could sacrifice animals if they were especially desperate to get their prayers answered. I tried it once, using a green Topper bird. Many people thought they brought good luck and could often be seen perching on the tops of trees, singing loudly. I was sixteen at the time, and it was right after my uncle's brutal punishment against me for trying to escape. I had beseeched the gods to lift the curse he'd placed on me.

One showed up that day, so I'd apparently got his attention. Unfortunately, he refused to help and said to have faith in the path set before me. I had no idea why he'd bothered to show up only to tell me that.

There would be no sacrifices today or probably ever again. I came about once a month, knowing full well no god would show up like that first time, but sometimes praying here gave me clarity—or at least the strength and resolve I needed to face my problems. My marriage prospects counted as worthy of a visit.

Shortly past the altar was a small pool of crystal-clear water. I removed my slippers, pulled up the bottom hem of my dress, and stepped into the cool depths. While one could choose not to make a sacrifice, one always had to cleanse one's feet before entering the main temple. All it required was taking three steps until reaching the other side.

After that, I found myself at the stairs of the white marble temple with four columns at the front. A wide entrance lay open in the middle, glowing from within. My wet feet slapped on the floor as I went inside. It was a reasonably large space with a square blue cushion directly in the middle and an empty throne at the back on a raised dais. Like the temple, it was constructed of white marble. If a god chose to visit, they always appeared in that seat, perched high above the person who called upon them.

I kneeled on the cushion and arranged my skirts before bowing my head. The priest who oversaw the temple had special chants for ceremonies, but at other times, we could speak our minds as long as we showed proper reverence.

"Please, nameless ones," I beseeched, my whispered voice seeming loud in the empty room. "Guide me about my marriage prospects and what to do."

Of course, nothing happened, but I continued to repeat the words and add more about my misery and worries. Was I doing the right thing by betraying my uncle and people to save my cousin? I closed my eyes, despairing over the impossible choices that overwhelmed me and kept me awake at night.

A loud sigh came from the direction of the throne. "Do you honestly think it's a choice?"

It was an ageless voice no fae could mimic.

"What?" I jerked my head up, shocked.

Sitting in the carved marble seat was the god I saw half my lifetime ago. He had short, black hair and almond skin, presenting a strong figure in his pristine white tunic and linen pants. There was bored amusement in his silver eyes that I didn't recall from last time.

He lifted an imperious brow. "I don't know why you are asking us for the answer. Your choices are to allow your cousin to die and marry a horrible man who will make the rest of your life miserable or to save your cousin and marry someone who isn't hard to look at and will bring adventure to your life. Doesn't seem like a difficult decision to me."

"It's not that simple," I said, my nails digging into my palms. "Our families have been killing each other for centuries, and he's my enemy. Plus, he's an arrogant ass. I'd be tying myself to someone who hates me."

He cocked his head. "So you think he's worse than Baron Elgord?"

"Well...no," I stuttered. "It's just that I wanted more for myself than either of these choices. Why are they my only two options?"

Was it so terrible to be upset about it? I'd received two horrible choices when I'd really hoped to settle down with someone who respected and loved me. Neither Elgord nor Darrow would ever care about me or see me as anything more than a pawn in their power games.

The nameless god shook his head slowly. "So what if he hates you now? Many successful marriages have started that way, but it doesn't mean they end the same."

"Yeah, it worked out so well for Darrow's parents," I said sarcastically.

He laughed. "Yes, well, I didn't say it always worked out perfectly. But there was this one time I joined with a rival goddess, and let me tell you, the sex is always good when you hate each other. It took three days before we could peel ourselves from each other's bodies."

Raunchy images flittered through my mind. Imagining two gods having sex was like thinking of your parents together in a similar manner—more than a little unsettling. "I could have slept better tonight *not* knowing that."

"Don't pretend you're a prude. We both know you're not the inexperienced girl I met last time."

Was he keeping track of my private life?

"So, what is my best option?" I asked. If anyone knew, it would be someone with all-knowing powers. He clearly understood how carnal aspects could play into my decision as well.

He rose from his seat and moved toward me, crouching low and tipping up my chin. "Which man caused your heart to race when he kissed you?"

Looking into his eyes was like seeing the whole universe inside them. I sighed, "Darrow."

He gave me a broad smile and stood. "We both know he's the better choice. Sure, he'll be an ass and likely frustrate you in many ways, but you'll always feel alive with him. Elgord will slowly extinguish the life from you until you're nothing more than a shell of yourself like your aunt. I can't have my favorite fae follow that path."

I barked out a laugh. "I am most definitely not your favorite. This is only the second time I've ever seen you, and you weren't exactly friendly the last time we met."

"You didn't need friendly last time, but cold hard truth." He settled back into his throne. "And just because you don't see me doesn't mean I'm not watching. It's not like anyone else in this realm can sneak out on adventures as often as you, and I enjoy your quiet strength. Perhaps you're not brazen and certainly avoid confrontation as much as possible—Darrow being the intriguing exception—but you've proven resilient. It's the reason I chose to come today."

That was...illuminating. The nameless god had been watching me then, too?

I swallowed and finally made myself commit to the less distasteful choice. "Fine. I'll marry my enemy."

"Good girl." He stood. "I'll enjoy seeing how it turns out and if the two of you ever do the tango."

"The *tango*...what?" I asked, having no idea what that word meant.

In a blink, he was gone.

I remained kneeling momentarily, trying to wrap my mind around the idea he'd shown up to make sure I chose the way he wished. Did he care? I'd always thought the nameless ones only concerned themselves with crucial matters. My marriage couldn't mean that much, yet something told me whatever was coming next in my life was much bigger than I could possibly imagine.

Chapter 9

Aella

I stepped out of the portal into the late afternoon sun at Tradain. It was equal parts a large village and a military training camp. Everyone who lived here was either in the Therressian Army, a family member of a soldier, or working to support them. The entire place was designed to be clean and uniform, without embellishments aside from our hippogriff crest, painted in golden yellow, on the walls of several buildings. As the story went, my family had used the half-eagle, half-horse for transportation thousands of years ago on the fae homeworld, but they weren't allowed to take them when they fled to Paxia.

The housing—all similar forest green two and three-bedroom homes—and the rows of barracks formed a circle around the training grounds. We had areas designated for archery, magic practice, sword and knife exercises, duels, and mounted combat drills.

One could find the stables, armory, and blacksmiths on the north end. On the opposite, one could visit uniform and clothing shops, tailors, and food and spice stalls. It only took five minutes to figure out the layout on one's first stay, despite the population being over ten thousand. That didn't include those only here for six-week reserve training most male and female fae received at eighteen years old. My uncle enacted that requirement when he became Lord of Therress as part of his mission to ensure the safety of his people. Of course, the active troops still did most of the defending since they trained full-time.

I found my friend, Sariyah, in the uniform shop. Her back faced me as she stood before an officer's uniform, sparks of magic flying from her hands as she coated the tunic and pants with protection enchantments. That was her specialty.

Those with enough coin could hire her to ensure arrows found it more difficult to penetrate the cloth or render their uniforms more impervious to offensive spells. Technically, she could make the clothing entirely invulnerable to damage, but that took a week, and she massively drained herself to do it, so she charged enough that it discouraged everyone except the richest high fae. It also didn't necessarily protect the wearer's exposed skin. Nothing was foolproof aside from avoiding battles altogether.

"Be with you in a minute," she said, not looking back.

Her rich brown hair was in a loose braid down her back, reaching her waist. One could make out her generous curves through her simple blue muslin dress. She exercised and trained frequently since her father was an officer and insisted on it, but she also enjoyed cooking and food. Sariyah was the most in-shape woman I knew while maintaining an enviable figure. She could take the obstacle course in the nearby woods like a champion.

While she received considerable male attention, she rarely returned it, preferring to be picky about where to spend her time. I'd known her for as long as I could remember since my father had also been stationed here until he died in battle. When I moved away, we began taking turns visiting each other.

I stood quietly waiting. There wasn't much to see since the front of the shop was small, with only a counter, and the space behind that had a rack for hanging uniforms. The back of the shop was considerably larger. Usually, several workers were sewing new uniforms and repairing old ones in that room. Sariyah didn't need much space for enchantments and enjoyed working with customers, so she often stayed up front.

Finally, she finished and turned around. "Oh, Aella! I wasn't expecting you."

"It was a last-minute decision," I said, spreading my arms as she raced around the counter to hug me. "But I was overdue for a visit anyway."

Sariyah pulled away and studied me. "Your uncle did something to upset you again, didn't he?"

She could always read me well.

"He's trying to marry me off soon," I admitted. While I wanted to tell my friend about Darrow, I wasn't ready to talk about it, even if he hadn't told me to keep it a secret. It was safest to stick with speaking about my other marriage prospect.

Her brows knitted. "Who?"

"Baron Elgord."

Sariyah bent over and pretended to wretch. "Lord Morgunn can't be serious. That elf gives me the hives every time he visits here, and I swear I've never seen anyone with worse breath. I thought about making him a mouthwash enchantment free of charge since it would be a public service."

"You should absolutely do that," I said, already relaxing in my friend's company. She had a way of lightening the mood no matter how dire the topic was, and I needed that more than ever.

She rubbed my arm. "Is he really set on the betrothal?"

I nodded. "He plans to petition King Worden when he returns from his village inspections in five days."

"Right, but surely His Majesty will have sense and refuse to approve it."

If I went along with Darrow, that was exactly what would happen. "I already prayed to the nameless ones about it and feel my prayers will be answered. The trouble is if the king does deny the petition, my uncle will blame me for it."

"Better that than being tied to Elgord for the rest of your days."

"True," I agreed.

We continued to chat, pausing only when customers came inside until I was reasonably certain training had ended for the day. I gave her a hug and hurried across the village to a familiar captain's home. Since he was an officer, he had small, private quarters near the barracks. It wasn't much since he wasn't married, but he had a living area, small kitchen, bathing chambers, and a back nook with a comfortable bed. I'd spent many nights here and planned to do the same on this visit.

I knocked on the door, and Camden answered a minute later. His muscular form filled the doorway, already missing his shirt since he must have been planning a bath. He was about four inches taller than me with rugged good looks, short blond hair, and lightly tanned skin. His pointed ears were easy to see and sharper than most.

We were a little over twenty years apart in age, so he hadn't drawn my attention until about four years ago. He'd volunteered to help me with my sword work when I was visiting Tradain to refresh my fighting skills, and by that night, I was in his bed. I didn't feel deep emotions for him, but he fulfilled my needs enough I didn't want anyone else.

"Need help?" I asked with a smile.

He grinned and took my hand, pulling me inside. The next thing I knew, I was in his arms with his mouth pressed into mine. It was hot and passionate, as always. I couldn't help but compare it to Darrow, though, finding the sparks weren't nearly as bright with the captain. At least Camden was safe. He'd never make demands of me that could put me in danger, and sex was pretty much all he wanted from me.

He pulled away. "I was hoping you'd visit soon."

In fact, it had been two weeks since I last came here, and I usually made it to see him more often than that. "Something came up with my uncle." I ran my hand down his bare chest, enjoying the feel of him. "I'll tell you about it later, but first, I want to help you with your bath."

He pulled me close. "Only if you join me."

"So demanding," I said, laughing.

His brown eyes turned heated. "That's what happens when you wait too long to visit."

"So you missed me?" I asked, cocking my head.

He began unlacing the front of my dress, pulling it from me with practiced ease. I stepped out of it, and he removed my shift next. There was nothing underneath that. I let him look his fill, feeling myself grow wet at his lustful gaze.

He pulled me close and nuzzled my neck. "Anytime I'm not buried inside you, I miss you."

Camden always knew the right words to say. I didn't let myself think about my impending marriage or anything that could take away from the present moment. This was my brief escape from all my troubles. "Then what are you waiting for?"

He scooped me up, and we were in his warm bath moments later.

Chapter 10

Aella

Darrow had kept his word and sent a sebeska with a note for me earlier in the day while I was in my garden. It had details of when and where to meet. Briauna and I helped Rynn slowly walk from her room to mine, thankfully managing to avoid anyone seeing us. Then, we'd let her rest for half an hour before crawling into the tunnels.

Maneuvering a sick girl through the passage had been the most challenging part, with each of us working to help my cousin. Once in the garden, she sat and caught her breath while I cleared the vines over the ring and channeled the portal. The darkness outside, along with the thickly covered trellis, would make it impossible for anyone walking by the garden entryway to see us. The familiar scent of my flora helped soothe my nerves at what we were about to do.

Briauna went first while I scooped up Rynn and carried her into the blue glow. I was eternally grateful for my enhanced elf strength compared to full druids because while my cousin was slight, especially after hardly eating for nearly a week, she wasn't a small child anymore. She rested her head on my shoulder, her breathing raspy. I couldn't wait to get her to the healer.

Darrow, Faina, and two other elves waited on the Veronnian side with horses next to them. They had their swords out, likely anticipating a trap, but they sheathed them as soon as they saw me carrying Rynn. She'd used all her energy getting through the short tunnel trip and was listless now.

"Thank you for bringing horses," I said, walking up to Darrow. "I didn't think to ask for them when we made the deal."

He guided the mount, whose reins he held, so that it stood parallel to me. "The journey is thirty minutes on horseback. I knew she couldn't make an even longer one on foot with the fever."

"Right."

"Get in the saddle, and I'll hand her up to you," he said, gently taking Rynn from me. He spoke impersonally, which felt strange since we were about to get married in a few hours, but I supposed that it was a matter of business—no romanticism involved.

I did as he requested, swinging onto the horse. He easily lifted my cousin, and I settled her in front of me. She rested her back against my chest, eyelids barely fluttering at all the movement. I braced an arm around her, keeping her close.

Darrow met my gaze. "You've already met my sister. The other two are Jax and Loden, who are close friends and loyal to me. They're here to help should we have any trouble along the way. This forest is known to have dangerous creatures that are more likely to attack at night, but the larger the group, the less probable they are to bother us."

That wasn't unusual for most of the woods in our realm.

"It's fine," I said, glancing at them but unable to make out much of their features with their hoods pulled over their heads and the trees blocking most of the moonlight.

He took a set of reins from his sister. "This horse is for you, Briauna."

"It's good to see you again, Darrow," she said, giving him a kind smile as he brought the mare to her. "We appreciate you arranging this."

"I can't say my reasons were entirely altruistic, but you're welcome."

Darrow moved to one of his friends, who held the reins of two horses and took control of his own. It was the same one I'd seen at the battle—a dapple-gray stallion. A minute later, we headed through a barely discernible trail through the thick woodland. The canopy overhead was so dense that it left the forest especially dark and creepy. I caught strange sounds in the distance and prayed none of them came closer to us.

When the path widened, Darrow let his friends take the lead and slowed to ride next to me. "I take it we're proceeding with everything as planned."

"Yes." I adjusted Rynn in my arms, thankful she slept. "I couldn't find any better options since I saw you last."

He gave me an amused look. "I'm sure you tried, though."

"Can you blame me? I still can't figure out why you suggested marriage, considering everything," I said, giving him a scrutinizing look.

Darrow's lips quirked. "You don't think keeping you out of the hands of an enemy who'd use you against me is enough?"

"My uncle uses me against you," I pointed out.

"True." His expression turned disgruntled. "But he doesn't sleep in your bed or take up your personal time like a husband would. I need you freer to slip away and assist me."

I supposed those were good points. "Fine. I get that, but marriage is forever."

"No matter who I marry, it won't be for love. I prefer a wife who will be useful to me in the long term," he said matter-of-factly.

I studied him for a minute, wishing I could figure him out. "Not the romantic sort of man?"

"No."

Based on his reputation, I supposed that made sense. "Good. That should make things easier between us if we keep emotions out of it."

"Yes, but be aware that I will be testing your channeling abilities soon, and they better be as good as you claim," he warned.

"They are," I said, giving him a sharp look.

How dare he accuse me of lying about something like that? Hadn't I proven myself enough by getting into his land numerous times despite the strong wards?

"Glad my future wife has such confidence."

I ground my teeth. "If it's a secret marriage, do we have to refer to each other as husband and wife when we're together?"

"It will be true." Darrow edged his mount closer to mine. "Or did sleeping with Camden two nights ago feel awkward knowing you'd be marrying me?"

I stiffened. "How did you find out?"

Darrow's lips twitched. "I told you before I have spies everywhere, so there's little you can do that I won't hear about sooner or later."

And so far, I hadn't figured out who they were despite paying closer attention.

"You said I could continue seeing him," I said, suddenly feeling uncomfortable. How many details did his spies give him, and how did they know? We were behind closed doors, though I supposed anyone could have seen me go to his place and not come out until morning.

Darrow guided his horse back over a few feet to put some distance between us again. "And I'm glad to see you took my advice. I'd worried our kiss might have affected you despite my warning. From all accounts, you've always preferred one lover at a time, so I wasn't sure if you could handle being with him and me."

"You..." I gave him an outraged look. "One kiss is not the same thing as sex."

"No. Of course not, but with how easily you responded to my touch, I have worried you'll eventually want more, and Camden won't be enough. Let me know if that's the case, and perhaps if you beg prettily, I'll consider obliging you."

He urged his horse forward, leaving me to sputter. "Arrogant prick!"

Darrow just laughed in response.

The rest of the ride only had one close call. Midway on our journey, a group of *chiggarbats* came out of the dark forest at breakneck speed, coming straight for us. Black scales covered their bodies, except their heads, which had dark fluffy fur inhabited by blood-sucking mites that could jump onto other victims. They also had broad wings and sharp teeth, able to cut deep into their prey. Fae, with any sense, avoided them at all costs, considering their viciousness.

Darrow lifted a hand and forced them into a different direction, but he didn't kill them.

"Why did you let them live?" I asked, surprised.

He glanced back at me. "They keep the *wiggarwart* population under control, so they have their uses. My aunt would wring my neck if she found out I harmed a single one."

Wiggarwarts were small, furry ground rodents that fed on plant roots. They were harmless to fae and other creatures but could decimate a forest if their numbers grew too great. Chiggarbats were their most active predator. Considering the rate at which we were losing fertile land, we couldn't take any chances. It made sense to let them live and do their work.

"I look forward to meeting your aunt if she strikes that level of fear into your heart," I said, grinning.

He grunted. "Durelle is possibly the only one with such power over me, but I've known her since I was a small child. It is doubtful anyone else will ever accomplish such a feat."

The implication that I'd never succeed at the same hung in the air.

"The rumors claim you have no soul." I didn't think that was true, especially if he cared about his aunt, but I barely knew him.

"Hmm, I've heard that, too," he said, then rode ahead to leave me in silence.

We didn't encounter any more dangerous creatures, though I continued to sense them nearby. It was a relief when a moderately sized log cabin appeared with lantern light filtering through the closed curtains. The place looked warm and inviting despite the eerie location. Trees surrounded it except the narrow road we'd used to reach it.

Jax and Loden dismounted first. One helped Briauna from her mount, which was good since she rarely rode anymore and had to be stiff and sore. The other took the reins of my horse from me while Darrow grabbed hold of Rynn.

As we made our way to the cabin, the door opened, and an older woman with gray hair in a bun appeared. She wore a dark blue dress that covered her softly rounded form. Her gaze immediately went to her sister, and a smile spread across her face. Briauna rushed as fast as she could on stiff legs, hugging her. They spoke for a moment before gesturing the rest of us inside.

Durelle accepted a kiss on the cheek from Darrow when he passed and then motioned for him to take Rynn into the next room, where I glimpsed a large bed with a silver metal frame. The cabin was cozy and warm, thanks to a large fireplace in the sitting area, which took the chill from my skin. Faina kissed her great aunt politely as well upon entering before settling on a small couch across from the hearth. Jax and Loden took seats at a sturdy wooden table at the back of the room where finger foods and drink pitchers had been left out.

Briauna guided me to her sister. "This is Aella. She is the one who requested you help her cousin, but I'm the one who suggested it."

The healer studied me for a moment. "I'll do my best for Rynn. I've no doubt if Briauna says she is worthy, then she is, but I should warn you there is a catch with doing this."

"What?" I frowned. "Darrow didn't mention anything."

"He wouldn't have said, I'm sure."

I took a deep breath. "Tell me."

She glanced toward the bedroom as Darrow came to join us, wrapping an arm around his aunt to give her a sweet hug. I was surprised by the gentleness of his expression when he looked at her. Not a hint of his usual coldness lurked in his gaze. He appeared like a doting nephew and certainly not someone lacking a soul. Did that mean he was capable of affection with more than just her?

"I'm only strong enough to do this one more time," Durelle said as she pulled away from him. "But this won't only be a healing. She will take my powers into herself as well, assuming the duty."

Briauna cleared her throat. "I talked to her about it before coming, and she understands the outcome. She's agreed to do it."

"Why didn't you tell me?" I asked, giving her an accusing look. That was a significant detail. My cousin would have the ability to cure diseases no one else could, and who knew how my uncle might use her if he found out.

She patted my arm. "You have enough trouble with other matters, and this was Rynn's decision. Not yours. Some regular healing powers come with it, so we should be able to hide the rest from everyone else."

I prayed to the nameless ones that she was right. "Is that how the gift is always passed along?"

Durelle nodded. "Usually. It was that way in my case, but if I died without transferring it, then the universe would have chosen who should take it after me. There is always one of us in the world."

"Okay, so what's next?" I glanced between the sisters. "Is there anything I can do?"

Briauna gestured toward a rocking chair by the fire. "Sit and relax. I'll assist my sister while the rest of you wait here."

I didn't want to let my cousin out of sight in a strange place, but I understood I'd only be in the way with such a small room. "How long will it take?"

"No more than an hour," Durelle replied, pulling away from Darrow with a kind smile for him.

With that, the two healers went into the bedroom and shut the door. As suggested, I sat in the rocking chair and stared at the fire. From the back of the room, I could hear Darrow and his friends eating and shuffling a deck of cards. At least they'd prepared a way to entertain themselves.

About ten minutes passed when Faina spoke from the couch where she lay comfortably. "So, is that the dress you're wearing to get married?"

"Does it look like I brought anything else?" I asked, not bothering to look at her.

If not for the wedding, I would have come in a tunic and pants, but knowing I'd see the king tonight, I'd chosen the newest of my riding dresses. It was a soft blue that hugged my waist, had tight long sleeves, and a full skirt. My favorite part was that it buttoned up to my neck, showing no cleavage. What was the point in wearing anything remotely flattering?

"Hmm, I assumed you'd dress up more," she said, sounding bored.

I had a feeling she only asked to irritate me. Undoubtedly, she would have nitpicked anything I wore. I'd agonized over my choice all day, aware someone would say something, but I'd chosen to be practical in the end.

I finally looked at her. "There's no point when it's a marriage on paper only, and no one is going to know about it except those of us in this cabin and the king."

Darrow's face was in profile to me, but I gave him credit for appearing as if he wasn't listening to us as he tossed cards on the table. At least he wasn't making any snarky comments. Perhaps he was letting his sister take over for him.

"You're right, of course. It's just that you only get married once, and you seem like the romantic type who'd want to make it special regardless of the circumstances." She sat up to look at her brother. "But you two must think alike because Darrow is also in simple riding clothes."

"It's called being pragmatic," I said.

Her brother turned to look at us. "Did I mention the king insisted we stay the night at the palace after the ceremony?"

"What?" My jaw dropped. "I thought we'd go home afterward."

"He's aware we aren't a love match, but he thinks we should spend some quality time together in the hope it could become one. Misguided as it may seem, he believes we should try to make it work if we want his approval. A room is being prepared for us," he said, amused—likely at the horror on my face. "But don't worry because nothing is going to happen in there."

Despite his words, I dreaded spending an entire night alone with him. It wasn't as if I could argue with the king, though. If he wanted us to spend time together after agreeing to a secret marriage, we had to go along with it. I only wondered how we would manage all this without anyone at court finding out.

"Fine." I met his gaze. "We'll just sleep and go our separate ways in the morning."

Darrow set his playing cards facedown and leaned back in his chair. "I must insist you don't seduce me while we're there, though."

Faina coughed to hide a laugh. The other two men in the room seemed abnormally interested in their hands and didn't look at any of us.

Fine. If he wanted to play games, then so would I. "Are you implying I could seduce you?" I batted my eyelashes. "Or are you hoping?"

Darrow lifted a brow, surprise in his gaze. "Only if you beg on your knees...again."

My jaw dropped. "You're such an ass. I'd rather be eaten by a sea snake than ever be touched by you...again."

He snorted and picked up his cards. "We'll see about that soon enough when we kiss before the king."

I ground my teeth and turned to face the fireplace. Though it seemed like hours, a short time later, Briauna opened the door and gestured at me. Her expression was calm. I rose from the rocking chair and went to the bedroom. Inside, I found Rynn sitting up with the color restored to her face and the blackness that had covered her hands gone. A blanket covered her feet, but I was sure they were also better.

"How are you feeling?" I asked.

She smiled. "Great...and different."

My gaze moved to Durelle in the chair by the bed. I found her complexion pale and her face drawn. Curing my cousin had taken a lot out of her. She seemed less vibrant, and her body slumped in her seat.

"Thank you," I said, hoping my gratitude showed.

She nodded almost imperceptibly. "Rynn is a good girl and will carry on my work. I'm glad you brought her."

"Will someone be staying with you after we go?" I asked.

"Faina and the two boys."

After we arrived at the cabin, I'd seen them in the light. They didn't look like boys to me but rather strong, grown men. Of course, almost everyone probably seemed very young to a woman over two centuries old. Life among the fae was dangerous, so few of us made it to that age.

"Good. I'm glad you won't be alone."

She let out a weak laugh. "I wouldn't have minded, but Darrow insisted. For a cursed man, he can be surprisingly protective."

"What curse?" I asked.

"She is being figurative," he said, coming directly behind me. "Rynn, how are you feeling?"

I stepped to the side, needing to put distance between us.

"Much better," my cousin replied, pulling away the blanket and swinging her legs over the side of the bed. "I can already feel the magic inside me."

She leaned down to grab her slippers and slid them onto her feet.

"We took a few minutes to explain matters to her," Briauna said, glancing at Darrow with an anxious frown. "I'll assist her with my sister's magic so she can properly hone it."

"Good."

Rynn walked over to us on steady legs, truly looking a hundred times better. "I'm ready to go when you all are."

Nerves churned in my stomach. I'd been looking forward to saving my cousin, but not the next part of this journey. Was I really doing this? Of course, because I had no other choice.

"Excellent. We'll leave in five minutes," Darrow said, spinning on his heels.

Chapter 11

Aella

It was nearly eleven at night by the time Darrow led me to a side entrance at the king's golden palace. We both wore dark cloaks he'd brought that covered us from head to toe. The few people we'd passed in the street on our way from the portal ring couldn't have possibly gotten a good look at us. Darrow merely nodded at the few guards we'd encountered, who hadn't seemed surprised to see him. I kept my head down, and they hardly glanced my way.

Once inside, he led me through a series of narrow corridors that were so plain as to be forgettable and likely only used by servants. Not once did he hesitate on which way to go. I wondered what he'd been doing with the king to know the palace so well.

Eventually, we stepped through a narrow door into an ornate room with cream walls, elaborate tapestries, and elegant gold and dark blue furniture. It was twice the size of our great hall at the Ivory Castle. I noted several instruments, including a harp in the corner. At best guess, the space was used for entertaining.

"Remove your cloak and give it to me," Darrow said, already taking off his.

My stomach twisted as I did as he requested, placing it in his outstretched hand. Why did it feel like I gave him something far greater than a simple overgarment? He carefully laid the cloaks across the settee with a blue floral print. The whole situation felt surreal.

We'd snuck through a side entrance into the royal castle and used a secret door to enter this sitting room. Somehow, Darrow had convinced the king to sanction this clandestine ceremony that would alter the course of my life, and I simply went along with it. Had I lost my mind?

Was I really going to marry this man who killed my people ruthlessly? He'd snapped Therressian soldiers' necks in front of me without hesitation, yet here I was, binding myself to him for life. Despite the fact I kept reminding myself of all his faults, it was hard not to be affected by his dark looks. He was far too devastating for his own good. Why couldn't he have the decency to appear as dreadful as his soul?

"How long are we going to keep this a secret?" I asked, trying to keep the worry from my voice.

Darrow met my gaze with a twinkle in his gray eyes. "Are you in a hurry to announce it to the world?"

"The opposite." I hugged myself. "The longer we can avoid the fallout, the better."

"We'll keep it quiet as long as possible." He moved closer and started fussing with my hair, loosening the braid. "I'm hoping for at least six months to a year, if possible."

I stiffened. "What are you doing?"

Darrow moved behind me and began finger-combing my locks. "We still have a few minutes until the king arrives, and I'm trying to make us presentable. Though he knows we aren't in love, I may have implied I have some affection for you. He was very adamant that I didn't coerce you into this."

He had failed to mention that particular detail at Durelle's cabin.

The way he touched my hair felt irritatingly good. "I can handle that myself, you know."

"Possibly." He leaned close to my right ear, warm breath fanning over me. "But you were very tense when we arrived, and after our last meeting, I discovered my touch relaxes you."

I suppressed a shiver. "You are the most arrogant man I've ever met."

"Dear Aella, I am only arrogant because I speak the truth." I started to step away from him, but he snaked an arm around my waist and held me still. "Pretend you want to marry me, or the king may refuse to officiate it."

"Easier said than done," I spoke through gritted teeth.

His body was like a wall of muscle behind mine, with his intoxicating scent of sandalwood surrounding me, and I was trying very hard not to be affected by it. This was all a game for him, but his touch had an impact on me—mentally and physically—I couldn't describe. He was like a force of nature, drawing me toward him despite my knowing the danger he represented.

Darrow spun me around and bored his gaze into mine. "Play the role for a little while and make it convincing. Afterward, we can stop pretending."

"But I can't just..."

He cupped my cheek and ran his thumb across my bottom lip. "I know. A week ago, I would have killed anyone who even suggested I marry you. I thought for certain you were no better than your uncle. It was only after you came and pled for your cousin's life that I realized you are not the same as him."

"I'm the opposite of my uncle," I said, gasping when he leaned down and ran light kisses along my neck. "What are you doing?"

"Relaxing you," he murmured.

What he was doing was sending my heartbeat into a gallop. "This wasn't part of the deal."

"Touch me," he said, nibbling at my ear as I suppressed a moan. "The king needs to think there's at least some passion between us."

I clenched my eyes shut, unable to believe what he was demanding. While I wasn't inexperienced, I wasn't ready to touch a man I'd spent my life fearing and hating. If he noticed my body responding, it would only prove his point at the cabin.

"You're only demanding I do that because I said I'd rather touch a sea serpent."

He pulled back a few inches, amusement in his gaze. "I knew you were lying."

"I hate you," I said, though my words lacked conviction.

"And yet, you still want me."

"I do not..."

He pressed his lips to mine and coaxed my mouth open. It felt so good as shivers raced up my spine that I couldn't resist. As the kiss deepened, he grasped my hands and guided them up his hard chest. Even through his tunic, I could feel his heat and the ripple of muscles underneath. It took a moment, but before I knew it, I was touching him of my own volition. Damn him for this attraction I felt. Why? It should have been easy to feel revulsion for him and everything he represented.

Darrow grasped the back of my neck to hold me in place, and his other hand made its way around my waist to cup my ass, squeezing one side. Heat shot straight into my core. Before I knew it, I was moaning as we continued to kiss. He was everywhere around me, scorching my skin with his brazen touches. Every part of me came alive and wanted more. I lost myself so completely that it took a moment to realize someone was speaking behind us.

I jerked back when I realized it was the king. He stood a handful of paces away, cutting an impressive figure in a golden doublet with intricate embroidery and black pants. His brown hair was cut short and neatly styled. His appearance wasn't what gave him away as a ruler, though. The waves of power emanating from him that filled the room and made everyone else feel small in his presence did it.

"Your Majesty," Darrow said, giving him a deep bow.

The odious man was calm and collected as if we hadn't been caught with our hands and mouths on each other. He didn't seem as intimidated by the king as me, but maybe it helped that he had a lot of power himself—and royal blood.

I quickly bent my knees into an awkward curtsy, blushing profusely. "My apologies, Your Majesty. I didn't hear you come in."

The stately man, who'd turned 114 years old a month ago, moved toward us with amusement in his azure gaze. "I can see why you wouldn't have noticed anything with how Darrow distracted you. It's good to see there's none of the animosity between you I anticipated."

Not at the moment, anyway. I was certain my cheeks were blazing with the heat of embarrassment. This was not my first time meeting the king or even the dozenth. I saw him at least once a year for the annual winter ball, and sometimes, my uncle brought me to the palace for other events. We weren't strangers, but I didn't know him well enough to be kissing and fondling someone in front of him. At least he didn't appear offended.

"I appreciate you taking the time to do this for us," I said, hoping to change the subject.

King Worden nodded. "More than happy to do it as long as you're both agreeable to your plan. I don't like the idea of it being a secret, but I understand the complexities of the situation. Every time I've tried to intervene and bring peace between your lands, it's proven impossible."

"I'm afraid there has been too much bloodshed to make it simple." Darrow drew me into his side, and I tried not to focus on where our bodies touched. "But Aella and I hope to resolve that issue when the time is right. For now, we must keep her out of Baron Elgord's hands."

It was all I could do to keep a straight face at the insinuation we had any plans to fix the war between our people. That topic had certainly not come up since we met. What had he told the king to make him agree to this?

His majesty frowned. "We must also consider the curse your uncle placed on you."

"Is it possible for you to order Lord Morgunn to remove it?" I asked hopefully.

"Not without consequences we can ill afford right now." He turned his gaze to Darrow. "You're going to have to bide your time and hope he makes a mistake. I cannot sanction you killing a lord without legal recourse, and since we aren't involving him in this marriage, that alone cannot justify it, either."

My soon-to-be husband nodded. "I remember everything we discussed before and will wait for my chance."

I went still. "You mean killing him?"

"The less you know, the better," Darrow replied, squeezing my waist.

I wanted to be angry at them for planning a family member's death without my say, but they were trying to free me from the curse. If I could have done it on my own, I would have by now, so I elected not to argue. Losing my uncle would not make me shed a tear.

The king glanced between us. "If your families don't take it well once the news is out, where will you live?"

"I finalized the purchase of a townhouse here in Porrine yesterday, and the renovations will start next week," Darrow answered, squeezing me in warning again.

He wanted me not to act surprised about it. Fine, I would go along with him for now, but we needed to work on communicating better. Something told me that would remain a problem as long as we lived apart, though.

"Excellent," King Worden gestured at a servant standing by the door. "Bring the papers so they may look over them."

The stoic elf carefully placed them on a side table, spreading them out. Darrow and I went over and began reading the documents. They laid out our marriage agreement in plain enough terms. The dowry had been waived, we'd share any property we owned, and we both agreed we could never cause the other any serious harm or death.

The punishment would be equal to the crime—magically enforced. So, if I stabbed him, the same injury would immediately appear on me. That was certainly a deterrent. Of course, it accounted for accidents and true intentions, so if something minor happened, like swatting him in the arm for being annoying, it wouldn't punish me. Our oaths tonight would bind that agreement for as long as we lived.

I took special note of the details on Darrow, such as his family line, which included the dark elf half and the fact his grandfather was King of Karganoth. It was something I knew, but it was still intimidating that he was technically royalty. I also noticed his birthday was in late summer. He would turn forty-six then, which meant we were about thirteen years apart since my birthday would come a couple of months before his. It was a reasonable gap, but it meant we'd have a long life together, barring mishaps. What choice did I have, though?

There were three copies of the document—one for the royal records, one for me, and one for Darrow. We took turns pricking our fingers with blood before pressing them to the parchment, with the king doing it last. Once he finished, the servant waved his hands over the documents, using magic to protect them from alterations. Technically, with that act, we were officially married now.

"Turn to face each other," Worden ordered.

Darrow took my hands, appearing solemn. He put on such a good performance that I wondered if I could ever truly trust anything he said or did because he appeared to take all of this seriously. I took a steadying breath, attempting to match his somberness.

The king led us through the simplest version of the fae vows. They didn't cover much beyond what was already written in the documents we'd signed. "Do you both vow to be loyal to each other above all others? Never to severely harm or kill?"

"Yes," Darrow said without hesitation.

It took me a moment before I could reply in a whisper. "I do."

Were we lying? I couldn't begin to predict how our future would go, but I knew there was magic with this ceremony that would make it very difficult to break the vows.

"You may now exchange rings."

I started to panic because I'd forgotten all about it, but Darrow pulled two simple bands from his pocket. He fitted one with tiny diamonds all around it onto my finger, then gave me the other one. With trembling hands, I placed his on him. Both were a perfect fit, but I'd felt magic in them. He must have spelled the rings so they'd mold to the correct size on the wearer.

"Very good. I now pronounce you permanently bound to each other as husband and wife," the king said, smiling broadly. "You may kiss."

As Darrow's lips met mine, sparkles of royal magic fell upon us. It was the king's blessing, but it held significant power. He'd made certain our vows would be especially difficult to break.

My new husband didn't hold back from our kiss, and I fell into it once more despite myself. How could I hate him so much yet melt against him like this? While he was overwhelmingly handsome, I wasn't one to fall easily for looks alone. With how he held me tightly, I wondered if it was entirely an act for him. Could he feel something, too?

Finally, we broke apart, and I had to clutch Darrow's jacket for a moment before I could trust my knees not to collapse. Everything about this night was leaving me confused and dizzy.

The king beamed at us. "Congratulations to you both. I hope you have happy, long lives together and trouble never darkens your doorsteps, though with Darrow, that's unlikely."

I laughed because at least he was honest.

"Thank you, Your Majesty," I said, curtseying low.

Darrow bowed. "You've been most generous with your time tonight, and we won't forget it."

"I'd expect not," the king said with a dark undertone.

Chapter 12

Aella

The same servant who handled our marriage documents led us to nearby chambers without anyone seeing us along the way. Inside, I found a large and beautifully appointed room with a massive, canopied bed on the far end. The color scheme was primarily burgundy and gold, with the curtains, furnishings, and décor all giving the space a dark, romantic atmosphere. To my left, a well-tended fireplace roared with flames. Darrow led me to the sitting area in the middle, where a small feast waited for us.

"Are you hungry?" he asked, pouring each of us a glass of wine.

I took mine from him and sipped it, finding the flavor rich and sweet. "A little."

He took a much longer drink. "We should eat some of this, considering the effort they put into the meal."

"I'm surprised they bothered this late at night," I said, thinking there was enough for five people on the table.

Darrow took hold of a chicken leg. "Perhaps the king thought we'd bond further over food."

"Doubtful," I muttered, sipping my wine again. The wedding band on my finger glinted and reminded me of another issue. "You know I'll need to take the ring off before I go home, right?"

He shook his head. "I had it spelled so no one can see it except those who know we're married. You'll also find it exceedingly difficult to remove."

That explained why the magic emanating from it felt too strong to be a simple sizing spell alone. He'd layered something else into it without consulting me. I set my glass down and pulled on the band, but it wouldn't budge. The bastard.

"Why?" I asked, glaring at him. We'd barely been married twenty minutes, and he was already making me question our nuptials.

Darrow gave me a sardonic smile. "So you won't forget about me during our times apart, dear wife. Why else?"

Dear wife? The term of endearment must be some sick joke to him, a mockery.

I gave him a scathing look. "Trust me. Being married to an arrogant ass who is also my enemy will always be at the top of my mind. I won't forget about you."

He finished his chicken and leaned back. "Tell me three things my spies wouldn't have uncovered about you."

Was he kidding?

I nearly had whiplash at his change of subject, but fine, I'd figure out the ring situation later. "Tell me who your spies are, and I'll better understand what they wouldn't know."

He laughed. "Nice try. Tell me something you hate."

"Besides you?" I asked, lifting a brow. "The color yellow."

"Hmm, why?"

"For one, most shades of it wash out my skin. For two, it's my uncle's favorite." It was on our banners and much of the upholstered furniture around the castle. Whenever we had a celebration, he insisted we all wear it, and it always ruined some of my enjoyment.

"Interesting." He studied me. "Then what is your favorite color?"

"Plum," I replied, grabbing a roll to try. "Your turn. One thing you hate and one thing you like."

"I prefer black above all other colors," he said, glancing down at his riding outfit, which was the aforementioned color.

I finished chewing. "Why does that not surprise me?"

"It's probably not much of a secret, but shockingly, we can agree on the worst color," he said with a wry smile. "Nothing annoys me more than seeing your yellow banner waving on the battlefield or when the king forces us all together for something or another."

"Why are you asking these questions?" Curious as to why he bothered when we'd go our separate ways in the morning as if we hadn't just gotten married. I took a bite of roasted potato while I awaited his answer.

Darrow served himself a slice of meat pie. "To ease the tension, and because I don't want to be completely ignorant of how my new wife's mind works. Ever since we last met, I've found it difficult to understand the dichotomy of you. Obeying your uncle on some things yet secretly defying him in others. I can't figure out if you're loyal to him or not."

"I'm loyal to my land and family," I said, sighing. "I also don't enjoy drawing my uncle's ire, but it doesn't mean I don't have a daring nature."

"Such as marrying me and your penchant for hopping around the world with your portals while he has no idea," Darrow observed.

I gave him an annoyed look. "It's not like I do that all the time. He doles out the holmium dust I need like it's more precious than gold. I can only hold a little back for my personal travels. Speaking of which, tonight's adventure has taken most of what I have left. If you want my services in the future, you'll have to provide me with more."

"Of course," he agreed readily.

We chatted about innocuous things for a few more minutes until we were both full. There was still a lot of food left. I hurried to the washroom to clean up, grateful to find a toiletry kit provided for us. Taking my time, I cleaned my face, brushed my hair, and brushed my teeth. All that was left was the matter of my dress. Sleeping in it would be uncomfortable, but the shift I wore underneath was thin.

It seemed stupid to agonize over my "husband" seeing me in my undergarments on our wedding night, but these were unusual circumstances. We'd mostly been polite with each other this evening. Despite that, we were entering the most awkward part. Then I considered that hundreds of people had seen me completely naked for the last dozen or so summer solstices when we drank heavily, danced, and let our inhibitions go. It wouldn't be a big deal if Darrow saw me in my shift.

I took the dress off. Examining myself in the mirror, I could see the faint outline of my nipples and the dusting of hair between my thighs, but it was only if I looked closely. Why should I be ashamed anyway? He'd likely seen many women's bodies, considering his reputation.

When I stepped out of the washroom, I found all the food cleared away and Darrow lying on the bed with his shirt and boots off. I allowed myself exactly one second to appreciate his corded muscles before meeting his gaze. It was unreadable. I doubted he even studied me in my shift since his gaze stayed on my face.

No matter how large the bed was, I wouldn't sleep there with him. I laid my dress across a chair and grabbed a throw to settle on the couch before the fire. It wasn't very comfortable with the stiff cushions, but I could make do for one night.

I barely heard Darrow's soft footsteps as he walked to the washroom, but he finished in there much faster than me. Through all this, I watched the fire, wishing I could ignore him entirely instead of being hyper-aware of his presence. When he returned to the bed, there was a slight creak, and the rustle of blankets.

"I'm not going to let you sleep on a hard couch, Aella," he said, sounding mildly amused.

Though he couldn't see my face, I still rolled my eyes. "It's my choice where I sleep, and it's not going to be with you."

"Worried I'll seduce you?" he asked.

Yes, and that I'd be foolish and give into it. As long as Darrow wasn't touching me, I could resist him. "No."

He chuckled. "Everything that happened earlier was for the king's benefit and had no meaning behind it. I'm not going to touch you, dear wife."

There he went with that term again, as if he had to remind me I belonged to him now.

I shifted uncomfortably. "Let me be, Darrow."

In the next moment, a weightless sensation took over my body, and I squealed as he lifted me into the air and guided me toward the bed. He watched my face with amusement as I struggled against his invisible hold. There was nothing I could do to get free. His powers were too strong, and using wind against him would only destroy the beautiful room. Considering we were in the king's palace, I could hardly do that.

A moment later, he settled me gently on the opposite side of the bed. I glared at him as the throw blanket flew to the floor with his invisible power, and the duvet came over the top of my body. He still hadn't freed me, so I was immobile and vulnerable.

"You can call me 'Dare' now that we're married," he said with a satisfied expression.

"Let me go."

He propped his head on his hand, lying on his side. The blanket only covered up to his stomach, giving me an up-close view of his impressive upper chest. A few jagged scars ran across the corded muscle, surprising me. I forced my gaze away from him. "I'll call you an overbearing jerk before I call you anything else."

"I'm ensuring we can at least say we slept together, should anyone ask," he replied. Then, a couple of the extra pillows moved to settle between us. "But have no fear. I won't fill you with my cock tonight or any night until you beg me for it."

"Do you have to be so graphic?" I asked, hating myself for visualizing him plunging inside me. He was the enemy and callous. I would not give in to temptation. Even now, he wouldn't hesitate to kill my people, and I couldn't forget that.

He chuckled. "Do you deny the thought hasn't crossed your mind?"

"Yes," I lied. "If you never touch me again, it won't be long enough."

"You overestimate your ability to resist me." An invisible hand pulled the hair from my face. "But I look forward to the day that your will crumbles and you submit your body to mine."

His hold on me eased, and I rolled to my side away from him.

"I thought you weren't interested in sex at all with me," I said as that invisible hand continued to play with my hair. Why wouldn't Darrow leave me alone? Was this another game of his to see how far he could push me and then mock me for any desire I showed for him?

The bed creaked a little as he adjusted his position. "That was before I dreamed about you on your knees like you were a few days ago, except this time, you used your mouth for more pleasant activities."

I rolled over, grabbed one of the center pillows, and flung it toward his head. He blocked it, laughing. It was then I noticed his black and brown hair was free to frame his face. If I thought he looked good before, he definitely drew the eye now.

"Just shut up and let me sleep," I demanded.

He lifted his brows. "Not until you call me, Dare."

"No."

"Would you like me to detail my dream about you further?" he asked, leaning a little closer. "Because I have a *very* vivid imagination and would love to describe every little nuance for you."

The man was infuriating! "Goodnight, *Dare*."

"That was too easy," he said with a sigh.

***

The next morning, I woke before dawn. We were both still far apart from each other on the bed. I was grateful neither of us had rolled past the pillow wall between us to create an awkward situation. To my surprise, though, I'd slept deeply despite him being a mere few feet away.

We dressed silently, ate a few bites of the breakfast delivered to our room, and Darrow kindly offered to let me leave first. One thing we could both agree on was not being seen together as we departed the palace.

He sat lazily in a chair with his legs splayed, sipping tea as I headed for the door. "Take care, Aella. I'll be seeing you soon."

"How soon?" I asked, pausing with my hand on the door latch.

"A week or so—long enough to miss me, I'm sure."

I turned to glare at him. "There is no way I'm going to miss you."

"We'll see," he said with a smug grin.

Perhaps his other goal with our marriage was to annoy me for the rest of my life as some sort of demented long-term revenge. Without another word, I fled the room and then the palace. I kept my cloak grasped tightly around me through the city to the portal ring, thankfully reaching it early enough that the first channeler of the day hadn't arrived yet. It was strange returning to Therress as a married woman—even if it was a secret. My life had drastically changed, but the world around me remained the same.

Chapter 13

Aella

I'd been married for a week, but life didn't feel any different. My uncle had returned to cast his usual gloom over the castle, and my aunt hid in her rooms again. Ulmar was out in the training field, challenging and defeating our soldiers for fun. My younger cousin, Tadeus, had escaped to Maradeyn—the largest city in Therress, about an hour's ride away. He would likely stay there a couple more days before his father forced him to return.

As for me, I'd chosen my own kind of escape by taking Rynn out for a ride on our horses. She was looking better and stronger than ever. Still, she needed to be closely watched during the coming months as she learned how to handle her new magic. While we already knew she'd develop a healing talent, there were other minor skills most fae could do once they gained their powers. She needed to develop her senses for them. I planned to help her with that while Briauna taught her about her primary gift.

In the distance, through the trees, I spied a hint of movement.

"Let's stop here," I said, reining in Astra.

Rynn did the same. "What are we doing?"

"This forest is full of creatures." I gestured around us. "Most are harmless, but there are vicious ones that you must anticipate coming well before they reach you."

She frowned, pointed ears twitching. "How?"

"Usually, riding this trail isn't a problem during the day. It's extremely rare that anything dangerous is out when the sun is high, but there is an exception in the spring. Do you know what that is?" I asked.

She shook her head and gazed around her, looking in the wrong direction. "No."

Clearly, she wasn't sensing anything, but that ability would take time to develop and only through practice. I'd felt the presence before pinpointing where to look. "Do you know what a *napaea* is?"

"A type of nymph," she said with confidence.

I nodded. "Yes. They're usually among the friendliest of the forest fae, but that isn't always the case in the spring. If one has recently given birth, they can become very territorial and protective."

She clutched her reins tightly. "I'm guessing you brought this up because there's one nearby."

"I sensed her several minutes ago and have been tracking her movements as she's crept closer to us. Even with your powers being new, you should be able to feel her now that she's nearby," I said, purposely avoiding looking toward the napaea. "Close your eyes and focus on what feels different...magical."

She did as I requested, brows scrunching. All the while, I kept track of the nymph. Like all her kind, she was very thin and wore just enough cloth to cover her private parts. This one's hair was a rich blue that fell halfway down her back. I hadn't caught her eye color, but it likely matched her hair. As for her skin, it was smooth, ebony, and flawless.

The closer she came, the slower she moved. I only tracked her from the corner of my eye while I waited for Rynn. So far, my cousin didn't appear to be picking up anything. I carefully dismounted Astra and moved to place myself nearest the impending danger.

"Got it!" Rynn shouted. "The napaea is that way."

She pointed in the correct direction, but her loud voice triggered the fae into leaping toward us sooner than she would have otherwise. I didn't have time to push the napaea back with my wind magic, and instead, I had to grab her lithe body as she attempted to skirt past me to my cousin.

All breeds of nymphs were strong but not as much as elves. She struggled in my arms, and I called upon my druid half to help calm her. I sang a sweet song in the old language, using my melodic voice. It was so rare I had a reason to use it these days. It spoke of life, beautiful meadows, and sunrises.

Rynn watched me with wide eyes but, thankfully, had the sense not to speak.

I continued my song until the powerful conclusion. By then, the napaea had calmed and rested her head against my shoulder. "You are okay. We wouldn't dream of hurting you, but it is time for you to get back to your baby now."

As further confirmation of my suspicion, the cloth covering her breasts was damp, and the scent of milk wafted from her. Her kind were great hunters who could understand language well enough but did not speak themselves. They preferred to hum, which is why I had chosen to sing. She looked up at me with her beautiful green eyes, and no malice was in them anymore.

I pressed my lips to hers in a brief kiss intended to show respect and friendship. The napaea smiled and drew away. Then, she turned and began gliding back through the forest in the same way she came, humming a sweet melody that copied the one I'd sung.

"Why did you kiss her?" Rynn asked.

"Growing up, I spent time with my mother's parents in Alavaar. Druids seek to be one with nature and animals as much as possible. They prefer peace. It's why they eventually withdrew to that land when the fae arrived long ago. They understood that we—the Seelie—had nowhere else to go after being expelled from our home world, so they sacrificed for us. Not all the inhabitants of Paxia were so gracious, but my mother's people didn't resist for very long."

"Oh, they sound nice," she said, curiosity in her gaze.

I nodded. "Yes, most of the druids are. My grandparents taught me how to interact with the forest races because our kind often resorts to violence when it's not necessary. Kissing the napaea sealed a friendship between us, so as long as I respect her, she will always trust me when I travel through this forest."

My cousin's expression showed awe. "Will you teach me things like that?"

"What do you think we're doing out here?" I asked, amusement in my voice.

"I thought we were going for a ride."

I gave her a patient look. "Haven't you ever wondered why you aren't allowed to go out alone and are only allowed to travel in groups?"

She shrugged. "I assumed people were just being overprotective."

"There are many dangers when you leave the safety of the castles and villages." I mounted my horse. "Some, you can handle like I did today. Others, you need to be prepared to fight for your life."

Rynn straightened her shoulders. "Then I will look forward to learning everything and training to fight."

Nearly dying had changed her perspective, for sure.

"Good. Because now that you have magic, that is going to be part of your daily lessons from now on, in addition to your regular studies with your tutor," I said.

Distant hoofbeats drew my attention. Someone was riding this way and quickly.

Rynn heard it as well, and we fell silent. Finally, far up the path, I glimpsed a large black warhorse and a menacing rider with short, red hair. I sighed. "That's Ulmar."

"I wish I had magic that could hurt him," Rynn said in a low voice.

Technically, a healer could cause harm using their powers in reverse, but she was nowhere near ready to learn that skill. I wouldn't be the one to tell her about it, either. Briauna would manage it when she was ready years from now.

"I could hurt him, but the price would be too high," I replied, guiding Astra to face my malicious older cousin.

She moved her mare closer to mine. "How do you resist?"

Rynn had mostly managed to stay off our uncle's radar, especially with me guarding and running interference for her. The few times she did draw his ire, he'd yelled at her but not harmed her. She didn't know the price I paid every time I stepped out of line, and if I could help it, she never would.

"Because I must," I whispered.

Ulmar pulled up his horse with an irritated expression on his face. "Did you two have to ride so far out?"

"Yes," I replied, grateful the napaea was long gone before he arrived. He would have killed her and left her baby motherless without a drop of remorse.

"My father wants you in his office now," he said, a malicious glint in his eyes. "He's enraged, and you're the cause of it."

"How is that?" I asked.

Ulmar smiled. "He prefers to tell you himself."

Lovely. It could be any number of things since, half the time, I was in trouble for activities I didn't even know were wrong. Sometimes, I assumed Lord Morgunn just decided they were offensive if he needed a target to vent his frustrations. I was his favorite person to berate whenever his youngest son wasn't around to draw his wrath.

The only thing that made me feel marginally better about my punishments was that Tadeus had it even worse, and a few times, he'd even taken mine to save me. If he hadn't had some of Lord Morgunn's features, I would have sworn he wasn't related to his father.

"Okay, let's go."

Ulmar led the way back to the castle, sending his horse into a gallop. We were only a few miles away, but he seemed determined to bring me before his father as quickly as possible. Rynn kept casting me worried glances along the route. I held my head high and refused to appear nervous. She looked up to me, and I wanted to set a good example rather than cower in fear.

Eventually, the high walls of Ivory Castle came into view, with their smooth white stones glinting brightly in the afternoon sunlight. A quarry was located about ten miles east of here, where my ancestors sourced the building materials. The keep was entirely self-contained, so there was no outer village. We even had cattle, grew sizeable crops to feed the inhabitants, and had a pond within the walls. If an army ever attempted to lay siege to us, they'd be waiting a while before we ran out of resources.

The heavy metal gates were wide open when we crossed inside. That was normal during the daytime as long as we didn't anticipate trouble. We followed the main road past the northern village on the left and numerous shops on the right. Beyond them were the front gardens with numerous vibrant spring blooms coloring the space.

Just before reaching the castle courtyard, we turned right to follow a path to the lord's stables. It only housed the highborn mounts and carriage horses. We kept all the ones for pulling wagons, working crops, or for soldiers southeast of the castle beyond the training area.

We handed our mounts off to the stable hands and hurried toward the castle. Rynn and I parted ways at the entrance as I turned toward my uncle's office near the front. Ulmar stayed behind me like a dark presence to ensure I didn't try to escape my fate. I couldn't figure out what would upset my uncle when I was positive he couldn't possibly know about my marriage to Darrow. Even if he'd found out, he would have come to the woods directly to punish me—far from witnesses. This was something else.

My cousin nudged me through the partially open door, finger poking into my back, and I stepped inside. Lord Morgunn was pacing behind his desk. He looked up upon my arrival, and his expression turned thunderous.

"The king refused your betrothal," he said, ice-blue eyes trained on me. "Do you have any idea why he would do that because I cannot think of a single one? Did you write him? Make a plea to him?"

Ulmar worked his way across the room to the window, but he listened closely. I had no doubt my uncle allowed him to stay because one of my cousin's strong magical abilities was detecting lies. It was another reason being near him always kept me on edge. One wrong slip of my words could result in me getting caught.

"I wouldn't dare write the king about that." I shook my head, choosing my reply carefully. "Didn't he give you an explanation?"

It was such a relief to know this was what had him upset, even if I couldn't show my true feelings on the matter. I'd assumed it would take at least a few more days before my uncle received the news. King Worden hadn't wasted any time.

He worked his jaw. "He only said that Baron Elgord wasn't suitable for a lady with your gifts."

"Oh," I said, unsure how to respond without angering him further.

Lord Morgunn began pacing again. "I had assumed this would go smoothly, and now I must think about what to do next. It is far past time you married. I must ensure the match will benefit me, and your future husband will keep a firm hand on you."

My hands clenched into fists, and I had to hide them behind my back.

Ulmar stood with his arms crossed, an amused smile on his lips. He loved nothing more than seeing me in trouble, though I'd never understood why. Lord Morgunn rarely became angry with him because he was just as sadistic.

"She needs someone strong enough to handle her waywardness," my cousin said, glancing at me with judgment in his eyes. He'd say anything to make his father happy.

Little did they know I was already married to someone who challenged me. Sure, I could hurt Darrow easily enough, but he had the capacity to kill me if he chose, at least before we spoke our vows. He couldn't harm me now, no matter how much he wished. The magic that bound us together ensured that, which ironically made me safer with him than with anyone else.

My uncle spun around to look at me. "I will search for another suitable match. In the meantime, I expect you on your best behavior so you don't make this any more difficult."

As if I ever did anything that would harm my marriage prospects—that my uncle knew about, anyway. "Yes, Lord Morgunn."

"Now, get out. I'll see you at dinner, and I expect Rynn to attend from now on since she has come into her magic," he said as I headed for the door.

We'd had to tell him she recovered from the fever, but I'd been delaying her presence at meals. Sometimes, they were tolerable, but other times, they could be volatile. I wished I could protect her from all of it for longer. Once she came out in the open, she'd be another target for our uncle to berate and cousin to torture.

"We'll both be there," I promised, forcing myself to leave gracefully from the office.

Chapter 14

Aella

Mealtime the last two days had been tense as expected. Lord Morgunn had desperately wanted me to marry Baron Elgord, and the king blocking it must have ruined secret plans. Maybe because finding a suitable prospect who would do what my uncle wanted wasn't easy? I didn't know.

He certainly wouldn't want to suffer the loss of my portal opening capabilities. I'd always assumed that would keep me safe from marriage, but the Lord of Therress clearly thought to use me in another way now. Aside from the mines, which he could have taken from Elgord if he chose, what did the baron have that he needed? I couldn't think of anything.

On the bright side, he hardly paid attention to Rynn at dinnertime when we all sat together. She'd taken my advice and only spoke if prompted. Ulmar tried to draw her into a verbal trap several times, but thankfully, our younger cousin didn't fall for it.

Now, I crouched in my garden, pulling weeds. It needed to be done, but it also helped relax me. The sweet scent of flowers, musky odor of the carnivorous plants, and freshly turned soil brought me a measure of peace I couldn't find anywhere else. Except for the cobbled walkway that ran down the middle, a variety of plants grew on either side at varying heights and colors. Each species hummed with the vibrancy of life in its unique way, spreading that sensation to me. They were mine, and I was theirs.

Being within the high ivory walls of my private sanctuary gave me a respite from the tension within the castle, which I desperately needed since my uncle's servant, Parzival, seemed to be watching me extra closely. He reminded me of a bird of prey waiting for his chance to pounce.

Finished with weeding, I grabbed a set of thick gloves—enchanted for protection—and a basket from the supply cabinet at the far end of the garden. I moved to my four snapper berry bushes in the back corner, which were producing an impressive harvest this season. The plant was known for being finicky and had difficulty surviving to maturity. However, once it grew large enough, it could last decades with proper care.

The bushes produced some of the sweetest fruit in all the realm. My uncle dearly loved pies made with the luscious red berries, so I was determined to gather plenty for tonight's dessert. Perhaps that would put him in a better mood. He would know I had a hand in it since no one else in the area could successfully grow them.

One of my secrets to keeping my garden flourishing was feeding the soil small tendrils of magic now and then to enrich it. My druid grandparents had taught me how to do that, but one needed to handle it precisely right, or the enrichment could go terribly wrong. Too much power would make them grow very fast and strong, rendering them aggressive and territorial. More than usual, anyway.

I started to pick berries when one of the yellow flowers with thick, curved petals snapped at my fingers. If not for my gloves, I would have lost a digit. Thankfully, I only felt the pressure.

"Stop it," I said, swatting at it. "Try that again, and I'll cut you off."

It withdrew, the petals drooping a little in resignation. They could be so moody.

As I filled my basket, a sebeska flew into the garden. It landed on the nearby ivory-stone birdbath, taking a drink while waiting for me. I admired its cerulean feathers. This one had a black head and black-tipped wings, but otherwise, it was all blue on top. I could barely see the patch of white on its underbelly.

I went to it, removing my gloves and holding a palm under its beak. A small scroll fell into my hand. My heart thundered as I unrolled it and read the neatly written script. It was my husband, wishing to meet later tonight. He'd warned me he would request my services soon, and it looked like that time was upon me. We had made a deal, after all.

I moved to the chest where I kept my gardening supplies. Inside, I also kept parchment and a pen. I quickly wrote a reply letting Darrow know I'd see him at ten tonight, as requested.

The bird took the note and flew away. As for my husband's note, I stuffed it inside a compost bin and buried it deep. Fire would have been better, but I didn't have any immediately available, and I didn't want to risk taking the message out of the garden. It was the only safe place where no one would enter, and even if they tried, they wouldn't live long enough to do anything about it.

Putting my gloves back on, I returned to picking more of the red berries. Another bloom tested my patience, so I plucked it off and threw it toward one of my other carnivorous plants. It plucked the flower up, chewed it thoroughly before realizing it wasn't tasty, and spat the pieces onto the walkway.

"Told you guys not to mess with me," I said, wagging a finger at the bush, and then returned to picking again. The rest of the yellow blooms cowered away from my hands as I worked. Sometimes, one had to show tough love to their plants when they misbehaved.

"Aella," a male voice called.

I turned and found Tadeus standing in the archway. He was just far enough back so the lavender crunchertrap flowers couldn't reach him. There was a time long ago when he used to come in here, but that was before I acquired some of my people-eating flora. He looked past his shoulder nervously as if he worried about being seen.

"You're back," I said, hurrying toward him while pulling my gloves. At least he hadn't shown up until I'd gathered plenty of berries, and he'd missed the messenger bird.

He ran a hand through his coppery-red hair. "Father summoned me."

"Did you enjoy yourself while away?" I asked, giving him a brief hug.

The nervous look eased, and a grin slowly formed. "More than you want to know."

"We all have needs." I shrugged. "Glad you got some time away, especially while your father is in one of his moods."

Tadeus nodded. "Is there a way I could come in? I'm not really comfortable standing out here and had hoped to speak privately."

It had to be serious for him to want to come into the garden, risking life and limb.

"Give me a minute." I glanced at my most cantankerous flora. "It's going to take a bit of coercion before they'll let you through without a fight. They're rather protective of me."

"That's one way to put it."

I couldn't argue the point, so I turned and put my hands on my hips. "All of you plants listen to me. My cousin is coming inside here for a visit, and I insist that none of you harass or harm him. If any of you do, I will pluck you out of the ground, chop you up, and feed you to whichever animal's dietary preference you meet. Nod if you understand."

As I ran my gaze around the garden, each sentient plant gave me an affirmative gesture. I supposed it helped that I'd already carried through with my threat earlier on one of them. That was still fresh in their leafy minds.

I took Tadeus' arm and guided him inside. The most worrisome part was getting him past the crunchertraps, but thankfully, they could be obedient when they felt like it. The plants near them were passive to avoid conflict. Then, we moved past the tract vines spaced out with three on each side. They were tricky. They only had two moods—friendly and deadly. To my relief, their flowers swayed in a gentle greeting.

We stopped near the back, where I kept a table and a workbench. Though Tadeus was in one of his nicer blue tunics and black pants, he didn't hesitate to sit. Thankfully, he wasn't averse to getting dirty when the situation required it.

"Water?" I asked, gesturing toward the pitcher and cup a servant had delivered to the safety of the entry arch earlier. It was hitting the warmest part of the afternoon. Spring liked to throw in hot days like this to prepare us for what was to come.

He nodded. "That would be great."

I refilled the cup I'd been using. If it bothered Tadeus to drink from mine, he didn't show it. He simply guzzled the water down, clearly thirsty. "Did you come straight here when you returned?"

"Yes," he said, setting the cup down. "I knew you'd be in here avoiding my father."

"More like avoiding everyone, but certainly him, too."

My cousin grew quiet, broodier than usual. "I think father is up to something bad...very bad."

I strained my ears to check our surroundings. Thanks to the high walls, noise didn't carry well, but the kitchen staff often came out during the hottest parts of the day to do some of their work where they could catch a breeze. That happened to be on the other side of the garden on the north end where we sat closest. As of now, I couldn't hear anyone over there.

"Why do you think your father is up to something bad?" I asked, keeping my voice low.

He shook his head and followed my lead with his tone. "I've just overheard small pieces of information that don't make sense, but I know marrying you off quickly is part of his plot. He's desperate to get you off the market, as it were, and with someone he can control."

I wished I could tell him it was too late for that. The trouble was that while we'd always had each other's backs, I'd never confided with him about some of my extreme activities. That was a step too risky to take. I was terrified of anyone finding out about my deal with Darrow and my uncle either locking me up permanently or killing me to keep me out of enemy hands. Even if he kept the secret, he could say the wrong thing in front of his brother and get caught in a lie.

"Well, at least he can't force me to marry Elgord," I said, sighing.

He nodded. "I was really worried about that, so I started checking into ways to save you from it. Almost anyone would be better for you than that elf. That's how I spent my days in Maradeyn while I was gone, and I even went to Porrine, trying to find a way around your curse mark since you could flee if you didn't have that. Everyone said it was impossible."

"Thanks for trying," I said, touched that he'd gone to those lengths for me. Little did he know that even Darrow and the king couldn't find a simple way to resolve it.

He shrugged. "It didn't do any good."

"Any idea what your father is planning?" I asked.

His ocean-blue eyes met mine. "Something big. I think that week he was gone inspecting villages was more than it seemed, and I overheard him mention he met with someone named Vaslav."

"That's an unusual name." It certainly wasn't common in Therress or even one I'd heard while at the Court of Porrine.

"Anyway, just be..." he trailed off and stood, slowly maneuvering toward the northwest corner of my garden with his gaze on the stones there.

I went rigid, realizing I forgot to have the vines cover that section before he entered. It was another of those big secrets I'd never told him because I didn't want to risk losing a portal ring that had taken me so much time and funds to build.

Tadeus stood over it with shock in his gaze. "How long have you had this here?"

"Well, uh..." I got up and moved closer to him. "A long time, but you can't tell anyone."

He shook his head. "You could have trusted me with this. No one understands better than I do how my father would react if he discovered this, and I know you must feel trapped. If this gives you a chance to escape every now and then for a while, I can't blame you in the least."

"Really?" I badly wanted to believe him.

He smiled. "I'm more upset that I could have used this too—with your help."

"Sorry." I gave him an apologetic look. "There were so many times I wanted to tell you, but it wasn't easy to get it in place. I was afraid of anyone finding out."

Though Briauna had known for a while, Rynn didn't learn about it until the night we used it to have her cured. I hadn't seen the need for Tadeus to be aware of it since his father allowed him frequent trips away. Most likely because he didn't like his son and preferred him out of sight. As long as my cousin used his powerful metal-working and enchanting abilities—mostly weapons—when needed, Morgunn didn't care where his youngest son went.

He narrowed his gaze on the circle. "Wait, I recognize those stones. They're the ones you had me work on...fourteen years ago. You said it was so you'd have them in case you needed to create a temporary portal, but you already had a set, so these were extra as a precaution. That's what I assumed, anyway."

"Yes," I admitted. "Those are your work, but the ring was the most difficult part. I had it commissioned in Porrine, then snuck it in here in pieces with a special spell that would bind them back together afterward. Anyway, it was all a pain, but it's been useful."

Tadeus patted my shoulder. "Just trust me. I would never dream of telling my father anything that could get you in trouble."

I believed that, but there were still some secrets he was better off not knowing.

"Thank you," I said, then glanced at the basket of berries. "Now, I've got to get these to the cooks if they're going to have enough time to make pies."

In fact, I'd picked enough the servants could make one for themselves. With food shortages worsening due to the blight, their allotment had grown smaller while my uncle continued requiring ridiculous feasts for his meals. I wouldn't be stingy with my fruit, though. The people here also deserved a treat to show that their hard work was appreciated.

He nodded. "Good idea. Maybe the pie will be enough to save us all from Father's grief for a night."

One could hope.

Chapter 15

Aella

I pushed the food around my plate, only able to eat about a quarter of it. Lord Morgunn sat at the head of the table, rigid and regularly casting dark looks my way. The topic was still my failed betrothal.

At one point, Ulmar joined in the conversation. He suggested that I visit the king and convince him to change his mind. My uncle seriously considered that but said the king had already been quite clear in his refusal, so they must think of an alternative. Several names were bandied about by the two of them as they speculated what to do next while I cringed at each option. Why couldn't they let it go for a while?

To my relief, the servants finally removed our plates and brought out dessert. Lord Morgunn took one look at the large slice of snapper berry pie they served him, and his ice-blue eyes blessedly softened with contentment. Some years were better than others for harvesting. Last year, it didn't grow enough fruit to make a pie, but the nameless gods smiled upon me this spring. Perhaps they did it to compensate for all the awful things they were putting me through.

As Lord Morgunn took his first bite, he let out a moan of pleasure. "Aella, the berries this season are especially sweet. Excellent work."

"Thank you, uncle," I said with a relieved smile.

Part of me wanted to preen at his rare compliment, but the other part wished he'd choke on the berries. Was I a terrible niece for that? Then again, I hadn't protested when the king and Darrow contemplated how to kill my uncle within the bounds of Zadrya's laws, so I had already begun heading down a dark path. I'd gladly walk it if it got me free of the madman.

Taking a bite and letting the flavor burst over my tongue, I could understand the reason for his compliment. That finicky, wrathful bush had produced the best berries yet since I planted it five years ago. It was almost worth the blooms always trying to eat my fingers.

My uncle looked at Rynn. "How is your training coming along?"

"Good." She pushed a piece of her pie around the plate with her fork. "I can already heal small wounds with no trouble."

"Briauna told me that she's developing her skills faster than most and will be a real asset for us," I added. Lord Morgunn would be kinder to his niece if he saw her as a vital resource—well, as kind as he was capable, anyway.

He nodded. "Good. Too many soldiers must endure days of pain, waiting on a healer to help them after a battle. Some end up permanently disfigured because they didn't receive treatment quickly enough. If we can reduce those numbers, we will have more who can resume their duties."

While my uncle had a point, he didn't have to be so callous about it. Briauna wasn't our only healer, but she was the best and handled the most grievous wounds. The trouble was that such work took a lot of energy from her. She could only handle a few serious injuries before needing a break for a few hours.

The others could help, but none of them were nearly as proficient at repairing internal organs or shattered bones. Often, a soldier would be left with permanent disabilities if they didn't receive treatment within the first day or two before the damage began to set. High fae could heal reasonably fast on their own and even better with help, but lesser fae were much slower. They made up the bulk of our fighting force.

The conversation continued for a few more minutes as everyone ate their pie. After dessert, I walked Rynn to her room. I didn't tell her I'd be away for most of the night since she'd only worry. She knew the bare minimum details about my deal with Darrow, and I wanted to keep it that way. It was a price I happily paid to see her alive and well.

Once back in my room, I still had an hour before I'd need to leave. Dinner was always late and ran longer than most of us liked. On the other hand, it had helped pass the time. I changed out of my dress and switched to a dark tunic and pants, adding a knife just in case. Darrow didn't tell me precisely where we'd be going in his note, but he'd said the location was remote and to wear something practical. In other words, there was a chance we could run into trouble. I only hoped I wasn't aiding in something that could hurt Therress somehow.

As time drew near, I hurried through the secret passage and then opened a portal to the same location I had used to reach Durelle. Darrow had told me that would be our standard meeting point unless circumstances required a different one. He probably didn't want me to see any more of his land than necessary. Ironic, considering I should be living there as his wife.

It was by contract only, though. It was doubtful our marriage would ever be anything traditional, even once it was public knowledge. While I had no interest in deepening our relationship, it still hurt to think I'd never experience what it was like to have a real husband who slept next to me each night and made love to me.

I arrived on the other side and found only Jax waiting for me, along with his horse that grazed on a patch of grass. The strong elf with shoulder-length brown hair, square jaw, and condescending eyes glared at me as I approached him.

When I last saw Darrow's friend, we didn't say a word to each other. Mostly, he'd just given me menacing looks that were not dissimilar to now. I had the distinct impression he disapproved of my marriage, and trying to win him over would be an unwinnable battle.

"Where is everyone?" I asked, forcing an even tone in my voice.

He leaned his back against a tree and crossed a leg. "They'll be here in a couple of hours once you've regained your strength. No sense in everyone coming and all of us having to sit with you."

Lovely. Jax wasn't even trying to cover his disdain, but I wouldn't sink to his level. "Fine."

I found a tree a short distance away, sat, and relaxed against it. Here, I thought Darrow would be ready and waiting with sarcastic remarks, but instead, he didn't want to see me until it was necessary. He'd sent his anti-social friend instead. I was more than a little annoyed, considering we'd been married for nine days, and he was already avoiding me even when he requested my services. If I complained about it, though, he'd sarcastically ask if I missed him.

Tired after a long day working in the garden, followed by a tense meal and verbal battles with my uncle, my eyelids drifted shut. I desperately needed a nap. Jax appeared awake and alert. If anything dangerous showed up, he could deal with it. That made it even harder to resist.

I spread my senses to be sure there weren't any threatening creatures. All I picked up were small, harmless fae animals. Safe enough. Despite being in enemy territory with a man who hated me, I drifted to sleep. I hadn't been getting much rest at night lately and couldn't help it. The druid side of me felt more at ease with nature, making it relaxing.

Sometime later, the sound of hoofbeats stirred me awake. I slowly rose and dusted off my pants. Darrow, Faina, Loden, and several others rode toward us. All of them wore expressionless masks.

That was fine. If they wanted to keep this cold and impersonal, I could do the same. After all, this was a business transaction. My husband held up his end of the deal, and now it was my turn to do the same. Of course, polite discourse was unnecessary when we were still enemies in every other way.

Darrow rode up to me and handed me a small sheet of paper, along with a bag of holmium dust. "That should be everything you need. Are you ready?"

"Yes," I said, staring at the paper with the symbol sequence and avoiding his gaze. I'd seen him when he came up the road and immediately remembered how his looks alone could make my heart race. Of course, he didn't have the same reaction toward me. It was all a game to him.

I moved to the portal. Darrow's rune sequence wasn't on my list, so I had no idea where we were going or what to expect. I wanted to ask what all this was about, but I knew they wouldn't tell me. Their closed expressions said as much. All I'd heard before was that this place was very difficult for anyone else with my gift to reach. I took a deep breath and drew upon my power until my skin tingled with the surge. Then, I sent the ray of light toward the runes and began channeling.

It was like hitting a wall. My chest tightened, and sharp pain drilled through my head as I slowly chanted the words to start the process. Wherever they wanted to go, it resisted my efforts. I could feel all their gazes on me as I pushed harder and mentally worked my way through complex wards and protection spells unlike any I'd ever encountered. Sweat beaded my brows after several minutes passed, then my hands began to shake, but finally, I made the connection.

A blue miasma appeared before me.

"I can't believe she did it," Loden murmured.

Someone grunted. "Guess Darrow won the bet on this one."

I stood back and gestured for them to go ahead, not bothering to look their way. There was no feeling of triumph when I had no idea what I'd just done beyond allowing them to reach a difficult location. They rode their horses through the ring, with Jax picking up the rear after he'd mounted his. I'd be the only one on foot.

Once they were clear, I braced myself and followed them. Travel took longer than usual and felt like nearly twenty seconds. When I came out, I discovered we were in a dark forest, and an unwelcome sensation crawled across my skin. Somewhere nearby, I heard waves crashing against the shore, and the scent of saltwater filled my nose. We were either on a coast or an island, but nothing looked familiar. I'd never visited a place that felt more ominous than this.

Chapter 16

Aella

I made myself look at Darrow. "Where are we?"

He didn't appear the least bit uncomfortable as his gaze slid my way, and he gave me a dark smile. "Jolloure. It's gone back and forth between belonging to Zadrya and Karganoth for many centuries, but the dark elves currently hold it. Technically, we're trespassing."

"You had me take you to enemy territory?" I asked, stunned. "And you didn't warn me?"

He shrugged. "The dark elves might hold it, but most of them can't stand to be on this island for more than a few hours, either. Magic here is...disagreeable to us."

"Is that why the portal was so hard to open?"

"Part of the reason," he said cryptically.

I crossed my arms and glared at him. "So what's next?"

Darrow turned his horse toward the others. "Koen will stay here with you. The rest of us will be back in a couple of hours, so you should have time to regain your strength."

I ran a nervous gaze at the hulking trees surrounding us. "Is it safe?"

"Sometimes we have no trouble, and other times we do. Stay alert."

Before I could ask anything else, he rode away. The rest of his people followed him, except Koen, who pulled his sword and glowered through the darkness. I had the distinct impression he expected something dangerous to appear soon.

I hadn't seen him before, but I imagined Darrow had many soldiers under his command if he spent most of his time fighting dark elves off the west coast along the Strait of Bajjep. This elf was on the shorter side, near my height, and heavily muscled with a block-like head and plain features. He had short, dark hair and lightly tanned skin. His uniform was standard Veronnian, a mix of olive green and black that blended well with our surroundings.

For the first few minutes, I let my senses take in the environment and absorb the strange place. Nothing felt right. It was dark and mysterious, with many things crawling through the forest that rattled my senses. I had the horrible urge to run far away, but that wasn't an option.

I needed to get a hold of myself because I wasn't some scared little girl.

Through a break in the trees where moonlight filtered down, I caught sight of a familiar plant. It was a beautiful eventide rose, which was difficult to find in Zadrya. It only bloomed at night and grew along coastlines under specific conditions.

I had the worst time locating them during the day because they naturally blended into their surroundings. In the dark, however, they produced beautiful, yellow, bulb-shaped flowers. On Alavaar, they had incredible value because they helped with various dragon ailments. My sister grew a crop yearly, but few made it to maturity despite her best efforts.

The ones I saw here were perfect. I began pulling them, shocked to find so many everywhere. Koen watched me with obvious irritation but said nothing. Even my temporary Veronnian guard couldn't find fault with picking flowers.

They were small, so I stuffed as many as possible into my pockets and kept moving to find more. They would need to be processed within two days or lose much of their vital properties. I'd need to sneak over to Alavaar tomorrow night to give them to my sister. The more I could bring her, the better.

It was difficult to stop when I kept spotting more, but after a while, I realized I had completely lost sight of Koen. Apparently, he couldn't be bothered to keep a direct eye on me. I wouldn't have minded if not for the stark gloominess of the island.

Telling myself I would only pick a few more, I was shocked when I came across another portal ring. I knew it wasn't the same as the one we entered because it was crafted with black metal, and some of the symbols were unlike the ones I knew well.

"What is this?" I breathed.

"You should stay away from that," a male voice said.

I spun around, unable to find the source. "Where are you?"

He slowly stepped out of the dark woods. The first thing I noticed was his pointed ears were entirely black—the trait of a dark elf. Next, I took in his tall, muscular form. He was the same height as Darrow, but his shiny black hair was long and loose, going halfway down his chest. His dark, gray eyes looked at me piercingly.

"You may call me Bogdan," he replied, cocking his head. "You're Darrow's new wife, are you not?"

I backed up a few steps warily. "How do you know that?"

A random dark elf on a mysterious, creepy island should not have that kind of information. I was more than a little disturbed.

"He sent me a message so I wouldn't be startled by your presence tonight." Bogdan began moving toward me, but when I stiffened, he stopped. "I'm not going to hurt you."

"Why not?" I asked, drawing my brows in confusion.

"Darrow and I spent every winter together on Karganoth while growing up, and we share a grandfather," he said, studying me. "I'm loyal to him and would never hurt his wife."

I'd had no idea my husband ever visited the dark elf continent. Then again, his mother didn't betray his father until after he'd reached adulthood. The peace deal likely included any offspring spending time with the other side of the family. Still, they were known for their cruelty and brutal ways of bringing up their children. How much of that had affected Darrow?

"If you know we're married, then you must know it wasn't for love," I said, still tense.

Bogdan nodded. "It couldn't have been, but I see you overcame the magical barriers on this island's portal ring. He was right that you must be powerful."

I hoped that meant he wouldn't be so quick to attack me.

"What about that ring?" I asked, gesturing toward the strange one standing twenty feet from us.

He shook his head. "You don't want to get closer to it."

"Why not?"

"It leads to Faelaria, where the Unseelie rule and other dangerous places that are not suitable for us," he said, giving it an uneasy look.

While light and dark elves had little in common besides some physical characteristics, we could both agree that it had been tragic when we had to leave our original world. According to the historical accounts I'd been taught, there was a great war. Seelie fae were losing, and hundreds of thousands had died before we fled.

If we'd wished to survive, we had no choice except to come here with only what we could carry. Some speculated that the Unseelie didn't completely eradicate us because they had taken heavy losses as well and couldn't afford to chase us here. Who knew what the truth was since I'd never met one to ask?

I looked at the ring, frowning. "Does anyone ever come through?"

"Now and then." Bogdan worked his jaw. "It's my job to live here and monitor it, but most are too powerful to stop. I report what I see to Karganoth and Darrow."

"How often exactly?"

He gave me a rueful smile. "I've already said too much, and your husband should answer that—should you earn his trust."

The dark elf implied Darrow knew a lot more. I could not figure out why he'd had me bring him and the others here tonight, but I doubted I'd get any satisfying replies on that matter. Why was everyone around me keeping secrets, and why did I get the feeling they would affect me, whether I knew about them or not?

"Aella!" Koen came stomping out of the woods with a furious look on his face. "I would have thought you knew better than to wander off this far alone."

I gave him an annoyed look. "What do you care? And anyway, I assure you I can defend myself if necessary."

"Doubtful." He snorted, then looked at Bogdan. "Did she give you any trouble?"

"None. She's certainly more tolerable than you."

Koen glared at him. "I have no idea why Darrow trusts you so much, but I never will."

"No, I suppose you won't," Bogdan said, stepping back and slowly fading into the woods. It was like he had natural camouflage because I could see a faint outline until he moved too far away.

A shiver ran through me. Aside from my initial reaction to him, I hadn't felt in danger while in the dark elf's presence. I didn't know what to think about that, but I hated being left alone with the other prickly light elf.

Koen grabbed my arm and began hauling me away. "The others will be back soon, and we must be there waiting for them."

We entered the near-pitch black woods. I swore he made a point of dragging me through the thickest brush and giving me no time to avoid the sharp vegetation. Soon, I had scratches littering the exposed skin on my hands, face, and neck. I tried to jerk from his hold more than once, but he had an iron grip.

"Let go of me!" I shouted.

He shot me a dark look. "No. I know you're just a tool for him, but he can't possibly care about a piece of Therressian trash."

I tripped over a fallen log. Koen yanked me over it, nearly dislocating my shoulder in the process. After another minute of stumbling to keep up, I'd had enough. While I couldn't use wind power while he held me, I could use a regular weapon. With my free hand, I managed to pull the blade sheathed at my belt. I slashed at his forearm, cutting deep.

Koen immediately let go, and I fell, losing grip on my knife.

"You bitch!" he said, backhanding me in the face.

My head swung to the side, and pain exploded in my cheek. He didn't break anything, but it was a brutal hit that left my mouth filling with blood from my teeth cutting me. I kicked him in the leg, sending him stumbling backward. The next thing I knew, he was on me and pulling my arms above my head as I struggled to knock him off.

"You asshole!" I screamed. "Get off me."

His face was red with rage. "Not when you're the one trying to spy on the island and attacking me with a knife."

"Because you were hurting me and wouldn't let go," I said heatedly, struggling against his hold. "I wasn't spying."

"Darrow doesn't like or trust you. He never will, and neither will the rest of us," he said, angrily staring down at me. "You're just a tool to use."

"Get off..." I began, but then he suddenly flew backward.

I watched in shock as he landed hard on the ground ten feet away, barely missing a tree. Turning my gaze, I found Darrow dismounting from his horse. He stalked toward Koen, picked him up with one hand, and began punching him with his other hand. Over and over, he hit him in the face with brutal force.

Scrambling up, I moved toward them.

Faina ran up and stopped me from getting closer. "Let me see where you're hurt."

"I'm fine," I said.

She lifted a mocking brow. "You don't look fine. Your cheek is swelling, and there are cuts all over you."

"What does it matter?" I asked, angry they'd put me in this situation.

"Koen was supposed to guard you, not hurt you. We would never allow that."

Darrow finished punching the soldier and hovered over him. "Do not ever lay a hand on Aella again. She is my wife, and you will treat her accordingly."

"She's the damn enemy," he said, cupping his nose where it bled profusely. "I caught her checking out the Unseelie ring and talking to Bogdan."

Darrow bared his teeth. "That doesn't give you the right to hurt her."

"She cut me with a knife, so of course I defended myself."

"No." I shook my head. I might take a lot of abuse from my family, but I refused to take it from anyone here. "You were dragging me through the woods into the brush and over fallen logs, not caring that you were hurting me, and refusing to let go when I asked. I had no choice except to fight back."

"It's not my fault you were too weak to keep up," he said, glaring at me through two swollen eyes. "But what should I expect from a Therressian whore!"

Darrow let out a growl. In the next instant, a blade glinted in his hand. He stabbed Koen straight into the heart, burying the knife to the hilt. The soldier slumped to the ground as all the color drained from his face. Everyone exchanged shocked looks.

He was...dead.

Did my enemy husband kill one of his own men because of me? I stared at the scene with incomprehension. Sure, the asshole had said some horrible things and hurt me, but I didn't think he'd get punished for it when they were probably all thinking the same way as him.

"Leave Koen here. The forest animals can consume his body for all I care," Darrow said, cold fury all over his face. "If anyone else hurts Aella or speaks about her the way he did, they die. Understood?"

The rest of the group nodded their head, gazes still stunned.

Then, he moved toward me with a determined stride, stopping less than two feet away as he ran his gaze up and down my body. "Are you okay?"

I stared at him, noting the anger still lining his features. "I'm fine."

"I'm sorry he hurt you." He brushed his fingers across my swollen cheek, and I flinched.

"Here," Faina said, handing him a clean cloth.

Darrow accepted it, gaze softening as he began dabbing at my cuts. He was gentle, but I was at my wits' end with all that had happened. The pure hatred I'd seen in Koen's eyes haunted me. My uncle and Ulmar might be vicious and cruel, but even they didn't look at me with such revulsion and venom. I hadn't even met that elf before tonight.

"What does it matter?" I asked, shaking as I tried to hold myself together.

He dabbed at a deeper cut on my neck. "I vow none of my people will lay a hand on you again."

"Please don't make promises you can't keep," I said, pulling away.

He sighed. "Koen should have known better than to do what he did, but it was my fault for not making your status with me clearer."

"Then make sure the others understand because that..." I pointed at the dead soldier's body, "...was not part of our deal." I spun away from him, unwilling to hear his reply.

Where was my knife? I was not leaving it in this gods' forsaken place. My gaze ran over the tousled brush and broken branches, searching frantically. A glint caught my eye. I snatched it up and quickly sheathed it. Everyone was watching me as I marched toward the portal. I ignored the pain in my cheek, the sting of my cuts, and my sore shoulder as I began channeling. This time, it wasn't as hard since the island's protections didn't stop people from leaving. I had it open in seconds.

Standing aside, I waved my arm for the group to enter. Though I felt their gazes linger on me, I refused to look at any of them. One by one, they passed until I was the last one left—not counting the dead elf.

With one last look at the gloomy island, I walked through the portal, allowing it to close behind me. Twenty seconds later, I stepped out the other side. Most of the others were already riding away. Only Darrow remained, dismounting from his horse. He pulled a wrapped bundle from his saddlebag and opened it. Inside, there was a metal container with bread, cheese, and dried meat.

"Are you hungry?" he asked.

He must have anticipated the massive amount of power I would use tonight would draw out my appetite, but it also felt like a peace offering. "I'll take some bread."

"You should eat more than that," he said, frowning.

I rubbed my cheek. "Not really up for eating much."

Darrow nodded in understanding, handed me the bread, and dug out a water container from his saddlebag. "Here."

"Thank you," I said, taking hold of them.

"How quickly do you usually heal?" he asked, gaze roving over my numerous wounds.

I took a swig of water first, not realizing how thirsty I'd become during my travels. "It will all be gone by morning."

Perhaps he wondered because of my druid side, but they healed as fast as high fae.

"Are you certain?" he asked, no doubt worried someone would see me and ask questions. We wouldn't want anyone to figure out I'm helping the enemy after all and ruin his plans—whatever those were.

"Yes, I'm sure." I had enough experience to know.

I sat down to finish my bread as he silently ate the rest of the food. A part of me wished he'd left with his friends, but he wouldn't dare leave me alone in his territory. At least the trip here hadn't drawn as much power, so I probably only needed another hour before I'd become strong enough again. Pushing my skills seemed to enhance them. Despite the fight beforehand, I didn't feel quite as drained as I expected.

Darrow set aside the food container. "I have heard that your uncle didn't handle it well when the king refused your betrothal to Elgord."

"No, it hasn't been pleasant to be around him. Now, he is trying to find someone else suitable for me, so we'll see how that goes," I said, taking another drink of water.

Being alone with him was strange when he wasn't baiting or teasing me, yet the tension between us was taut. I was angry about the fight with Koen, and maybe he felt guilty about putting me in that situation. Before tonight, I wouldn't have guessed it might bother him, but to kill one of his soldiers and abandon him like that revealed—at the very least—that he didn't want to see me hurt. I couldn't decide how I felt about that. The scene continuously replayed in my head from when his rage became so great that he stabbed the elf.

"Perhaps it will take your uncle a long time to find anyone willing and worthy," Darrow said, staring at me in a way I couldn't read.

I shrugged. "It's my problem, not yours."

"It's both of ours now."

Oh, sure. He'd choose which things we handled as a married couple and which we didn't. I refused to dignify that with a response and stared into the woods instead. Physically, I was exhausted and couldn't wait to go home and sleep for a few hours.

I checked my pockets and was grateful the flowers I'd stuffed in them were still there. The rest I'd held in my hands were lost during my struggle with Koen, which frustrated me almost more than my wounds. Those buds could have done so much good for the dragons.

"Will we be returning to Jolloure in the future?" I asked.

He nodded. "Yes."

"Can I ask why?"

Darrow stared at me for a moment. "No. At least, not yet."

His answer didn't surprise me. Then again, with all the bad blood between our lands, did I want his trust? This marriage had nothing to do with that. It was simply business to get what we both needed, and I didn't have to know what he did as long as it didn't hurt my people. Only one thing continued to bother me.

I sat up straighter and cocked my head. "Why didn't you kill me that day on the battlefield?"

A smile stretched his lips. "I probably would have if not for you blowing a kiss. It was a challenge I couldn't resist, so I retaliated in kind."

How ironic. I never did things like that, but doing it that one day likely saved my life.

"You could have removed the one person capable of transferring Lord Morgunn's forces across your border without warning." I shook my head. "It seems short-sighted."

His expression turned thoughtful. "Believe me when I say I questioned my choice afterward, and when you showed up almost a week later, I thought I had my second chance at finishing you. Then, you gave me an opportunity I couldn't resist."

"To use my portal opening abilities for yourself?"

Darrow nodded. "And to see how you responded to a real kiss."

I sighed and looked away. His light chuckle filled my ears, but I refused to look at him again. We spent the rest of our time sitting in the woods in silence. To my relief, nothing came out of the night to bother us. As soon as I felt myself regain enough power, I stood. Darrow watched me open the portal home but blocked me before I could go through it.

He leaned forward and kissed my forehead, surprising me. "I'll contact you when I need you again, Aella."

Then, he stepped away and nudged me toward the portal. I didn't bother looking back.

Chapter 17

Aella

I t was four in the morning when I returned to my room after the Jolloure trip. I had hoped to sleep in late since I didn't always eat breakfast with the family anyway, but a mere four hours later, my uncle sent a servant to tell me I needed to be downstairs in ten minutes. He had news.

I forced myself to dress in a simple lavender gown with short sleeves and braid my hair. Fatigue weighed my body down. Anytime I had to open multiple long-distance portals, it took a lot out of me. My muscles were even sore, but one look in the mirror confirmed that the signs of my fight the night before had healed as expected. I merely had to wash away the final remnants.

Hurrying downstairs, I found my uncle and cousins at the table. They were already midway through their meal. Rynn gave me a discreet smile, Tadeus nodded his head, and Ulmar smiled cryptically at me. Lord Morgunn had a distinct look of impatience.

"It's about time." He set his teacup down with a *click*. "By the nameless ones, Aella, you look dreadful."

"I had trouble sleeping last night," I said, already prepared with an excuse.

I took a seat next to Rynn, and a servant delivered food to me a moment later. My breakfast preferences rarely changed, so they knew what I wanted. The plate had a biscuit with jam, two eggs, and a bowl of fruit. I was starving and planned to eat every bite of it now that my face didn't hurt anymore.

He lifted a brow. "What could have possibly kept you up?"

Um, that was a good question I hadn't expected. He usually didn't care.

I supposed I should go with something that made sense in his diabolical mind and wouldn't trigger Ulmar's gift of detecting lies. "I was concerned about my marriage prospects, my lord, as I know it has been troubling you."

Thankfully, I had been thinking about that last night.

"It's good to hear you take such matters seriously." A slow smile formed. "I happened to receive a message before breakfast from one possibility, and I think you might appreciate it."

Not likely if it made him happy. "Who?"

"The Prime Chief of the Andalagar tribe. They tend to be reclusive, but they have some of the fiercest warriors in the realm. The leader is searching for a suitable wife," he said, a pleased expression on his face.

My mind raced. I was familiar with the tribe since their main branch resided within Therress, but they mostly acted autonomously within Zadrya. My uncle left them alone on the condition that they paid quarterly tithes and promised to join our forces should a war break out. He often lamented that it would be better if he could use their warriors beyond that agreement, such as for raids on Veronna.

The Andalagar tribe had been here long before the fae arrived, and like the druids with their dragons, they had something precious that we didn't—Pegasi. According to our early years on the planet, the Seelie attempted to take some of the winged horses for themselves, but they would not tolerate fae on their backs.

Nothing our ancestors tried made them more amenable. As a result, many of the beautiful Pegasi were killed during the Seelie's attempts to tame them, and they eventually had to concede that only the native tribes could use them. Their most significant advantage was the ease with which they flew over the Sobaryan Mountains and bypassed any wards without triggering them. Of course, any fae lord would love access to them and their riders.

"They always marry within their tribal system," I said, genuinely surprised. "Why would the leader consider me?"

Lord Morgunn sat back in his chair, finished with his meal. "It astonished me as well, but the message inquired about your portal channeling abilities. Chief Orran recently lost the only person he had who could open distant ones. Also, because you are half-druid, it makes you more palatable, I suppose."

While druids were also native, I hadn't thought that mattered to them.

"When will we meet him?" I asked, bracing myself.

If I wasn't already married and knew this deal could never go through, I might have been a little excited at the prospect. There was a chance the leader would be better than anyone else my uncle might choose. On the other hand, the tribes had an entirely different culture that I didn't understand. I'd never had the opportunity to visit them, so for all I knew, life there could be worse. Who knew how they treated their women? My lessons growing up only taught the bare minimum, as if the tribe held little importance.

My uncle's expression became stern. "His message said he wishes to meet and evaluate potential marriage prospects this summer. They will expect you to demonstrate your battle prowess—with magic and weapons. In the meantime, I'm sending you to Tradain to improve your skills before you visit. No need for you to embarrass me because you fail to practice enough."

I held back a wince.

While he could have been kinder with his words, he wasn't entirely wrong. I tried to train occasionally but hadn't dedicated myself to it for several years. With everything happening in my life, it was a good idea to hone my weapons capabilities and try to improve my light magic. We didn't have the necessary setup on the castle grounds for me to work on that particular power, but they did at Tradain.

"I will work hard on it, Uncle," I said, adding a little enthusiasm to my voice.

The training part was a good idea, anyway. I also hoped to see a Pegasus up close, but I didn't look forward to proving myself before the Andalagar or finding a way to discourage their leader from marriage.

He nodded approvingly. "Very well. Spend the rest of the morning organizing for an extended stay at Tradain. I have already sent word to expect you there early this afternoon."

That soon? I was barely going to have time to pack my things and prepare my garden for my absence, never mind my lack of sleep. It took all my control to rein in my panic. "Thank you, uncle."

I finished my breakfast quickly and hurried back to my room. First, I needed to preserve the flowers I'd managed to save the night before so they didn't wilt further before I saw my sister.

Next, I'd have to rush to the garden. The regular spring rains would be enough to keep everything sufficiently watered, so I just needed to feed my carnivorous plants from my insect traps to hold them for a while. I could return periodically for a few hours to tend them while at Tradain. I'd also ensure safe passage for Rynn so she could check on them in between. Most of my plants had shown affection for my younger cousin anyway and wouldn't hurt her.

I'd barely left the dining room before Ulmar caught up to me. "You better train well, Aella."

I didn't like the sound of his menacing voice. "I am planning on it, but why do you care?"

"We need strong alliances." He gave me a look that made my skin crawl. "It's up to that pretty face of yours to help us build them, so do whatever it takes to win over that chief."

It wasn't easy, but I managed to resist punching him. "Why aren't you marrying anyone then? You're over twenty years older than me and a firstborn son, so it makes even more sense for you."

"Oh, you're not the only one, but unlike you, the king approved my betrothal. We are merely waiting until later this summer to announce it as a few matters are sorted out," he said, giving me a smug grin.

I felt sorry for whoever he'd marry. "Good. I'll look forward to meeting her."

With that, I hurried away from him.

Chapter 18

Aella

Leaving the dining hall after dinner, I headed back to the barracks. I'd only practiced for a few hours since I didn't arrive at Tradain until after one in the afternoon, but I already felt sore from all the sword and knife drills. It would get worse before it would get better.

I entered through the main entrance and turned to my right. The barracks were two floors, but I was lucky they assigned me a ground-level room. I opened the door, passing through the ward I'd already put in place to keep people out. The space was tiny and narrow. It only had a small bed, a chest sitting at the foot of it, and a nightstand. The empty floor space was a mere two by six feet, which didn't encourage guests.

I liked having the room to keep my things, but I rarely slept in the barracks, preferring to spend the night in Cam's roomier officer quarters instead. He knew better than to expect me this evening, though. I'd told him I had plans to see my sister and wouldn't return until late, so I'd come to his place after training tomorrow.

Opening the chest, I grabbed the cloth-wrapped flower buds. A brief assessment confirmed that the preservation spell I had placed on them had held so far. I looked yearningly at my bed. It would be another long night without much sleep, but it couldn't be helped. Not only did I need to see my sister, but I could also use one of the sebeskas in her village to send a message to Darrow without anyone knowing. I'd promised to update him on anything affecting our agreement, and he certainly needed to know about the latest developments with the Andalagar.

No one questioned me when I left Tradain and walked a half mile toward the portal ring. Two male guards dressed in the Therressian army's brown and forest green uniforms stood next to it, alert and watchful. They nodded when I approached but didn't question me. Most soldiers could recognize me from my channeling them to and from battlefields.

I pulled my stash of holmium from my pocket. My uncle had given me extra in case he needed me to open portals while I was at Tradain, and I'd combined that with what Darrow provided. Drawing in the necessary elements, I pushed my power into sequencing the runes on the ring. Seconds later, blue light shimmered before me. Giving the guards a wave, I stepped into it.

Though the portal had to transport me from south-central Therress across the narrow Carsiyan Sea and onto the southwestern coast of Alavaar, the distance was still shorter than going to Siggaya, where Darrow and I made our deal. I estimated that about eight seconds passed.

When I stepped out, I found myself in barren woods devoid of wildlife. Despite the warm day, goosebumps ran up my arms, and waves of melancholy and emptiness swept over me, clawing at my mental energy. A few trees in the distance had a smattering of brown leaves that would fall soon, but most stood barren of any foliage. It was one of the areas worst hit by the blight in Alavaar. I hated walking through these pockets of death where even the scents of decay burned my nostrils.

All the races of Paxia took energy from the environment to perform magic, but the planet struggled to reabsorb the waste produced by spells. The fountain helped act as a filter and generator, but the longer it was gone, the worse things became. I'd heard other worlds didn't need one, but ours couldn't survive for too long without it for reasons lost to time.

We hadn't realized how deleterious the effects would be during the first few centuries because they were subtle. Mostly, there were small pockets of land where the environment felt off or wrong. In the last two hundred years or so, the issue began to intensify as fertility rates dropped for fae and animals, and the land began to die. It worried me to think of how much worse it might get. In times past, couples would produce six or more children, but they now averaged half that number, with even fewer surviving to adulthood due to faebor fever.

The darkness pushing at my mind grew worse, urging me to run from this place.

I quickly began my trek west, following a barely discernible trail through the dried vegetation. It took about ten minutes before I escaped the barren land. Relief filled me as healthier trees and brush surrounded me, and birds tweeted beautiful songs. I eagerly breathed in the floral and pine scents.

The line I'd crossed was where the druids concentrated on renewing the land to prevent the spread of decay, but they could only do so much. Keeping populated areas safe was their top priority. After a few more minutes, I finally spotted the first thatched houses. It was a small village of about 570 people, and they spaced their homes widely apart to allow room for gardens and workshops.

In the distance, the trees opened to reveal the coastline with waves crashing at the shore. The fresh scent of salt filled the air, invigorating after my walk through the woods. I stopped to ask about my sister, and an older woman hanging laundry told me Priyya was up at the ridge. That didn't surprise me.

I weaved between homes, heading south into vibrant woods filled with bright green leaves and blue pine. Small, furry animals scurried through the brush almost everywhere I looked. A brown spurmel poked its head around a nearby tree and chirped at me. They were small creatures with fluffy fur, long tails, and cute little faces. Most were shy, but some could be domesticated and even kept as pets if one didn't mind a little chaos in their home. They had a great deal of energy due to the amount of time they typically spent in the wild hunting for the fruits and berries that made up their diet.

As for other nearby creatures, I didn't worry about them posing a threat while I walked. Alavaar had little dangerous wildlife due to the dragons eating or scaring them away from most areas. Even hazardous plants had been cleared from the vicinity of population centers and well-traveled roads. Aside from the dead zone pockets, I always felt safe and at peace while visiting, unlike in Zadrya, where I always had to stay on my guard.

Fifteen minutes after leaving the village, I made my way over a bridge with a river's rushing water beneath it. Past that, the land opened to a verdant field covered in blue-green grass and tiny purple flowers called mayzies. Green and yellow striped bees flitted between them, performing nature's hypnotic dance as they sought pollen. The warmth of the sun was welcome as it heated my skin.

Near the ridge farther ahead, a massive sky-blue dragon nuzzled its nose against my sister's chest. The sound of her melodic laugh was welcome to my ears. Sometimes, it was easy to forget that I once had a complete family with constant love and laughter.

My father had generally been a stern man and didn't tolerate impertinence, but he'd encouraged family bonding and happy moments. His own childhood had lacked it, which wasn't a surprise with Lord Morgunn for an older brother. Mother had alternated between having a single-minded focus on an important project and being carefree with her children. It hadn't mattered that my siblings' ages and mine were far apart. In most ways, she'd treated us the same. It was a period of my life I still recalled fondly before it had crashed around me.

Sometimes, I envied Priyya for having nine years more with our mom than I did, but those feelings never lasted. She was so much like Nerine that they could almost have been twins. My sister also deviated between seriousness and uncontained joy. Right now, she was the latter.

Priyya stood before the dragon, her dark-blonde hair flowing loosely down her back, wearing a simple dark blue dress with white lace trimming. Like me, her ears weren't as pointed as a full elf and rounded a little at the top. We both had green eyes, but whereas mine were pear green, hers were sea green. She was much more petite than me—as if she barely remembered to eat.

My sister patted the dragon's nose and hurried toward me. We hugged, and I drew in her fresh, flowery scent. It was always comforting to me. We might have lost our parents and elder brother, but we still had each other.

She pulled back and scrutinized me. "You look tired."

"Not enough sleep lately is all," I said, shaking my head.

"What's our uncle done this time?" she asked, sighing.

Priyya couldn't stand Lord Morgunn and had tried to find a way to save me from the curse years ago, but she never found one. It was amazing how many people had tried and failed, making me wonder if Darrow would have any better luck. There might not be bars caging me, but I still felt like a prisoner.

I stared toward the ocean, which lay a couple of hundred feet below the ridge from where we stood. Waves crashed against the rocks with a loud spray. "First, he tried to make me marry Baron Elgord, but thankfully, the king refused to approve the betrothal."

Priyya wrinkled her nose. "I remember him. He was awful and had the coldest eyes."

"Terrible kisser, too," I said, then explained all that happened with him and the newest plan with the Andalagar.

Before coming, I'd thought long and hard about whether or not to tell her about Darrow, but I decided against it. She'd throw a fit and ruin the couple of hours I had to visit her before returning to Tradain. It was better to wait until another time, when I felt more comfortable with my circumstances and had more time with her, though I had no idea when that would be, given my new schedule. I was usually allowed one trip a month, but Lord Morgunn sometimes revoked that privilege when it suited him.

My sister pulled me into another hug. "I wish there was a way I could save you from it."

"I know, but it helps to see you and know you're here." It truly did, since she had a way of bringing peace to my turbulent emotions.

Priyya wasn't a fighter. In fact, she hated weapons so badly that our father gave up trying to train her. Her druid side was so much stronger, and the one thing she did have was a major stubborn streak. She'd chosen to live in the village of Fionbor because it was where our grandmother lived, and she wanted to be close to her. I didn't have time to visit our Nan today, and would probably have to avoid her for a while since she had a way of getting secrets out of me. She wouldn't find it strange since I often avoided her. The elder druid was also rather intimidating and more than a little scary at times with her razor-sharp mind.

My sister also chose this area because there were a lot of dragon nests in the southern area of the continent, and her passion was taking care of them. Druids had a symbiotic relationship with the massive beasts that couldn't be easily explained.

Even as I thought that the sky-blue dragon ambled toward us. The ground trembled with each step. She was so big that with her head up, I couldn't reach her nose. I'd never seen this one before. She was lovely, with her scales glinting in the waning sunlight and her wings tucked into her sides.

"What's her name?" I asked.

Priyya's magic involved communicating with nature, including animals. She could even soothe their pain and heal most types of wounds for them. It was one of the reasons my father realized she wasn't meant to fight and to let her come here instead. None of her magic was conducive to battle.

"She is called Dagra," my sister said, smiling at the massive creature. "She wants to know if you'd like to go for a ride."

A thrill ran through me. Not all dragons liked being ridden, particularly if they didn't know someone well. I didn't get enough time around them to be familiar with most. It was a rare opportunity if one offered, especially at the first meeting.

I grinned. "Absolutely. It's been ages since I've been up in the air, but first..." I pulled a small, wrapped parcel from my pocket. "...take this. It's eventide roses."

"Where did you get those?" she asked, eyes rounded with surprise.

"I went on a portal exploration last night and found a place with plenty of them." I paused as she exclaimed over the number and quality I had retrieved. "It wasn't a very safe place, so I can't go back often. Just glad I came away with something to make the trip worthwhile." She was well aware of my penchant for exploring various portal locations and didn't question me further on it.

"Thank you so much. These will go a long way since I've had trouble getting them to grow here anymore," she said, unsurprised when the dragon dropped her giant head down to sniff at the flowers.

"I'll keep looking for more when I go out," I promised.

She nodded, folding the cloth back. "Now, go for that ride before it gets dark."

Priyya didn't have to tell me again. A moment later, Dagra lowered herself enough for me to climb. Still, it wasn't easy because the apex of her back was about fifteen feet from the ground. It was steep and uneven getting up there.

Once at the top, I found the natural seat and grabbed hold of the spikes jutting from her shoulder joints. She lifted into the air in one of the smoothest take-offs I'd ever experienced, gliding right over the sea. As we rose higher, I caught the sun beginning to kiss the horizon. It was incredibly stunning, with the orange and red streaks painting the sky in splashes of brilliant colors. For a moment, I could let all my worries and fears go. Flying high was definitely worth the trip here.

Chapter 19

Aella

I woke up cradled in the heat of Camden's arms. After two weeks at Tradain, I'd become accustomed to sleeping in his quarters every night. It had been a long time since I'd regularly had my needs fulfilled, and I appreciated the *mostly* sated feeling.

Since marrying Darrow, though, it didn't feel the same anymore. I had to remind myself that he didn't care about Camden and even encouraged us sleeping together. He was no doubt waking in the arms of some other fae right now as well. Not to mention, we remained enemies, and I had no reason to be loyal to him—even if he did kill a man for hurting me. I still couldn't get that scene out of my head, but I tried because I couldn't make sense of him doing it.

Most of all, it was hard to comprehend that I had a husband, except each night when I slept. I saw him in my dreams and remembered that first kiss by the portal. Then, the one in the room where the king performed the ceremony. I hated how good and right it had felt to have his mouth on mine, as if we were made for each other.

I slowly rose from the bed, completely naked. Camden's brown eyes opened as I rifled through my things, following my movements as I gathered a few items to take to the bathing chambers with me. His gaze heated.

"Come back to bed, Aella. It's barely past dawn," he said huskily.

There was a time when I wouldn't have hesitated.

"Sorry, I want to get out early to work on my light magic. I feel like I'm getting close to figuring out how to use it more safely, or at least less dangerously," I sighed, running a hand through my tangled blonde hair. "It will be a useful offensive weapon if I can perfect it."

He groaned and glanced down at his hard cock, which begged for attention, then back at me. "You've been working at that every morning since you arrived. Waiting another half hour won't make much of a difference."

Camden had a point. Looking at him lying there with his dark blond hair sticking up in different directions and bedroom eyes full of lust, it was hard to resist. I supposed some of my hangups lately had been whether I was betraying him by not mentioning I was married. He'd been on the battlefield that day when Darrow had faced off against us. I was lucky the captain wasn't one of the soldiers who'd died.

What would he think when he found out? It was inevitable since I couldn't keep it secret forever, but right now, I only wanted to delay that revelation as long as possible. Not to mention, the fae side of my libido protested at the very idea of going without sex for long.

So, I set down the things I'd gathered and crawled back into bed, climbing on top of him. For however long this lasted, I would make it worthwhile for both of us. He groaned when I sank onto him, already wet and ready. He took hold of my hips. We began slowly at first, with me rising and falling to tease us both in a sensual glide that built our need higher and higher.

Before long, neither of us could take it anymore. We rolled over, and he took charge, speeding the pace and pounding into me so hard the bed rattled against the wall. I closed my eyes, concentrating only on the pleasure and not on the errant thoughts that distracted me regularly. Camden had learned long ago the perfect rhythm to make me orgasm fast, and he came with me when I exploded. We had morning sex down to an art.

He nuzzled my neck. "I'm going to enjoy you for as long as I can before that Andalagar chief decides to marry you."

I swallowed hard as my guilt rose back to the forefront.

"What makes you think he'll choose me?" I asked. Of course, I had to tell him the reason my uncle sent me to Tradain, so at least I wasn't lying to him about everything.

"He'd be crazy not to choose a beautiful, talented woman like you," he said, pulling away to look down at me with his brown eyes. "If I thought your uncle would approve it, I would have offered to marry you."

I frowned. "Really?"

His gaze drifted toward the curtained window, and his jaw hardened. "The thought crossed my mind a time or two, but I've always known my time with you was limited."

I wasn't sure what to think of that. Camden was a lowborn fae with limited magic, so he wasn't wrong that Lord Morgunn would disapprove of us becoming husband and wife. Aside from that, I'd never considered something serious with him. I enjoyed sex with him immensely, and we could talk about nearly anything, but he didn't tug at my heart like I wanted. Perhaps no one ever would.

Giving him a peck on the cheek, I slid out from under him. "I've really got to get going now, but I'll see you for lunch?"

"Yes," he said, still lost in thought.

I grabbed my things and headed for the washroom.

***

The place I used for my light magic was not within Tradain. Instead, it was a mile outside the village and consisted of a deep pit with stone stairs leading to the bottom. This was where those of us with dangerous, volatile magic could practice without the risk of harming others. There were also layers of protection spells to prevent the walls from collapsing.

I had a two-inch stone on the ground as a target. It was the latest of many that had suffered a terrible fate. I had no problem hitting the rocks since I had an excellent aim, but I always destroyed them into tiny fragments. What I really wanted was to make precise cuts that left the rest intact.

For the umpteenth time, I extended my hand and focused my power. A narrow beam of red light extended from my index finger, slow at first, before moving so fast it hit the stone and pulverized it in a spray of dust and pebbles. I sighed. Other channelers could do something similar, but their powers were so much weaker that they had limited range and damage they could inflict. It didn't compare, so I couldn't ask them for help. They didn't need to rein in their magic like me.

I focused on the next stone and tried once more. This time, I slowed down the extension of the beam a little more, but as soon as it came near the stone...*boom*! It was dust. There were a lot of piles in this pit, sitting on newly formed glass I'd also made from the heat of my magic.

"You could kill many enemy soldiers doing that," a condescending voice said from above.

I drew a deep breath and slowly turned to look at the top of the pit, finding Lord Morgunn there with an arrogant expression. Of course, he'd show up to witness my failure. "It will also cut through anything behind my targets."

He worked his way down the steps toward me. "Yes. The destructive power is promising, but it is almost useless without control. Don't show the Andalagar Chieftain this unless you become more proficient."

"I've been practicing every day," I said, hoping that counted for something.

He grimaced. "Then it will likely be a long time yet before you master it...if ever. I'm not sure you have the mental acuity for it."

I gritted my teeth. It would likely kill my uncle to say something mildly encouraging, so I didn't know why I expected anything less than a disparaging remark. He constantly complained about my portal abilities not progressing fast enough, though I was okay with that since he didn't know I'd far exceeded his expectations.

This was different, though. I'd been incompetent at my light magic for years, aside from when I entwined it to channel portals, but singling it out was a mess.

It was like how I was right-handed, so everything was smoother and more precise when I used that side. It represented my perfected skill with wind. As for my left, I could use it, but most things I did ended up sloppy and unrefined. That symbolized my light powers.

"To what do I owe the pleasure of your visit?" I asked, deciding to change the subject.

He smiled like he knew exactly what I was doing. "We will raid Veronna tonight, an hour after sunset. You'll be transporting the troops from here, so I thought I'd come to Tradain to inform you and see how you're doing."

How very thoughtful of him. He'd likely watch me the rest of the day, making me a nervous wreck, and then I'd have to help him attack my husband's territory. There was no way to warn Darrow in time, though I wouldn't anyway since that would result in us losing more of our forces. It was a no-win situation. If this went badly, my uncle would unknowingly violate my agreement with Darrow and force me to help Veronna retaliate against my people.

I painted a calm expression on my face. "I'm always at your service, my lord. It's about lunchtime if you'd like to walk back with me to Tradain."

"Yes." He nodded. "Let's do that."

Chapter 20

Aella

Anxiety filled me, and my stomach felt like it had twisted into knots. I sat astride Astra next to the ring as mounted troops disappeared through it. There were a lot of them—far more than usual.

While channeling wind and light to keep the massive portal open, I tried to keep count. Finally, those on horseback had all passed, with the centaurs and foot soldiers coming next. Lines of five or six at a time marched into the blue miasma with stoic expressions and weapons in hand. By the time the last disappeared, I estimated at least five hundred, almost double what we usually sent for a raid.

My gut churned with dread.

Taking a deep breath, I guided my horse through the portal. We zoomed through space in a whirl of colors. I arrived on the other side, approximately a mile from the village of Parvayn, situated on the southeastern edge of Veronna. Its population was just under nine hundred, with only a small contingent of soldiers to guard it. I knew because I'd researched all the border towns when my uncle started having me channel his troops there.

The last time we targeted this town was when our forces still physically traversed the mountain passes, as it sat near the southernmost crossing between our lands. The people here would be quickly overwhelmed, considering half of them were elderly, infirm, or children, and many others were either miners or sheep herders with limited fighting skills. The last time we came here was ten years ago when my uncle slaughtered dozens before I intervened. He d promised he wouldn't do it again.

I found myself surrounded by thick woods with a narrow dirt road running alongside the portal ring. It was dark since the moon was only a sliver tonight, but most of our soldiers had powered their glow stones to see better. There were many soft lights, primarily in shades of blue or green, so that no one would see them from far away. Armed fae and horses were scattered everywhere. The captains called out orders and quickly reorganized them.

Tadeus joined me off to the side of the ring. "This is going to be a long night."

"Why do you say that?" I asked.

"My father hopes to steal a few crates of blue burst gems the Veronnians plan to ship to Juvarn tomorrow, and he'll do anything to make certain he gets them instead," he said, voice grim.

My eyes widened. Those gems were rare, with the mine near Parvayn producing over half the total for the realm. They amplified spells that could be protective or destructive. Once activated, the stones only worked once before becoming inert dust, so there was always a demand for more, making them quite valuable.

Therress didn't have direct access to blue burst gems, but our northern neighbor, Raumandia, had a small mining operation. They gave us twenty percent of their output in exchange for taking some of their people because their land was suffering from large sections of dead zones—both in the sense that nothing grew there and the magic was fully depleted. Fae could die quickly on land devoid of life and energy.

Within our own land, we had spots that had either died or would soon, but nothing like Raumandia. Even the dead pocket near my sister's village hadn't lost all its magic yet, or else the portal wouldn't work anymore. They would have to move it before long, though. I noted it was weakening during my last visit.

I gripped my reins. "You know Veronna is going to retaliate."

"Father plans to triple the border guards for a while."

Two soldiers, both strong elves, rode up to us as all the rest headed south toward Parvayn. The tallest one met my gaze. "Your uncle has asked that we guard you."

Leaving one elf with me wasn't unusual, but two plus my cousin didn't sit right with me. With some trepidation, I moved with them away from the ring to avoid the risk of someone coming through and noticing us. We stopped behind a grouping of trees and brush that provided ample cover for us and our mounts, especially in the darkness, but still offered a direct view of the ring. Should anyone use it, we'd ascertain their identity first. If they were innocent civilians, the guards would grab and hold them until we left. Threats would be dispatched right away.

My wedding ring had grown warm on my finger over the last few minutes. It was almost as if it could sense my guilt at being here and my part in the raid, reminding me that I was attacking my husband's land. The four of us dismounted, tied off our horses, and found comfortable places to sit. My uncle, Ulmar, and the rest of the forces would be gone for at least another hour.

At first, it was dark and quiet as we sat silently, but after a while, I could have sworn I heard screams. My hearing was better than most. I stood and strained to listen closer, twitching my ears. A moment later, I heard the tortured cries of women and children.

"He's killing people," I said, furious.

Tadeus ran a hand through his hair. "I told you he'd do anything to get those gemstones."

I glared at him. "You knew about this and didn't tell me?"

"You wouldn't have opened the portal if I did, and Father would have punished you."

I dashed toward my horse, fury filling me. "He doesn't need to kill innocent people to get the stones. We both know he does it to be cruel."

Just before I mounted, one of the guards grabbed me. "I can't let you do that."

"Let me go." I struggled against him. "I have to stop this!"

I slammed my head into his jaw and elbowed him in the stomach. He let go, but the other soldier grabbed me before I could reach my horse. They roughly pulled me to the ground, with one elf pinning my arms and the other my legs. Then Tadeus came over and placed an iron bracelet on my wrist, shutting down my magic before I could use it against the guards.

"Sorry, Aella, but my father made it clear we couldn't let you interfere." He shook his head. "If you go there trying to stop him, he'll punish us as well."

I glared at him. "You traitor. Innocent people are dying while you do nothing."

"No, I'm protecting you. We both know what he'll do if you get in the way, and I don't want to see you hurt like that again," he said, trying to speak to me calmly.

I didn't care. He had let the guards hold me down, and he'd cut me off from my magic. Tadeus was supposed to be the good cousin who always stood by me. I struggled some more, but it was no use. Both guards were too strong. For a while, I just lay there breathing heavily, enraged and unable to do anything, as more screams and shouts filtered toward me. In my mind, I could envision what was happening with each pained cry revealing another victim of my uncle's ruthlessness.

Then, a slight *pop* of air drew my attention.

We looked over and saw the portal glowing with its soft blue light. I couldn't see much through the brush from my position, but a moment later, I froze as I heard my husband's furious voice shouting commands. He was instructing his troops as they arrived on where to go and what to do. Based on the amount of noise, he must have brought hundreds. As soon as the portal closed, they rode hard for Parvayn. I wanted to shout at him but knew that would only get me in worse trouble with both sides.

My uncle wouldn't expect Darrow to arrive with soldiers this soon. Therressian forces had only arrived at the village forty-five minutes ago, and it wouldn't take more than ten minutes before Darrow reached them. With him in the lead, both sides could suffer heavy losses.

"You've got to let me up," I said, looking at my cousin.

He shook his head. "Not until they're returning."

"The iron is suppressing my magic. If you don't take the cuff off now, there is no way I will regenerate enough power to hold the portal open," I argued, giving him a pleading look.

It was true, and he knew it. Our only hope was that the energy I built before he cut me off, along with what I gained starting now, would be enough to get our troops through the ring when they returned—if they moved quickly. It would be a struggle, though at least I didn't have to push through any wards on the way back.

Tadeus cursed. "Very well, but don't try anything."

"With the Veronnians here, it's too late for that," I said, relieved when the guards let me go and I could sit up.

"Go watch for Lord Morgunn's forces returning," my cousin ordered one of the elves. "Let us know immediately when you see them so Aella can begin channeling."

He hurried away, hugging the trees and brush as he maneuvered parallel to the road.

Tadeus knelt beside me and removed the iron bracelet, dropping it into a special cloth bag. "Do you think you'll be able to get us out of here?"

"It will be cutting it close if they come back soon," I said, rubbing my wrist—iron made my skin burn.

"Just do the best you can."

I swallowed. We would lose enough people from Darrow's wrath tonight, but I hoped more wouldn't die if I couldn't hold the portal open long enough for our forces to flee. For now, I could only wait and pray to the nameless ones that I'd regain enough magic to save everyone.

Chapter 21

Darrow

The bastards were everywhere. Therressian forces had lit half of Parvayn's homes and shops on fire with torches, and they continued to spread the flames to every structure they could reach. My blood boiled in rage. As soon as I'd arrived, I'd begun killing anyone with the yellow hippogriff on their breastplate. Some I slaughtered with my blade and others with my powers, whichever got the job done most efficiently. My soldiers were everywhere, battling just as hard as me to save our people.

I could hardly see through the smoke and damage as I pursued more of Lord Morgunn's troops. Too many people were running in every direction, forcing me to be cautious about who I targeted. It meant getting up close to verify identities before striking.

An elf in a forest green and brown uniform across the street struck a woman so hard that she crashed to the ground. When he bent over her with the clear intent to mount her, I didn't waste a moment gripping his head with my magic and crushing his skull, then flinging his body into a nearby Therressian centaur galloping my way. The half-horse, half-man crashed to the ground, tangled with the dead soldier. Riding over, I thrust my sword into his throat, finishing him as well.

I searched for more targets as I guided my horse between mutilated bodies and fire, nostrils burning from the acrid stench in the air. The flames made the heat in the village nearly unbearable. I was grateful I'd brought a gnome who already worked to extinguish the blazing inferno.

Through the murky haze, I caught movement just beyond the village. Though I couldn't discern distinct features, I knew my men wouldn't be fleeing, so it had to be Therressians. I gestured at a handful of my troops, beckoning them to pursue the enemy with me. Lord Morgunn's forces appeared to be coalescing as they made a hasty retreat. They would not leave until I had taken down as many as possible.

I worked my way toward them, coughing from the smoke. My mount and I struggled to maneuver swiftly through the fires, bodies, and debris. There was so much destruction and death. I protected what was mine, and fury coursed through me at the sight of so many slaughtered innocents. They would pay for this.

Once I finally began closing the gap, I noted several men on horseback carrying familiar small crates. They had taken our latest batch of blue burst gemstones. The numerous fires and slaughter of innocents had been a diversion from their true intent. I wished I had a spy within Lord Morgunn's inner circle so I could anticipate attacks like this, but that was impossible. Aella's uncle didn't even inform most of his officers of the plans until the same day they would occur. He was annoyingly cautious.

The value of the goods the Therressian lord plotted to steal could not be overestimated, and the last thing I wanted was for them to obtain the powerful gems. I pushed my stallion harder to reach them, encouraging him to leap over bodies and fallen debris. They were well ahead of me on the road to the portal. When my soldiers and I finally cleared the village and reached open ground, the enemy had a substantial lead.

We gave chase, but most of the fleeing forces were beyond my range to target in the murky darkness. I consoled myself with picking off Therressian stragglers, one of whom happened to have one of my crates. After he flew from his mount into a tree, I ordered two of my people to grab the gems where they fell to the ground and take them somewhere safe. They did as ordered, dashing through the woods to the west in the one direction the enemy hadn't infiltrated.

Hot embers rained down from above, singeing me and my stallion. The enchantments on me and my horse prevented severe damage, but the cinders still hurt and distracted us. My mount stumbled at the first volley, though he recovered quickly.

I twisted around in the saddle and noted more of the enemy coming behind us. Several launched magic spells our way. The most dangerous was an elf throwing blazing starbursts at us, sending one of my men screaming from his horse. Those could slice through a body with brutal efficiency. They were thin metal with seven sharp points crafted in large quantities at forges and then distributed to specialized troops. Those soldiers used their powers to transform the deadly weapons into blazing hot projectiles. It was one of the most common magics that a lesser fae soldier might master for use in battle.

I hated to let the remaining gemstones out of my sight, but we had to deal with the enemy at our backs or risk many more of us dying. I forced myself to turn around and ordered my squad to do the same.

We faced the incoming soldiers. The ones in the lead wielded battle magic, with one of them hitting us with a spell that stunned our bodies with intense pain.

Another had flames building in her hands that she planned to launch our way next.

I pushed through the agony consuming my body—for once grateful for my torturous training on Karganoth—and grabbed hold of the front row, cracking all their necks in one fell swoop. They tumbled from their horses, and the pain faded from my squad and me. The troops beyond that first line barely managed to veer around their dead comrades before colliding with them.

My side sent the next volley of magic at our foes. We hit them with ice daggers that speared into their chests and lava balls that scorched into their bodies. One of the Therressian soldiers put up a shield, but it only protected him and the elves on either side of him. Half a dozen others fell. I spotted numerous enemies racing through the woods to the east, attempting to avoid confrontation. My squad and I couldn't handle that many at once, but they didn't have much time left to flee.

Aella couldn't have had much longer than an hour and a half since she transported her army here. She wouldn't have recharged enough to keep the portal open long, so I only needed to delay as many of her people as possible. Pulling on my magic, I began felling trees on either side of me to slow the Therressian soldiers while my team continued to hit the ones on the main road. After about ten minutes, we didn't see any more, and the rest of my army was catching up with us. They'd only do that if they'd cleared the village of Lord Morgunn's forces.

I turned my horse toward the portal. "Let's go!"

We rode hard, heading north. In the darkness, I could barely make out the enemies running on foot to make their escape. I considered grabbing some of them with my powers, but then I caught sight of the portal's blue glow. As Therressians raced to leap into the ring, Aella was on her knees with shaking hands extended toward it. I was impressed that she'd held it this long. As I came closer, I caught the sound of her ragged breaths.

Using my power, I forced her arms down until I broke her channeling magic. She turned her face toward me with tired, mournful eyes and cheeks streaked with tears. I sighed. This was going to be complicated because if she were anyone else, I'd have killed her right then. People would wonder why I didn't do so now—or at least make an example out of her. Though I might not feel anything other than some lust toward my beautiful wife, I couldn't harm her. My vow prevented it, but also because she and her abilities were vital to my plans.

One of the elves riding with me headed straight for her with his sword raised. No doubt, he thought he was doing us all a favor by killing her. Still, it surprised me how much rage built inside my chest at the thought of her being harmed—the same as that day on the island.

"Stop," I ordered.

The elf paused his blade mid-strike. "Sir?"

"She's mine. Split up our forces and seek out all the lingering Therressians. Finish them and then gather all the bodies and bring them here. The lady Aella will open a portal to transport them back when she's sufficiently recovered," I said.

One argument I could make was that by the king's law, we had to return the bodies of our enemies. There were so many tonight that transporting them through the mountain pass to the border for Therress to collect would require a lot of time and effort. Using Aella to open a portal would be far more efficient.

He nodded and began shouting orders to the others. I used my power to scoop up my wife and put her before me on my horse. A sweet, floral scent with a hint of spice hit my senses. I had to grind my teeth to ignore the reaction it evoked in me. She trembled so hard that I had to hold her tightly to prevent her from falling.

"What...?" Aella asked, twisting to look up at me.

"That was the second time you've been on your knees before me, you know," I said, giving her a grim smile.

She stiffened and looked around at my forces working to do my bidding. Her voice came out in a whisper, "How are we going to explain this?"

An idea had already begun to take shape in my mind, but I couldn't tell her the precise truth, or it wouldn't work properly. "I suppose I'll have to keep you prisoner."

"You wouldn't," she said, eyes rounding.

I shrugged. "First, you must recover enough to send your dead home through the portal ring, and then I'll decide for certain."

"I'm sorry I couldn't stop him, but I tried."

The remorse I'd witnessed in her eyes had told me as much, but I couldn't forgive her role entirely. Aella would pay a price for it. "When the time comes, you'll have to open a portal into Therress for me to exact my revenge."

She pulled away from my chest and averted her gaze. "Of course."

If I'd had a heart, the resignation in her voice would have bothered me. Good thing I didn't. "Glad you understand."

I took Aella to the village and forced her to witness the death and destruction her uncle had wrought. Smoke and the cries of the dying filled the air. Her eyes grew watery at seeing the bodies of slain men, women, and children. Many of them were maimed in inconceivable ways. I made her look at all of them because she needed to see the reason I had to exact retribution and why she must assist me with it.

My wife didn't say a word and kept her back straight, as far from me as feasible while riding astride together. I drew my arm from her waist and avoided touching her as much as possible, too. She'd never be a real spouse to me, but I had a feeling

I'd eventually lose my internal struggle to avoid bedding her once my anger over this battle abated.

I might be heartless, but I wasn't blind to the pull between us, and by law, she belonged to me. Eventually, we would consummate our marriage. Her response each time I kissed her told me she wouldn't refuse if I put my full effort into convincing her. Every time I saw her, the urge to claim her grew stronger.

My forces spent two hours gathering and transporting the dead Therressians to the portal. We'd lost more than seventy innocents and thirty soldiers. Sixty-two troops died on my wife's side. My fury grew by the moment. As we surveyed the destruction, I barely spoke to her.

I would have preferred not to have her warm, beautiful body close to mine for so long, but it couldn't be helped. Some of my people would kill her, given the chance. They certainly gave her enough scathing looks after the word spread about who rode with me. As we returned to the portal, she kept opening her mouth as if to say something and then closing it.

Finally, I had enough. "What?"

She startled and shook her head. "Nothing."

"Say it." I was rapidly losing patience.

Aella sighed. "As soon as I heard their screams, I tried running to the village to do something. I'm sorry they wouldn't let me."

"How did they stop you?" I asked, thinking if she could shove me into a wall and hold me there, nothing should have held her back.

She clenched her hands. "My uncle had two guards stay with me to keep me safe, but I usually only have one. I should have known something was wrong, and he also left my cousin to watch me. They held me down and cuffed me in iron."

I cursed. She would have been powerless, but it made no sense. "Why would they be prepared for you to cause trouble?"

"Because the last time I discovered my uncle was ravaging this village, I used my wind power to stop as many of his soldiers as I could," she said, staring out into the darkness of the passing woods. "Afterward, I told him if he did it again, I would refuse to open any more portals to Veronna for him."

That explained why it had stopped for years, though not long enough. "So, will you cease aiding him now?"

"I'll try, but he has ways of forcing me."

I grunted. Aella's response seemed rather hollow if she wouldn't commit fully. The victims of tonight's tragedy wouldn't be satisfied with that answer, nor would I.

"Trying isn't good enough," I said, beginning the next stage of my plan for her.

"But I..." she began.

"Don't," I interrupted. "Perhaps the best place for you is confined here in Veronna, where your uncle cannot use you anymore."

I stopped the horse just before the ring and pile of bodies. A dozen of my soldiers waited to begin pushing them through, and most had pointed glares for Aella. She held her chin high, which surprised me under the circumstances. I dismounted my horse and pulled her to the ground.

"Open the portal," I ordered.

She took a few steps forward, drew her bag of holmium dust from her trouser pocket, and began spinning her magic toward the ring. In seconds, she had it open. The male and female soldiers immediately started work, moving the bodies into the soft glow. They had to toss them hard to ensure they'd not pile in front of the other end and block the way. We had no way of knowing if anyone was on the other end to receive them.

Once they were through, Aella stepped forward as if she thought to escape.

I grabbed her arms. "No, you're not going back."

"The curse," she said, touching the back of her neck with her free hand. "If it perceives that I can't or won't return, I'll be unconscious until my uncle retrieves me."

I smiled. "That's what I'm counting on happening."

"Please don't do this," she begged, shaking with fear.

"You're staying in Veronna and not going back. It's the only way," I said as she lost control of her channeling, and the portal closed.

A moment later, she slumped into me. I lifted her into my arms. It was time for my father to learn the truth and help me with the next stage of my plan. Aella wouldn't know or remember it, but she was about to be the first Therressian visitor to Darynia—Veronna's capital—in many centuries. I was bringing my wife home.

Chapter 22

Darrow

Crystal Castle was located in the heart of Darynia on an island in the middle of a massive lake. Beyond that, marshlands extended for miles, making the location difficult to reach by land. Numerous other islands dotted the waters around my family's home. Each served a different purpose—housing, markets, barracks, armories, farm and pastureland, orchards, parks, and much more. To reach any of them, one must take a boat. We had numerous types to fit our various needs so that transport for any purpose could be easily obtained.

The portal ring sat on one of the perimeter islands at the south end. The small rise of land could barely fit a hundred soldiers at a time if packed tightly. Invading Veronna's capital from that point would be nigh on impossible without risking excess troops drowning in the nearby waters or swamp reptiles coming up from below to eat them. Only protection spells kept them from creeping more than a few feet onto inhabited land.

As the sun's rays slowly broke across the city of islands, I waited for a boat to transport myself, Aella, and my horse. For security reasons, we rarely kept more than one or two small crafts near the portal. We'd also dispatched other vessels to take the eighty soldiers who'd accompanied me while the rest remained back at Parvayn to return home once they'd finished assisting with recovery efforts at the village.

After the portal channeler I'd used to transport us to Parvayn regained his strength, he sent us to the capital near dawn. I thanked the nameless ones that I happened to be home when I detected Aella's arrival in our territory, or else I wouldn't have had access to the troops I needed or someone to move them quickly. My father had wondered how I could know about the attack, and now he'd get his answer. I'd had no time to explain before we left.

Finally, a sleek gray boat arrived, pulling up to the wooden dock. I carefully laid Aella on a bench seat at the front before returning to retrieve my horse. The stallion was used to traveling this way and easily kept his footing as I stopped him at the back end, where up to two equines could fit in a small pen. A couple of castle soldiers who'd come with me last night were up front already to balance the weight, but the vessel wasn't large enough for many more to ride. The rest of the troops would wait for the longer crafts, which would take them directly to the barracks and officer housing island.

I joined Aella on the bench, placing her head in my lap as we drifted into deeper blue-gray water. We passed multiple rises of land along the way to the castle. The one full of flower gardens made me wonder what my slumbering wife would think if she could see it now.

Next was the army training area to our right and the open market fair to our left, currently shuttered at this early hour. The last we passed included a sizeable island with middle-class housing to the west and the soldiers' quarters on the land mass to our right, but straight ahead past the stretch of blue-gray waters were the high walls of Crystal Castle, where I'd been born and raised.

The towers and ramparts were constructed with glimmering, crystallized rock, only found in abundance on our lands. My ancestors used most of it more than a thousand years ago to build the impressive structure. It glinted like blue and lavender diamonds in the dawning sunlight.

As soon as the guards on the dock saw me, they ordered the front gates open. My vessel's captain glided us to a stop and tied our craft to a pillar. One of the soldiers led my horse away to the stables while I carried Aella in my arms. We entered the keep, where the inhabitants were only beginning to stir for the day, giving me curious looks as I passed them. I hurried across the glimmering cobblestones reflecting the dawn's brilliant colors toward the castle at the center.

It was three floors high and sprawled outward with two parallel wings on each side to house family, guests, and servants with rooms left to spare. The central wing comprised common areas such as the great hall, kitchen, and library. Crystal stones formed the outer walls, but since they were nearly as clear as glass, white quartz was used for the interior to provide privacy. The all-around effect was stunning, though I'd long grown accustomed to the sight.

My father burst out of the black, double-front doors. The Lord of Veronna was a tall, stout man who still cut a strong figure at over a century old. He had warm ivory skin, brown hair short enough not to hide his pointed ears, and a trimmed beard. Today, he wore a fitted black doublet with silver buttons running up the front, matching pants, and freshly shined leather boots.

He took one look at the woman in my arms and stopped stiffly at the top of the steps. "Who is that?"

"Lady Aella of Therress."

He glared at me. "You should have killed her, not captured and brought her here. The number of lives that her death could save is countless. Never mind that her uncle couldn't use her anymore to defend against our attacks."

"If you give me the privacy to explain, you'll understand exactly why she must remain alive," I said calmly.

Cradled in my arms, completely helpless, I continued to find myself surprised at the protectiveness that surged within me for the woman I held. Absolutely no harm would come to her if I could help it. The fact that she felt right while cradling her close hadn't escaped my notice.

I couldn't begin to understand the reason, having never experienced such a sensation before. Even with my Aunt Durelle, I didn't feel anything quite like this, though I still had memories of loving her as a child before the curse took hold. The connection between Aella and me was a mystery.

My father narrowed his gaze. "Give me a reason now, or I'll slit her throat on these steps."

Over my dead body, he would. I pulled Aella closer to my chest as I leaned toward my father and whispered furiously, "She is my wife, and you won't touch her."

"What?" He took a step back as shock transformed his features. "When did this happen?"

"Twenty-five days ago."

"Curse the nameless ones, Darrow. Have you lost your mind?" he asked, fury in his hazel eyes.

I shook my head. "If you'll allow me to install her in a guest chamber—not to worry, she is currently in a deep sleep and can't wake—I'll explain why she is exactly what we've been searching for all these years."

Lord Gannon stared at her as he likely tried to determine what I saw in her. Eventually, light dawned in his gaze, and a slow smile spread across his face. Though no one stood too close to us, he gestured at everyone working in the courtyard to leave. They were gone in seconds.

"She has gotten past our most powerful wards time and again, which means she is no average portal channeler," he said in a low tone. "While that is significant, how can you be sure she's strong enough?"

I gave him a cunning smile. "What if I told you I know for a fact that Aella can open any portal on this planet?"

"That can't be true." He stiffened. "She wouldn't have restricted herself to our border villages if she could go deeper."

"I tested her and assure you she hasn't come to Darynia only because she doesn't know the rune sequence. She can open any portal where she does have it. As for her not going deeper, she walks a fine line with her uncle. She does enough to stay in his good graces but lies about how much she can do. He has no idea she can transport him much farther."

My father rubbed his jaw. "Why is she asleep?"

"Lord Morgunn placed a curse on her long ago, so if she ever tries to flee from him—willingly or not—she is rendered unconscious until she is returned to him." I shifted Aella in my arms. "As soon as I told her she would not be allowed to leave Veronna, she passed out. Hasn't stirred since."

"That explains why you didn't take her from Morgunn after marrying," he surmised, studying her delicate features. "She doesn't do anyone much good like this."

I nodded. "Yes."

There were other reasons my father didn't know, but I'd let him think what he liked.

"Take her to one of the chambers near yours, then meet me in my office," Lord Gannon said, spinning on his heels and heading back into the castle.

I did as ordered, choosing the room next to mine. It probably didn't matter where I put her since she'd never know the difference, but she was vulnerable. I wanted her close during her stay to ensure her safety. The door between our chambers, usually convenient for my mistresses, would give me that peace of mind. My plan would require at least two or three days to enact. She'd stay on this bed until it was time to return her.

I gently laid her on the mattress, ensuring her head rested comfortably on the pillow. Next, I pulled her blonde braid over her shoulder and folded her hands over her stomach. She appeared utterly peaceful, sleeping there, even in her plain battle garb. It was such a dichotomy with how she looked at me while awake—full of suspicion and annoyance. I couldn't wait for those expressions to return because this version of Aella made her seem far too innocent for my liking. Unable to help myself, I leaned down and kissed her forehead softly.

"Try not to dream of me, will you?" I whispered and forced myself to walk away.

After locking the door with a key, I moved swiftly to my father's office. I found him inside with a glass in his hand. "Perhaps you should explain from the beginning why you decided to marry our enemy's niece. As you know, with your mother, such alliances often do not work out. This arrangement won't even bring us peace since it's too late for that bargain."

I detailed the night Aella appeared at the tavern in Siggaya, leaving little out. Then, the days that followed leading up to our marriage. "She is powerful and brave, though I don't trust her, of course. It is why I had her ring spelled for concealment from her family, and so I could always track her location within a quarter mile."

"I would have talked you out of this if you'd brought the plan to me first," Lord Gannon said, a stern look on his face.

"Yes," I agreed. It was why it was better to ask forgiveness after the fact.

He rubbed his face. "But then, I wouldn't have seen the two of you together."

"What does that have to do with anything?" I asked.

"She's your true mate, though I can't imagine a worse possible pair."

I stiffened. "That can't be true."

"Very few know this, but I can sense true mates if I spend a few minutes close to a couple. My first wife was mine." He shook his head, lost in memory for a moment. "I couldn't love her, of course, but something still breaks through our curse, making us very protective of the one fated for us. I could see it clearly by how you held her when I came close to you."

That explained so many things, such as why I could not truly harm her even before our vows, and possibly the same reason she hesitated with me on the battlefield and in the tavern. True mates could not seriously injure one another, and normally, it would only take a kiss to recognize the connection. My family's paternal line curse ensured we could not do so, nor could our intended. At least, that was what my father and grandfather had always told me.

"How is it possible you have that gift, and it works with us?" I asked, confused.

He shrugged. "I have no idea, except it is mostly useless. It did help me recognize my first wife when choosing a bride, and despite everything that followed, she was perfect for me. I'm only sorry my lack of love and understanding ultimately made her miserable."

"I've made it clear to Aella that our marriage will be one of business and convenience," I said, glad I'd told her as much from the start.

My father gave me a rueful smile. "Your souls will still call to each other. For you, strong feelings won't be part of it, but you'll still want to protect her and be with her physically. I couldn't get enough of my first wife. As for Aella, she will feel the pull toward you as well. You're her other half, so she won't be able to resist that for long, though living apart will help delay the inevitable. Ultimately, I'm sorry to say, you'll make her miserable as all the men of our line have done to our wives."

That was something I was well aware of since my grandfather had explained it to me in detail when I came of age. Lack of love wasn't our only curse, but also failed relationships.

"Perhaps fate had mercy on me by granting the one woman who might be able to help us end this problem," I said, pacing the floor. "We know the Naforya Fountain is not on this planet, and we continue to find clues to where it might have gone, but none of that will mean anything without someone powerful enough to open a cross-galaxy portal."

My father nodded. "You could be right about her, which is why I'll allow this misdeed to go unpunished. I can hardly argue your intentions when they will benefit our family, as well as the planet. Just last week, we discovered another area in the south is beginning to die faster than I've seen before. Spring crops that had begun to grow withered within days."

I swore under my breath. Normally, it took weeks or months for that to happen. Finding the fountain would solve so many problems. For the last ten years, we'd seen the damaging effects on Paxia rapidly get worse. It was impossible to guess how much time we had remaining before it would be too late.

"Until we can break Aella's curse, I do not want her uncle to know she's married to me. We can't keep her away from him for more than a few days since she cannot eat or drink in her current state. She will grow weak before long. If we give her back, and he is aware I'm her husband, I suspect he'll punish her for it or possibly kill her. I cannot abide by that."

"And we don't have legal justification to kill him overtly," Lord Gannon said, grimacing.

"It would solve so much if we could." I raked my hand through my loose hair. "I'd hoped to catch him on the battlefield yesterday, where I could have killed him without breaking the king's law, but as always, he proved elusive once again."

We began suspecting years ago that once the Lord of Therress entered a battle, he donned glamour to blend with his troops or perhaps hid somewhere. Our spies also reported that he always kept a soldier with strong shield powers close to him to keep him safe. That combination made it next to impossible to kill him.

My father drummed his fingers on his desk. "We must also save face with our people if we return her without telling them the truth. The only thing I can think of is to exchange her for the fury, Csilla, and the elf, Quim. I've been trying to find a way to free them for the last year since they were captured, so perhaps your wife is the answer to those troubles, at least."

I could hardly argue with him. While the two Veronnians we'd lost when we attempted to assassinate Lord Morgunn a while back were important to us, we'd had nothing of equal value to trade. I couldn't say why they weren't executed immediately, but my spies told me they were still alive, though suffering greatly. If there was a way to free them, we had to take it.

"Considering his niece's rare and powerful gift, we can also ask for holmium powder," I said, considering the matter further. "The nameless ones know that he makes it difficult and expensive to acquire since Hisgar is the only other land to produce it, and they only sell meager amounts beyond their borders. Not to mention, we must nearly freeze to death, acquiring every allotment the ice giants give us, and portal hop our way there and back."

Lord Gannon appeared to mull it over. "Yes. That is a good point. Your sister was due to take her turn next month, so you'll make her happy if she can put it off a while longer."

That was my thought exactly. Faina always became ill-tempered when dealing with the northern fae, and it was a wonder they hadn't killed her as a result. She lacked a certain finesse with her words. Our father felt she needed the experience anyway, so he kept her in the rotation no matter the potential consequences. I'd gone last month, and my older brother, Hagen, the time before that.

"I will send a message to Therress," I said, giving my father a pleased smile.

It had been a while since we could agree on much of anything or have a conversation that didn't end in a fight. I'd thought for certain I'd have to work a lot harder for him to see the advantages with Aella, but he was undoubtedly tired of our curse and more of our land dying as the years passed.

Aside from the newest patch of dying land he'd mentioned, a section in the north where the vegetation had withered away years ago finally lost its magic last month. Thankfully, we'd already moved all the fae out of there before it became too deadly to stay.

The harshness of Lord Gannon's features softened. "You've done well, son. This plan could very well save us all if we handle it carefully."

"Thank you. With luck, we'll have our assassins back within the next few days."

I left out the unsaid part. We had no way of knowing how Lord Morgunn would react to his niece's capture and the sacrifices he'd have to make to get her back. She may very well pay a price for it, but the only other choice was to keep her here, wasting away until she died. That, or break the curse. The whole reason Therress had prisoners of ours to exchange was from trying to kill her uncle surreptitiously once before, so trying again on short notice wouldn't be possible. I could only monitor Aella the best I could through my spies once she returned.

Chapter 23

Darrow

I stood in my father's office, reading the missive from Therress that Lord Gannon had just handed me. It had taken two full days of negotiating back and forth, but we'd gotten what we wanted. In eight hours, we would meet Lord Morgunn's son, along with a small retinue of his soldiers, at the border to make the prisoner exchange.

"It's ironic he believed our threat about killing Aella and has no idea that legally, she belongs to us," I said, shaking my head.

Lord Gannon snorted. "For someone who is so protective of his wife that he won't let anyone near her body, you did provide quite vivid imagery for what you would do to her before killing her should Lord Morgunn delay any longer. I think that likely convinced him to agree to the deal."

"Sometimes, my dark reputation works in my favor," I said, scowling. "I've never forced a woman, much less a sleeping one, and I certainly wouldn't slit her throat afterward."

My father lifted a brow. "Are you going to have difficulties returning her to our enemy?"

"Yes." I ground my jaw, imagining handing her over to those bastards. "But I have no choice in the matter. Somehow, I'll find a way to free her from that place for good."

He patted my shoulder. "I know you'll do what's best for Veronna."

"Don't I always?" I asked. I wasn't bitter but certainly frustrated.

Lord Gannon grunted. "Not without arguing and second-guessing all my orders. You've always had difficulties doing things in any way other than your own."

Only my father could reduce me to the young boy I'd been decades ago. Little did he understand how my time away in Karganoth had left me sour and angry, as my mother's family worked to extract every ounce of weakness from me during my visits. They'd been brutal—physically and mentally. Dark elves took pride in producing strong children who didn't flinch in the face of pain or danger, and my grandfather had made certain I wouldn't bring him shame.

"I only argue when I believe there is a better way."

"Or do things behind my back so I can't stop you," Lord Gannon said, giving me a wan smile. "Such as getting married."

I lifted a brow. "You can't argue now that it wasn't the right call to make."

"Begrudgingly." He took the missive from me. "Now go prepare your wife for departure. We must begin our journey in two hours if we hope to arrive early."

I nodded. "Of course."

Wasting no time, I exited his office and headed upstairs. There wasn't much I could do to prepare Aella, but I'd checked on her more often than necessary during her stay. Having her here physically but not consciously wore on me.

I entered the room and found her lying on the bed, the same as before. On the first night after her arrival, I'd had my sister—the only other person I trusted—wash and change Aella into a simple plum-colored dress. I didn't know if she could sense the state of her body, but I didn't want to leave her dirty from her travels.

Faina had kept my wife's undergarments on her through the process, so I could at least say we preserved her modesty. It would still leave Lord Morgunn wondering who'd bathed and changed his niece while with us. I hoped it deeply upset him to think what might have happened.

Now, I stood over Aella and gave her one last kiss, breathing in her natural floral scent. The gesture was always brief yet impossible to resist. I kept hoping she'd magically wake up, but her curse was obviously different from the old fables I grew up hearing. Nothing I did here would make those beautiful green eyes flutter open.

"She's so quiet right now," an ageless voice said from behind me.

I stiffened but didn't bother to turn. "What are you doing here, nameless one?"

The dark-skinned god came to stand beside me, looking down at Aella. "Checking on my favorite fae."

"I assume that is her," I said with a dark chuckle. He'd only visited me a few times in my life, but usually, he had little nice to say.

The nameless one grunted. "For once, you assume correctly."

"You wouldn't be willing to remove the curse on her, would you?" I asked, figuring it couldn't hurt to make the request.

"She asked for the same thing the first time I met her." He gestured toward Aella. "You can see where that got her."

I raked a hand through my hair, frustrated with the god as always when he visited. "You can surely see us clearly enough from wherever you usually inhabit, so why come down now?"

"To warn you."

"About what?" I asked, jerking my gaze from Aella to him.

"Beware the Unseelie. They have become more active recently, and I fear they'll undermine your plans," he said.

I let out a growl of frustration. "They've taken enough from us already, so what do they want now?"

"Their thirst for power is unending and can never be satisfied, but every time they reach for more, a price is exacted from them in return. Now, they seek a way around the troubles they've brought upon themselves. I fear you and your new wife will draw their attention if you don't take care."

"In what way?" I asked.

"Vaslav knows, though I doubt he'll tell you." Before my eyes, he vanished.

I clenched my fists, hating that he always came with cryptic messages that left me with more questions than answers. Everyone on Zadrya knew to beware the Unseelie. It was hardly news worth sharing, except a nameless god wouldn't have troubled himself to say that if it wasn't especially dire this time. What were they planning now? And he was right that even if I found Vas, he wouldn't share a shred of information. He never did, but he likely knew.

Chapter 24

Aella

The sun burned my eyes as I woke up outside, cradled in someone's arms. It took me a moment to focus, considering how weak my body felt. My mouth was dry, and my stomach was gnawingly empty. Finally, my vision cleared enough to make out the details of my cousin Tadeus' face.

"Where am I?" I asked.

"Just outside Reshirk."

I twisted around, looking up at the Sobaryan Mountains, where the foothills were a short distance away. The trail to the pass that crossed from Therress to Veronna wasn't far away. At the very top, I spotted a group disappearing over the ridge, but they were too far to identify.

I turned my head in the other direction and spotted my uncle. "Lord Morgunn?"

"You're home now," he said coldly. "I hope you're pleased with what you cost us."

"What?" I asked, still confused.

"We just got you back from Lord Gannon and his son after you got yourself captured, foolish girl." He took a step closer to Tadeus and me. "I'm letting this slide because witnesses corroborate that you couldn't have escaped under the circumstances, but next time, put yourself before my soldiers if you can't hold a portal open long enough. They won't cost me the way you have."

I flinched. "I'm sorry."

"Sure you are," he said, turning away.

Next thing I knew, he was on his stallion with a retinue of soldiers riding behind him.

Rubbing my head at my fuzzy memories, I looked up at Tadeus. "The last thing I remember is trying to hold the portal open when Darrow used his powers to stop me. He forced me to it again after they retrieved our dead, but once they were gone, he said he wasn't letting me go. Then I blacked out."

My cousin carried me to a waiting horse. "Can you ride on your own?"

"I think so." Everything was so disorienting that I could barely make sense of it all as he helped me mount Astra. "How long have I been gone?"

He knew how my curse worked, so he didn't ask any questions I couldn't possibly answer about my time away. I couldn't be sure of anything except that at least a day had passed, considering I was very thirsty and hungry. Also, someone had changed my clothes. A chill ran through me, considering I now wore a dress that was my favorite color—a detail my husband knew from our wedding night. Had Darrow seen my nude body while putting it on me? The thought horrified and angered me, yet I couldn't complain because he had the legal right.

Tadeus handed me a water flask. "Almost three days. It took some negotiating to get you back, and Father wasn't happy with what he had to trade."

I made myself drink slowly so I wouldn't get sick. "What did Lord Morgunn give up?"

My cousin mounted the horse beside mine. "Two Veronnian prisoners we've been holding in the dungeons who attempted to kill him a year ago and two barrels of holmium powder."

"He gave up that much for me?" I asked, shocked.

"You're valuable, Aella. We also didn't have the luxury of time, considering you'd die in a week or so without food and water." He sighed and shook his head. "Father made certain you couldn't even accept sustenance while knocked out from that curse."

That was something I knew very well.

He gestured, and we began riding toward the village. "How did the exchange go?"

I could only guess Tadeus handled it at the mountain border because my uncle wouldn't dare get too close to the Veronnians at a planned meeting. It had been just over a year, but I remembered the two assassins who worked together to attempt killing him at the dinner table with all of us present.

They nearly succeeded. I'd had no idea they were still alive, but if Lord Morgunn kept them in the dungeons all that time, they must have been in terrible shape. He would have made certain their fate was worse than death.

"It went smoothly enough, though I swear Gannon's son, Darrow, was reluctant to hand you over." Tadeus shook his head as he led the way into the village. "He gave me the strangest look before releasing you to me."

I twisted in the saddle, pretending surprise. "Really?"

"Yes. Then, he took charge of the holmium and rode off, leaving the rest of us to finish the exchange," he said, frowning. "I can't say I wasn't glad to see him go, considering he scares me with those cold eyes of his and all that power he inherited. We were terrified of what he might do to you if we didn't make the exchange quickly."

I wanted to laugh at the irony of what Darrow must have made them think but managed to hold a straight face. "As far as I can tell, I'm fine other than hungry and thirsty. I'm more worried about what Lord Morgunn will do to me for getting caught. He isn't really going to let it slide, is he?"

"Father is furious, but I argued it was hardly your fault since you had to get as many of our soldiers home as possible. He shouldn't be angry at you for doing the job he tasked you with and saving lives. None of us could have predicted Darrow would show up that quickly with a large force." He stopped his stallion in front of a local pub with the tantalizing scent of cooking food wafting from it. "We're all trying to figure out how he knew we were there."

I glanced down at the ring on my finger that no one else could see except those who knew about the marriage. Magic throbbed within the metal. I'd assumed it was only the concealment spell, but now I wondered if it didn't have a way to track me, too. How else could my husband have responded that fast?

Regardless, I found the idea didn't bother me. If Darrow hadn't shown up when he did, more innocent people in the village would have died. I didn't mind him knowing my whereabouts—at least for now—since I had no plans I needed to hide from him. Additionally, his having my current location when sending messages would reduce the chances of them getting intercepted. I wouldn't let him know I'd figured it out, though.

"Please tell me you brought me here to eat, Tad," I said.

"Yes." He dismounted and came over to give me a hand. "After what I did with the iron cuff, I wanted to make it up to you. If I hadn't restricted your magic, maybe you would have had the strength to escape in time."

It was tough to stay mad at Tadeus when he showed true remorse. If I were honest, he tried to protect me from my uncle's wrath that night. I only knew then that I couldn't hide away and do nothing, no matter how illogical it was to try stopping my uncle's forces.

"Thanks," I said, giving him a look that hopefully conveyed my appreciation.

He nodded. "Of course."

A wave of dizziness swept over me as we walked toward the tavern door. My cousin took my arm to steady me. We entered the dimly lit establishment, which was relatively empty mid-afternoon, and sat at a table near the side wall.

A full-sized pixie whose head would almost reach me mid-chest if I were standing came to take our orders. She had a riot of curly blue hair and freckles on her pale skin. Her purple blouse was conservative, but her short skirt left most of her legs bare. She gave us impatient looks.

"What'll ya have?" Her voice was high-pitched with an accent.

"Two meads and a bowl of gruel for Aella," Tadeus said.

I scowled at him. "Gruel? Are you serious?"

"Briauna's orders. She said you've gone too long without eating and shouldn't have solid food right away, so take it up with her if you don't like it. I just don't want to see you throw up the first meal you've had in days," he said, giving me a pointed look.

"Welcome back," the server said, giving me a sympathetic look now that she knew my identity. I didn't often visit this area of our land. "We worried 'bout what they might do to ya over there, considerin'..."

"I was unconscious, but it's scary to think I was at their mercy the whole time." I shuddered a little because until I saw Darrow again, I wouldn't even know what he did with my body while I was there, except change my clothes. "But my uncle managed to exchange me back."

An amused smile pulled at her lips. "Bet it nearly killed the big lord to hand over his would-be assassins and holmium for you."

This woman was more forthright than most, but I liked that about her. Most people would only sing my uncle's praises. He didn't try to be too scary to anyone beyond the castle, but those who spoke too loudly tended to have bad things happen to them. Either they disappeared, or they acquired a nasty curse. I wasn't sure which was worse.

"Yes, I'm sure I'll hear all about it for at least a week," I agreed.

She patted my shoulder. "I'll pray to the nameless ones for you."

The server walked away with a sway in her step. I turned my attention to Tadeus because I preferred to know now how bad it would be when we returned home. "Tell me what to expect."

"You'll spend the next few days at the castle to recuperate. But in the morning, after breakfast, you will meet him in the office, where he'll basically lecture you on how you failed him, even though we all know there isn't a thing you could have done differently that night."

I let out a sigh of relief. "That's nothing I can't handle."

"Yes," he said.

The server returned a few minutes later with our drinks and a bowl of gruel that looked like they'd added a bit more sweet spice to it just for me. It was usually plain and one of the cheapest menu items aside from a chunk of bread, which she also brought with a wink. Nameless ones bless her.

I began eating right away.

"Take it slow," my cousin cautioned.

I forced myself to do as he suggested, though it was hard with an empty pit for a stomach. "Any other news?"

A twinkle lit his blue eyes. "You won't have to return to Tradain until after the summer solstice celebration in four days. I expect it will be as wild as ever."

"That is something I can look forward to," I said, grinning. It was my favorite holiday because it was one of the few times I could completely let go of my worries and enjoy myself. Plus, I loved the dancing.

"You and me both," he replied with a grin.

Chapter 25

Aella

With the sun low in the sky, I stepped out of the castle gates with my friend, Sariyah, and cousin, Rynn, by my side. Our feet were bare, grounding us as the magic thrummed in the air and the earth. Solstice was always when it was most potent, but fae enjoyed the burgeoning life around them even more with summer.

Torches lit the way to the open south field where the celebration occurred. Sariyah had donned a lavender dress with thin straps over her shoulders and a bottom hem that only reached her knees. Rynn wore a pale pink halter dress that left much of her back bare, but the skirt fell to mid-calf. She'd be allowed to stay until midnight when we sent away the adolescents and the adults allowed their passions to take over.

As for me, I'd chosen to wear an ice-blue strapless dress that fell to mid-thigh. The material was thin, so a hint of my nipples showed through the fabric. It was a daring ensemble compared to my usual attire, but perfectly normal for this night. Some fae went so far as to harken back to the old days when we only used leaves strung together to hide our intimate parts. I saw several men and women adorned that way as we hurried toward the field. Tonight was about releasing inhibitions and becoming one with nature.

We reached the end of the torches and stepped onto the crowded field full of merriment. All day, we'd fasted without food or drink. My greedy gaze fell on the handsome centaurs walking around on four legs with platters of food and mugs of spiced wine. Their bottom half resembled a horse, but the upper half was all beautiful and muscular man.

Rynn gaped at the server's very exposed genitalia, much larger than most other types of male fae, that protruded between his legs. I laughed. It was her first solstice that we allowed her to come to the field, and likely her first glimpse of a centaur up close. They never wore clothes, but she hadn't visited where their herds lived. I remembered the same shock when I joined the celebration for the first time. Fae couldn't attend until they gained their magic, but we wouldn't shield her from most things anymore.

Uncaring of the male server's exposed parts, I grabbed a mug from the platter and began drinking right away. Sariyah did the same while Rynn hesitated.

"Don't be shy," I said, gesturing at the male centaur. "He's not going to hurt you."

She shifted foot to foot before taking the leap and grabbing a mug. The large fae gave her an amused look. They preferred their own kind for copulation, but they knew the effect they had on all of us. They were innately sexual beings when they weren't in the middle of a battle.

As the centaur moved away, we drank down the contents of our mugs. They disappeared as soon as we finished, spelled to return to the kitchen where they'd be washed and refilled. The wine loosened my body and made me feel lightheaded. I knew I should eat, but I desperately wanted to dance first. The others followed me as I crossed the field toward the massive bonfire in the middle. Dozens of fae danced around it.

Taking Rynn and Sariyah's hands, I formed us into a circle. The nearby musicians played a lively beat with drums and stringed instruments. Before long, we fell into step with it. Music and magic flowed through our bodies until the joy of our movements sent us into a mindless trance. I couldn't have said how long we danced, but the sun had set, and the buzz of the wine had worn off by the time we stopped. Each of us was coated in glistening sweat, our hair wild and loose.

"Hungry?" I asked, chest heaving from exertion.

Rynn jerkily nodded her head.

Sariyah put a hand to her stomach. "Ravenous. Every year, I swear I'll eat first and just observe others until the food settles." She gave me an accusing look. "And each year, you thwart my plans."

"Then you should learn not to follow me," I said, laughing.

She sighed. "Easier said than done when you make it so much fun."

We headed toward a female centaur who wore no more clothes than her male counterparts, leaving her voluminous breasts bare. She held a platter filled with various foods to satisfy anyone's appetite. I took the whole thing from her.

"Thank you."

She dipped her head. "Enjoy."

Though it was large and cumbersome, I insisted on carrying it until I found a quiet place near the tree line to sit. We settled around the platter and gorged ourselves. The meats were warm and delicious, the fruits sweet and luscious, and the pastries practically melted in my mouth. Food always tasted the best on solstice.

After finishing, we sat back to watch everyone else. The music had changed to a slower pace. Over a dozen male and female faeries, clad in revealing garments, formed a line and danced hypnotically, moving in perfect sync. It was mesmerizing to witness. At first, they were separated, but then they paired with each other. None of them touched, but they were a breath from each other in a teasing glide that taunted their audience, making us wait with bated breath to see if they'd do more.

Warm hands touched my shoulders, and I turned to look up. Camden smiled at me. He wore dark blue pants and nothing else. I couldn't help admiring his bare, muscular chest.

His lips quirked at my admiration. "Sorry, I couldn't wait to join you any longer."

I'd asked him to give me time with my cousin and best friend before finding me. "It's alright. Have you eaten yet?" I gestured toward the platter, three-quarters empty. "We still have some left."

"I've already eaten," he said, then settled behind me and pulled me into his warm body.

It felt good having him here. I twisted in his arms and angled for a kiss he didn't hesitate to give. "Glad you're here."

"You're beautiful tonight, Aella." His gaze was heated. "It's twenty minutes before midnight."

I knew exactly what he insinuated and looked at Rynn. "You should start heading back now."

Some other adolescents gathered nearby, as they would walk together for safety. Most fae were good-natured and wouldn't dream of harming them, but there were always a few with dark tastes who might take advantage of their vulnerability. It was a hard rule for none of our younger participants to be left alone on solstice night. They would enjoy a smaller celebration inside the castle grounds, complete with dancing and music, for those who wished to stay up late.

She nodded and rose to her feet. "You all have fun!"

We watched as Rynn made her way to the group, not letting her out of our sight until she and the others reached the torchlit path. Several guards who weren't participating escorted the group. All the while, Camden ran his fingers over my bare shoulders and arms, teasing me for what was to come. Sariyah left us, going on the hunt for a partner of her own.

The mood changed over the next few minutes as the music's thrum grew louder and magic swirled through the air, stimulating our bodies. We rose to our feet, kissing and swaying to the beat. Camden's hands ran up the backs of my thighs under my dress, kneading my butt. My fingers traced the hard lines of muscles across his chest. Despite hundreds of fae everywhere, it was as if the universe shrank to only us.

Slowly, we moved into the trees, our mouths and hands too busy to break apart. We didn't make it farther than thirty feet into the forest before my dress fell to the ground, and I was yanking his pants off. As soon as Camden stepped out of them, my mouth went to his cock. He moaned as I closed over it, licking and sucking him wantonly.

More fae entered the woods around us, ready to be one with nature as well. Some paused to watch us, but I barely noticed before he nudged my head closer, urging me to take all of him. I obliged, needing to drive him wild with pleasure.

Before long, Camden pulled away from me and pressed me onto the ground. I spread my thighs for him, aching and wet. The fae who'd been watching us moved on, but we were surrounded by others feeding their passions. The eroticism in the air was tangible and growing thicker by the moment. I could hardly think beyond longing and need.

His thick cock thrust inside me, filling me. I moaned and pulled him closer. He started slow and teasing, but before long, he quickened his pace. My body was more than ready. With each thrust, my need heightened until I was exploding and screaming my pleasure. Camden followed close behind. More shouts and cries rang through the woods as so many others hit their peaks simultaneously. It was music to our ears and the power of the magic that night.

We kissed and touched, watched others, and fucked again and again before finally passing out on the soft grass in a tangle of limbs. I couldn't have said how much time had passed before a familiar voice broke my slumber.

"Aella."

I thought for sure I must be dreaming. "Hmm?"

"Aella!" he said, annoyed.

My head jerked up to find Darrow staring down at me where I was lying naked and tangled in Camden's arms. I scrambled to pull away from my lover and draw my knees up to hide my body. "What...what are you doing here?"

Something dark and possessive lurked in my husband's gaze, giving me chills.

"Looking for my wife," he said coldly.

Chapter 26

Darrow

I needed to speak with Aella. A wiser man would have sent a sebeska with a message, but I couldn't help taking advantage of the one night a year when it would be easiest to infiltrate Therress. The spell of solstice night took over everyone except the border sentries. They wouldn't be a problem either, with the way I planned to reach my wife.

My sister and I had just finished visiting my Aunt Durelle and having dinner. She was long past the age when the celebrations interested her, so she was happy to have us over instead. We chatted and kept her company until nearly midnight. Since she didn't get many visitors, and I didn't want to infiltrate Therress until after magic rose to its highest, we didn't leave right after eating. Instead, we chatted and played cards until she'd had enough of us.

"Are you sure about this?" Faina asked, raising her brows skeptically.

We stood a short distance outside my aunt's home. Since she lived at the edge of the Sobaryan Mountains, we couldn't get much closer to Therress from the Veronnian side.

I gave my sister an imperious look because she shouldn't doubt me after all this time. "We won't have to fight anyone, and if you do your job, no one will be concerned with us."

"Yeah, but this is going to drain you, Dare. You'll be more vulnerable."

"I can still fight, if necessary," I said, trying to be patient with her. As twins, we tended to be protective of each other.

Of course, she had no idea that I often used my secret ability for the king's tasks. She would throw a fit and worry if she found out, and I had pledged to tell no one until matters hit a certain point, but I knew what I was doing. True, it would drain me most of the way, but I'd planned this out carefully, so I'd have a small measure of power if an unanticipated situation arose.

"Fine." She took my hand. "But if we get killed, I'm going to be really angry with you."

I didn't bother responding to that. Instead, I concentrated on a forest located between the Sobaryan Mountains and the Salmar River in Therress. Gripping

Faina's hand tightly, I pushed my magic to that point. We became weightless for several seconds before our feet touched the ground again. It was a strange sensation to dematerialize and then become whole once more, but I'd grown used to it over the decades. Faina immediately let go of my hand to retch on the ground.

I snorted and turned away from my sister to give her privacy.

A variety of pine trees, along with the occasional mistarr tree, surrounded us. We were a couple of miles from a border village I attacked with the Veronnian army nearly twenty years ago. Since I could only teleport to locations where I'd physically been before—flights with sebeskas not counting—I had to choose a place that would get me more than halfway to Ivory Castle. Now, we would stop for a couple of hours so I could regenerate my powers before I took us the rest of the way.

"Ahhh," Faina said, straightening. "Now I remember why I've never been jealous of your inheriting mother's gift and not me. That way of traveling is dreadful. You are going to owe me for this, brother."

I could have gotten myself most of the way if I hadn't brought her, but I needed my sister's abilities to put everyone to sleep while I spoke to Aella. The plan was to get there and back without anyone the wiser.

"I already told you I'd owe you a favor," I said, pulling a canteen from the pack I'd brought and handing it to her.

I'd anticipated her body wouldn't handle it well. Also, I'd need to eat at breaks during the journey, as using this ability multiple times would take a heavy toll on me. By the time we reached Darynia tomorrow morning, I'd have to sleep for nearly a full day. It was one of the reasons I only used teleporting if I could do it with little chance of being caught. I didn't like being vulnerable or anyone outside of a select group knowing I could do it. Even then, all my contacts had sworn a blood oath to never speak of it.

Faina handed the canteen back to me. "Why can't you just send a message? You know she's going to be with Cam tonight, and you do not need to get in the middle of that."

How could I explain the driving need to see my wife after handing her over to Lord Morgunn less than a week ago? I'd had her in my grasp, but only a shell of her true self. She was still under the sleeping spell when I last saw her. With each day that passed since she'd returned to Therress, the urge to see her and make certain she was doing well grew stronger.

Also, I was still frustrated with the role she played in attacking Parvayn. We'd lost many good, innocent people from that. Catching Aella off guard tonight would be part of her punishment while also informing her of my plans to get revenge on Therress for what they did to Verona.

Faina and I took turns napping during the two hours we waited for my powers to return. A few creatures tried to creep up on us during my watch, but I quickly discouraged them. I was grateful when it was time to get moving again. The longer we sat there, the more my mind turned to what Aella might be doing at that moment with Camden. My overactive imagination didn't do me any favors, but surely, I didn't feel jealousy.

I'd never experienced such an emotion in my life. What did I care if she slept with another man? Yet, I found myself disturbed by the thought and wanting to ensure it never happened again.

Our next stop would put us at a thirty-minute walk from our destination. I'd never been to Ivory Castle because the risk was too significant, and there were wards on the lord's keep to prevent teleportation there. That didn't mean I couldn't get close, though.

Long ago, when I developed my spy network, I'd snuck into Therress with Jax. He'd used his invisibility to hide us whenever we came near guards. We'd traveled to a forest between Maradeyn and Lord Morgunn's home so that I'd have a private place to meet with my contacts. While my friends didn't know about my specific dealings with the king, they assisted with my information gathering within the realm.

Jax had helped me obtain several other points throughout the land for the same purpose, and I'd been using them ever since. Teleporting did have a downside aside from the power drain, though. I couldn't see if anyone was there before I arrived. More than once, I'd had to draw my sword right away and kill the witness so they couldn't alert anyone.

As I gathered my powers once more, I hoped I wouldn't have to do that tonight. As long as my sister had time to put them to sleep, it shouldn't become necessary. That was my other reason for bringing her.

We touched solid ground in another dark forest with slightly shorter trees than the previous one, but the brush was much thicker. The place I'd selected was a small clearing, nowhere near any homes or even a stream that might attract animals and fishermen. I'd never seen anyone other than my spies at this location, making it one of the safest to use.

Once more, we sat down to rest. I didn't dare begin the journey to find Aella until I regenerated most of my power so I could leave quickly afterward. In the meantime, my sister and I shared the cheese and rolls I had brought, with me taking the larger portions due to my increasing hunger. I would have to consume a whole feast once we got home and then sleep for at least twelve hours, if not more.

The solstice magic began pumping through my veins soon after eating, turning me hard and frustrated. We'd taken an herbal concoction at my aunt's home to dull the effect, but my heavy use of power was causing it to wear off more quickly than usual. My skin itched with the need to find my wife and have my way with her, but I knew that wouldn't be happening tonight. I began to wonder if it had been a good idea to see her after all, but it was too late to turn back now.

After fifteen more minutes had passed, I stood. "Let's go."

"Finally. I'm ready to get this over with and go home," Faina said, rising and brushing off her pants.

I checked the map to locate Aella's general direction and then headed that way. We moved carefully, winding our way through brush as we tried to find animal trails to follow. Once we came closer to the celebration, we slowed further to scan our surroundings.

Some fae were so busy they never looked our way. Faina left them alone since it hardly seemed fair to put them to sleep while they were in the middle of their pleasure. Only when they weren't busy or looked directly at us did she knock them out. Two men and a woman were going to wake up in a very awkward situation, all because one of them faced us as we passed. It would only last for half an hour without my sister maintaining a magical hold on them, but that would be more than long enough.

My ring grew warmer as we drew closer to Aella. "She's just up ahead."

"I'll stay back and make sure you're not disturbed," Faina said, stopping by a tree.

She had a look of concentration as she touched the minds of everyone within a hundred feet of her. This part of the journey would push my sister to her limits, but she needed a good challenge now and then to keep her skills sharp. Of course, she'd leave Aella and Camden alone, as we'd previously discussed. Since she knew both of them, she could recognize them, though I had no idea how that worked for her.

I rushed forward, finding my wife sleeping tangled in her lover's arms. Soft moonlight glinted on her creamy skin. I couldn't help admiring her full breasts, the curves of her hips, or her beautiful, long legs. She was absolutely stunning and perfect for me—except that another man held her.

An unfamiliar feeling of jealous rage swept over me. Though I knew very well I'd encouraged this, seeing it up close sent me into an angry spiral. Camden had clearly enjoyed Aella all night long while I wore myself out reaching this place to see her. She likely hadn't thought of me once while she allowed a man who wasn't her husband inside her again and again. He'd had liberties with her I'd never had, even though we were married.

I forced myself to take a deep breath and calm myself. This was neither the time nor the place to pick a fight with someone who had no idea his lover was married to another. Still, it was all I could do to resist the urge to snap his neck. I had enough power at the moment to do it easily and still teleport a healthy distance away.

"Aella," I said from where I stood ten feet from her.

She moaned but didn't respond, nuzzling her face into Camden's bare chest. I clenched my fists. "Aella!"

She jerked her head up to look in my direction, eyes widening when she saw me standing close and staring at her. I almost felt amusement as she jerked out of her lover's arms and pulled her knees to her chest. Now, she wanted to be shy?

Likely, everyone nearby had seen her nude, and she had to realize I'd looked my fill before waking her. No one out here tonight expected any sense of privacy, so even if we weren't married, I'd done nothing wrong by appreciating her body. She'd chosen to expose herself.

"What...what are you doing here?" she asked in a shaky voice.

I didn't hide the cold possessiveness in my voice. "Looking for my wife."

Aella scrambled toward her dress that lay just out of reach. I felt like a wolf that had sighted its prey. Her body was mine, even if she didn't recognize it yet. As she crawled for the thin piece of cloth, Camden stirred and sat up.

His gaze found mine, and then he began frantically searching for his clothes, finding his pants within arm's reach. I let him draw those on while grabbing Aella with my power and dragging her squealing form across the ground toward a tree. Holding the pressure, I secured her bare back and arms against the rough bark before she could pull the cloth over her head. She wouldn't be able to move much, but I gave her enough freedom to breathe and turn her head. It was the best I could do with the irrational jealousy fueling my fury.

She would not hide that luscious body from me just yet. "You stay right there, *wife*."

"Wife?" Camden asked, shocked gaze darting between us.

I gave him a hard look. "Yes, as of a month ago."

"Don't act like you didn't specifically give me permission to keep sleeping with him," Aella said with a glare. Her embarrassment had transformed into outrage on her lover's behalf. Did she worry I'd kill him? Ironically, I was tempted despite knowing it wouldn't be fair under the circumstances.

"I did," I agreed, then returned my attention to Camden, not bothering to hide my homicidal thoughts. "But now, my consent has been revoked. Stay away from Aella, and don't *ever* touch her again...or I will kill you in a way that will shock even the most sadistic of individuals."

I meant every word. Tonight would be the only free pass I gave him.

Aella trembled. "He's going to tell someone you're here. My uncle..."

"No, he won't. Will you, Cam?" I asked with a pointed look.

The other elf shook his head vehemently. "No, sir. Of course not."

　　　　　　　　　　　　　　SUSAN ILLENE

"Then get out of my sight," I ordered.

Camden didn't waste another moment before disappearing into the woods.

I sauntered over to Aella, running my gaze up and down her body. Her light-golden skin appeared creamy in the soft moonlight and utterly touchable. She truly was magnificent. When I stopped before her, I took my time memorizing every bare inch before lifting my gaze to meet hers. There was a mixture of lust and fear in her green eyes.

"It's about time I saw my wife naked, though I would have preferred it under different circumstances," I said with a wicked smile that likely disturbed her.

Aella lifted her chin with mutiny in her gaze. How adorable.

"Don't pretend like you didn't change my clothes while I was asleep and helpless for days. That plum dress was a message, loud and clear. You probably looked at my body all you wanted while I couldn't stop you."

I almost regretted behaving myself during her stay, but I had tried to be honorable.

"Oh no, dear Aella." I let out a dark chuckle and leaned an arm on the tree above her head. "As much as I was tempted, I asked my sister to handle that. She was the only one to see your body, though your undergarments remained on the entire time, and her tastes don't run that way. I wanted you to be fully aware when I saw you naked for the first time."

Relief flashed in her eyes, quickly followed by anger. "Let me go, Darrow."

"Dare," I said, wanting to hear it from her lips. It implied more intimacy between us, which was likely why she didn't like using it. I enjoyed making her uncomfortable and challenging her.

"Fine, *Dare*." She glared at me. "Let me go!"

I released my power over her, having made my point. Now, it was time to test what she did with her newfound freedom of movement. I leaned a little closer to see if she tried to scoot away or stand her ground. It was her choice. Interestingly, she stayed firmly in place and licked her lips as she gazed up at me nervously.

"By the looks of it, you've enjoyed the evening's festivities. Your lovely hair is a wild mess with twigs in it." I paused to pluck one out. "And your skin is quite flushed."

Aella had pinkened even more since I began hovering close, which made me wonder if her body responded to my proximity. Now that I knew she was my mate, I was aware we'd both have a hard time resisting each other. The pull between us grew more undeniable with each meeting.

"There are people everywhere who could overhear us and see you," she said, green eyes darting left and right.

"Faina is nearby, keeping them asleep." I ran my fingers down her cheek and along her jaw, pleased at the way she drew in a breath at my touch. Still, no sign of resistance. "As for Cam, he is one of my spies, so you can rest assured he won't tell anyone...if you're still worried about that."

Her jaw dropped, incredulity written all over her face. "You're joking. He can't be, or I'd have known."

It was so much fun revealing that bit of news to see her reaction. Though we didn't plan it, I'd known about their relationship since it began four years ago. Camden never kept that from me. It wasn't his mission to spy on her specifically, but he did relay any information she gave him if it pertained to her uncle or other family members.

Now and then, it proved useful. He was a gentleman, though, and didn't go into detail about his intimate activities with Aella. I'd never cared until recently. Now, I hated that he'd had all that time with her—knew my wife in ways I didn't.

"Would I joke about it or let him live otherwise?" I asked, lifting a brow.

It was true that if he'd been anyone else, my restraint might not have been so resilient tonight. All I could think about now that I had Aella this close was touching her. The magic was getting under my skin more and more as the herbal remedy wore away to almost nothing. It didn't help that her floral scent with that vague hint of spice teased me, while the musky aroma from her lover made me want to cover it with my own.

"Well, I..."

I pressed my lips to hers before she could finish, pleased when she let out a moan. She didn't fight it when I dipped my tongue inside her mouth, and instead, kissed me back with impressive passion. My wife was most certainly receptive to my touch despite what else she'd been doing tonight. I placed a hand on her hip. Feeling her bare skin there sent a jolt through my cock, making me long to do so much more. She couldn't possibly understand the filthy thoughts running through my mind or the overriding need to claim her until she thought of no one except me.

Pulling back a few inches, I looked deeply into her green eyes. "For three days, I kept your sleeping body in the room next to mine. I'd check on you often to be sure you were safe and press a kiss on your forehead, hoping you would wake like in the fables, but of course, you never did. Tonight, I realized I don't want to share you with anyone else because I want you all to myself."

A mixture of lust and uncertainty filled her gaze. "I bet you're still sleeping with other women, though."

Aella had no idea the effect she had on me—curse or no curse. I hadn't been faithful to her after we married, but the pleasure was fleeting and hardly fulfilling. Since I'd had her in Darynia for those three days, I hadn't wanted to touch another woman again, but she didn't need those details. Nameless ones knew what she'd do if she realized the power she held over my desire for her. Given a bit of time, this woman could bring me to my knees. I didn't need to love her to want her above all else.

"Only until you submit yourself to me, and then, I'm yours alone," I swore, though it was already true.

Somehow, I'd have to find a way to control myself because this was getting dangerous.

She shook her head. "You're insane. We are not sleeping together, so forget it."

Aella was in denial, but she'd come around with time. Once I had a chance to fully enjoy her body and bind her to me, this overriding need would surely stop. My father had implied as much. Of course, gaining her cooperation would take some convincing.

I let a smile play on my lips. "If you're not interested, then why do you always return my kisses with such passion?"

"Because I'm a fool."

"If your thighs weren't filthy from another man's use, I'd test your resolve right now," I said, running a finger along her bare stomach up to her breast. She was so utterly tempting like this.

Would she feel dirty letting me fondle her after she'd been with her lover tonight? I couldn't help testing her. Damn if I cared what she'd done in the hours before this point. Her beautiful body was calling to mine, begging to be caressed. I paused my touch just below her left nipple and waited to see her reaction. She didn't push my hand away or protest, only breathed more heavily. Good. She was waiting to see what I did as anticipatory lust filled her gaze.

I took hold of her nipple and pinched it hard. Instead of complaining, she gasped and trembled. Her hands clawed at the tree behind her as if she didn't dare let them stop me from the sensual torture. Did she know she was doing that? It wasn't as if my power held her still anymore, so she could easily stop me if she wanted.

My lips spread into a pleased smile.

Taking it a step further, I cupped both her full breasts and squeezed them hard, curious if more pain would turn her on the way it did me. She moaned and arched into my touch as I kneaded them roughly. There was no sign whatsoever that she minded. If anything, the scent of her arousal grew stronger with the increasing pressure I put on her tender flesh. It was then that I knew she was truly made for me.

Aella's gaze moved from her breasts in my hands to my face, perhaps realizing how easily she'd fallen into my seduction. It no doubt galled her that I had proved my point. She had no idea about the plans I was currently formulating in my head for when we could be together fully. Now that I knew she enjoyed a mix of pain and pleasure, the possibilities were endless. I wouldn't try too much at once and would ease her into it, but I had no doubt she'd respond beautifully.

"It's only the solstice magic affecting us," she said breathily. Her ridiculous denial was returning because she wasn't ready for me quite yet...but soon.

I gave one last squeeze that made her gasp again, and then I let go. "Hmm, we'll test that theory another time."

With luck, she'd lie in bed every night remembering what I'd done to her in the darkness of these woods and wishing for more. Let that ache build until the day she submitted to me fully with her beautiful, bare body spread before my gaze in invitation.

"Why are you here?" she asked, voice shaky.

It was encouraging that she didn't try to cover up or move away from me. How far would she let me go? I hated that I needed to switch the topic to the business side of my visit. Someday, I'd make time to focus on the intimacy between us instead.

"To tell you that I will be requiring your channeling services." I glanced at the sky with a frown, estimating the time by the alignment of the stars. "It's two hours until dawn, so we'll meet at nine tomorrow night. That gives you a day and a half to prepare. Coming now was the only way I could meet you in person to speak since everyone's guard is down for solstice. It's time you help me get my vengeance."

Her expression turned bitter. "Like you didn't know exactly how you'd find me when every sane adult would be enjoying the night, not infiltrating enemy territory."

"Maybe I did." I shrugged because she wasn't wrong. "Perhaps having my wife in my home for several days made me reconsider our marriage, and I felt the need to make a point."

She shook her head, blonde hair falling over her pert breasts. "You can't want me that much with the history between us."

"How I wish that were true." I leaned forward, making certain my possessiveness of her was quite clear. "But I've decided that you're mine, and if someone else touches you from this point forward, they die. Understand?"

Shock flashed in her eyes, but it quickly changed to ire "If you think I'll ever let you touch me again after you force me to help you attack my people, you're wrong."

I pulled away, giving her a knowing smile. "You will help me because that's the deal we made, and you'll still want me afterward—even if you hate yourself for it."

Of that much, I was certain.

"Fine." Her features tightened. "I'll see you tomorrow night."

I held her gaze, making certain she understood the gravity of my request. "Don't be late. As you see, I can always find you, dear wife."

Though it wasn't easy, I made myself walk away from her without looking back. Time was running short. Faina and I needed to begin our return journey to Veronna before my exhaustion set in and forced me to sleep.

Chapter 27

Aella

I was in one of the castle's sitting rooms with Rynn, Tadeus, and Briauna after a tedious dinner with Lord Morgunn, who forgot about my birthday. A custom he followed every year. We each had a piece of murtberry cake that the kind kitchen staff had baked perfectly. It was my favorite kind—unlike my uncle's. The small tree from which the main ingredient came was one of many varieties that grew in the castle orchard, producing round, lavender fruit. It wasn't very pleasant if eaten fresh, but sweet and delicious when baked in bread or desserts.

"Thank you for this," I said to my older cousin.

Tadeus shrugged. "You always do something special for our birthdays, and I felt bad I wasn't here last year to do anything."

Per his father's orders, he'd been away at court, so it was hardly his fault.

"Do you like our gifts?" Rynn asked, blue eyes dancing with light.

I nodded. "Absolutely. I couldn't have asked for anything better."

She'd given me a beautiful diamond barrette, which had to be worth a fortune. It was from her mother's collection that she'd inherited. I'd tried to refuse, but she insisted, saying I more than deserved it for the sacrifices I'd made for her. If it reduced her guilt, then I supposed I couldn't turn it down. Also, it was perfect and could be paired with almost anything. I'd told her as much, which made her happy.

My cousin had given me new gardening supplies, which had sat by the arched entrance this morning when I arrived to tend my plants. My favorite was a sack of the best fertilizer in the realm from the Isle of Penoria. It was located off the northwest coast of Zadrya's mainland and home primarily to the faeries. They didn't sell much of their rich compost, but when they did, it was ideal for growing fruit and vegetable plants. I could only imagine how much it cost him since I hadn't tried purchasing any in years on my budget. The price only grew with the blight and crop failures.

Briauna had woven me a beautiful shawl that matched my green eyes exactly. She knew I often used one while reading on my window seat, but mine had become worn and threadbare. I was touched by the thoughtful gifts the three of them gave me.

"How does it feel to be thirty-three now?" Tadeus asked with an amused look.

I shrugged. "For a couple of months, I'm only a year younger than you, so how do you feel?"

"Like time is passing too fast and also too slow," he said with a laugh.

"That sums it up perfectly," I agreed.

I wished Sariyah could have been here as well, but my best friend had to return to Tradain yesterday evening after recovering from the summer solstice celebration. They'd only let her off work for the holiday, but she'd promised she'd have a gift waiting for me when I returned in a couple of days.

Finishing my cake, I set the plate down. "Thanks, everyone, for remembering me, but I think I'm going to retire early tonight. Maybe curl up with a good book."

"What?" Tadeus asked, surprised. "We usually enjoy a good drink on the north tower roof after cake."

I wished we could tonight as well, but I had to make my excuses, whether I liked it or not. "Not this time. Camden and I broke things off, and I just want to be alone."

Rynn leaped to her feet, anger in her youthful features. "You two were fine on solstice night. What did he do?"

"It's complicated," I said, giving her a meaningful look. "You know…with my upcoming potential marriage and all."

She looked confused for a moment before light dawned in her eyes. Rynn might not have known Darrow had shown up that night, but she knew about my marriage to him and that I had to open portals for him frequently.

"Oh." She settled back in her seat. "Yeah, I can see how that might make things weird."

Briauna, the only one who knew what I really needed to do tonight, slapped her thigh. "We should leave Aella to it. If she wants to be alone in her room on her birthday, who are we to stop her?"

I gave everyone hugs, took my gifts, and hurried from the room.

***

A little over an hour later, I exited the portal into Veronna. It was the same location I'd used to reach his great-aunt's house the night we got married. As a precaution, I wore a thin black cloak and some light glamour to conceal my features. The last thing I needed was for anyone to know who was opening portals tonight, aside from my husband and his inner circle.

I only found Darrow's sister, Faina, waiting for me. Why was I not surprised? I moved to sit against the tree next to where she rested with her legs crossed. Since she was in black battle garb, I assumed she'd also be fighting this time.

"Which of my villages am I assisting you in ruining?"

"Petosty," Faina said, picking up a branch from the ground and pulling a knife from a sheath attached to her belt. She began carving into it as if she planned to make a stake.

I clenched my eyes shut. It wasn't as if I had a favorite village, but that one crafted some of the finest furniture in all of Zadrya. How much would they destroy? Almost eight hundred people lived there, and I worried for their safety.

"How long until the others arrive?" I asked, listening to the sounds of the night and her carving.

Faina sighed. "Half of them will be here in two hours."

"Half?"

"The rest are traveling through the mountain pass right now to take out the sentries, and they'll wait until we've finished the ones on the ground before coming down." She paused her carving. "Darrow is making sure our attack doesn't incriminate you in any way."

How very thoughtful of him.

She went on to detail the plan further. We would use the portal two miles from the village within a forest, which they somehow knew was rarely guarded. It would be easy to sneak a few soldiers, especially with the right magic, to take out the tower at the base of the pass. The two halves could join in the woods near the village without anyone seeing them before that.

I could understand why they'd chosen the location because it was the easiest to attack without anyone figuring out a channeler had helped them. At least, it was great for me, but not so much for the people there. I was helping to destroy their lives.

"Yes, glad I factor into his plans beyond aiding his attack on my people," I said, bitterly.

Faina stopped carving. "Not the way you expected to spend your birthday?"

I stiffened, unable to read her expression.

"No." I leaned my head against the tree. "I'm surprised you knew it was today, though it looks like Darrow doesn't know...or is this his version of a morbid gift?"

She shrugged. "My brother has never been good with birthdays, so I doubt he realizes yours is today. I only knew because he had me look into you after you married, and I'm good with dates."

"Do you think it would matter if he did know?" I asked.

Why I expected anything from a husband who married me to keep me out of enemy hands and to use my skills was beyond me. Never mind his possessive claims the other night because that didn't mean he cared. He was like a child who didn't want to share his toy.

Faina was quiet for a moment. "Darrow is cold but not callous. He would have likely chosen a different day if he'd known."

"But you didn't bother to point it out," I said, annoyed.

"Why should I?" She lifted a brow. "You're not my friend, nor do I like you, and it's better you see my brother for who he is now rather than later."

I narrowed my eyes. "What is that supposed to mean?"

"There's a curse on all the males of my father's line. As soon as they come into their magic, they become incapable of love—that includes family. Even their other emotions are dimmed a little."

Faina paused and sighed. "It has ruined every marriage for them for generations because they are charismatic and possessive despite the curse, and even if warned, their wives always fall for them eventually. Why should I have told him about your birthday when it's better he doesn't do anything for you that might make you feel something for him?" She resumed carving the wood. "I wasn't supposed to tell you, but that secret is my gift to you."

Her revelation was more than unexpected. "Can the curse be broken?"

"Every curse has a way to break it, but this one isn't easy, or it would have been done centuries ago," she said, not looking at me.

"How?" I asked, impatiently.

"It's not for me to say, but you're welcome to ask my brother."

I snorted. "Think he'll tell me?"

She gave me a scornful look. "It's doubtful Dare will anytime soon since he doesn't trust you, and for good reason."

I decided I'd had enough of talking to Faina and didn't respond. Even her telling me about Darrow's curse seemed to have ulterior motives. She couldn't possibly care about protecting my feelings, so there had to be some other reason. I just didn't know what that could be.

The time passed in silence until hoofbeats began shaking the ground. Faina and I rose to our feet upon their approach, and she mounted her horse. I saw Darrow in the lead. Bracing myself, I met his gaze as he pulled his mount to a stop. Heat filled his gray eyes as he looked me up and down—a blatant reminder I was naked the last time we met. I stood my ground, refusing to let his hot gaze bother me. At least with my glamour and cloak, he couldn't see much of the real me.

"Good of you to join us, Aella," he said, reaching out a hand.

"As if I had a choice." I let him pull me onto his stallion before him, trying to keep a sliver of distance between my back and his chest.

Darrow leaned close to my right ear. "Too bad you chose to don your clothing this time, as I thoroughly enjoyed the full view yesterday morning."

He snaked an arm around my waist and pulled me close. Anger poured through me at his audacity and the reminder of everything we'd discussed while he'd had me pinned naked against a tree. I still wondered how he had gotten into the heart of Therress so easily, even on solstice. There were no reports of attacks or deaths. I knew since I'd listened closely for any related news, but everyone said it was quiet on the border that night.

"You mean you enjoyed seeing me nude in another man's arms?" I asked tauntingly. Two could play at this game.

He tensed. "At least he was one of my people, and he won't be touching you again since he takes his orders very seriously."

I gritted my teeth, unable to help myself by taunting him. "Then I'll find someone else in a place you can't reach."

"There is nowhere I won't follow when it comes to you, and like I told you last night, I'll kill any man who touches you. Do you want to be responsible for that?" Darrow asked mockingly.

I hated that I didn't truly want anyone else. "That wasn't part of our deal."

"If you have needs," he said, moving his hand inside my cloak to rub a thumb just under my left breast, teasing so close to where he'd touched me last time. "I'll be happy to take care of that. Say the word."

I wanted to leap off the horse so badly. First, he ended things between me and Camden, and then he ruined my birthday by forcing me to help his army attack my land. While I usually couldn't resist his touch, I forced myself to remember what we were doing tonight. I would not fall for his seductive words and caresses this time. He was forcing me to betray my people.

"You are literally the last elf I want to have sex with now or ever."

His tracing fingers paused. "I'll let that go under the circumstances, but I promise I'll prove those words wrong soon enough."

"We'll see," I vowed.

"Time to open the portal to Petosty, Aella," Darrow ordered, handing me a hefty bag of holmium powder—far more than I needed. I could have sworn there was relish in his voice when he gave me the command.

Pinching some between my fingers, I tried to hide the tears that pricked my eyes at what I was about to do—the betrayal I was committing against my people. It wasn't fair, but I'd agreed to this. Like it or not, I had to do it. So I chanted the damning words and pulled at my wind and light power, opening the gate in seconds since it was one of mine with no wards to slow me down and the closest one to my current location. Only the mountain range and a stretch of forest stood between.

A small *pop* broke the air, and the soft blue glow of the portal filled the ring. Darrow began shouting orders as I held it open for his troops. Even as I channeled, I started counting them. He hadn't held back from this attack.

Their line was far longer than I'd been able to make out in the dark woods, but by the time the end of them came near, I counted over two hundred. I hadn't seen the other group, but Faina said half had already crossed into the mountains. That was a hefty force for a village of eight hundred. I didn't think we had more than twenty soldiers there since it hadn't been attacked in at least a century.

Darrow continued to hold me closely as he guided his horse through the portal. Once on the other side, he handed me off to his friend, Loden, who would stay with me during the attack. My callous husband led the rest of his troops through the forest away from us.

Once they took care of the tower guards at the foot of the mountain pass, the village would be next, and there would be no one to send a warning to my uncle or his military commanders. They'd have free reign to do what they wanted. I wouldn't be able to see any of it or know if Darrow kept his promise not to kill civilians until reports came tomorrow. Whatever happened, though, it would still be my fault.

There was a tree stump with a broad base about twenty feet from the ring. I moved over and sat on it, sinking my face into my hands as I began to cry. This whole marriage plan had seemed tolerable before, but now, I was second-guessing myself. I should have negotiated harder against opening portals to my land.

Loden dropped a hand on my shoulder. "You shouldn't feel guilt over this."

"Easy for you to say," I mumbled without looking up.

"At least you're honorable enough to keep your end of the deal." He pulled his hand away. "Half of us thought you wouldn't show up, and Darrow would have to lead the attack without your help. Of course, that would have led to many more deaths as punishment to you."

"How do I know he won't kill everyone regardless?" I asked, finally looking up at him with a tear-streaked face.

Loden looked at me sympathetically. "Because he's trying to earn your trust, and that would be a bad way to go about it when you just extended yours."

I wiped my hand at my face, trying to dry it. "Why would he care if I trust him?"

"Because what we're doing tonight is not why he wanted your portal abilities."

That was hard to believe. "Then why else would he want them?"

"Keep earning his trust, and you'll find out," Loden said, walking away to settle onto his own spot.

Several hours later, Darrow and his half of the soldiers returned. I refused to look at him and simply opened the portal once they reached the ring. He stopped his horse beside me, watching his people disappear inside the blue glow.

Now and then, I felt his gaze, but I stood firm and kept mine on the blue glow. He could fall off a mountain for all I cared. As the end of his troops neared, I noted the last ones performing a spell that restored the ground to how it looked before our arrival. There would be no way for my uncle to know they'd come from this direction.

"See you again soon, dear wife," he said with one last look before disappearing with all the others—arrogant ass.

I let the portal close and waited a minute to collect myself. Though I couldn't know the condition of the village and didn't dare walk down there to look, I felt a weight on my chest that made it hard to breathe. No matter what anyone said, I'd done this. Every death, every destroyed structure, and every life ruined was on me. I'd never think of my birthday in the same way because it would always remind me of the terrible thing I'd done this night.

Searching within, I found I had just enough energy to get myself back to my garden ring. It was helpful already being inside Therress. All I wanted to do was climb into bed, burrow into my blankets, and shut out the world.

Chapter 28

Aella

The next morning, all anyone could talk about was the attack on Petosty. I made myself get up at my usual time to avoid suspicion. Uncle Morgunn was furious since the news didn't reach him until after dawn. That was likely due to the Veronnians setting loose the messenger birds without missives and all the scouts put to sleep for hours.

At breakfast, he said he announced plans to visit the village and bring Briauna with him for her healing powers. Early reports he'd received so far indicated half a dozen soldiers had died, and the rest were moderately wounded. Only a few villagers sustained injuries. Those consisted of people who'd resisted Darrow's forces herding them to the village school or worship temple. Every home and shop burned to the ground, so only the two structures remained standing. The enemy soldiers surprisingly set all the animals and chickens loose before torching everything. I appreciated that they were spared, though it didn't reduce my guilt by much.

I barely made it back to my room after eating before breaking down in tears. Sure, they'd minimized deaths as promised, but they'd destroyed cottages, workshops, and almost everything else. It wasn't something we could rebuild in a week or two. Families had to be relocated, and many would need to start all over again. I'd done that to them.

After opening a portal for Lord Morgunn and his retinue to visit the village, I opened another for Tradain. My uncle insisted that I return to training, as he'd already arranged for a channeler to meet him at Petosty for the return trip.

It was lunchtime when I arrived, so I headed straight for Camden's officer quarters. A part of me hoped he wasn't there, but he opened the door on the first knock. We stood staring at each other for a moment, silent.

I cleared my throat. "Can I get my things, please?"

"Of course, I've put them together already," he said, stepping back.

I came in and stared at the bag in the corner of his sitting area. When he shut the door with a *click*, I jumped. How awkward was this? My husband had damned

Camden and I both for things we didn't know the other was doing, which made it hard to be mad or forgive.

"So, how did Darrow convince you to marry him in secret?" he asked, curiosity in his gaze. There was also a hint of betrayal.

I grabbed my bag and sat in the chair, figuring we should work this out now, so we didn't have to speak to each other again later, or be left wondering. "Rynn had faebor fever and wasn't going to survive. I discovered Darrow's great aunt could cure her, so I found him in Siggaya to make a deal."

"For marriage?" he asked, aghast.

I snorted, imagining if that had been my opening line. "Hardly. I offered my portal services—with limits, but he wanted marriage so a future husband couldn't track me so closely that I couldn't keep my end of the deal with him."

Camden ran a hand through his dark-blond hair. "I can't believe he would even suggest that with as much as he hates your family."

I explained the gist of what was said that first night and how we managed the wedding. "Until last night, the deal seemed worth it."

"You portaled his army to Petosty," he surmised, shock in his gaze. "It's why you look exhausted and guilty right now. You are the last person I would have thought to betray Therress."

I flinched, my guilt growing. "It was part of the deal. As long as my uncle didn't use me to attack civilians on Veronna's side, I didn't have to portal Darrow and his army to my side. Then Lord Morgunn ruined it, and I had no choice. Darrow threatened to do much worse if I didn't help."

Camden sat in the chair opposite me, taking in my story with incredulity. "You shouldn't have married him. I admit my allegiance to Therress, but he's half dark elf and ruthless. I would have advised you against it if you'd come to me first."

"What was my other choice?" I asked, chest tightening. "Let Rynn die and be married to Baron Elgord instead? A man who swore he'd break me and use my body, whether I liked it or not, to birth a bunch of his children. At least Darrow hasn't forced himself on me."

Not exactly, anyway. I fully cooperated with his kisses, and while a small part of me had been embarrassed by him catching me nude, another part had enjoyed his heated gaze and rough hands on my body. It was causing me to lose sleep at night. Of course, that was before he used me to attack a Therressian village on my birthday. Now, I would do everything I could to banish him from my mind and forget his touches.

Camden grunted. "Admittedly, you had no good choices, and it does explain the king's immediate refusal of the betrothal. I hadn't thought he'd care enough about a lady he hardly knew to stop it. Of course, this means your next potential suitor won't work, either. He's going to get suspicious."

"I'm trying to buy time before the truth comes out," I said, fiddling with the handle of my bag. "With luck, I'll find a way out of it without the king needing to deny Lord Morgunn again."

"It's a dangerous game you play," he said, genuine worry in his gaze. We might have been forced to break up, but it was hard to stop caring about someone in a matter of days—even with betrayal on both sides.

I shook my head. "You're one to talk. How are you even his spy when you've been here for as long as I can remember?"

"My father's brother lives in Veronna, and we visited once every couple of years. I began to learn the truth about our history, so by the time I was a teenager, Lord Gannon's spymaster had already recruited me. Later, Darrow and his inner circle took over my handling. Mostly, I pass them information and try to mitigate civilian casualties when we must fight on Veronnian soil."

That made sense, I supposed. They reached him when he was young and influential.

"Thanks for explaining," I said, glad we could handle this civilly.

He nodded. "You're as deep into it as I am now, probably more. Please watch yourself with Darrow and try to avoid any emotional entanglements. He is very good at manipulating women to get what he wants, but rumor has it that he is incapable of feeling anything in return for them. The way he looked at you on solstice tells me he isn't going to refrain from seducing you for long, especially since you legally belong to him. I've never heard of him being possessive like that, which is concerning. You shouldn't matter to him that much."

Darrow had made some rather shocking and colorful threats if Camden touched me again. I couldn't decide if my husband was truly jealous or simply trying to make my life more difficult. Was it another game?

"His sister explained some things to me last night, but there's still a lot he's hiding." I swallowed. "Darrow and his inner circle don't trust me. I know they have some secret plans they hope to bring me into eventually, but I have no idea what they might be."

Camden's brows knitted. "I have no idea, or I'd tell you. Please be careful."

We hugged, and he held me tightly for a moment, both of us ignoring my frustrating husband's threats. Despite everything, part of me wished it didn't have to end this way. Maybe we didn't love each other, but Camden had always been good to me, and I enjoyed his company. It was hard to end it just because Darrow suddenly decided he wanted more from our marriage, even though he'd never feel anything real for me.

With one last look, I left, knowing I'd never step foot in the quarters again.

I went to my small barracks room, put away the bag, and changed into training gear. For the rest of the afternoon, I spent my time practicing with my sword and dagger. I had so much anger and resentment inside me that I managed to finish a good workout before quitting for the day.

Sariyah found me in my room shortly after I'd returned from a shower in the community washroom. My hair was still wet as I combed through it. Her rich brown locks flowed loosely around her, beautiful as always. She'd donned a light summer dress that hugged her figure and made me wish I'd brought something aside from training and sleep clothes. Sometimes, it helped to look extra nice when one needed a morale boost.

"By the look in your eyes, something is wrong," she said, concern in her hazel eyes.

I nodded. "How about we grab food and wine from the dining hall and take it to the river?"

"Ah, I see, it's *that* bad."

I set my brush down and began to braid my blonde hair into a thick plait. "Very. There are some serious things I haven't told you, but I desperately need to talk about them now."

"It felt like you were holding back lately," she said, moving behind me to take over doing the intricate braid I preferred yet could never do right myself. "I figured you'd tell me when you were ready."

"Yes," I agreed.

As soon as she finished, we made good on our plans, and within half an hour, we were settled at our favorite spot along the Salmar River. The fast-flowing water was wide and deep enough that one would have to swim hard to cross it. People drowned in it every spring when the winter snow thawed, causing it to swell and become too turbulent for anyone to enter except the strongest and most experienced.

It snaked through much of the western half of Therress, starting at the Sobaryan Mountains and ending at the Pazakian Sea. A rocky outcrop with a few flat boulders near a dense tree line made for the perfect place to eat and relax. It was secluded and private. We set up in our usual spot, opening the cloth sack that held wrapped chicken sandwiches larger than I could hope to finish in one sitting. We also poured wine into tin cups.

Sariyah and I ate silently, watching the occasional fish swim by from our perch. A pack of wild boars tried to come close to us from downriver, but I pushed them hard enough with my wind magic to discourage them. It was never a good idea to let them get too close.

"Are you going to tell me what has that sad and hopeless expression on your face?" Sariyah finally asked after I set aside the remains of my sandwich.

I couldn't meet her gaze and stared at the river instead. "I married Lord Gannon's son, Darrow, about five weeks ago. We agreed to keep it a secret from everyone except a select few and the king, who presided over the ceremony."

Might as well tell her the most significant part of the story first.

"What?" my friend asked, dropping the water container in her hand. It tumbled down the rocks, barely stopping before the river could take it. She didn't seem to notice. "You're joking, right?"

"Nope," I said, leaning down to retrieve the canteen. "I agreed to it because he has an aunt who was able to save Rynn from faebor fever and to avoid marriage to Baron Elgord."

She took a moment to let that news sink into her mind. "And what did Darrow get in return?"

"My portal channeling whenever he wants and almost anywhere he wants."

Sariyah climbed off the boulder and paced as much as one could along a rocky shore for a few minutes. She fired rapid questions after she collected herself, and I answered them truthfully. The whole time, I barely looked at her, preferring to keep my eyes on the water that was as chaotic as my emotions. My guilt from last night's attack colored everything I'd told her, making me feel like a fool and worse.

Finally, she sighed and settled back onto her seat. "Please tell me the dark elf is at least pleasing to look at."

"Enough that I wish to the nameless ones that he was uglier," I admitted, finally looking her in the eyes and giving her a wan smile.

She cocked her head. "Is he a good kisser?"

I'd told her we hadn't had sex, but not much more.

"Also, too good," I said, leaning back on my elbows. "Darrow said it would be purely business between us when we negotiated, but he's definitely changed his mind, and now I have a feeling it's going to take every ounce of strength I have not to give in to him."

"What about Cam?" she asked, brows furrowing. "I know you've been with him since you married."

I told her what happened on Solstice night after she went to seek out her own partner, leaving out only that Cam was a spy. Instead, I said I made him promise not to tell anyone. She thankfully bought that story. I couldn't betray my former lover even if he were betraying Therress. It wasn't as if I had room to judge, and maybe someday I'd find out what turned him against our land. He'd said something about history, but I hadn't wanted to ask about it then.

Sariyah moved closer and hugged me. "That's a lot, Aella. I don't know how you held it all in for this long, but I understand why you did. Thanks for confiding in me."

One thing about my best friend was her easygoing nature and willing acceptance of others. She wasn't mad that I didn't tell her sooner, but rather, understood I'd needed time to come to terms with it. I loved her dearly for that.

"So what are you going to do now?" she asked, sympathy in her eyes.

I shrugged. "Try to survive and hope things don't get any worse."

"I'll do what I can to help you," she vowed.

"Thanks," I said and gave her another hug. It felt good to have her on my side.

Chapter 29

Aella

The early afternoon sun beat down on me as I moved through my warm-up drills. Summer in Therress was always brutal, but we'd reached the worst heat now, which was unforgiving. I'd changed my pants and tunic during my lunch break. The new set now soaked up the sweat pouring from me as I lunged and parried against an invisible target. Was it still a warm-up if you were already baking?

I paused momentarily to pull out a handkerchief and wipe my face. Across the practice ring, I spotted Camden working with a pair of new trainees, helping them practice their knife-throwing skills. He caught my gaze and gave me an almost imperceptible nod.

Since a month ago, when Darrow ended my relationship with Cam, we hadn't spoken after I collected my things. We didn't even exchange greetings. I didn't mind losing the sex nearly as much as a friend. Until we'd been forced apart, I hadn't realized how much I'd enjoyed spending time and discussing things with him. Maybe that was the real reason we'd lasted for years.

I forced my gaze away, wondering who else might be a spy around Tradain. Camden couldn't be the only one, but none of the others stood out so far. I hadn't even narrowed down anyone else in Tradain with loose ties to Veronna. If there were any, they kept those details quiet.

I'd only seen Darrow once since the night he made me betray my people with the attack on Petosty. We'd met a week ago when he'd had me take him and his inner circle to Jolloure again. This time, his dark elf cousin, Bogdan, sat with me while the others did whatever they did on the island. He didn't say much while I picked flowers for my sister, but at least he didn't look at me like he was plotting my demise. That was refreshing.

After I brought everyone back to Veronna, Darrow stayed with me until I had enough power to return home. He'd tried to get close, but I'd vowed never to speak to him again if he touched me. Thankfully, my husband had the sense to back off and leave me alone.

I forced myself to resume my warm-up drills as others nearby began sparring. Every day I came out here, I felt stronger and more confident that I could defend myself even without my magic. That was good since I was still struggling with my light-wielding skills after nearly two months of focused effort. My only improvement so far was splitting stones in half instead of pulverizing them, but the concentrated beam continued to go beyond my target.

"Looks like you need a sparring partner," a sardonic voice came from behind me.

I swung around, gripping my sword tightly at the sight of my cousin. Ulmar stood with his arms crossed, leaning against the wooden fence surrounding the practice field. His dark red hair appeared freshly cut short, but he'd left a few days' worth of stubble on his face. Combined with his piercing blue eyes, fitted navy tunic, and black pants, he appeared absolutely menacing. He might not have bulky muscles, but he was still tall and strong.

He usually didn't come to Tradain unless we assembled for battle, but Lord Morgunn bided his time right now and hadn't retaliated for what happened at Petosty yet. He'd focused his efforts on cleaning up the aftermath of the destroyed village and consoling his people. I had a feeling he planned something big against Veronna, but needed time to organize and wanted to catch them off guard. Dread filled me at what that might mean.

"No, thank you," I said, lifting my chin. "My partner is coming now."

I gestured toward Sariyah, who headed our way. She took the afternoon off work to train a few times a week, and we practiced together. Today, my friend ran a little late. I'd extended my warm-up while waiting for her.

Sariyah, wearing a deep red tunic and beige pants, grabbed one of the practice swords from a nearby rack and marched toward us. She couldn't stand Ulmar. The flat look she gave him made that clear, though he already knew. With her father being the commander of the Therressian army and King Worden's nephew, Ulmar had to watch his level of sneering and snide comments.

"Oh, look. It's the *almost* princess," he said mockingly.

Or maybe he didn't care today.

She lifted her brows at him. "Jealous?"

"Considering your mother was a low-born mongrel, hardly," he replied. It was a cruel taunt, considering her mom died when she was sixteen from a strange malady that swept the land that year, sickening most fae and some not surviving the ailment. Her grandmother didn't overcome it, either. Both had Andalagarian blood, which many of the fae considered lesser.

I grabbed Sariyah's arm before she did something she'd regret. She had excellent sword skills, but her magic couldn't compete with Ulmar's. Aside from his ability to detect lies, he could also inflict pain on his enemies. It was exceptionally debilitating for those who weren't intimately acquainted with the levels of agony he could produce.

"Can you sink any lower?" I asked him, moving to stand before my friend.

My cousin gave me a derisive look. "It depends. Will you let me test your skills, or is your friend going to fight your battles for you?"

I suspected my uncle had sent him here, and I'd have to duel with him whether I liked it or not. He just couldn't be straightforward and say as much. Ulmar loved creating drama.

"Get a sword," I said, refusing to show a hint of fear. "But we do this with the traditional practice rules."

In other words, we couldn't use any magic for the first two minutes. That forced opponents to test their physical skills first. After that, we could attack with anything in our arsenal—blades or magic—as long as we didn't maim or kill. I'd only fought Ulmar twice, both times years ago, but I'd never won. He was cunning and ruthless.

As my cousin grabbed a practice sword—made of sturdy wood with a blunted tip—I moved into my fighting stance. Today, he would not get the best of me. I'd make him hurt the way he'd done to me often in the past, usually outside the practice ring.

He returned to face me. "Very well, traditional rules it is, Aella. Let's see if you can stay on your feet this time, hmm?"

Ulmar wasted no time swinging his sword at me, but he broadcasted the move so much that I easily ducked as it sailed over my head, missing me by inches. I thrust forward, stabbing him in his exposed stomach. It didn't penetrate his tunic, but the breath *whooshed* from him due to the force, and he stumbled back. Getting hit with a blunt tip still hurt.

My cousin growled at me. In the next moment, he lunged forward and began a series of strikes that left me on the defensive. He had incredible speed that could rival the best swordsman. I kept my eyes trained on his blade, blocking and ducking each attack. This was how he got me to the ground the last time we fought, but I'd spent these previous weeks practicing for this very strategy. I'd had two people attack me at once, so I'd have to accelerate my reactions.

Ulmar killed time by not giving me another opening. He didn't have great stamina but had enough endurance to buy time until he could use magic. I estimated that I had fifteen seconds before that happened.

When he spun to build force for a particularly devastating strike, I ducked and rolled past his legs, kicking him in the knee as I went. With him already unbalanced as he rotated, he went down hard. I leaped to my feet as he began to rise and slammed my sword into the side of his head, ringing his ears.

"Who is on the ground now?" I asked, looking down at him.

He sneered. "Not for long, little cousin."

I noted a crowd had gathered on the other side of the fence, watching us. Sariyah's father stood over there with a stoic, analytical expression. He was about as serious as a person could get, but in private, he doted on his daughter. After losing his wife, his only child meant everything to him. I envied their close relationship. The way they chatted amiably at dinner when I visited reminded me of how things were before my parents died.

As Ulmar struggled to his feet, Sariyah called out, "Time!"

I didn't hesitate to gather my wind magic and send my cousin flying down the ring thirty feet away, crashing into the fence. He let out a pained grunt as his back struck one of the support posts enhanced with magic so it wouldn't give under any pressure. The farther I stayed away from him, the better. That was my strategy. For once, I wouldn't let him get the best of me, and I *would* win.

Per the rules, I waited for Ulmar to return to his feet. He did it slowly, but the moment he was up, he stretched his hand toward me. Pain burst in my head. I winced and backed up because every foot of space I put between us reduced the intensity. Unfortunately, he quickly moved in step with me.

I'd endured this agony many times before, so I pushed through it and sent a curve of wind that hit him from the side and sent him sliding across the dirt. The pain vanished momentarily as he rolled onto his hands and knees and pushed off the ground to stand. I sent another forceful gale at him until he slammed into another fence post, head flying back as he struck it.

Sariyah flashed me two fingers, indicating we had two minutes left. It wasn't long, but it was also an eternity. A lot could happen during that time. I jolted as pain sparked inside my head again, directly behind my eyes. My vision blurred as it worsened.

"Ahhh!" I screamed.

Ulmar had hit a cluster of nerves that felt like a thousand tiny needles had stabbed me. I pressed my palms onto my face, willing myself to work past the agony. It went on and on in ever-intensifying waves. My knees shook, but I refused to fall to the ground the way my cousin wanted. He'd sworn to take me down. I couldn't give him that satisfaction because he would not win this time. I was tired of losing in so many ways.

His solid footsteps came close. I braced my feet and removed my hands, attempting to see, but my vision didn't clear. A fist struck the side of my head, and more pain exploded in my cheekbone. I tilted to the right but caught myself from falling. Lifting my arms, I managed to block the next blow and blindly kicked outward. My boot struck his leg.

As he stumbled back, the pain let up enough for my vision to clear a little. Now that I could spot his location, I decided to put a new secret weapon into action.

I drew in the air around me and spun my hand in small circles. Wind swirled around Ulmar like a whirlpool, lifting him and turning him. As long as he wasn't on the ground, I didn't have to stop. It would make him so dizzy that he wouldn't be able to see anything to target me again. Let's see how he liked it.

I'd developed the idea a couple of weeks ago while alone in the pit and practiced with stones when I grew tired of failing at my light magic. I hadn't planned to reveal it today, but he'd left me no choice.

The wind picked up the dirt underneath, along with a few stray rocks and twigs from last night's storm that had blown into the ring. Ulmar's body continued to spin fast through the whirling vortex. Breaking through the torrent of noise, I heard him grunting and crying out as the debris struck his exposed skin. His shirt lifted, and after a few moments, it tore from his body to join the other spiraling items.

I kept my eyes on him to maintain the speed of my wind magic, but I heard the shocked and impressed murmurs around me. No one had done anything like this before. Wind in Zadrya usually flew straight or at a slight curve, but it never spun like this. I'd stolen the idea from a natural whirlpool near mine and Sariyah's favorite spot by the Salmar River. It had seemed like something that could work with air as well.

It didn't tire me to keep the spin going since I hadn't used my magic all day, so I found I could even move around my wind swirl to get a good lock at the vortex from all sides. Something like it could prove useful on a larger scale in the future. It was fortunate that this wasn't a natural phenomenon, though, because it could easily destroy whole villages.

Commander Norvin, Sariyah's father, gestured at me. "It's over. You won, Aella."

I stopped spinning my hand and flicked out my fingers, letting Ulmar crash to the ground. He huddled there in a ball and began heaving his lunch onto the hardpacked ground. My cousin was covered in dirt, bloody cuts, and red marks.

After the horrible things he'd done to me over the years, I didn't feel the least remorse. He'd fully recover within a few hours from the minor injuries, whereas I constantly had to hide my scars from others so no one outside my family would know what he and my uncle had done to me.

"Excellent display of power, Aella," Commander Norvin said, coming over to pat me on the back. "If a situation is ever dire enough, I may call you forward to launch such magic on a larger scale."

I lifted a brow. "How do you know I could make it bigger?"

"The fact you're not out of breath tells me you've expended very little energy to perform that maneuver." He chuckled and leaned closer to me. "It was nice to see your cousin put in his place for once, with how he abuses my soldiers with his powers."

"You couldn't have possibly enjoyed it more than me," I whispered back. Despite my win, I didn't dare gloat too loudly. Ulmar was unforgiving, and if he found an opportunity, he would exact revenge for today.

Sariyah ran up and hugged me. "That was amazing. I'm so glad you finally beat his ass, Aella."

My cousin finished retching and lifted his head to glare at me with a promise of vengeance in his bloodshot gaze. I gave my best friend a wan smile. "Thank you."

I'd have to watch my every step for a while. The trouble with Ulmar was that he could also be very patient and wait weeks or months to strike when I least expected it. I wondered if I shouldn't have taken a beating instead of what might come later.

Chapter 30

Aella

Five weeks had passed with daily training for my weapons and magic since I'd last seen my husband. He'd only asked me to open a portal that one time since the attack at Petosty, and I supposed he took the hint that night that I needed space after our last meeting.

The break from him had finally ended with a sebeska finding me while I worked on my light magic at the pit this morning, thankfully without an audience. I was terrified of seeing Darrow tonight because it had been over two months since I'd last had sex, and my physical urges grew with each passing day. Thoughts crept into my mind of his promise to fulfill my needs if only I asked, as well as memories of him touching me. My dreams were especially vivid, leaving me frustrated and panting when I woke.

I had to remind myself that it was nothing more than a game for Darrow. He only saw me as a means to an end. How bad would it be to fall for my enemy whose heart was as cold as ice and would never thaw for me? It would be the ultimate vengeance against me and my family, with no way to escape due to our marriage vows.

I braced myself as I stepped from the portal onto Veronnian land near Durelle's cabin. The forest was dark and silent, except for Darrow standing ten feet away. He'd pulled back half of his brown and black streaked hair, and his face was mesmerizing in the moonlight. Additionally, he wore form-fitting, black leather pants and a matching tunic that left a tantalizing glimpse of his muscular chest. No matter how much I tried, I couldn't deny my attraction to him. Even my anger had abated with time.

Two months ago, my fury was like rock-hard ice. I could clench the jagged ball in my hands to remind myself of what he'd made me do to my own people, but it had melted over the weeks and slipped through my fingers no matter how hard I tried to hold onto it. The fact of the matter was, he'd kept his promise, and loss of life had been minimal—far less than the deaths from my uncle's malicious attack.

The woods appeared empty aside from Darrow, making me stiffen. "Where is everyone else?"

"It is only the two of us tonight." He took my hand, his warm and rough, and led me away from the ring.

"What?" I tried to pull away from him, but he wouldn't let go. He continued to guide me through the darkness to a place just past the trees. "I thought you summoned me here to portal you somewhere."

We stopped a short distance beyond sight of the ring, where his horse fed on some foliage, and a blanket lay across the ground. Moonlight filtered through an open spot in the canopy to shine upon the silver cloth. "You will be transporting us to a meeting once you've regained enough energy to open a portal to Jolloure."

"Why is there a blanket there?" I asked warily.

He gave me one of those taunting smiles that made my thighs clench. "I thought we'd have some quality time as husband and wife while we waited. I even took the time to scare all the dangerous creatures far away so we wouldn't be disturbed."

"No." I shook my head, backing up a step. "We are not doing that."

He moved fast, pulling my body into his strong arms and surrounding me with his scorching heat. The scent of sandalwood and leather filled my nose. "Why not?"

"Because I'm being torn by two sides, between you and my uncle, and you're never going to truly care about me or what I want."

Darrow nuzzled my neck, sending a shiver down my spine. "I do care about your well-being, Aella. If you ever need me, don't hesitate to ask. You'd be surprised what I'd do for you."

Only for his own benefit. He was well-known for his ability to seduce women.

"I don't want to fall for you, Dare," I said, finding it hard to think with his lips and breath teasing my skin. What was wrong with me that I didn't want him to stop?

He pressed kisses below my ear, along my jaw, and then my mouth before pulling back a tiny fraction. "We'll be married the rest of our lives, Aella. At some point, everyone will know, and then we'll have to share a home together. Do you really think you can go on forever resisting me and feeling nothing?"

"I know you can't love me back," I said as one of his hands roamed toward my backside. Annoyingly, I had no desire to stop him.

He met my gaze, only inches separating our faces. "Who told you?"

"Does it matter?" I asked.

A flash of annoyance crossed his features before he smoothed them again. "Very well, it's true that I'm cursed and cannot love. I can still care, as well as feel lust and possessiveness for you. Isn't that enough?"

"Not when it means you can use my feelings to manipulate me while I can't do the same to you," I argued.

He gently took my hand. When I didn't resist, he pressed it against the front of his pants, shocking me with the hardness there. "You're manipulating me even when you're not around to see it. All I need to do is think about you, and my cock gets hard."

More like stunningly rock solid and far too tempting.

"You can get anyone you want, so use some other woman," I said, pulling my hand away.

Darrow shook his head. "I've grown bored with the others, which is certainly your fault, yet I gave you a break from me so you could come to terms with our arrangement. No other woman has touched me during that time."

I couldn't help being a little satisfied that he was also suffering on some level. "I'm not having sex with you in these creepy woods at night. Forget it."

"What if I promise only kissing and touching?" he asked, fiery need in his eyes.

Trying to deny the lust he clearly felt, or my own, for that matter, was impossible. I needed to remember why I should hate him, not want him badly. "You stand for everything I hate, *Dare*. All Veronna wants is to force Therress back under their rule again, and that includes me."

"Oh, I definitely want you under me in every way possible, but as for the rest, it is all lies," he said fiercely.

"Do you deny that five centuries ago, Veronna taxed the people within my land twice as much as those west of the Sobaryan Mountains?" I asked, pointing out one of the strongest arguments we had for rebelling.

He flashed his teeth. "If your tutors had bothered to tell you the whole story, you'd know your people agreed to that deal in exchange for not having to provide soldiers to fight against Karganoth. Our side of the range took the brunt of the losses while yours enjoyed peace and safety."

I opened my mouth to say something, but I couldn't refute it without looking into the matter more fully. It made too much sense to argue until I knew for sure. Pushing that point aside, I grabbed at another one. "What about taking ninety percent of the holmium from the mines and only leaving us with ten percent?"

He arched a brow. "We were fighting a war with the dark elves, and you of all people understand how critical holmium is to moving armies quickly. Therress didn't need it as badly as us, but the irony is that when your side decided to rebel, you began sending a quarter of what you mined to Karganoth and have ever since."

My jaw dropped, and I finally managed to pull away from him. "Now, I know you're lying."

"Am I?" He stepped into my personal space again. "There are no holmium deposits in Karganoth, but if you were to visit, you'd find they have no trouble using their portal rings. The ice giants would never deal with them, so where are they getting their supply?"

I glared at him. "The king would never allow my uncle to do that."

"True, if he could catch him in the act, but Lord Morgunn is quite adept at sneaking those shipments out without being caught. Even the few times we have intercepted a boat, it mysteriously caught fire and erased the evidence before we could see what was on it," he said, shaking his head. "Your family has been doing that for centuries, aiding the dark elves in their cause to get a foothold in Zadrya. Veronna and Juvarn to our north are the only ones fighting to stop them."

I looked away. The things he'd said made more sense than I liked to admit and unraveled a history I'd always been taught to believe. I had no way to disprove him at the moment, and I didn't dare ask my uncle. Even posing questions along those lines would send him into a fit of rage.

"How can I verify what you're saying?" I asked.

He searched my gaze. "You could choose to believe your husband, or if my word still isn't good enough, you could check the histories at the royal library in Porrine."

"I'll do that." When I found the time and opportunity.

Darrow caressed my cheek. "I wouldn't lie to you about this."

"Not even so that I'll give my body to you?" I asked, raising a quizzical brow.

His lips quirked. "You barely spoke to me for two months after I made you assist with my attack on Therress. I wouldn't dare lie about this and risk your wrath once more. We will be married for the rest of our lives. I'd rather not test how long you can hold a grudge if I tell you falsehoods about our lands' history, especially since you will be able to find the truth now that you know to look for it."

"Okay," I said, feeling my resolve against him cracking.

"I want you, Aella, in any way I can have you tonight," he said in a husky voice that sent deep awareness through my body.

I realized at that moment that he was seriously desperate to have me, and that gave me some power over him. Maybe I should turn the tables on my husband for once. It didn't have to be emotional, and I didn't have to let him always take charge. Gathering my courage, I kissed him, making it as deep and passionate as possible until he was groaning and holding me so close I could feel his cock straining against his pants. Then, I pulled back to meet his gaze.

"Here's my offer. Take off all your clothes and lie on that blanket. I get to touch you wherever I want, but you can't touch me," I said, running a finger down his chest. "If you behave yourself, I promise you'll enjoy it and be totally satisfied when I'm done."

Behind his gray eyes, I could see his mind working furiously. "What about after that? Can I touch you then?"

"No." I shook my head. "This only works one way tonight—take the deal or leave it."

He worked his jaw. "Don't think I won't find a way to return the favor at the next opportunity."

I tossed my hair over my shoulder and smiled. "We'll see. Now, get undressed, *Dare.*"

His gaze heated even more at hearing his name on my lips. He took his time, keeping his seductive eyes on me as he removed his black leather tunic, boots, and pants. I didn't hold back from studying his hard, masculine form. Through the moonlight, I caught sight of several scars on his chest that I'd noticed on our wedding night, and continued to wonder how he got them. Had he suffered abuse from his family, too?

While I wanted to ask about it, we were nowhere near a point where we could dive into our pasts. Even if my husband were willing to tell me about his old wounds, it would open me to having to explain my scars that he'd see if I removed my tunic now. There was no way I was going to tell him about those.

Finally, he stood before me naked and proud, without a hint of modesty. I circled him, taking in every inch of his body and memorizing it. Dear nameless ones, he was incredible. The rest of my life wouldn't be long enough to touch and explore him. How could a half-dark elf as dangerous and manipulative as him be so alluring? Why did I want him so much?

I stopped behind Darrow and pressed a kiss between his shoulder blades. "It took three months of marriage before I could do this."

"You could have done it sooner," he murmured in a deep, seductive voice.

I continued raining kisses along his spine while squeezing his tight, muscular ass. It was so satisfying to hear him groan from my touch. Maybe he'd begun to think I was shy, but I'd been having sex for over fifteen years. The only reason I'd held back was because of the history between our people and to protect my heart. It felt good to be in control for once, doing what I wanted. This was different since I was seducing him while he had to endure it without reciprocating. It was much safer and more empowering.

"Maybe I should have tried this sooner," I said, moving around and taking his right hand. I lifted it and brought it to my mouth. While staring into his eyes, I sucked on his index finger.

He drew in a breath, gaze fixed on my lips. "Hmm, much sooner."

I let his hand go and wrapped my arms around his neck, fingers threading into his hair as I pulled him down for a kiss. He hesitated for only a moment before returning it with vigor. It was hot and electrifying. As soon as his hands began to touch me, I pulled back.

"Ah, ah, ah." I shook a finger at him. "No touching."

Heated amusement reflected in his gray eyes. "You make that very difficult."

"Lie down on the blanket," I ordered.

He slowly lowered himself so he reclined on his elbows, and I couldn't help admiring his cock. It was larger than expected, and I knew it would completely fill me if I ever allowed it. Wetness gathered between my thighs at the thought. I wished I could let him relieve the ache, but I refused to give him that part of me yet. I would wage a campaign against him for now, which would give me all the control. That was far safer.

Kneeling next to him, I ran my hands along the hard contours of his chest as he watched me intently. I admired his muscles and how they moved under my caress. He was behaving well and letting me explore.

"Are you enjoying yourself?" he asked, clenching his fists as my fingertips came temptingly close to his cock that rested against his flexed stomach. He had a dark trail of hair leading downward.

I smiled at him. "Yes."

For several minutes, I teased him by skimming my hands close and then edging away from that part of him. The strain on his face intensified the longer I taunted him. Finally, I took him into my hand and stroked him once. He groaned, and his head fell back.

It was hard to believe this was the same man who could kill half a dozen soldiers with little more than a thought, and he'd surrendered his body to me. How did I have him lying naked on his back, willingly letting me do whatever I wanted to him? I never would have believed this could be possible a few months ago.

To reward him, I leaned down and took his cock into my mouth, running my tongue over the tip before sucking hard. My hair fell onto his stomach, blocking my view of his face. By the moaning sounds he made, I had complete confidence he enjoyed my careful attention.

Lifting my head, I pulled his legs apart and moved to kneel between them. Now, I could watch him clearly while letting my blond locks curtain either side of me and fall to tease his hips. The gaze in his eyes turned wild now as I gripped his cock in my hand.

"Does it bother you having a Therressian giving you pleasure?" I asked, squeezing him.

His lips stretched into a smile. "Not when it's my beautiful wife."

"Hmm, good answer," I said and took him in my mouth once more.

He began stroking my hair, and I allowed it.

"I vow that by the time I'm done with you..." He gasped when I took more than half of him and sucked hard. "...there won't be any Therressian left in you."

I pulled back to give him an amused look. "That's mighty arrogant of you."

"It's not arrogance. The more you touch me, the more determined I am to make you mine in every possible way, so your loyalties lie with no one except me," he said with a vehemence that shocked me.

"You assume I'm that easy to conquer."

He traced my bottom lip with his thumb. "No, not at all. I look forward to the challenge. It wouldn't be fun if you made it easy, would it?"

If I ran right now, would he chase me? A playful side I'd thought was expunged long ago considered the idea before discarding it. He'd surely catch me, and I doubted I'd be able to resist what he did next.

"No touching," I reminded him, giving him a warning look.

Darrow dropped his hand. "This time, you have me at your mercy, but do not doubt I will have you begging and screaming when it's my turn."

"I'd have to agree to it first," I said. Inwardly, I prayed to the nameless ones that I had the strength to deny him that privilege for as long as possible.

Relentless promise filled his gaze. "Oh, you will."

To shut him up, I took him into my mouth again until his cock hit the back of my throat. He bucked as I bobbed my head up and down, sucking and pulling his length while his hands fisted in my hair. There was something truly satisfying about having him mindless with pleasure. His balls tightened, and I sucked hard as he came into my mouth. Darrow's shout of pleasure echoed through the woods as I swallowed every drop of him.

I pulled away once he finished and licked my lips. "Feel better now?"

He worked his jaw as he studied me.

"Not until I have you naked and at my mercy," he said.

I shook my head. "That's not going to happen."

Darrow grazed his fingers across my cheek. "You've only solidified my resolve. I vow to all the nameless ones that I will have you—mind, body, and soul, Aella. You won this battle with that delicious mouth of yours, but I'll win the war."

The tone of his voice told me that he meant every word. I may have made a grave mistake tonight, but I'd never guessed a man known for going through women like shots of alcohol would become fixated on me.

"Get dressed." I caressed his chest one last time. "I'm ready to take us to Jolloure."

Chapter 31

Darrow

I kept my attention locked on Aella as I slowly pulled on my clothes. Her green eyes held defiance, but desire swam underneath as she shamelessly stared at my body. She knew as well as I did that she could only resist me for so long. Hunger and longing always simmered in her gaze whenever I had her close, but especially now that she'd gone over two months without another man's touch. I enjoyed the thought of her need for me growing by the day, slowly torturing her.

Tonight, she'd attempted to wrest control. I wholly approved of her methods, but she'd also proven that her resolve was weakening. She had blazing passion burning within her that couldn't be denied for long, and I would continue to wear away at the protective walls she'd built around herself. She would surrender to me before much longer.

The nameless ones knew I'd given up on being with anyone else. Try as I might, I'd found little pleasure with any other woman since marrying her. It was always Aella's face that I saw in my mind's eye, and it was her that I had to envision when I found release. Of course, my curse kept me from having deep feelings for her. It was likely just as well since the physical need I had for her was more than enough, not to mention the jealousy and protective urges she invoked.

I sat to lace my boots. "You look strained, Aella. Is there something I can do to help with that?"

"No," she said, turning her attention toward the woods.

"My tongue is quite skilled, I assure you. It would only take a few minutes."

She tensed, and I wondered if she grew wet at the thought of my mouth between her legs. "Please stop, Dare."

Even when she was angry or frustrated, I enjoyed hearing her say my name.

I finished with my boots and stood. As I moved toward Aella, she grew even stiffer, if possible. That didn't deter me. I took hold of her face and kissed her tight lips. She didn't respond at first but gave in quickly, as always.

Her body melted against mine, and she clutched at my tunic. If I kept going like this long enough, I knew she'd lose all resistance. My wife might not know I was her true mate, but her soul recognized our connection. That worked to my advantage.

Unfortunately, our time to play had come to an end. We'd be late if we didn't leave soon. I would have to save my seduction plans for next time, but Aella would explode under my touch once I had her alone again.

"Let's go," I said, taking her hand and guiding her to the ring.

She said nothing more until she began channeling. A stream of golden light hit each of the runes before the wind joined it to suffuse the entire circle. Then, she murmured in a low voice as she built the power necessary to bridge the two locations. As always, when we went to Jolloure, the portal took longer to open than anywhere else, but I swore she cut a second or two each time. Aella's powers were incredible. I hoped they would continue to develop enough for what I had planned for the future, because that would require far more strength than reaching the island.

The air popped, and a blue light shone from the ring. I took her free hand, guiding her through it with me. After a dizzying ride, we stepped from the other side to the shadowy island where few could survive for long.

It had an unwelcome presence, but the dark half of me enjoyed the feral magic soaking the atmosphere here. If I allowed it, the feeling could take over my mind and body, but I'd avoided doing that again for a long time and had no intention of allowing Aella to see it. She'd run screaming from me for certain.

"Come," I said as the portal closed behind us.

She frowned. "Aren't you leaving me here?"

"Alone? No." I tugged her along. "Believe it or not, I didn't meet you tonight only to seduce you, but also because someone requested your presence."

"Who?" she asked warily.

If I told her, I'd likely never get her to cooperate. Best not to ruin the surprise. "You'll see."

She dug her heels into the ground. "Darrow, if you're taking me to see someone dangerous…"

"I would never do that." I stopped and turned to face her. "Get this through your beautiful head. I will never put you in unnecessary danger if I can help it. Despite everything, I want to protect you, not only because you're my wife or our vows. I want you to be safe. Whatever happens, I wouldn't have brought you if I thought any harm might befall you."

Uncertainty swam in her green eyes. "I must be a fool because I want to believe you."

I had the sense that she didn't speak only of this matter but also of the other discussions we'd had tonight.

"You're not a fool, Aella." I sighed and traced my thumb across her cheek as if my touch could somehow convey my intentions. "Trust in the fact that I need you alive more than anyone else in this world, and I've known that since the night you showed up in that tavern begging me to save your cousin's life."

"You threatened to kill me that night, and so did your sister," she said, green eyes flashing.

I couldn't help but chuckle as I dropped my hand from her. "That was part of the show. Neither of us had any intention of killing you, but we needed you to think we did for bargaining power."

Aella took a step back. "So, how do I know you're not lying now?"

The road to earning her trust wasn't going to be easy, especially since I needed her to earn mine before I could tell her everything. Only then could she understand my true intentions, but that wouldn't happen tonight. I could only do and say so much.

I sighed. "Very well, you may stay here. I'll tell her you refused to come."

With that, I turned away and began heading down a narrow westerly path. I had to make some decisions for Aella out of necessity, but I tried to give her as many choices as possible, recognizing that she needed them. Her uncle allowed her too few. I most definitely had no desire to be anything like him. If she were to come with me now, it had to be her choice.

"Dammit, wait."

A smile formed on my face when I heard the sounds of Aella's soft steps behind me. I didn't bother to turn or acknowledge her at first, letting her catch up at her own pace. When her hand joined mine, relief filled me. Perhaps I was making progress after all.

While the island wasn't massive, it was big enough to take time to cross, with thick vegetation that made traversing it slow. We had to travel nearly the length of Jolloure to reach our destination, which took over half an hour. Now that we'd reached the height of summer, the humidity was high, and the oppressive moisture clogged the air. When we broke through the trees to the western beach, we both had a light sheen of sweat glistening on our skin. Aella's blonde hair lay wavy and limp against her shoulders and back.

We spotted a lone woman in the distance, staring at the tide and wearing a black halter dress that reached her feet but left her back bare. It was covered only by her long, dark locks that lifted with the breeze from the Bassaci Sea. She looked young from this distance, but in truth, she was nearing middle age for a fae at seventy-five years old.

"Who is that?" Aella asked in a whisper.

I pulled her along as she grasped my hand tightly. She was nervous and clutching at me for strength—further progress. "That is my mother."

She shot me a look. "But I thought you never see her anymore since…you know."

"Don't be ridiculous." I slowed my pace so I wouldn't have to drag her along as her steps slowed. "She betrayed my father, not me or my sister."

"You know what I mean," she said.

"For a while after the treachery, I didn't see her, but eventually, we began exchanging messages through sebeskas and meeting here twice a year. It's a pain and time-consuming to reach this island by boat, so it was only when I gained your assistance that I could visit her more often," I explained.

Aella's eyes rounded. "So that's who you visit every time you come?"

"Usually," I hedged. She wasn't ready to know much more yet, but I could give her some of the truth. Not that my mother gave me much choice.

We finally came close enough that I could make out the fine lines of Zareen's brows as she watched our approach. She was still considered a beauty, but time and life's difficulties had worn her down. It was there in her dark gray eyes that matched mine. Despite that, she held herself with a straight posture and moved with grace as she closed the distance.

"Darrow, it's good to see you, son." She leaned forward and kissed my cheeks before pulling back to study the woman beside me. "And you've finally brought your wife for me to see. I am Zareen, by the way," she said, extending her pale hand with bejeweled fingers.

To her credit, Aella kept her expression neutral and clasped my mother's hand. They squeezed and let go. It was a very formal greeting among high-fae women.

"I'm afraid your son failed to tell me who we were meeting until a few minutes ago, so I'm at a disadvantage, but I am pleased to meet you," she replied, giving her a tight smile. I could detect the annoyance by her stiff shoulders, but she didn't direct her feelings at my mother. She was irritated with me.

Zareen sighed. "Darrow has always been good at keeping secrets and surprising us. I apologize that he didn't prepare you better, but I'm pleased to meet you all the same. He has told me how powerful you are with your channeling abilities. I was quite surprised you could bring him here with so little trouble. Even our people struggle to open the ring on Jolloure without the extra wards you must bypass."

In fact, the dark elves only had one who could do it, and he was quite old. Only if the King of Karganoth needed his services for himself or someone on a critical mission did he bestir that channeler. My mother would not reveal such critical intelligence, though. She had an alternative means of travel that was simpler.

"It was more challenging than any others I've encountered in recent years," Aella admitted, glancing over at me. "But it gets easier each time."

My mother lifted a brow. "So your powers are still growing?"

"I'm only thirty-three, so yes."

Zareen's eyes twinkled. "What a lovely age. Not so young that you lack experience, but not so old you must rush to have children."

"Oh, well, Darrow doesn't want..." I gripped her arm before she could finish that sentence.

"She means such matters will come later," I said, shooting her a warning glance because I didn't want my mother to know all the details of our relationship. She'd only meddle. "But for now, we have other priorities."

Aella's jaw stiffened. Of course, I'd said when we first made our bargain that there would be no sex or children, but at the time, I hadn't thought I could stomach sleeping with anyone from Therress—no matter how beautiful. It had been better to shut down those notions. Since then, I had been rethinking many things and how she fit into my long-term plans.

My mother frowned at us. "Well, if you want that option to remain, I suggest you keep your marriage and the scope of her abilities a secret as long as possible. It will be dangerous once word gets out."

"What do you mean?" I asked, though I had my suspicions and already worked to keep Aella's abilities from becoming common knowledge.

Zareen's face darkened. "Vaslav has been sighted a few times recently. I believe they've sent him here with a purpose that won't bode well for us or Zadrya."

"Did he come to you?" I asked, tensing.

She hesitated. "Yes, and he asked about you."

"Wait." Aella glanced between us. "Who is Vaslav?"

"He is a dangerous Unseelie prince from Faelaria." He was also my oldest half-brother, but she didn't need to know that yet. It got into complicated matters that I didn't have the time to explain. Not to mention, it would dredge up painful memories for my mother. Vas was her firstborn, but she'd conceived him under difficult circumstances.

My wife glanced between us. "So Bogdan wasn't joking when he said they sometimes come here?"

"He rarely jokes."

My mother snorted. "Sadly, but he has his reasons."

"Wait." Aella's brows drew together. "A few months ago, Tadeus told me he overheard my uncle mentioning someone named Vaslav. I only remember because the name isn't common here, but my cousin seemed to think Lord Morgunn met with him."

I stilled and glanced at Zareen, whose face paled. "This confirms what we thought. Therress is working with the Unseelie as well as the dark elves."

"But..." Aella shook her head. "Why would he do that? It's a betrayal to everyone in Paxia if he's helping them, too."

My mother put a hand on my wife's shoulder. "We don't even know what the Unseelie want with our world since they're doing an excellent job of hiding their plans. It's best not to jump to conclusions until we can ascertain why Lord Morgunn met with one of them."

"Do not try to find out more," I said, giving her a warning look. "It is a dangerous game you're ill-equipped to play."

She crossed her arms. "Only because everyone keeps me in the dark about it all."

"Be grateful for that." Zareen dropped her hand. "It is likely what has helped keep you out of harm's way for this long."

"Just because I can't feel the spider crawling up my back doesn't mean it can't bite me," she replied stonily.

Aella had a point, but I couldn't let her statement stand. "Avoiding a spider web is often a wiser course of action than walking through it if you have a choice."

"Only if you know where the web is located to evade it."

I sighed, begrudgingly approving of Aella's cleverness. "I appreciate you offering the information about your uncle when you certainly could have kept it to yourself. If you should learn something else pertinent without drawing attention or putting yourself in danger, I would appreciate you sharing it."

"Now, you're making more sense," she said, finally satisfied.

My mother gave us a rueful look. "The two of you have a long road ahead of you, I see."

She wasn't wrong, though she had no idea by how much. Aside from my intense need, I'd also seduced Aella tonight so that our scents would be mingled. Otherwise, my mother would have known we weren't as intimate as a husband and wife should be after several months of marriage—even if we did live apart at the moment.

"Why haven't I heard about the Unseelie being here before if they're coming and going so much?" Aella asked.

Her question was valid. We didn't have them visiting Paxia for nearly two millennia after they forced us from our home world, but within the last century, they found a way. They'd been surreptitiously meddling in our affairs ever since.

"We don't discuss it openly because it would only arouse fear if the general population found out," I replied.

"Why is Vaslav specifically concerning?" Aella asked.

My mother glanced at me, and I nodded, letting her take the lead. "We can't be certain of his motivations, but his presence here means he's likely on a mission for the newly crowned Unseelie king—his father. Darrow and Vaslav have had a few confrontations over the years that became quite violent. I would not put it past him to use you to get to him."

While my elder brother and I had different powers, we were equally strong and destructive. We'd battled twice and nearly killed each other in the process. I'd sincerely hoped two years ago was the last I'd see of him, but I should have known better.

Unlike other Unseelie, he had enough of our mother's blood to prevent him from standing out too much while in this world if he used some light glamour. In hindsight, it was likely the reason they'd wanted my mother to give birth to him. The magic and climate of this world weren't compatible with most Unseelie, which was why our people chose it as a new home nearly two thousand years ago. Even for us, it took time to adapt.

Now, there was a grave problem on Faelaria, according to the nameless god, and they needed us for something if they wished to resolve it. Despite deploying considerable resources, I hadn't determined what they sought.

The only thing I knew for certain was they would covet Aella's abilities if they found out about them—nearly anyone in power would. It was likely why her uncle was trying to hide her away, marrying her within his borders. He could keep using her while giving her to someone likely to restrict her movements and keep her out of broader social circles. It was a guess, anyway. I still couldn't be sure based on my current information.

I worked my jaw. "Vaslav is one more reason to keep our marriage a secret for now and avoid him learning about Aella's abilities. She may be strong enough to infiltrate their world, which the Unseelie would not appreciate. No one in Paxia has been born near her power level in many centuries, perhaps millennia."

"We can't know I'm that strong." Aella shook her head. "Accessing the portals here is one thing, but I can't imagine channeling to different worlds."

"Breaching the ring here was a test put in place long ago," my mother said, eyeing my wife shrewdly. "Only the most powerful with your ability can do it. All strong channelers can travel to nearby realms, but a rare few can even go to distant planets across the galaxy. The question is, how far can your gift take you?"

Aella's mouth opened and closed wordlessly. She truly had no idea what she'd stepped into by marrying me. I'd already ascertained her uncle kept her ignorant of the darker side of our politics and affairs. Her world would get much uglier soon, but I'd ease her into it as much as I could. It was why she hadn't met my mother sooner. I had put it off as long as possible, but we were running out of time for so many things.

I brushed a loose lock of blonde hair from her face and gently touched her arm. "We will have to figure it out eventually. For now, try to avoid any male elves with silver hair. He could be wearing glamour since his is such an unusual shade among our kind, so be wary of that as well. Look deeper with anyone who approaches you that you don't know."

"What have you gotten me into?" Aella asked, though I noted she didn't pull away from my touch. Good. I wanted her to get *very* used to it.

My mother laughed—a thread of irony laced into her tone. "You poor girl. What a luxury to make it thirty-three years without seeing the true level of darkness and corruption in this world, especially with your talent and power. I cannot abide your uncle, but I must credit him for that much."

Zareen had a point. One of her gifts was the ability to see into a person's heart, discerning their level of innocence or corruption. She'd wanted Aella here to ensure my instincts about my wife were accurate, and I'd been right based on how my mother was behaving right now. She was being more open than expected.

For whatever reason, Lord Morgunn hadn't wanted his niece to know how corrupt matters truly were within the realm. He likely felt it kept her more amenable. Her innocence was so refreshing that I almost felt guilty about altering her worldview, but I needed to prepare her to some degree because she might be the only one capable of saving the whole of Paxia.

Aella stiffened and pulled away from me to face my mother. "You know nothing about me or what I've experienced."

"Pain and loss?" Zareen lifted a brow. "They are not the same as what you'll soon learn about our world and how much your life has been influenced by it."

Aella crossed her arms. "Why don't you tell me, then?"

"Soon." I pulled her to my side, not wanting to overwhelm her tonight. "You'll learn everything you need to know when the time is right, but we must return home before it gets any later."

My mother sighed. "Yes, but hopefully, we will have the opportunity to speak again before long." She pulled a folded paper from a hidden pocket in her gown, handing it to me. "Take care, son. I'll send word when it is time to meet again."

I didn't have to look at the parchment to know it would give me vital intelligence to further my quest. It would also affect Aella, but I still didn't want to involve her until absolutely necessary. She might not be corrupt like her uncle, but I didn't feel I could trust her with sensitive information yet. It would only take one slip of the tongue to ruin everything.

"You take care as well, Mother," I said, giving her a nod.

Taking hold of Aella's hand, I guided us back the way we came. She was quiet for most of the walk through the woods. Whenever I sensed something threatening nearby, I pushed at it with my powers to scare it away before she saw it. We didn't have time to deal with the dangerous creatures of this island when it would be nearly dawn before she returned home.

Aella opened the portal to Veronna in seconds, though it helped that I'd permanently removed the wards against her on the ring near my great-aunt's home to ease the power draw. Still, we'd only been on Jolloure for an hour and a half.

She should have struggled harder, but instead, she continued to become faster. That was a good sign for my long-term plans.

After we stepped out of the ring on the other side, I guided Aella to the nearby copse of trees. "You've learned a few secrets tonight that I need you to keep."

"Who would I tell without incriminating myself?" she asked, irritation in her gaze.

I backed her into a large tree, placing my hands on her hips. "True, but you could ruin everything if you told the wrong person."

She stiffened, and anger flashed in her eyes. "I won't tell anyone, but do we need to be this close?"

"Does it bother you after what we've already done?" I leaned closer to her. "It is only a kiss."

Her breath caught. "What if I don't want it?"

I brushed my lips along her jaw and then down her neck as she trembled. "Lie to yourself, but don't lie to me. I'm not asking for your body right now, only your mouth, which you've freely given in more ways than one tonight."

In fact, I would lie in bed tonight reliving the memory of her mouth on my cock. She'd been utterly entrancing. While I'd been with many women, none had brought me such a devastatingly complete release. I wondered what it would feel like to be inside her.

"Darrow, I don't..."

I cut off her words with my lips. Her body relaxed in my hold, and she wrapped her arms around me. My only goal for now was to get her used to my touch. Each time we met, I'd work on her more, endearing her to me. It was the only way I could be certain of her cooperation and loyalty in the future.

Was it right to do such a thing to my wife when I couldn't love her in return? Likely not, but our world's fate relied on Aella's willing assistance and her discretion. I wouldn't feel guilty for manipulating her when the alternative would be so much worse for us all, and it wasn't as if I wouldn't ensure her safety and well-being along the way. She mattered to me more than her abilities alone.

As I caressed her body, testing her resolve little by little, I was encouraged when she moaned at my touch. She could deny her attraction, but tonight proved I'd own her entirely before long.

Chapter 32

Aella

It was nearly three in the morning when I returned to Tradain, stepping through the portal onto the dark formation field. Darrow's kisses had left my lips swollen, and his hands had made a mess of my hair. He seemed to have a newfound fascination with running his fingers through it. The ache between my legs throbbed, my body hating me for not giving in to him all the way.

What kind of game was my husband playing? Did he truly want more for our marriage, or was it something else? How was I supposed to resist him when the moment he touched me, I lost my senses and reasoning? The one thing I did know was I needed to find some control.

Darrow had so many secrets, and I was only beginning to realize how much. Meeting his mother tonight had been an enormous surprise. I'd desperately wanted to ask why she'd betrayed Darrow's father all those years ago, but they'd revealed so much startling news during the short meeting that I didn't have a chance. I needed time to make sense of everything they told me, so hopefully, I could prepare myself better the next time I saw Darrow.

"Where have you been, Aella?" My uncle's angry voice came from behind me.

I jumped and spun around, having been so lost in thought that I'd missed him and Ulmar standing behind the ring. They'd waited where they knew I wouldn't see them right away. My mind skittered with possible excuses.

"I went to see a lover," I replied, which was truthful enough not to come out as a lie.

He looked me up and down disdainfully. "Clearly, but I thought you had one here."

"We ended things a couple of months ago," I said, slowly maneuvering around the ring to face him and my cousin.

Every part of my body was strung taut. Something in the two men's demeanor told me they were especially furious tonight, and I'd missed something important if they'd been looking for me. I'd been with Darrow, so I felt reasonably certain Veronna couldn't have attacked.

Ulmar narrowed his gaze on me. "There are hundreds of available men here, yet you chose to find one that required a portal? At a time when you should be focusing on your betrothal?"

"Not to mention we needed her here tonight," my uncle growled. He took a menacing step toward me. "We woke the entire village searching for you tonight while our troops waited for your assistance to transport them. Do you know how embarrassing it was when we failed to produce or locate you?"

My heart skipped a beat. Everyone in Tradain would know I'd snuck away, and the army would expect Lord Morgunn to punish me accordingly. They'd been unable to go forward with their campaign. The only reason they couldn't was if he'd finally planned to retaliate against Veronna for destroying Petosty. Had Darrow's spies figured that out? Was that why he'd chosen tonight to summon me? A thousand thoughts raced through my mind, none of them good.

The tension in the air was palpable. "I'm sorry, uncle. I didn't know you needed me tonight."

"You shouldn't have left for any reason without consulting me first." He moved closer like a dark cloud about to release its stormy wrath. "I am beginning to question your loyalty, Aella. The king denied your first betrothal, which I find suspicious. Our last raid on Veronna was a disaster, with them arriving too quickly and capturing you, forcing terrible concessions from me. Then, their forces led a masterful attack that destroyed one of the border villages. We had no word of it until hours after it was over. Now, tonight, you were nowhere to be found when we were ready to retaliate."

I gulped. "If you'd told me, I swear I would have..."

Slap! Pain burst in my cheek, and blood filled my mouth.

"The only thing I want to hear is your lover's name and where you went," he said, grabbing my arms forcefully. "That is the only way you can save yourself."

There was no way to lie with Ulmar standing there, so I went with blatant defiance. It was my only option despite the consequences it would bring. "Who I sleep with is my business."

He slapped me hard again. My ears rang, and stars danced in front of my eyes. So badly, I wanted to use my magic to protect myself, but I couldn't fight them both without exhausting what remained of my powers after channeling. Not to mention, they made me pay heavily the last time I fought. They would again if I resisted.

"Tell me," he said, gripping me hard.

I hung my head. "I promised I wouldn't."

Lord Morgunn dragged me to the front of the ring. "Here's a little test. If you can open a portal back to the castle, then you didn't go far. If you can't, I'll assume you were in Veronna—likely spilling our secrets to them. I assume you must have some spare holmium if you can sneak away without my assistance."

I gulped, glad I'd grown stronger in recent months. "Okay."

He swept an arm out toward the ring. "Do it."

Ulmar had followed us to the other side of the ring with his arms crossed. The gleam in his eyes told me he couldn't wait to exact revenge after our last duel. I'd suspected I'd pay for defeating him a month ago, but I'd hoped he wouldn't find an opportunity before I escaped this place.

Pulling a small bag from my pocket, I pinched some holmium in my fingers. Lord Morgunn swiped the rest from my grasp. At least it wasn't my whole supply since I'd broken up Darrow's generous allotment into multiple pouches and hidden them in different places.

I concentrated hard, pulling as much power as I could muster, and sent the energy to hit each of the runes in the sequence I'd known for much of my life. All the while, I chanted low to direct the magic. It didn't come as easily as usual. My abused cheeks throbbed, and my hands shook as I tried to concentrate, knowing what I'd face at Ivory Castle. Just when I thought I wouldn't manage it, the air popped, and a blue light shone within the ring.

Chest tightening, I gestured toward the portal. "Done."

My uncle ordered Ulmar to go first, and then he gripped my arm and pulled me along with him. I wished I knew of a ring in a remote location because I would have been sorely tempted to send them to it if I thought I could escape before entering. Unfortunately, there weren't any I knew about that would work, and I'd barely had the strength to channel a ring close to us.

When we reached the other side, Lord Morgunn marched me past the barracks and armory to the outer entrance of the dungeon. It was an unassuming black metal door on the southwest side of the castle. Dread filled me. The last time I came here was years ago, and I'd done my best to avoid returning until now.

Lord Morgunn shoved me inside, and I had to grab the side wall to avoid falling down the steep stairs. It was dark, with only one torch midway to lighten the gloomy atmosphere. Before he could push me again, I hurried to the bottom.

My uncle handed me off to Ulmar while he went into a side room. A few moments later, he returned with an iron armband he clasped on my bicep. What little power I had faded away. I trembled and wanted to cry, but I refused to give either of the men the satisfaction. They'd enjoy it too much. Instead, I did my best to hold myself together.

My cousin dragged me down the corridor, passing half a dozen closed doors on either side that were dungeon cells. As far as I knew, we had no prisoners at the moment. I'd spent time in them before and prayed I wouldn't go in one tonight.

We reached the end of the passageway, which opened to a wide space with metal shackles hanging from the ceiling. Ulmar shoved me toward them, forcing my wrists into the magically enhanced manacles that tightened to my size. Lord Morgunn stood at the corner with a chain in hand. As he pulled it, my arms yanked upward until I could barely touch the floor with my feet. He fastened the chain to a hook so it would hold.

My cousin tossed my hair over my shoulder, pulled out his dagger, and cut the back of my tunic straight down. I gritted my teeth to keep from screaming when his blade nicked the skin near my spine in the process. Once finished, he'd bared me from shoulders to waist.

"Father, may I be the one to whip her?" Ulmar asked, giving me a malicious smile. His opportunity for revenge had come, and he'd have no mercy.

My knees shook despite my desperate attempts to calm myself and hide my fear.

Footsteps sounded as Lord Morgunn came around to face me with cold cruelty lining his features. "Yes. Don't stop until Aella confesses where she's been, or I tell you it's enough."

My cousin chuckled as he moved back behind me. "Luckily for me, her stubbornness should hold out for a long time."

I clenched my eyes shut, wanting to plead with them, but it would make no difference. Neither of them had a heart. I'd interrupted their important plans to kill innocent people and wouldn't explain where I'd gone, so there would be no escape from this punishment.

The sound of the whip cracking the air came a split second before an explosion of pain struck across the middle of my back. Ulmar waited a moment, pausing to see if I'd scream. I didn't because I always held out as long as possible, but it wouldn't take him long to push me past my tolerance. He'd strike harder and harder until I gave him the desired response.

He whipped me a second time in the same location, and I yelped as my skin broke. I counted to five before the third came, crisscrossing the other two. Blood trailed down my back now as he lashed me two more times with brutal intensity.

Lord Morgunn held up a hand. "Ready to talk?"

If I told them the truth, they'd either kill me or keep me in the dungeon for years.

"No," I said in a pained whisper.

Ulmar came around so I could see him with his whip coiled in his hand. "Why are you protecting your lover? It can't be worth it."

I pressed my lips shut, refusing to respond.

"Very well." He moved back to his previous position. "Don't say we didn't give you a chance to end this sooner."

My cousin began to whip me in earnest. The lashes came so hard and fast that I was screaming before long. He only paused his strikes to use his powers to send blinding pain into my head. Back and forth, he switched until all I knew was pure agony. By the time my uncle called it off, I was sagging in the manacles with my blood pooling on the floor at my feet and badly blurred vision.

Ulmar grabbed hold of my waist while his father released me from the bindings. I whimpered from the pain of his arm pressing against the lash wounds. My cousin carried me roughly, eliciting more pained moans from me as he climbed a different set of steps to the inner castle. In a journey that seemed to take forever, he finally brought me to my room and dropped me on my bed.

I quickly rolled onto my side and caught Lord Morgunn standing at the doorway as a blurry figure. There was nothing except coldness in his voice, "I'll send Briauna in shortly to clean and bandage you, but for now, you're confined to this room until I decide otherwise. Ulmar will bring you one meal a day unless you decide you remember your lover's name and the location where you met."

With that, they left me bleeding with an iron cuff that would slow down my ability to heal. The outer lock to my door slid into place, ensuring I wouldn't escape that way. Tears filled my eyes. I wondered if it would bother Darrow to know what he cost me for tonight's visit and the pleasure I gave him. Probably not, since I was little more than a tool to him—the same as my uncle.

Chapter 33

Darrow

My head ached fiercely. I sat hunched over on the couch in my loft, maintaining a connection to the sebeska currently flying around Lord Morgunn's castle. For the last few days, I'd been searching for Aella with no sign of her. The day after I last saw her, my spies reported that she never returned to Tradain and that her uncle was furious when she wasn't there to transport his soldiers for a surprise attack on Veronna.

I hadn't known he planned one, but I couldn't say it didn't please me to discover I had thwarted him by absconding with his niece. My only fear was what he might have done to her as punishment. The fact that I couldn't find her with the sebeska and my spies couldn't locate her didn't bode well. Her uncle must have confined her somewhere, but my locator spell only revealed she was somewhere inside or near the castle.

Flying over her courtyard garden and using the bird's vision, I noticed the plants appeared parched. Their colors weren't as vibrant, and many sagged in the afternoon heat. It hadn't rained for the last two weeks. With summer at its height, they needed regular watering.

Since marrying Aella, I'd used my birds to monitor her from a distance regularly, and she had never neglected her plants before, even while at Tradain. The fact that she did now indicated that something had prevented her from reaching the garden. I wished I could see inside her bedroom window, but they'd spelled it shut and darkened the glass. Until this week, it had been clear. Was she inside, or was something else going on? I didn't like not knowing.

Aella had no idea I could mind-link with sebeskas, so she wouldn't worry about that for privacy. It was a rare gift that I kept secret from all except a few closest to me, as it gave me an advantage in spying. I'd never used the ability as much as I had recently. The protective urge I had over my wife drove me to find out what happened to her, and I hated that none of my usual avenues for information worked. She was mine to keep safe, yet I was failing her.

Resigned that she was nowhere easily accessible, I let my control of the bird go and returned to myself. I rubbed my head. The migraine would pass in an hour or two, but I was too worried to rest. I needed to find a way to draw out Aella so I could be certain Lord Morgunn hadn't hurt her. There had to be a way without storming the castle.

An idea struck me.

I stood abruptly, wincing as a stab of pain hit my temple. Once it eased, I hurried to wash and change. I'd begun the search shortly after breakfast and only took a break once to relieve myself, never bothering to change out of my nightclothes. Searching every nook and cranny of Ivory Castle grounds and listening to hushed conversations took hours, and I'd lost track of time.

After I'd groomed myself and put on a midnight blue tunic and black pants, I hurried from the loft and headed toward Siggaya's portal ring. A channeler would be there in twenty minutes to open it, and luckily, the destination at this time of day was the Court of Porrine. The king was the one person I knew who could force Lord Morgunn to bring out his niece. It was in his best interest to assist me on this matter.

***

My migraine had finally eased by the time I arrived at the palace. I spotted the king's eldest son passing through the formal reception area with a determined stride. He appeared to be heading outside.

Armin was nearly as tall as me, though slightly leaner. His ears were the same as all light elves, pointed and matching his beige skin. He kept his dark blonde hair slicked back and trimmed at the nape. Most would consider him handsome, but he rarely smiled or laughed anymore.

Since he was only two years older, the king often asked my sister and me to visit when we were growing up, as well as other highborn children our age, so that we might form long-lasting bonds. There was a time when Armin and I were quite close, but he'd become withdrawn after his wife died in childbirth four years ago, the baby passing with her.

It was a common problem since the Naforya Fountain was lost and had worsened over time. Armin had taken it particularly hard since he'd loved her dearly. Now, his only focus was on serving his father and the realm. I hated watching him live a half-life, but he'd resisted all my efforts to socialize and bring him out of his melancholy.

"Prince," I said, giving him a short bow. "How are you?"

Armin stopped, surprise on his features. "I'm well, thank you. What are you doing here?"

"I came to speak to your father about a personal matter," I replied.

He frowned. "Come with me."

The prince led me out of the reception area and through an ornately decorated corridor to a small sitting room. After we entered, he closed the door firmly behind him and whispered a privacy spell. I was surprised he went to such lengths without knowing why I visited. He was known to have some foresight, though. Could he have guessed?

"Tell me your troubles," Armin commanded.

I clasped my hands behind my back. "It's a complicated matter."

"If it's about your wife, I'd imagine so."

I jolted at his words. "You know?"

He nodded. "My father informed me the day after he married the two of you since I need to be aware of such matters. He worries about the future of the realm."

"Yes, that is true," I agreed.

Though it still surprised me, I understood why the king chose to tell him. Armin was excellent at keeping secrets and would never betray our trust. It only worried me as more and more people learned about my marriage that it could eventually leak out before we were ready.

The prince looked at me with azure eyes that matched his father's. "I believe you chose wisely with Lord Morgunn's niece. She is powerful with a good heart, but I sense something may have happened to her."

"Aella hasn't been seen in five days, and all my attempts to locate her at Ivory Castle have failed. None of my spies have been able to provide any information, either," I said and went on to explain what happened the night she disappeared.

Armin frowned. "So you wish us to help by summoning her?"

"Yes, I do."

"As you know, the summer ball is in two days. We sent invitations to all the lords and ladies over a month ago. Her uncle confirmed his attendance but not hers. I can have my father insist she be here. Morgunn can hardly refuse, and if you're there, you can see her for yourself."

Relief filled me. I'd forgotten about the ball with so many other matters on my mind, but it was the perfect way to see Aella without drawing suspicion—as long as I was careful. "How soon do you think your father can get word to Lord Morgunn?"

"I'll make certain he sends a sebeska by this evening."

"You have my gratitude," I said, glad I'd run into him. It didn't hurt to have the prince on my side as I navigated my complicated marriage, and I needed to rebuild our relationship in any case.

Armin nodded. "Then I suppose you should prepare yourself for the ball."

"Will you be there?" I asked. While serious about his duties, he often skipped social events. He and his wife had six years of being at the center of them, constantly proving to be the happiest couple in the realm as they danced the night away. Those times were past now.

The corner of Armin's lips twitched. "I hadn't planned on it, but in light of this turn of events, I believe I will attend. It would be well worth it to watch you and your wife in the same room, playing a rather dangerous game."

At least it was some consolation that my struggles helped him. "I will look forward to seeing you."

Chapter 34

Aella

Briauna entered my room, bustling quietly. It was dark due to the spell on my window because my uncle felt I shouldn't even enjoy natural light or look at my garden. Not that it mattered since I didn't have the strength to leave my bed except to use the chamber pot. Even with that, I needed help.

The iron cuff on my arm slowed my healing down so much that it was pure agony to move with my back shredded and the wounds only beginning to close. If I jostled them too much, they reopened and bled again. Briauna had changed my sheets numerous times over the last week.

Lord Morgunn came once daily at the same time as the healer to ensure she didn't knit them back together with her magic. All she'd been allowed to do was clean and rebandage them. Ulmar came at other times to fill my head with intense pain, taunting me all the while that I must never embarrass him again like I did that day in the training ring. He didn't stop until blood ran down my nose. My life revolved around pain, misery, and wondering if my husband had willfully brought this torture upon me.

"Where is Lord Morgunn?" I mumbled from where I lay on my stomach, finally noticing my uncle wasn't in the room.

The healer took a seat beside me, sympathy on her face. "You've received a reprieve. The king insisted you attend the ball tonight, so we only have six hours to prepare you. When your uncle received word, he ordered a dress but wouldn't let me prepare you until now."

I lifted my head. "Why would the king demand I be there?"

"I suspect your husband has something to do with it," she said, pushing a golden lock of hair from my cheek.

A sigh escaped me. "Then Darrow must need something, or else why bother? It's not as if I matter to him. He probably kept me away that night so my uncle couldn't attack, knowing it would get me in trouble."

Had he laid there in the woods that night, letting me pleasure him while fully aware of the trouble I'd be in when I returned home? That question had plagued me for days as I lay in pain and misery in my bed.

"Don't say that, dear," Briauna tsked. "I refuse to believe he'd wish harm upon you."

Of course, she'd defend him, being her sister's favorite and all.

"How much can you heal me?" I asked, knowing the damage was too severe to manage completely in one session. My entire back was ravaged. Every day, my uncle would tell me how I could end my suffering if only I told him where I went that night. Of course, I never answered him.

Briauna grimaced. "I can heal them most of the way, but they'll still feel raw and tender. They've lingered long enough that I won't be able to prevent scarring, though they'll blend with the older ones before long anyway. We'll have to give you a tonic to ease the pain and use glamour to cover them."

The first time I'd been left with permanent lash marks, I'd been horrified. Since then, I'd stopped caring as much because there was no way to fix the mutilated skin on my back. Adding a few scars hardly made a difference at this point.

"Everyone there will be powerful and able to sense the level of magic we'll need to hide the damage," I said, thinking ahead. "We'll have to add an outer spell, so no one suspects anything." I didn't want anyone to know what happened this past week if I could help it, but I could only alter my looks in subtle ways. We needed someone who specialized in flashy glamour.

"I've already thought of that and have someone coming once you're ready."

I relaxed as she began the healing treatment, working from the top down. It hurt having my skin knitted back together, but knowing the worst of the pain would be gone soon helped me lay still. I'd barely been able to eat the one meal Ulmar brought daily. Though that likely had to do with him torturing me first before handing over the food.

Finally, Briauna finished. Her face was ashen from the power required, but I knew she'd done her best work. Nearly all the pain was gone, with only a lingering tenderness. I sat up for the first time in a week without nearly passing out in agony.

"Thank you," I said.

She stood, hands trembling a little. "I'll have the bath drawn for you now."

***

I'd only attended the annual summer ball at the Court of Porrine a few times. Most years, my uncle didn't bring me because he worried I'd find a suitor who wasn't one of his approved allies, and this event was optional for the high fae. He preferred to keep me close within his sphere of influence and avoid me developing friendships outside Therress that might tempt me to visit other places. Little did he know how well-traveled I was anyway.

As we entered the ballroom, I looked up in awe. The dome ceiling swirled with a miasma of colors that constantly moved within the glass—an effect of some magic spell they'd crafted. A glance around the rest of the room revealed more than two hundred fae had shown up for the event, including elves, faeries, pixies, gnomes, and so much more. The walls were painted pale green at this time of year, with vines and yellow flowers growing along them. I appreciated the amount of nature the king and queen incorporated into the theme.

Our current monarchy was among the best we'd had since the formation of Zadrya. About a hundred and fifteen years ago, it had been far different. The king back then was a tyrant who held the entire realm at his mercy. All it took was looking at him the wrong way, and he would kill the offender. He'd come from a line of air wielders who could suck the oxygen from a room or a single pair of lungs. No one was safe from his wrath.

Those who lived during that time said it was terrible. Only after an uprising did the old king lose his position and life, along with most of his family. The few who survived fled. They only managed it because they were distant, weaker members who'd been at the bottom of the assassination list. No one bothered to track them down, as far as I knew.

Then, King Worden's father took the crown with the resistance followers he'd spent years gathering. He'd had to be firm in the beginning to get rid of those who'd either supported the previous monarch or others who wanted to take the position instead.

Once he'd cleared out the worst of them, he began restructuring the realm to be a fairer, more prosperous place. It wasn't perfect, such as him being unable to end the conflict between Therress and Veronna, but it was far better than what we'd had before.

He passed away of old age thirty-two years ago, not long after I was born. His son took his place and continued his father's work, further improving Zadrya. I doubted we'd ever had a fairer king. With any law he enacted, he insisted on abiding by it himself because he asserted that a good ruler led by example and held themselves to a higher standard. It was why he wouldn't stop my uncle until Lord Morgunn did something to instigate punishment.

Ahead, on the dais, the king and queen sat in their finery as they watched the dancers on the floor. Everyone wore vibrantly-colored garments that revealed as much as they hid. It was a tradition of the summer ball, as the heat could be quite intense.

I was in a royal blue strapless dress. The bodice ran straight across my chest, revealing a hint of cleavage. From just beneath my breasts, my skin was visible through intricately woven lace that hugged my stomach and lower back. It stretched to a few inches below my belly button. Then, sheer blue silk flowed downward to my ankles except for a slit on my left side that began at my hip. Every step revealed most of my leg, so I couldn't wear undergarments.

The only other items I wore were matching slippers with a one-inch heel and two diamond and sapphire-studded combs that swept up my blonde hair. A maid had curled my locks so they cascaded nearly to my waist. As a final touch, we'd glamoured every inch of my skin to sparkle. No one would suspect another spell covered the tender wounds on my back.

While Lord Morgunn despised spending more coins than necessary, he never skimped for royal balls. The fae adored fashion and style at these events, and my uncle wouldn't have brought me in anything less than a stunning ensemble. He had to show off to the other lords and ladies that he was prosperous. I didn't have a say in the garments I wore to such events. Despite that, I would have enjoyed wearing this particular dress and having countless eyes drawn to me, but not tonight. It all felt so superfluous after a week of pain and torture.

He clasped my arm now while Ulmar and Tadeus followed behind us. We worked our way toward the dais, stopping ten feet from the green carpet steps to bow and curtsy to the king and queen. I kept my head down until the king spoke.

"It is good of you to make it, Lord Morgunn." He nodded at me and my cousins. "Lady Aella, my son has requested your first dance if you would be so kind."

My gaze ran from the king to Prince Armin. He wore the standard style of all the other men for the summer ball, with fitted pants and an open vest that revealed hints of his muscular chest. The primary difference between his attire and others was the sheer amount of intricate gold embroidery along the front with a leafy design. While the garment colors varied among guests, I noted Armin was the only one in black.

As usual, his handsome features were serious, but I caught a glint of amusement in his azure eyes. One of his dark blonde locks had fallen across his brow, giving him an almost rakish look. When was the last time I saw him? He was usually away when I visited, so it occurred to me that our last meeting was when I attended his wife's funeral pyre.

My uncle stiffened, but he let go of me, and we both bowed to Armin.

The prince stepped forward and took my hand. I'd never had a reason to dance with him, and we'd never spoken beyond the occasional greeting. The first time I even met him was almost twenty years ago at his older sister's wedding, attended by all the high fae in Zadrya.

It was all I could do to keep my composure as he swept me toward the dance floor.

The tune was a moderate one that required us to clasp hands and move through intricate steps. I was grateful for the mild pain reliever tonic Briauna had given me before leaving, so I managed not to wince as I moved. There was some discomfort, but it was manageable.

Armin's gaze never left mine until the dance called for us to move closer. He leaned toward me. "We were worried about you, Aella. Is all well?"

I blinked, shocked at his question. "Oh...yes. I'm fine now."

"Your husband said he couldn't locate you this past week," he whispered, once again surprising me with his knowledge of my marriage.

The healer had been right that Darrow orchestrated my attendance here, but I wondered what had motivated him. "My uncle was upset with me and confined me to my room."

"For disappearing with Darrow when you should have been in Therress, I presume."

I nodded. "Lord Morgunn refused to let me out until I told him where I was that night. Obviously, I couldn't without making matters worse."

Armin put an arm around my waist and dipped me backward, sending pain through my tender wounds. He caught my expression when he brought me back up. "Are you hurt?"

"It's nothing," I said in a whisper.

He frowned. "If you need assistance, please do not hesitate to ask."

His kind words made me want to cry. Unfortunately, the prince couldn't help me any more than what his father had already accomplished. "There is nothing anyone can do, but I'll be fine."

At least, I hoped. Lord Morgunn had barely spoken to me during the journey here, so I had no idea what was in store for me upon my return. He could be rather unpredictable. Regardless, I couldn't ask the crown to intervene. While the king had considerable power, using it to punish someone outside the bounds of law would undermine the independence he sought to give each of the lands in our realm. How a highborn male handled his female relatives was entirely his business, except in the cases of marriage or murder.

"Perhaps your husband will have better luck assisting you," he said, concern remaining in his gaze. "He comes now."

"What?" I began to ask, but it was too late. The music changed to a slow rhythm.

As the prince let me go, Darrow took my hands. "You look beautiful, Aella. I've got half a mind to strip you right here and take you on the floor—damn the consequences."

He acted as though nothing bad had happened over the past week, but he'd just made it worse. Dancing with the prince hadn't been too suspicious, but those of us from Therress and Veronna never danced together. At least, not the highborn.

"Are you mad? My uncle is going to have a fit seeing us together," I said, purposely schooling my expression to outrage so that Lord Morgunn would believe I wasn't willingly dancing with our enemy.

Already, I'd caught him taking a step forward before the king promptly drew his attention. Truly, I was beginning to love Zadrya's monarch more than ever.

"I needed to see that you were well after you disappeared," he said.

Darrow twirled me around before taking me into his arms again. If I thought the prince looked handsome in his attire, my husband appeared devastating. His open burgundy vest barely covered the large muscles of his chest and arms, and I couldn't help but appreciate his flat stomach and narrow waist. Interestingly, his scars didn't show, so he must have applied a light glamour I couldn't sense.

"Did you know my uncle planned to attack that night?" I asked in a furious whisper, continuing to show my fury that wasn't fake at all.

His expression hardened. "No. I wouldn't put you at risk that way."

I desperately wanted to believe him, but how could I? "Not even to save your own people?"

"Believe what you will about me," Darrow said, grip tightening on my waist dangerously close to my healing wounds. "But I would much rather face your uncle on a battlefield than risk him suspecting and harming you. I told you that your safety matters to me, and I meant it."

I closed my eyes and took a breath.

Despite myself, I believed him. The vehemence in his tone had rung true. It also helped that he'd orchestrated bringing me here, which proved Briauna right. Would he have bothered if he'd purposely kept me away from Therress that night?

Silence fell between us while we had to separate and circle each other. The way he moved with me through the dance was like a dream after all I'd been through. By some miracle, he never touched my wounds. When he pulled me close once more, we fit together perfectly.

"Where were you this past week?" he asked in a low voice.

I gave him my best haughty look to keep up the charade for my uncle. "Didn't the locater spell on my wedding ring tell you?"

His gray eyes lit up in surprise. "You know?"

I sighed. "You could have told me from the beginning, and I would have been fine with it."

"Would you?" Darrow appeared skeptical.

"Yes. Because I have nothing to hide and want you to trust me." He had no idea the pain I endured to keep our secrets. I could have admitted my marriage and told my uncle everything I learned to save myself, but I didn't.

"Why hasn't anyone seen you until now?" he asked.

I told him the same story as the prince, but his expression was skeptical as I finished. "Thank you for your concern, but I am fine."

"Are you certain?"

I could have sworn his voice held genuine concern, but surely he couldn't feel that for me. "Yes. I'm alive and well."

The look in his gaze turned intense. "The dance is about to end. Wait half an hour, then when the entertainers appear, make an excuse to refresh yourself. I'll find you."

"It's too dangerous," I hissed.

He gave me a smug smile. "Not to worry, your uncle and cousins will be quite distracted so that you can slip away."

Chapter 35

Darrow

I stood in a small sitting room, waiting for Aella to pass by from her trip to the privy. The anticipation was almost more than I could bear. For the last half hour, I'd had to watch her dance and converse with others. Some of them had looked upon her with lust in their eyes, which made me seriously contemplate crushing their skulls. Of course, the king would have undoubtedly frowned upon such a course of action.

Being unable to claim my wife in front of the High Fae Court had taken supreme self-control. She was far too lovely in that blue dress, especially every time it opened to reveal her luscious bare leg and hip. While dancing with her, I'd known it would only take one slip of the hand to touch the warm center between her thighs, and it had driven me mad. At least, until she accused me of purposely keeping her away from Therress so her uncle couldn't attack my land. I'd thought I'd gained enough trust from her by now that she wouldn't come to such a terrible conclusion.

Finally, I heard the soft *click* of her slippers against the tile. Peeking out, I confirmed it was her. I grabbed her a moment later and pulled her inside, relieved to finally have her all to myself.

"This has to be quick," she whispered.

I locked the door and set a privacy spell before turning to her. "The king and prince have arranged for special entertainers who will distract your uncle and cousins. I am told they include beautiful males and females who are nude and quite flexible when they dance together."

It was a pity we were missing it, but I had something else in mind for my wife.

"They didn't arrange that for us, did they?" she asked, eyes wide.

"No." I guided her farther into the room. "But they did coordinate the timing with me and instructed the dancers to focus their efforts closest to your family members."

I stopped us next to a lounge seat, sat, and pulled Aella onto my lap. When she squirmed, I adjusted my hold until she settled. I would reciprocate what she'd done for me at our last meeting.

"Darrow, we can't..."

"I told you before to call me Dare," I interrupted, pulling her face close to mine.

Panic tightened her features. "Fine, but we can't do this here."

"I don't think you understand how much I want you right now. Watching you in that dress as you danced with other men after me nearly drove me wild, especially knowing we still haven't consummated our marriage," I said. My need to stake my claim on her had never been higher, and I would make certain Aella left here fully satisfied by my touch, and my touch alone.

"This is not the place for that," she argued, though her voice was weak, and she'd begun to relax in my hold.

"Perhaps." I traced her bottom lip with my thumb. "But there are other things we can do for now, dear wife."

Before she could protest again, I kissed her. She only hesitated a moment before succumbing to the press of my lips. Our tongues melded together. At first, I did nothing more than seduce her with my mouth until she was completely pliant in my arms.

Then I found that lovely slit in her dress and traced my hand up her calf, along her knee, and onward along her hip. The soft noises she made told me she enjoyed it. When I moved toward the space between her legs, she opened them without hesitation. A feeling of triumph swept over me as I finally took my chance to touch her there for the first time.

I found her drenched. Pressing my fingers to her clit, I began lightly playing with the soft nub. Her moans intensified, and her thighs parted more, giving me greater access. I slid my finger downward until I reached her entrance, and then I teased the area all around it, taunting her. It was nothing she hadn't done to me the other night.

"Dare, please," she begged.

Enjoying her squirming, I didn't immediately give her what she wanted. Instead, I continued circling her with my fingers while pressing kisses along her neck. She clutched at my shoulders. Only when she began whimpering incoherently did I give her what she wanted. First, I inserted one finger and then two, gliding them in and out. She worked her hips with me, eyes closed as her head fell back, and her riot of blond hair cascaded over my arm where I held her. While I could bring her to climax this way, it wasn't my plan.

Using my powers, I resettled her across the lounge while continuing to work her with my fingers. Her eyes opened, green gems full of lust. I opened her dress further so I could get my first full look at what lay between my wife's legs. Something I'd fantasized about many nights.

She was perfect and glistening. I pulled out my fingers and watched her surprised look as I leaned forward and dipped my head to lick her clit, once, then twice. Nameless ones above—Aella tasted like the sweetest nectar. She lay her head back and gripped the edges of the lounge.

I took my time exploring and savoring her, pleased at how she responded so readily to everything I did to her. I'd handle Aella gently for tonight because something lurked in her gaze that told me she needed tenderness more than roughness. We could save the other for later, but satisfaction filled me at her complete surrender to my ministrations despite her earlier anger.

Sensing her pleasure building, I pressed my fingers inside her once more as I continued to lick and suck. She lifted her hips, giving me better access, and I took advantage. I noted every place she responded with a pleasure-filled cry, memorizing each for future use.

No man would touch her again except me, but I would do my best to satisfy her in every way possible. I was shocked at how much the need for that drove me. When I first proposed wedding each other, we hadn't kissed, and it all seemed more straightforward. Our marriage would be one of convenience. I soon realized there was nothing simple with her. She was mine, and with every moment we spent together, I would make that clearer.

My father had warned me about what would happen with my mate. He'd said he knew he was endearing his wife to him, making her fall madly in love when he could not return the sentiment. Still, he couldn't help himself. He'd desperately wanted her bound, heart and soul, yet all he could offer in return was his protection and passion. She wasn't happy once she realized her husband was cold toward her outside of bed after he owned her completely. I wished I could resist repeating that mistake with Aella, but I was no saint, and my control with her was limited.

As her pleasure built, I worked my fingers inside her faster and lapped at her sensitive nub as she screamed her release. I worked to keep it going until she collapsed, panting.

"Dare, I...that was..." she stumbled over her words as she looked at me with sated passion. Then she opened her thighs wider in the sexiest move I'd ever seen. "You need release, too."

Dear nameless ones, she tempted me like no other. I wanted nothing more than to plunge my engorged cock inside her right now.

"No." I reluctantly closed her legs and pulled her skirt over them. "If we do that, our scents will fully mix, and everyone will know it."

Fae noses could be quite sensitive about some things, and the powerful aroma of sex was one of them. I would thoroughly wash my face and rinse my mouth before returning to the ball, but at least she had little of me on her. Nothing would make me happier than to take her, though. I'd triumphed with another step in the right direction tonight—she'd finally offered her whole body.

"Of course," she said, sitting up with a blush. "I don't know what I was thinking."

Tightness filled my chest. Aella had been so beautiful and passionate that I wished I didn't have to return her to her uncle. She appeared fine, but occasionally, while she'd danced, I'd noted a flash of discomfort in her gaze. Something was wrong, even if I couldn't see it.

"Did your uncle hurt you?" I asked, leaning over to cup her cheek.

She hesitated, gaze dropping. "He...he slapped me when I refused to tell him where I'd been. Twice, actually, but I'm fine. It didn't hurt too much."

Something told me she lied about the severity. I dropped my arm and clenched my fists, wishing I could run into the ballroom and kill him right now. The curse he laid on Aella would be gone with his death, but it would be considered an unprovoked murder. Since her uncle didn't know about our marriage, I couldn't use his abuse of my wife as a valid excuse.

When I arrived at the palace earlier, the king had made it very clear that I must not start trouble, no matter what we discovered—even if Aella had been harmed. If I did so, he'd reveal our marriage to make my punishment lighter, but I would still have to serve time in the royal prison. It was in a remote location up north in Hartoll where they'd force me to spend years of my life alone with my magic suppressed and no contact with the outside world.

Then, my Unseelie brother would surely hear about Aella's channeling powers while I couldn't protect her. He would likely want to kill her or steal her for himself. Neither was a palatable option. For now, she was safer with her uncle, appearing to have no ties to me, like it or not.

"Send word if you need me for anything," I said, forcing her head up so she looked at me again. There was misery in her gaze. She usually hid those emotions, but I'd gotten closer to her tonight in every way. "I'll do whatever I can."

"Okay," she said.

I pulled her into my arms and kissed her deeply one last time, unsure how long it would be before I could call on her again. It wasn't easy to let her go when my need to claim her was still so strong. Perhaps next time we would have a chance.

Withdrawing from her, I stood. "Take care, Aella."

Then, I walked away.

Chapter 36

Aella

Three days had passed since the ball and seeing my husband. My uncle had questioned me about dancing with him, but I'd managed to make up a believable story that Darrow had done it to taunt us. As for my restrictions, my uncle kept me confined to the castle and training area. The guards were instructed not to let me anywhere near the ring without his advance permission.

I might not have been allowed that much freedom, but Lord Morgunn received word that he must bring me to see the Andalagar Prime Chieftain. After all the abuse I'd suffered, I'd needed every moment to get back in shape.

We were about to head to their territory now, and I was more than a little nervous after several months of preparation for this day. I wore a new outfit my uncle had tailored for me. It was different than anything I'd worn before because it used animal skin rather than cloth. The brown pants were thick and tight, and the matching top was a flattering halter style with ribbing for armor that would protect my chest and most of my back from blades. I also had a custom belt and leg harness to hold numerous weapons.

It was a surprising splurge for Lord Morgunn to have it made when there was no guarantee the betrothal would happen, but he certainly had high hopes. I didn't look forward to disappointing him.

He'd stopped acting cold and furious with me, but it wouldn't take much to anger him again. The strain was evident every time we spoke to each other. Unknowingly, the Andalagar had saved me from further punishment.

We walked toward the ring outside Tradain, accompanied by half a dozen soldiers. My uncle had exchanged back-and-forth messages with the leader these past months while I'd been preparing at Tradain and had finally received the invitation for a visit. Lord Morgunn made it abundantly clear that I had better do well at this meeting. I had little idea what to expect other than being tested in some way that they kept secret from outsiders.

The trip through the portal took about seven seconds since the tribe's lands were on the northeast corner of Therress. When we stepped out of the ring, a beach stretched before us with the Pazakian Sea's waves crashing gently to shore.

The water was crystal clear with a cerulean blue tint, the same as the other end where the druid continent, Alavaar, dwelled.

"Aella," my uncle called sternly.

I spun around and gasped. In the sky, there were several Pegasi with riders. Having never been on Andalagar tribal lands, I'd never seen the winged horses. It had been centuries since they'd had a reason to leave their home territories.

There were three other tribal land sections in Zadrya, but this was the only one in Therress. The borders were negotiated more than thirteen hundred years ago after centuries of war with the natives as the Seelie fae fought to obtain enough land to thrive after being forced from the fae home world. The Andalagar, with their Pegasi, were impressive, honorable warriors who certainly fought valiantly, but their magic had more limits than ours. It put them at a disadvantage, which cost them dearly when facing us.

I clasped my hands behind my back as a beautiful dapple-gray Pegasus landed first with a large, muscular man riding him. He wore a brown vest and pants made of animal skins like mine. His belt also had two daggers strapped to his hips and a sword scabbard.

The power emanating from him told me this was the Prime Chief of the tribe.

As he leaped off his winged horse, I took in his full appearance. He was about the same height as Darrow, who was quite tall, but this man had even broader shoulders. The muscles in his arms and chest were also well-defined. Multiple scars crisscrossed his dark, honey-colored skin, proclaiming him an experienced warrior. I looked up at his strong face, framed by wavy russet brown hair with single braids running from each of his temples. One of his ears protruded from his locks enough for me to see that it was rounded rather than pointed. His gaze was deep and intelligent as he assessed me just as thoroughly as I did him.

I tried to keep my expression neutral, unsure of what would help gain his approval. As far as I knew, no Therressian lord had ever successfully married one of his female relatives to an Andalagar leader. Only the occasional lowborn fae had ever intermarried with the tribal folk, but not their chiefs. There was no precedent for me to rely upon. Both sides felt they were superior to the other.

Several more Pegasi landed behind the Prime Chief, carrying men who had similar skin tones, though their hair ranged from brown to black shades. All of them appeared battle-hardened with many scars. I wondered who they could have been fighting since we certainly didn't bother them.

"I am Orran," he said, moving toward me with strident steps. "Prime Chief of all the Andalagar tribal sects."

Meaning that the other three throughout Zadrya also answered to him.

I dipped my chin. "I am Lady Aella, niece of Lord Morgunn."

He held out a hand. "Come, meet my mount, Stradii."

"Thank you." I placed my palm in his, and he led me toward the large Pegasus.

It was several hands taller than any horse I'd ever seen, with a larger body and thicker muscles than other equines and massive wings that it had folded upon landing. A smooth black saddle rested on its back. The halter and reins were also black, except for the silver metal pieces to link the leather straps together.

It was an intimidating animal with feral ice-blue eyes that watched me closely. As all druids could do, I called upon inner feelings of calm, letting them emanate from me to the beast. Within seconds, the Pegasus relaxed, and its eyes softened as it dropped its head to greet me.

"Good boy," I said, running my hand down his forelock. "Aren't you beautiful?"

He nickered.

Orran gave me a surprised look. "Hmm, he does not normally allow strangers to touch him, especially elves. I half-expected him to bite you when you reached out."

One way to greet an intended bride was by putting them in danger. I should have known this was the first of many tests today. My uncle had warned me that the Andalagar leader would put me through a series of them without direction or warning. It was frustrating that I had to endure these trials even though I would never marry this man. On the other hand, seeing a Pegasus up close almost made it worth it.

I scratched Stradii's forehead, and he nuzzled me. "I'm half druid, so I used the same calming technique as I do when meeting dragons."

"Have you ever ridden one?" Orran asked, curiosity in his gaze.

My uncle said my druid side was the main reason I was being considered as a potential bride at all. Perhaps the Andalagar leader didn't know I visited Alavaar often to see my sister since that was the only place on Paxia where they lived. I didn't know what exactly Lord Morgunn had told him.

"Yes, a few times over the years. It is not easy to gain their acceptance since they don't see me often, but I've learned how to befriend some of the more amenable dragons. They can be a pleasure to ride."

He smiled. "Yes, I can imagine."

"I heard you bond with your Pegasi. Is that true?" I asked.

"For some of us, yes." He patted his mount. "They can choose to have only one rider, and if we bond, we can sense each other's emotions and desires. No words are exchanged, but there is communication between us, nonetheless."

I continued petting Stradii. "Those who bond with dragons on Alavaar can speak with theirs, but a few can speak with all of them. My sister is one of those as a beast healer."

"Interesting." He turned and shouted at his men in a language I couldn't understand, then returned his focus to me. "We will go for a walk now."

"What about my uncle?" I asked, turning my gaze to Lord Morgunn. He stared at us with annoyance and impatience, probably because Orran had failed to greet or acknowledge him.

"My men will take him to the village where he may eat and rest until we arrive," the Andalagar chief said, taking my hand.

He guided me toward a wide path in the nearby woods. I suspected this would be my next test, and I widened my senses to prepare myself. No way would it be a simple stroll, especially when an ominous feeling overtook me as the tall, thick trees enveloped us. It was almost like nighttime, with little sunlight reaching the ground.

Orran didn't let go of my left hand, keeping a tight grip on it. A thrum of magic ran between our palms, but I had no idea what sort of spell he used. It didn't seem to affect me in any way I could discern.

"Are you an obedient woman, Aella?" he asked, voice breaking the silence of the still woods. No birds sang, and I couldn't make out any sounds from insects or small animals.

I knitted my brows. "Obedient?"

"Yes." He squeezed my palm. "And tell me truthfully."

This had to be some sort of test, and since I had little to lose, I chose to be forthright. "I straddle a line. In front of my uncle, I'm as obedient as possible, but I admit to doing things he would disapprove of when he isn't watching."

"Hmm." Orran's expression was neutral, giving nothing away.

"Is that what you're looking for?" I asked, unnerved at how hot his hand had become. "An obedient wife?"

Mirth transformed his features, and he let out a deep chuckle. "I doubt there is such a thing—at least not among women worth having."

Well, that was a refreshing answer.

"Glad to hear that," I said, but then something dark and sinister crept at the edges of my senses. My stomach turned at its malevolence. I pulled on his hand, bringing us to a stop. "Wait."

Orran gave me an amused look. "What is it?"

"Something is out there."

He still wouldn't let go of me, so I needed to choose between using wind power or a blade as a weapon. It would help if I knew what I was facing, but it hadn't shown itself yet. I kept my free hand next to my sheathed knife. If necessary, I could pull it fast.

Movement darted between the trees to my right, roaming swiftly. It was barely visible as a grayish figure floating off the ground. It came closer, perhaps fifty feet away now. I squinted, and when it shifted again, I realized I could see through the creature. It was a wisp.

Most were green or blue and harmless as long as you didn't follow them. There were some, though, that came from evil spirits. They were either gray or red. The fact that this one was gray meant that it hadn't fed from anyone's energy in a long time and must be ravenous. If it touched either of us, it would devour our magic and then our life force until we died.

Physical weapons were useless against them. Most of the time, when one saw a wisp, the best thing to do was run or start a fire because they hated flames. I had another option—my light power. While I still hadn't mastered using it with pinpoint focus, that wasn't necessary in this case.

The hungry creature darted straight for us—now only twenty feet away. I drew on my light magic as I did every time I opened a portal, except I didn't funnel my wind powers with it. As I lifted my hand, bright illumination spread from my palm, and the wisp ran straight into it. A loud, screeching wail sounded before it faded to nothing. Most likely, it wouldn't be able to regenerate for weeks.

I dropped my hand and let go of my magic with a sigh of relief.

"Impressive," Orran said, looking down at me with surprise. "I expected you to drag me into a run."

This was all a game to him, of course. He hadn't seemed worried for a moment.

"Could you have taken care of it yourself?" I asked.

The corner of his lips lifted. "You'll never know now, will you?"

He gestured forward, and we resumed our walk through the woods. I kept my eyes open for anything amiss. It wasn't long before another creature came along—a leprechaun with bloody teeth and a deer haunch he threw at me. Orran and I dodged it. As he came closer, I used my wind power to slam him into a tree.

The Prime Chief still wouldn't let go of my hand, so I had to pull him along as I dashed for the snarling creature. I stabbed the leprechaun in the throat and didn't pull my blade out until he breathed his last breath. This one must have had a gold stash somewhere nearby because they didn't attack so viciously without cause. I had a feeling that despite the clear trail, few ever entered these treacherous woods. Perhaps they only used it for tests like mine.

For the next hour, I ran into several more attackers of various types as we covered at least a mile. Then, we stepped into a sunlit clearing. The blue-green grass was soft as we walked through it. I sensed no danger, relieved to leave the oppressive darkness of the woods.

"Few make it through that walk without my assistance," Orran said, finally letting go of my hand.

I rubbed my palm, attempting to wipe away whatever magic he'd used on me. "Has anyone ever died during your test?"

"Yes," he admitted, regret in his golden gaze. "About one in four. It is not only used for potential chief brides but also for those who wish to be elite warriors. With them, they must travel alone to this point."

"Where do we go from here?" I asked, glancing around me.

He headed toward a boulder where a large sack sat atop it. "Normally, we'd take a trail on the other side of this clearing to reach the village, but you are going to open a portal for me to the Andalagar tribal lands in Juvarn."

"What?" I frowned, calculating the distance. "If I do that, we'll have to stay there for two hours until I regain my strength."

I would barely have enough power to make it that distance now since I'd had to use a little fighting the various creatures who attacked us. It never occurred to me that I'd need to open a portal this soon, much less one so far away, but perhaps I should have known. My gift would always be the factor that made me valuable to everyone.

"That's all the time it will take?" he asked, stunned.

I nodded. "As long as I don't have to use my powers for anything else."

"You won't, but the question remains whether you can open this one or not." He gave me an inscrutable look. "It is far more difficult than others."

I straightened my shoulders, tired of everyone doubting me. "There is no portal in Paxia I can't open."

"That remains to be seen." Orran grabbed the cumbersome sack from the boulder and brought it to me. "Here are the supplies you'll need, and this is the rune sequence." He also drew a folded piece of parchment paper from his pocket, giving it to me.

The bag was so heavy I nearly dropped it.

I dumped the contents onto the grass. A thin, four-inch-wide metal coil with fused algodonite stones fell to the ground, along with a pouch of Holmium. I pocketed the small bag and spread out the other item, finding the silver circle stretched to a ten-foot diameter. It was slightly smaller than the temporary portal ring I kept stored away at Ivory Castle for occasional use. Since this type was not grounded to a specific place, and the metal that linked the runes was much thinner, it required more power and concentration to travel far. It didn't even have its own rune address since it wasn't permanent, so we couldn't use it to return and would need to use the main ring by the sea when it was time to come back.

"Do you have a channeler here?" I asked as I adjusted the circle to smooth it against the ground. Every minute that passed brought me closer to fully recharging, so I didn't rush the setup. "My uncle said you were short one."

He nodded. "I took one from one of my other territories since the other passed, but he cannot open a portal for long distances more than once daily. I must always plan to stay the night if I visit other lands."

"At least he can do it. Most of ours can only channel within Therress, except one who is like yours. She can open to longer distances but needs about eighteen hours to recover," I said, standing back to check my work. It looked perfect.

He lifted a brow. "Is it ready?"

"Yes."

I pulled out the parchment to study the rune sequence. I realized I didn't have it in my records, though I did have another for the Andalagar tribe in Juvarn that led to their main village, so there must have been more than one ring there. Where would this one take us?

After pinching a healthy dose of holmium powder, I gathered the necessary elements together. Orran kept his gaze focused on me as I worked. I extended my hands and pushed the light magic toward the runes on the ring. It struck each of them, one after another, until all five stones glowed, and then I intertwined my wind to begin channeling.

I pushed more power to form the connection to the other side. My hands shook, and it took all my attention to force the magic to reach the desired destination. It was so much harder than with an established ring that was properly grounded and had better conductive metal.

My muscles ached and strained as I pushed and pushed as if trying to move a mountain. When I finally reached the receiving end, I found layers of glowing, intricately woven wards. Gritting my teeth, I quickly began working my way through them before I ran out of energy. My power burned through me faster than usual because these couldn't be broken or bypassed like most others, but rather, had to be solved like a riddle.

I'd only run into a few like this in my life, though not nearly as complicated. I was grateful for the practice I had with them since the experience helped guide my intuition now. These wards were more complex, but somehow, I could easily visualize how to unravel each one with a little concentration and patience. It wasn't a skill that could be taught.

After nearly a minute of furious work, a *pop* sounded, and a blue glow formed over the grass where the circle sat. "Hurry, go!"

"See you in a moment," he said, giving me an impressed look.

Orran stepped into the ring, sinking downward until his body disappeared. Heaving for breath, I pushed the last surge of power remaining in me. Weakness assailed my body. I stumbled forward and entered the portal, grateful to let go of my magic as my feet disappeared into the swirling depths.

The distance was quite far since it spanned much of the continent. As my body glided through a swirling tunnel of light, I had more time than usual to study the beautiful color patterns. They were incredible, like a rainbow surrounding me and dancing to a silent tune.

I estimated that thirty seconds had passed before I exited the other side of an upright ring. Stumbling over rocks, I managed to right myself and get my bearings. We were high up in the Sobaryan Mountains, with their lavender peaks and hazy clouds surrounding us, making it impossible to see the land below. The ring had to be in the northeast corner of Juvarn, which was near the ice giant territory of Hisgar.

The air was chill at this elevation so far north. I hugged myself, trying to preserve my body heat since I had grown accustomed to summer's scorching temperatures. The animal skins kept my legs warm, but the halter top did little for my upper body. Not far from us were patches of snow that never melted, telling me it must not ever get hot here.

"You truly are impressive, Lady Aella," Orran said with unrestrained astonishment. "I hadn't expected you to succeed despite what I'd heard about your power."

What had my uncle told him? Lord Morgunn shouldn't have known the depth of my abilities, yet the tribal chief acted as though he'd expected me to be far above average, though not quite talented enough to reach this secret place. Did I need to worry about Orran's enthusiasm? Darrow and his mother had mentioned I should keep the breadth of my skills quiet, but I couldn't imagine the Andalagar being a problem since they'd never align for the dark elves or Unseelie.

I drew my gaze to him. "What do you mean? I told you I can reach any portal in Paxia."

He shook his head. "This one is heavily warded since it is where the Naforya Fountain stood before it was stolen. A channeler used to train for years before assuming the responsibility of transporting guards and special visitors here. As far as I know, no one has managed to open it on a first attempt, much less while starting with a temporary ring."

"What?" My eyes rounded as I took in my surroundings with a more critical eye, spotting a raised rock platform on the next rise over from us. "I had no idea."

He'd set me up to fail because, apparently, reaching this place should have been impossible. I would have been furious had it not been for the importance of our location. I'd memorize the rune sequence on the paper and then destroy it.

"This area has always been a secret to all except its oath-sworn guardians, even after the fountain went missing." Orran's mouth formed a grim line. "But I needed to see if you could reach it because no other channeler has succeeded for centuries, and without someone like you, we can't acquire and reestablish the fountain even if we locate it."

It confused me that, of all the tests he could administer to a marriage prospect, he would choose this one. "What does this have to do with the bride trial?"

The Andalagar leader strode toward me, took my face in his hands, and kissed me. For a second, I was so shocked at his lips pressing into mine that I did nothing. Then, some instinct had me pressing my hands against his chest.

I felt nothing for this man. Instead, it was Darrow's face that came to my mind. For reasons I couldn't explain, he was the only one I wanted anymore. When had that happened? I couldn't resist my husband, but apparently, I could resist anyone else—even handsome tribal leaders.

With a hard shove, I pushed Orran away. "No. I can't do this."

My uncle was going to be furious with me, but I didn't care.

"Good." He smiled. "That was another test."

"Test for what?" I asked incredulously. This man had a profound love of putting unsuspecting women through ridiculous trials.

"To see how loyal you are to your husband, Darrow."

My jaw dropped. "How do you know?"

"He requested a meeting months ago and told me of your secret marriage and the dilemma it presented. At first, I wanted nothing to do with the matter until he told me of your channeling abilities and that you might be the answer to retrieving the fountain. It is why I contacted your uncle and expressed interest in you."

Darrow had said he'd get involved in the matter. When he never mentioned anything about it again, I'd assumed he'd left it alone. Instead, he'd found a way to buy us months without my uncle being able to marry me to anyone else. I'd even had plenty of time to train and improve my magic, which I suspected I would need in the future. He'd been looking out for me without me realizing it. As much as I hated to admit it, that touched me.

Then again, he was also keeping a lot of secrets if he'd set this up so early in our marriage, likely in the first week. Not once had Darrow mentioned it despite my having a right to know, and he'd had plenty of opportunities.

I struggled to formulate a response for the Prime Chief. "What do I have to do with the fountain?"

That was also news to me.

"This world is slowly dying because the fountain was hidden on another planet." His golden eyes bored into mine. "You may very well have the power to open an intergalactic portal to the location where it currently resides."

My husband had suggested the traveling part when we visited his mother, but I remained unconvinced. Channeling here took a lot out of me. How could I possibly open a portal to a distant world, and how did they know it was on another planet? My mother had never mentioned that, but I had been young at the time. She didn't share everything with me.

"Do we even know where it might be?" I asked.

"Not yet." Orran sighed and ran his hands through his shoulder-length hair. "I know your mother was trying to find out, especially after she realized her daughter might be the one to finally reach it."

"I hadn't even come into my full channeling abilities when she died," I said, shaking my head in denial.

The Prime Chief was quiet a moment, as if mulling over some matter. "When Nerine first brought you to Alavaar after your birth so her parents could meet you, a druid seer visited. She predicted you'd have portal magic, and it would surpass any others of our time. Even so, most of us didn't think it would grow to your current level. Your mother was the only one who believed your gift could rival all who came before you."

When I was born, Orran was only seven years old and certainly didn't live in Alavaar. "How do you know that?"

"My father was the leader of the tribe then, and he told me many things before he passed." Orran gave me a kind smile. "The Andalagar and druids have been close allies for a very long time, and this was certainly something that concerned us both. I have sections of land beginning to wither and die. It appears to progress faster with each passing year, and I fear it will worsen significantly soon. Retrieving the fountain has become one of our most vital objectives."

"So you've been testing me as a potential portal channeler rather than a marriage prospect?" I asked, lifting a brow. That was both vexing and a relief. I didn't have to pretend to be interested in him as a husband anymore, but it annoyed me that he couldn't have been more forthright from the beginning.

He shrugged. "I needed to make it look official, so I put you through trials for both. Darrow is right that we must conceal your abilities and divert attention away from you for as long as possible. There are forces at work who will target you if they know you exist."

My chest tightened, as this was the second time I had heard this. "What forces?"

"I'll leave it for your husband to explain."

I clenched my fists in frustration. "You realize Darrow tells me very little despite the important role I apparently have to play in all this?"

I was tired of everyone being vague and unwilling to share important information.

"He is wise to do so." Orran gave me an apologetic look. "As long as you're in your uncle's care, it is best you know as little as possible, especially with a cousin who can detect lies."

A sigh escaped me. I couldn't entirely argue that point, but the chief didn't know how much pain I had already endured to keep secrets. When it came to the fountain and preservation of this world, I'd do anything to protect that knowledge. It was too bad no one could have more faith in me.

"But surely Lord Morgunn would want the fountain returned as well," I said, gesturing toward the empty platform in the distance. "His lands are affected, too."

"He is a man with questionable allegiances, Aella. Never trust him."

I didn't, not really, but it felt wrong to believe others whom I hardly knew. "So, what now?"

"We wait for your powers to regenerate enough for us to return to my lands." He nodded at the nice, sturdy portal behind me. "Then we continue with this farce of courting each other a while longer so your uncle doesn't move on to a less desirable prospect."

"You're truly willing to help us?" I asked, surprised.

He gave me a grim smile. "Now that I am certain of you and what you can do, yes. Continue to train as much as possible because I suspect many battles lie ahead, and you'll need to be strong and prepared for them. You have proven reasonably adept, but there is always room for improvement."

He wasn't wrong. I'd been lucky in my battles today because they were singular creatures in the woods, most of which I already knew how to face through experience and studies. On a larger, more complicated scale against other fae, I'd have more trouble.

"Okay," I agreed, no longer feeling the cold as I tried to absorb everything he'd told me. "Is there any chance you'd allow me to ride one of the Pegasi?"

He let out a deep laugh. "If you return the fountain to us, I'll let you try."

Chapter 37

Aella

A week and a half had passed since I visited the Andalagar chief. We'd returned to my uncle after leaving the mountains, with Orran praising my battle skills and magic. He'd done an impressive job showing interest in me, which wasn't all false since he saw me as vital to returning the fountain to our world. While we'd waited for me to regain my strength, I'd explained how much pressure my family placed on me to do well at the visit. The Prime Chief had taken it to heart.

Lord Morgunn was so pleased with Orran's report that he said I could return to the castle and continue my weapons practice at the garrison training field instead of going back to Tradain. He didn't even mind that we hardly saw much while at the tribal lands, or that he'd mostly been sequestered to a few key places in the village. The Andalagar took their privacy very seriously with outsiders.

Since then, I spent my mornings practicing with my swords and daggers, but each afternoon, I spared two to three hours for my garden. The plants had been in poor shape due to a lack of attention over the last few months and the high heat. Rynn had watered them now and then, but she was busy with her studies and practicing her new magic, so she hadn't been able to make it by there often. I'd snuck into the garden when I could as well, but it hadn't been enough for my high-maintenance plants. They could have used their own nanny if the risk of that person getting eaten wasn't so high.

After being snapped at several times, I'd had to wear gloves to protect myself. Only after they'd all received rich mulch, had the weeds picked from around them, and been given regular waterings mixed with vital nutrients, did they finally forgive me. There was no way to explain to them that I would never neglect them willingly.

I also acquired plenty of mice and rats from the castle rodent catcher for the carnivorous plants. He was a kind, older gnome who thoughtfully held them in cages alive until I could collect them. It deeply touched me to see how good some people here were despite my evil uncle.

Now that all the plants were nourished and happy, I had turned my attention to pruning the ones that required it. To keep certain varieties healthy, it was necessary to trim any foliage near the ground to reduce the risk of disease. It didn't happen often since the garden courtyard was mostly closed off, but a couple of times over the years, a contagion had found its way inside.

I wasn't always able to save them in time. Though my plants could be antagonistic toward each other, they mourned if any died, and I'd spend a week dealing with sagging, depressed flora. They were like siblings that way.

My mardizold plants were a prime example of needing careful tending. As they grew larger, they also became bushier but were susceptible to contagion brought down by rain and mixed with the earth. I had to keep their foliage at least six inches from the ground.

They were well worth having if they were healthy and well-tended since the orange blooms produced a soothing, fragrant scent that could calm anyone—people, plants, and animals—within their vicinity. Their scent turned putrid and sour if I allowed them to become sick or withered.

After finishing the pruning, I spoke and comforted each plant so they knew I still cared. I had been doing it each day since returning. The positive energy in the garden had improved to almost where it had been in the spring. That lifted my spirits as well.

Finally, I left to bathe and prepare myself for dinner. I'd play nicely with my uncle and other family to avoid suspicion, and then later tonight, I'd make a surprise visit to Siggaya. It was Darrow's forty-sixth birthday, and I wouldn't forget his like he did mine. Revenge was best served with unexpected gifts.

***

I stepped from the portal into the Veronnian trade city an hour before midnight. It was still quite warm outside, so I was glad I'd chosen a low-cut sleeveless gown with wide shoulder straps, a tapered waist, and a skirt hem that only reached my knees. The fabric was royal purple, and fine lace accentuated the bodice.

It was a little strange dressing up for a man who'd been my husband for nearly four months, yet we'd never had sex. Still, after what he'd done to me at the summer court ball, I wanted to finally consummate our marriage—to find out if it would be as good as I imagined. Of course, I would have stood out in my attire, so I wore a thin black cloak that covered me from head to toe. Darrow would see the dress later.

With that thought, I moved to sit on one of the benches in the courtyard so I'd be less conspicuous, figuring my husband would find me soon enough when his tracking spell alerted him of my arrival. He should realize my uncle wasn't crazy enough to attack a city this size and that it would only be me.

While I waited, I watched the night butterflies flit between flowers in the garden beds dotted throughout the area. They were beautiful, glowing in various pastel colors as they danced together. I rarely had the opportunity to appreciate them since I often didn't visit gardens in the evening, and they didn't dare enter mine since it was too dangerous. One of the plant varieties I had there produced a scent that discouraged them from getting close, which was its intended purpose. I didn't want my carnivorous varieties eating the beautiful, harmless insects.

A dark figure entered the courtyard and immediately cast his gaze on me. I stood, moving toward him. Darrow met me halfway with suspicion in his eyes, which was disconcerting, but I wouldn't let that get to me. I walked right up, rose on my toes, and kissed him. His mouth tasted of alcohol, which wasn't unexpected. He stood frozen for a moment in what I suspected was shock before warming and returning the gesture.

We pulled apart, him with a frown. His voice was low as he asked, "What are you doing here?"

"It's your birthday," I said, following his example and whispering. Just this once, I wanted to be the one planning and acting first. Maybe he couldn't ever love me, but he could feel many other emotions. I wanted to test them all and see where it led.

His gaze changed to one of surprise. "How did you know?"

"I saw the date on our marriage contract."

"Thank you for remembering, but you shouldn't be here." He took my hand and guided me toward a copse of trees at the back of the courtyard, where the shadows were deeper. "You'll be in danger if you're seen."

We continued to keep our voices low.

"Which is why I'm wearing a cloak," I replied, drawing it closer around my face.

He worked his jaw. "Yes, I see that, but every moment you're here puts your life at greater risk. It's not worth it...even for my birthday."

I couldn't help feeling a little hurt, considering he'd forgotten about mine and then didn't want to see me on his. It was frustrating. At the ball and Jolloure, it seemed like he wanted more from our marriage, even if it was only physical, but now he pushed me away.

"Fine, I should be able to go home in an hour." Shoving my hands into my cloak pockets, I pulled small, wrapped gifts from each one. "These are gifts for you and your sister."

I pushed them into his hands as he gave them a bewildered look. "Why would you give us gifts?"

"Do you really have to ask? This marriage is a secret now, but it won't be forever, and I'm just trying to make it work," I said, growing frustrated with him.

He shook his head and put the gifts back into my cloak pockets. "You should save those efforts for the future when things are safer."

"Are you serious? Every time I come to you, I take a risk, but I do it anyway because you ask it of me. Even after my uncle caught me, and everything that he..." I clenched my fists, unwilling to tell him what I'd endured since he probably didn't care regardless of what he claimed. "Anyway, I'm fully aware of the repercussions, but since the ball, I thought you'd at least be open to this."

He sighed and ran a hand through his loose hair. "Those were different circumstances where I had everything planned and coordinated. This city is full of spies for nearly everyone in the realm, and I have no way to shield you from them all, especially without adequate warning. You might have made it through here once without being noticed, but it's unlikely to happen again."

"Yes, we wouldn't want anyone to suspect we're married, such as the leader of the Andalagar tribe," I said in a scathing voice.

His lips twitched. "So he told you about that?"

"Yes." I lifted a brow. "After he kissed me."

Darrow stiffened, and his eyes narrowed. "He did *what*?"

"Orran had me open a portal to where the Naforya Fountain should be located. We were discussing it, and then he kissed me out of nowhere," I said, shrugging. "Guess he wanted to see how committed I am to you."

Darrow turned his face away, but I managed to catch a glimpse of his anger. The hard line of his jaw told me he was fighting a much stronger reaction. His voice came out cold, "Did you enjoy his kiss?"

I let out a low, bitter laugh. "Does it really matter when you don't want to see me on your birthday or accept my gifts?"

"You're still mine, dear wife. No one touches you except me," he said, voice menacingly low.

"Then why don't you take me somewhere and prove it?" I challenged, trying to turn the situation around. Why couldn't anything ever be on my terms?

He let out a growl of frustration. "Because this isn't the time or place, and you should know that by now. If someone sees you, it could ruin all my plans, which are more important than a damned birthday."

Yet, obviously, he could sit around drinking with others. Just not his wife. Despite everything he'd said recently, he likely still saw me as the enemy. Playing with me could only be on his terms, never mine. Red, hot anger poured through my veins.

In that moment, I was sorely tempted to punch him. "Tonight, I was prepared to consummate this marriage, but thanks for making it clear that even fucking me isn't worth your time." I pulled the gifts back from my pockets and shoved them into his chest, but he let them fall to the ground. "Hope you have a happy birthday, Darrow."

His expression hardened. "You're being ridiculous."

I backed away toward the ring, letting him see all the rage in my eyes. I'd taken a whipping to protect this marriage and lain in horrific pain for a week, but this was how he greeted me when I tried to do something nice despite everything? Now, I felt as ridiculous as he claimed.

"So you know," I said, now halfway to the ring. "I pushed Orran away the second his lips touched mine because all I thought of was you, but I see now how stupid that was to do since I doubt you really care beyond some ridiculous possessiveness. I'm nothing more than an object for you to use at your whim."

Then, I spun around and moved to face the ring. A tear ran down my cheek as I lifted my shaking hands and began channeling. I hadn't regenerated my powers enough, but I pulled everything I had anyway. It only needed to stay open long enough for one person to pass, and there were no wards on the portal to my garden. The distance was the only thing that made it more difficult. My knees began to shake next as I kept trying to find scraps of power to complete the connection.

Darrow had moved from the trees, stopping just within my line of sight. "It's too soon. You're going to burn yourself out."

I couldn't respond to him as I continued chanting. The frustration on his face only made me want to leave that much sooner, so I dug to the bottom of my well and found the last bit of magic I needed. The connection snapped into place.

He stepped closer. "Aella, I..."

"Fuck you, Darrow."

The blue light appeared, and I stumbled toward it. My legs barely wanted to cooperate because I'd used everything. My well was almost dry. I continued pushing with everything I had as I fell to my knees and crawled the rest of the way. If Darrow reacted, I couldn't say at that point, but I made it across those final few feet and entered the portal. It closed right behind me.

Shortly thereafter, I popped into my garden courtyard. I dragged myself toward my vine plants and sobbed. Several blooms leaned down and brushed the tears from my cheeks. The mardizolds released their soothing fragrance, giving me a measure of calm. I lay there for a while, letting my flora comfort me until I regained the strength to return to my room.

Chapter 38

Darrow

S unlight filtered through a break in my curtains directly on my face. I groaned as I rolled over to avoid it, head pounding. Last night, I'd drank far too much. Most of it was a blur, but I was still fairly lucid when my wife arrived in Siggaya. Fear for her had hit me immediately. The risks were greater now than they had been four months ago when she first visited the city, and we made our deal.

Dark forces were plotting and maneuvering, and every side had spies watching locations like city portal rings. I didn't find anyone after she'd left last night, but that didn't mean they hadn't been there at some point, or they may have had very effective concealment spells.

Forcing my eyes open, I stared at my nightstand where I'd set the wrapped gifts Aella had brought with her. She hardly knew me or my sister, so I couldn't help but wonder what she'd given us.

I found the one with my name labeled with beautifully written script. Unwrapping it, I sat up quickly when I saw what the package contained—a white clarity stone. They were extremely rare and valuable. My father had one that he let me borrow once, but that was under exceptional circumstances. He usually kept it hidden away, using it only for himself. Holding the stone in your hand would allow you to see through any glamour.

Aella must have held onto it from her mother's collection. Only druids had access to the difficult-to-reach location where they could be found, and precious few of them could perform the enchantment successfully. They were also reluctant to sell or trade them to fae. Yet my wife had come to Siggaya at great personal risk to give me a near-priceless gift, and I'd admonished her and attempted to give it back. She'd had to shove it at me. Then, I upset her so much that she drained herself of her powers to escape. I let out a stream of curses.

A knock sounded at the door.

"What?" I barked.

Faina opened it, sticking her head inside. She must have just risen because her long, brown-black hair was loose and wild around her face. "What are you cursing about?"

I grabbed her gift and tossed the package at her. She caught it easily.

"Oh, brother, you needn't give me anything other than your charming personality," she said, stepping further into the room. I was thankful that she wore a black robe covering most of her body. Sometimes, when hungover, she strutted around in nothing more than underwear, giving me nightmares for days. I might have shared a womb with her, but thankfully, I had no memory of that.

"It's from Aella," I growled, still holding my gift. "She brought them here last night."

She grinned and quickly unwrapped hers. When she pulled out an iridescent gold stone, she squealed. "Oh, I've always wanted one of these, but they're out of my price range unless I want to sacrifice buying anything else for two years."

It was an amplifier that could make a spell twice as powerful. They were similar to blue burst gems, except stronger, and they could be reused with a twenty-four-hour break between. The basic stone could be found on Alavaar and the Isles of Mannoth, where most gnomes, goblins, and gremlins lived in the far south. Druid enchanters were the only ones who could spell them to work, though. Since they were somewhat more plentiful, there were more in circulation, but they were still expensive and uncommon to find. Aella had gifted a woman she hardly knew with something precious because Faina was my sister.

I rubbed my face. "She arrived last night, wishing me a happy birthday and bringing these gifts, and I yelled at her for coming."

"Well," Faina said, still gazing at her stone. "It's far better than what you did for her on her birthday."

"What do you mean?" I asked, not realizing I'd done anything for Aella on her birthday or which day it was since I hadn't thought it relevant at this point in our marriage.

My sister gave me a pointed look. "You forced her to open a portal to Therress so you could attack her people."

I closed my eyes, regret pulling at my chest. "I had no idea."

"Clearly. Even I hadn't thought you could be so cruel, but how could I know you didn't bother to learn your wife's birthday? I figured that curse of yours must have made you not care, which is why I told Aella as much while we waited for the attack to begin."

I narrowed my eyes. "So, you're the one who told her?"

"It was my gift to her since I thought you might not have said anything, and she had a right to be aware of it, especially when you pretty much ruined her birthday," she said smugly, pocketing her stone.

For a moment, I was quiet as I considered everything. Some people took their revenge using violence or destruction. Aella took hers by making a person feel like shit about themselves while she came out looking sweet and benevolent.

That was certainly her druid side since elves didn't plot quiet and thoughtful strategies—light or dark. How well played, and yet, it didn't make me feel any better about what I'd done to her.

I lifted my stone. "She gave me this as a gift."

"You cannot be serious." Faina moved closer with shock in her gaze. "I'm half tempted to kill you for that."

"You could try," I said, pulling my hand away before she tried to snatch my gift from me.

My sister made a tsking sound. "As much as I want to hate Aella, I have to say you don't deserve her. She's far too good for you."

I grimaced. "I've begun to realize that."

There was no way I'd mention to my sister that my wife had even planned to seduce me last night, so we could finally consummate our marriage. That was a subject I certainly didn't want to discuss with a sibling. A part of me wondered if I shouldn't have brought her to my loft. She was already in Siggaya at the time, so the damage was mostly done, but I'd worried my oldest brother might have been watching the loft. Who knew what the Unseelie was doing right now?

"Maybe you should start thinking of a way to make it up to her before she decides to hate you forever," Faina said, expression thoughtful. "We need her on our side, and you're ruining it, Dare."

She wasn't wrong.

A loud pounding on the door sounded before I could respond. I hurriedly grabbed a clean tunic, glad I'd passed out in my pants, and rushed to the sitting room. Only one person ever came to my home and knocked like that. My sister had vanished, aware of who the visitor must be as well.

I opened the door to my father, who appeared irritated. He barged inside and took a good look around my place. "Who else is here?"

"Only Faina."

"Good." He swung around. "What was Lord Morgunn's daughter doing in Siggaya last night?"

That explained the extra-fierce pounding and my father's mood. "Apparently, surprising me for my birthday."

"Does she actually like you that much?" he asked, skepticism in his voice.

I sighed. "She did until I lectured her on the dangers of coming here. How did you know it was her?"

"My spy told me she was the only one who came through the portal, and she re-opened it less than forty minutes later, which should have been impossible." Lord Gannon glared at me. "I had to kill him to keep that secret from spreading further."

Lovely, someone had died so Aella could wish me a happy birthday. I really should have kept her here for longer, but I didn't believe she'd be able to open the portal successfully until it was too late. At the time, I'd figured she'd fail, and then I'd figure out what to do with her until she regained her strength. When she succeeded, I was too stunned to stop her.

"I told you she was powerful, but she surprised me as well," I said, gesturing at my father to take a seat. "She was so weak by the end that she crawled through the ring to leave."

If not for the fact that it would have landed me in the heart of enemy territory, I would have carried her. The problem was she'd burned herself out, and when one did that, it took at least a day to recover. She wouldn't have been able to send me home for some time. As a result, I had no choice except to stand there helplessly as she left on her hands and knees.

"The only reason I'm not angrier with you is because last night proved she's the answer to getting the Naforya Fountain back." He reclined and rested an arm on the back of the couch. "My spy didn't get a good look at her or know who she was, so anyone else watching wouldn't have either, but you're going to need to be extra cautious because if anyone else saw, they'll come to the same conclusion as us."

"I'm rather certain she's furious with me," I said, pulling out the clarity stone. "This was the gift she brought me, and I sent her away crying."

My father's eyes rounded. "That must have been left over from her mother's collection."

"Yes." I went on to explain some of the other details from Aella's visit and what Faina had told me.

Lord Gannon turned contemplative. "Your sister is right, as much as I hate to admit it. You need to make amends with your wife and start using her resources to help us find the fountain. It isn't only her portal skills that are an asset, but also her access to Alavaar."

"What's there that we need?" I asked, frowning. My father could be the worst of us all when it came to doling out information like breadcrumbs.

"Libraries," he said with a smug smile. "I've exhausted nearly all the other ones where we have access, but I suspect at least some of the answers we seek must be in Tuireen."

I hadn't considered that before—to my annoyance—but he was right. "Aella is due to visit her sister in about ten days."

Assuming she stayed on schedule. It varied sometimes, but I didn't see any reason the timing of her next trip would change. My spies were quite effective in their roles and would have reported otherwise.

Lord Gannon nodded. "Do it then, so you'll have more time to accomplish what you need—and make amends with her."

"Of course," I agreed.

Now, how to regain Aella's good graces? I'd need all the time I could get to plan for that.

Chapter 39

Aella

The night after my disastrous birthday trip to see Darrow, heavy rain poured down on us. It was rare for late summer and sent my plants into a growing frenzy while also encouraging weed growth. Two days later, I set aside time to pull weeds and prune bushes. Sariyah had taken a week off to visit me at Ivory Castle and joined me in the garden. She understood how much I needed a friend right now with everything happening in my life, and I loved her for it.

"If this plant licks my cheek one more time, Aella," she began, clenching her eyes shut as it did it again. "I'm gonna..."

"Be grateful it likes you so much," I finished before she said something to offend the tulipworm.

The plant was very affectionate and harmless as long as she didn't upset it. If she did, the saliva, for lack of a better term, could insert an element into its secretion that would make her skin itch for days, no matter how much she washed. Sariyah hadn't spent enough time in my garden to know all the species' personalities. She only knew which ones were carnivorous to avoid them. It was the reason I had her pulling weeds near the less volatile plants.

She sighed as she pulled more errant sprigs. "I know this is all my fault. If I hadn't given you that snapper berry bush seedling for your twelfth birthday, maybe you wouldn't have morphed this garden into such a hazardous place. Honestly, the elf who sold it to me said they were difficult to keep alive, but it would be fun to watch you try."

"I love you to this day for that," I said, bumping her shoulder with mine. Our hands were filthy from digging in the dirt, or I would have patted her on the back.

She cast her gaze skyward. "And I've cursed myself ever since for that terrible idea."

"Aella," Tadeus called from the archway. "Is it safe to come in here?"

I beckoned to him. "Sure. Just bow to the crunchertraps before you pass them."

"Bow?" he asked.

"Think of it like a secret password," I said, sharing a sly grin with Sariyah. "I've been teaching them, so they're less hostile to people I like."

He gave me a dubious look. "I feel better when you threaten them before I try entering."

"Tadeus, stop being a baby and get in here."

My cousin eyed each of the crunchertraps warily, then gave each of them perfect bows that would have done justice to the king. Then, he straightened and marched forward. He nearly jumped out of his pants when both plants leaned forward to rub themselves against him as he passed, but I suspected they were merely pleased with his show of respect. My plants had feelings, after all.

As Tadeus continued, he eyed some of my other cantankerous plants and gave them bows as well. Sariyah and I watched him, bemused, as he slowly made his way toward us, carefully using the stepping stones since we were about ten feet off the main cobbled path.

"Honestly, I think you grew this whole place just to vex me, Aella," my cousin said as he stopped a few feet from us. One of the tullipworms reached out and licked his hand, making him shout. "Ahh!"

I sighed and shook my head. "It's not my fault you are at odds with nature."

"At least I grow friendly plants back home," Sariyah said, giving me a pointed look.

"Anyway." Tadeus gave us perturbed looks. "I came to tell you that Orran sent an invitation for you to visit this evening and have dinner with his people. My father already has plans and will be leaving within the hour—no idea what he's doing—so I'm to escort you there."

That was rather last-minute notice, but if the Andalagar leader wanted to see me, he must have a good reason. "Fine, but Sariyah is coming with us. Her grandmother was from the southern tribe, so he shouldn't object."

"Do you think I'll get to see a Pegasus?" Sariyah asked, eyes lighting up.

I nodded. "The Andalagar have hundreds in this territory alone, so they're hard to miss."

"Oh, I'm definitely coming with you."

"That settles it." Tadeus looked us both over. "You ladies have two hours to bathe and change before we go, so I suggest you finish here quickly."

***

We stepped out of the portal onto the Andalagar territory. As before, the waves crashed onto the beach a mere fifty feet away with the current tide. A cerulean turtle slowly worked its way along the sand, paying no attention to us as we passed but often lifting its head when the water touched its feet.

This place was such a serene location that I wondered who put the ring here long ago. Most others were placed more strategically, depending on the area's needs. I was certain this one was built in this location for the beauty that unfolded around it.

Turning away from the sea, I found Orran and several of his warriors flying toward us, though they were still a few minutes away. We'd arrived a little early. One thing I could say about Tadeus was that he hated to be late, so he'd pushed us to hurry.

Sariyah gasped. "Those are the Pegasi!"

"Yes," I said, enjoying her wonder. "Just take care once they land. Orran told me they aren't fond of most strangers and will bite."

"Like your plants?" she asked, lifting a brow.

"Something like that."

The Andalagar tribespeople landed and dismounted. Their horses folded their wings and began to graze as their riders left them. Orran moved to me first, kissing each of my cheeks. Except for a first meeting, this was their standard greeting.

When his gaze ran over my companions, I cleared my throat. "This is my cousin Tadeus, the second son of Lord Morgunn. I'm afraid my uncle couldn't make it on short notice."

Orran studied him for a moment. "You're not like your father."

"No." Tadeus' lips twitched. "In fact, we rarely get along."

"Excellent. Then you've already grown in my esteem."

My cousin let out a chuckle. "I could say the same of you. Those who like my father tend to be rather unpleasant."

"You're unafraid to speak the truth, even at risk to yourself." Orran squeezed my cousin's shoulder. "Perhaps I will insist on you representing your father from this point forward."

"Lord Morgunn won't like it, but you'll hear no argument from me," he replied with amusement.

I gestured at my best friend. "This is Sariyah. We grew up together and have always been close. Her grandmother was from your southern tribe."

The Andalagar chief's eyes warmed. "Have you visited there often?"

"Only once when I was a child, I'm afraid." Sariyah met his gaze. "My father decided the journey was too treacherous and didn't allow it again."

Since half the tribal lands were in the Oarwar desert and the other half in Veronna, it was risky for her to travel by land. Neither was safe for a three-quarter elf from Therress as far as routes went, and they had heavily warded their only portal ring.

"Couldn't Aella have taken you there?" Orran asked, frowning at me.

"Oh, she could now, but my grandmother and mother passed before Aella's abilities were strong enough to get us there, and my father had no interest in letting me go without them," she said, a note of defensiveness for my sake in her voice.

"Ah. Then, I will not hold it against either of you." He studied her for a moment. "But perhaps you should visit us more often so you might know more about your heritage."

She smiled. "I would like that."

Something about how they looked at each other made me think an attraction was developing. It wouldn't be the worst thing in the world. Sariyah tended to keep her relationships with men as minimal as possible, aside from casual sex. She was behaving very differently with Orran than with others. I'd have to watch their interaction and see how it went during the visit to be sure if I was imagining things.

"I was told you invited us for dinner?" Tadeus asked.

Orran nodded. "Yes, though that won't be for a little over an hour. Since you have not visited us before, my men will give you a tour of the village so you might learn a little about us. If you find that amenable?"

After hearing my uncle's description of his tour from last time, it probably wouldn't take long since they kept it rather limited, but I didn't point that out. It would still be more than what they let me see of the village previously. I only saw one building—where we ate a simple meal with Orran—before it was time to return to Ivory Castle.

"Of course," Tadeus agreed.

"I thought I might take Aella on a walk so we can speak further about the future," Orran said, then frowned at Sariyah. Obviously, my friend hadn't factored into his plans.

"She should come with us." I turned to give him a look, urging him to trust me with my eyes. "Sariyah practically knows me better than I know myself. You could ask her questions."

Comprehension dawned in his gaze. I was implying that I didn't keep secrets from my best friend, and he could speak plainly about whatever he needed to tell me. Thank the nameless ones, he understood.

"Very well, that does sound like an excellent opportunity."

Orran gave his men orders, and Tadeus obligingly followed the warriors. Thanks to my first visit, I knew the main village was only a twenty-minute walk from here. Orran lived at a more distant location, but this was the place where they preferred to host outsiders. They'd allow the Pegasi to graze since they could always beckon them with a special horn, each mount having a unique blowing pattern to summon them.

Sariyah and I followed Orran as he led us down the beach. I was glad he was taking the scenic route since I hadn't seen much of the coastline during my last visit. The shore was smooth here but became rockier, with swaths of purple moss covering everything as we moved south.

A few minutes passed before the Andalagar chieftain spoke, looking at me. "I assume I can speak openly in front of your friend?"

"Yes. I've told Sariyah everything, and she keeps my confidence," I said, giving her a thankful look.

She nodded. "Aella is only six months older than me, so we can't remember a time when we didn't know each other. I would never betray her."

"Good." He glanced between us. "Everyone should have friends like that."

"What made you request my presence on such short notice?" I asked.

Orran worked his jaw. "My spies informed me this morning of a secret meeting on a shore near Balzour that your uncle plans to attend this evening."

That was near the mines where we acquired the holmium dust I used for opening portals.

I frowned. "What sort of meeting?"

"My sources reported a group of dark elves arrived last night and have hidden in the cliff caves in anticipation of speaking with your uncle tonight." He pressed his lips together. "This is by no means the first time such clandestine meetings have taken place, but I fear they are escalating ill-fated plans that will not bode well for Zadrya."

My eyes rounded, and a gasp from Sariyah told me she was also shocked. "Are you saying my uncle plans to betray the king with the dark elves' help?"

Also, it amazed me that he was sharing this information. Was he like Darrow and had spies within the keep to know I had little loyalty to my uncle? Did my being secretly married to a known enemy of my land make me more trustworthy? Or was this his way of starting a mutual exchange of information for each of our benefits?

"Yes." Orran stared out at the water with a troubled gaze. "From what I've discerned, Lord Morgunn has never been fond of the king, though he is adept at appearing loyal. I've yet to confirm it, but I believe he wants the monarch gone."

"But to work with the dark elves is ludicrous." Of course, he did it once years ago, but I thought that was an isolated incident in his attempt to weaken Veronna. I couldn't believe he'd maintain a relationship with them, especially since he often cursed them at mealtimes. Was that part of his ruse?

And did everyone have spies all over the kingdom except me? I felt like my tutors skipped a lesson that I should have received, and perhaps given me a book titled *Introduction to Building Spy Networks in Paxia.* Maybe the Ivory Castle library had a copy, or certainly Porrine.

The Andalagar chieftain gave me a rueful look. "Says the woman married to a half-dark elf."

"You apparently trust Darrow more than my uncle," I replied.

There seemed to be so much more happening than I could begin to understand. The night I had visited my husband for his birthday, I'd hoped to ask a lot of questions after seducing him. I thought he might be more pliable then, but that plan went horribly wrong.

Orran nodded. "Darrow and I have exchanged critical information in the past. His intelligence has proven impressively accurate. I wouldn't say I trust him implicitly, but I do believe he has Zadrya's best interests at heart. He's playing a dangerous game doing all that he does, though."

Frustration filled me that I still didn't know much about that.

"I've met his mother and can only guess what role she plays in all this, considering she conspired with my uncle years ago," I said. It was another mystery as to why she'd done it, but the one time I'd asked Darrow after the meeting, he'd quickly changed the subject.

The chieftain studied me. "So your husband still hasn't explained anything to you?"

"No." I shook my head. "But I've only seen him once briefly since you and I last met, and there wasn't time to get into that sort of discussion."

"It's not my place to bring you fully into this intrigue, but I fear you're already in it to some degree, whether you like it or not. Press Darrow the next time you see him because, otherwise, you could be caught off guard, and that may result in deadly consequences."

I sighed, wishing I could explain how angry I was with my husband at the moment. That was definitely something that wouldn't be suitable to mention to the Andalagar chieftain, though. We needed to keep our marriage issues to ourselves. Well, except Sariyah, but talking about relationship troubles with best friends was always appropriate.

"I'll do my best," I promised.

"Good." He turned his gaze to Sariyah. "I have noted the look in your eyes and wonder if you might have something to add?"

She hesitated. "It could be nothing."

"You'd be surprised how often nothing is something. Our people have excellent instincts, and you likely inherited some of that gift," he said, giving her a generous smile.

"Well." She swallowed. "I've just noticed certain officers at Tradain sometimes leave with no notice for days and then come back without reasonable explanations on where they've been or what they were doing. It's always struck me as strange."

"How long has this been happening?" Orran asked, cocking his head.

"For several of them, as long as I've been paying attention—so over a decade—but a few more have joined in recent years, and they're disappearing more frequently. For example, it's almost once a month over the last year. Before, it was maybe every six months."

"That is suspicious," he agreed, brows drawing together. "Perhaps you should begin visiting me more often and providing details on such matters. Names and their magic specialties would be particularly useful."

Part of me wondered if we should be this forthcoming with Orran, considering we hardly knew him. I couldn't say what made him feel more trustworthy than most, except this had always been his homeland, as it had for part of my and Sariyah's family lines. The Andalagar would have a vested interest in protecting this world more than most. Maybe that was why it felt natural to speak openly about matters we might have otherwise kept quiet.

Sariyah blushed. "Are you asking me to be your spy?"

"Only if it might coincide with courtship," he replied, turning to face her and grasping her hands. "But first, you would have to pass the trial."

She glanced at me, and I nodded approvingly.

"Fine, I will consider it, but you'll have to prove worthy for me as well," she said, lifting her chin.

Orran laughed. "Pass the same initial trial as Aella, and I'll be happy to see what challenge you give me."

I wished I was allowed to watch, but they had to take that journey alone. It was why only the chief and I walked through the woods during our first meeting.

"Should I leave the two of you alone?" I asked, grinning.

"No," Sariyah said quickly, blushing.

Orran shook his head with amusement in his expression. "Not now, but I am grateful this meeting proved more productive than anticipated. Perhaps we can all find a way to work together toward a common goal. While Andalagar tribal lands will always be my priority, the fate of Zadrya certainly affects us. If we wish to keep peace, we must rely on assisting each other."

"Why are so many of you covered in scars?" I asked. The question had been niggling at me since we last saw each other.

The chieftain gestured for us to turn around so we could begin the journey back. "That is complicated. Some are from challenges among each other, many are from fighting dangerous beasts, but others occurred in service to a greater cause. Talk to your husband and get answers, Aella."

I nodded. "I am planning on it."

"Good. Let's discuss the feast we are about to enjoy," Orran said, positioning himself between me and Sariyah.

I listened quietly as he detailed the meal, where we would sit, and what behavior to expect. It sounded as if it wouldn't be one of the sedate dinners at the castle for sure. There'd even be fire and a lot of dancing. The trip here would be worth it for that alone if it got my mind off other troubles.

Chapter 40

Darrow

The sun shone down on us with a vengeance as we crossed the Oarwar desert. It was a barren wasteland with only the occasional rocky outcropping and dry shrubs to break the blindingly bright terrain. I spotted a pile of bleached bones ahead, many broken into jagged pieces, and amended that thought. Those were frequent features as well.

Death stalked this place, breathing dark promises of a terrible fate if we didn't turn back. Those relentless whispers on the wind weren't wrong. Only the strongest survived this hostile desert. Even then, there were no guarantees.

Threats were numerous and varied, including massive stinger bugs that flew in swarms, scorpions the size of wolves, and a scorching sun that grilled the inhabitants so intensely even the native animals needed frequent breaks during the day.

The first time I'd come here, I'd only been eighteen years old. King Worden had held a contest for those coming of age, awarding a hefty sack of gold for whoever first reached an ancient black obelisk that stood a hundred feet high in the middle of the desert. It'd hummed with powerful magic.

No one knew for sure how it had gotten there, but stories abounded that the nameless ones may have erected it. All I knew was that, when I'd touched it, I'd gained the power to mind meld with sebeskas and control them. It had shown me a vision, so I'd know what to do. Not everyone who encountered the square, onyx pillar received a gift. It was unpredictable. Sometimes, it extinguished their life, so they fell dead on the ground, or even made them vanish entirely, but it was part of the requirement to complete the contest.

To reach it, I'd spent three days crossing the unforgiving terrain on foot, fighting off attacks from vicious creatures and fellow contestants. In the end, I'd won the five thousand gold coins in the heavy sack and gained a clandestine job with the king, but over half of those who started the journey had perished.

Of those who survived and made it to the end after me, most chose not to touch the obelisk after seeing what it did to the first who died, but Worden waited there and watched. He gave smaller rewards to those who proved brave.

We never found the bodies of several who disappeared during the race. I'd brought back the head of a satyr to make a point. He'd set up a trap mid-journey, using his earth powers to move sand and bury me. The fool hadn't considered that, with my telekinesis, I could lift the mound off. I'd left the rest of his body for the circling vultures to devour.

Others had come at me as well, but that one had annoyed me the most, which was why I took his head. I couldn't very well carry any more decaying trophies through a hostile environment, though. That would have been ridiculous.

This time, I didn't travel on foot. We'd acquired large desert cats from a border village a mile inside the Oarwar desert, each of them varying shades of beige and brown. They could easily hold the same amount of weight as horses, had large paws that moved well over sand, and were surprisingly easy to tame despite being utterly vicious against predators. We started out with them yesterday at dawn. It became too hot by late morning to continue, so we took a break until early evening.

We'd spent most of last night traveling, but that had held other risks. Desert spirits came out to cast illusions that tricked the mind into going straight into danger. I'd used the clarity stone Aella gifted me to see through their effects and guide the rest of the group. If not for her timely present, we would have ridden into a fire lake and burned to ash with only our souls left to haunt the desert forevermore.

The foothills of the Sobaryan Mountains lay ahead in the distance. I could barely make out the high lavender peaks to the north that faded into mute copper as they descended south. The most powerful seer in generations lived in a cave there.

He was a troll and should have been dead long ago, considering he'd far exceeded other fae life expectancies and made it to nearly three hundred years old. I knew he was alive only because he still had supplies delivered to him every month. The nameless ones only knew why anyone would willingly make that journey so often, but perhaps he made it worth their while somehow.

Only an hour of daylight remained, and a handful of miles stood between us and our goal, but we'd entered the most dangerous section of territory. It was the place where Aella's mother died in her effort to reach the elusive seer.

"This journey cannot end fast enough," Jax said, grimacing toward the rugged hills where we headed.

I lifted a brow at him. "Don't forget the trip back."

He scowled. "Which is why I wanted your wife to come along with us so we could portal out once we got the information. We could have brought a portable ring."

"She's still angry with me for yelling at her on my birthday," I pointed out, shaking my head. "Also, I'm not so insensitive that I'd bring her to the place where her mother died. We will share the information with her once we have it, reveal our plans, and show her that her mother's journey wasn't in vain. Perhaps that will help me win her favor back."

We wouldn't have known to look here if not for learning the real reason Nerine and the other druids came to the desert, which had been kept quiet for a while after her death. That was vital intelligence I'd finally gleaned a few years back, but it took even longer to find out where the seer lived since I had no desire to wander the desert for weeks searching.

My mother had uncovered that final bit of information and gave me the details the night I brought Aella to meet her on Jolloure Island. From what she'd discovered, if the troll didn't wish to be found, he could camouflage his home. The clarity stone would aid us with any illusions he might cast. So many pieces of the puzzle had to come together before even considering this trip.

"Dare," Faina said with urgency in her tone. "The ground is moving suspiciously over there." She pointed to a spot several hundred feet ahead where the earth rippled and rose. Surprisingly, it barely made a sound.

Jax rolled his eyes. "Anytime the ground here moves, it's suspicious. Just say to look that way, and we'll get that danger is coming."

"You're such an ass," she said, glaring at him.

Loden narrowed his eyes. "The way the sand is disturbed, it has to be one of the giant worms."

The last time I was here, I'd managed to avoid them by taking a southerly route to the obelisk—far from their territory in the north-central part of the Oarwar Desert. I'd suspected I wouldn't evade them this time.

"Everyone get off your cats and toss your packs to the side," I said, dismounting as well before addressing my sister. "Do you think you can make the worm drowsy?"

Her ability to burn enemies with flames would be worthless against this creature.

Faina nodded. "I'll try."

We'd researched as much as possible about them before coming. While they were called "sandworms" by the natives of this planet long before fae arrived, they technically weren't anything like the smaller, harmless varieties. These were an odd species with traits from multiple other types since they had bones, excellent eyesight when topside, and teeth.

While they weren't entirely impervious to magic, all accounts described that most powers were dulled considerably against sandworms. It would need to be a group effort to bring down the massive creature. Even the desert cats seemed to understand the direness of the situation as they backed away from the incoming threat but also crouched in a way that indicated they'd attack when the opportunity arose. Their teeth and claws would be an asset in this battle.

Most likely, they'd traveled to these parts many times before and had experience facing such menaces since they were often loaned to travelers. We'd been assured that if we failed to return, the felines would have no trouble finding their way home without us. I had an odd suspicion that such an event had occurred before.

"Loden, start using your light magic the moment it appears aboveground and aim directly behind the head," I ordered before turning my attention to Jax. "Try to get on the worm's back and stab its spine as many times as you can."

Hopefully, that would limit its movement if he could get through to the bone.

"What are you going to do?" my sister asked, narrowing her gaze as I tossed my pack onto the pile with the others.

I grinned. "Face it from the front and keep it distracted from the rest of you."

She glared at me. *I hope you know what you're doing.*

I spent a significant amount of time considering the best method of attacking the worm before we left. This will work, I promised her through our twin telepathic connection. I needed to appear fully confident. We had to do this because failure wasn't an option.

She let out a dramatic sigh, tossed her brown and black braid over her shoulder, and faced the incoming sandworm. It was massive, based on the piles of disturbed earth left in its wake. Our only advantage was that it traveled slowly underground and gave us time to maneuver into the best positions. Once it surfaced, it would be able to move faster.

It began to swerve toward Jax, who was finding the best spot to jump on once the creature passed him. I recalled that the worm had excellent senses and could detect movement. Calling out loudly, I ordered my friend to hold still and began stomping the ground.

The disturbed earth immediately shifted my way. I took measured steps backward as it approached—only fifty feet from me now. Everyone else settled into their positions, unmoving as I drew our target my way. In the worst-case scenario, I could teleport, but I hoped it didn't come to that. Even short hops took nearly a quarter of my power each time. I'd already used some of my magic crushing stinger bugs that attacked us an hour ago and hadn't fully recharged from that. This battle would require a judicious use of my abilities.

At twenty feet away, its head blasted out of the earth, hanging suspended for a moment before crashing to the ground as it continued its forward momentum. Sand sprayed everywhere and covered us in a thin layer that stuck to our skin and clothes, which were already coated in sweat from the desert heat. I wiped my eyes to clear my vision.

Wisely, everyone kept their curses to themselves as I continued to back up and draw the worm's attention. The creature was beige with dark brown stripes. Its body was at least ten feet wide, and so far, at least fifty feet long, but the backend hadn't emerged from the ground yet. I wouldn't have been surprised if it were twice that length.

All over, the massive worm had malleable spikes that shifted to help it move across the terrain. My feet stilled when it opened large, black eyes and stared directly at me. Its gaze was cold and hungry.

A moment later, their sharpness dimmed as my sister held out her hands and pushed her powers to make the worm drowsy. I estimated at best that it would only make the creature sluggish, but that was far better than fast and alert. Even its forward momentum slowed.

It let out an ear-splitting shriek as Jax grabbed its spikes to climb on top of it, and Loden began hitting it with his light powers, with little effect against the tough exterior. I'd suspected any heat-based magic wouldn't work well based on desert survivor tales, but it had been worth a try.

The worm's breath was rotten, and I nearly gagged as the fetid odor reached me.

I spotted multiple rows of needle-sharp teeth at the top and bottom of its mouth. Not wasting a moment, I targeted those with my powers. They were small and easy to yank out despite the worm's resistance to magic. I plucked the teeth one row at a time as the creature began to thrash and made more pain-filled sounds. Blood dripped from the rapidly multiplying holes in its mouth.

The desert cats joined the fight, ripping and tearing into our target's sides more effectively than magic or swords. The sandworm twisted and tried to chomp down on the closest felines. One of them didn't dodge fast enough. I'd just finished removing the last of the creature's teeth when the cat disappeared inside the massive mouth.

I cursed under my breath, but a moment later, the worm opened its maw and spat the animal out. The cat snarled and growled as it rose to its feet before rejoining its brethren with fresh ferocity. New gashes and spurting blood in the worm's throat explained why it didn't keep its prey. Without teeth, it hadn't stood a chance against the fierce animal.

I used my powers to crush my target's eyes next until they were nothing more than empty orbs, and then I focused on the hint of brain matter beyond that. Before now, the worm's skull and other organs blocked my powers from reaching that vital location. I had a direct line of sight to it now and sensed the difference in my ability to latch onto it.

Also, the creature was weakening. Jax, Loden, and the cats had worn it down with numerous injuries. On the other hand, Faina heaved for breath and shook her head at me. The toll it took on her to keep the sandworm sluggish had become too much. Even heavily damaged, the creature would put up a stronger fight the moment she dropped her magic.

I locked onto its brain and focused with all my might, outstretched hands shaking, until I felt the organ crush under the weight of my power. It took nearly every drop I had left to do it, but the worm slumped as life left its body.

"Damn, that was a wild ride," Jax said, leaping from the limp worm.

Loden shook his head. "I've never seen anything resist my light power like that. I barely did any damage, no matter how much I tried."

The elf half of him was low fae, which was likely why he only had one prominent gift, but we had no idea of the strength of his druid father. I suspected he was on the powerful side since my friend had a better command of his power than he should have. Still, he was nowhere near Aella's magical ability. Her lineage on both sides gave her an incredible advantage.

We watched for a moment as the desert cats continued to tear into the sandworm with their extended fangs, consuming the creature's meat. They were due for a fresh meal anyway, and it would save us the trouble of hunting for their food. The rest of us pulled open our packs and took the opportunity to drink water and eat some dried meat.

After half an hour, we resumed our journey. The sun waned on the horizon, leaving us little light to complete the last few miles. It was full dark by the time I spotted the cave opening with only the glow of a half-moon to guide us. As I'd expected, the entrance was hidden with glamour, so it appeared as nothing more than rock and dry bushes. As soon as I pulled out the clarity stone, I was able to spot the path leading up to it.

"Follow me," I ordered the others as I guided my cat toward the trail.

It wasn't an easy route, but the agile cats managed it in less than ten minutes. A squat troll with deep, brown skin, heavy wrinkles lining his face, and frizzy gray hair sticking out in all directions stepped outside. He didn't appear the least bit surprised to see us. I supposed with his abilities, that was to be expected.

"Well, it's about time," he said in a grouchy, shrill voice. "Leave the cats outside and come in for tea."

We did as requested and found a delicate set of white porcelain cups with pink floral print waiting at a center table not far from the cave entrance. The place was surprisingly cozy with rugs covering the floor, comfortable furniture scattered in no discernible pattern, and the stone walls were nearly hidden by shelves upon shelves of dusty old books. A narrow opening at the back likely led to other parts of the cavernous home.

"Sit, drink," the troll ordered.

We reluctantly did as he requested. I took a sip and grimaced at the bitter, foul taste, but our host looked so pleased that I resisted the urge to spit it out.

The others had a similar reaction, though Jax turned his head to gag after swallowing.

I cleared my throat. "We came to inquire about the Naforya Fountain's location," I said, hoping to get through the meeting quickly. There was no telling what the troll might try to give us next if we lingered for long.

"Ah, that. It's on a planet far, far away—across the Milk Stone Galaxy. It won't be easy to reach," he paused dramatically. "But I know you've found the right person to help with the portal, so there is hope you can manage it."

"Yes, but a name for this planet would be helpful," I said, knowing we needed a designation before we could research how to reach it by portal. Hence, the perilous trip here.

He made a clucking sound and shook his head. "All in good time. There is much to discuss before you leave, and I must make sure you know all of it." He frowned and stared at his bare feet. "Where did my shoes go?"

Loden sighed. "You weren't wearing any when we arrived."

In fact, all he wore was a loose, gray tunic that reached his knees, failing to cover his hairy legs.

"Oh, well, I must find my slippers." He turned and headed toward the rear opening. "It gets cold at night."

As soon as he disappeared, Faina began banging her forehead on the table.

I leaned forward and rubbed her back. "I'll try to get the information we need quickly when he returns."

"You better." She lifted her head with exhaustion lining her face. "Because I don't know if I can keep from killing him otherwise."

Something told me the journey through the desert was the easy part of this quest.

Chapter 41

Aella

The summer heat was finally becoming more bearable as we edged toward autumn. Unfortunately, my uncle's recent behavior kept us all on edge more than usual. He'd grown moody, erratic, and short-tempered. I'd tried listening outside his office door this morning while he and Ulmar spoke alone, but he'd used a silencing spell. None of the stones I had left from my mother could counter the magic.

Whatever was said in there, though, left my uncle in an especially foul temper. He exited the office with a parting comment for his eldest son, spoken in a low tone I could barely catch. "Make them see reason, or this is all going to fall apart. I need you married to her as soon as possible to solidify this alliance."

My jaw dropped as I listened from the alcove where I hid.

"I'll suggest a quiet ceremony for sometime soon," Ulmar replied in a mollifying tone I strained to hear. "The king won't know."

Lord Morgunn grunted. "See that you do."

As they passed by my hiding spot, unaware of my presence, I stood perfectly still and mulled over their conversation. Ulmar had said he planned to get married, but there had been no further mention of it since. From the sounds of their discussion, his intended wife wouldn't be someone the king approved, yet he'd told me he already had permission. High fae couldn't wed without a monarch's permission, but in certain circumstances, it didn't have to be Zadrya's. What if it were Karganoth's instead?

I peeked around the corner. Rynn happened to be walking in the opposite direction as our uncle stormed down the corridor and crashed right into her. She barely managed not to fall. Then, he slapped and berated her for being in his way.

As she sobbed and cupped her cheek, my uncle marched past her. I ran to comfort her once he was gone. It took several minutes for Rynn to calm down, so I decided it was best if we went for a ride to escape the madness. What was my uncle planning, and why was it upsetting him? I hated that I'd lived my life naively for so many years without noticing his scheming and treachery.

How I wished to the nameless ones that I could leave this place for good and take my sweet cousin with me. If only I could get rid of my curse. Short of killing my uncle, there was nothing I could do.

The thought had crossed my mind, but I couldn't kill family—not even the awful ones. Not to mention, if I succeeded, I'd have to face my cousin, Ulmar, who would most certainly kill me without hesitation, and my uncle's loyalists would help him. I couldn't fight them all, nor spend the rest of my life hiding from them.

Rynn and I quickly secured our mounts and rode out to the forest. I wished Sariyah could have joined us. Things had seemed a little less daunting with my best friend here, but she had to return to work at Tradain a few days ago.

Interestingly, she seemed rather excited about spying for Orran and not the least bothered about helping him against my uncle. Her father was the commanding officer for Therress' army, but Norvin had never behaved suspiciously. I'd always seen him as quite honorable, most especially with his treatment of his family. Sariyah and I had discussed it briefly and decided he couldn't be helping Lord Morgunn in whatever scheme he'd hatched, particularly as King Worden's nephew. He'd always been loyal to the crown above all else, especially after his father's disappearance just over three decades ago. A mystery that had never been solved.

Something scratched at my senses as we followed a well-worn trail. I took a slow look around us, unable to pinpoint what bothered me. As our horses continued at a sedate pace, the feeling grew a little stronger, though I still couldn't identify the source.

Rynn stiffened. "I think something is hiding in the woods."

"Yes," I agreed, glad she was paying attention. "I'm not sure what, though."

Both of our horses' ears twitched, and their steps slowed. They didn't want to go any farther forward. I gestured at Rynn, and we brought our mounts to a stop. It was always dimmer in the woods because of the overhead canopy of foliage, but it seemed to be getting darker by the moment. I handed my reins to my cousin so I could dismount.

All the insect noises and birds chirping stopped as I took a few steps. If something attacked, I wanted to appear the most vulnerable to give Rynn a chance to run with the horses.

A loud, baying noise rippled through the woods, bringing a chill to my bones. My heart shot up to my throat as I looked for the source, but saw nothing. The sound felt like it came from everywhere and nowhere at the same time.

"Don't move," I said.

It tore through the air again, longer this time. I'd heard stories about this beast, but I'd never come across one. Few who heard it lived to tell the tale. Though it usually gave itself away with three haunting barks, one couldn't run fast enough to get away. It would kill us and the horses if I didn't take it down first.

"What is that?" Rynn whispered, eyes rounded as she sat still on her mount.

The final baying sound filled the woods, much closer this time.

"It's a Cù Sìth."

Shock filled her gaze. Most fae could go their whole lives without seeing one, but they were a bedtime story told to children so they wouldn't wander off alone. Everyone knew about them. We just hoped they stayed a myth and never made an appearance.

I pulled my dagger, knowing we'd get no further warning. A Cù Sìth moved without sound and didn't appear until the moment before it attacked. According to the stories, they were black, shaggy dogs the size of a cow with glowing silver eyes. Their unkempt fur hid powerful muscles underneath that could tear a person apart. No one knew why they came out sporadically to attack, as there was no discernible pattern to their prey. Men, women, young, old, strong, and weak, all were vulnerable to the fabled creature.

"As soon as it attacks, take the horses away quickly," I ordered in a low voice.

"But..."

"Just do it, Rynn."

Gathering my magic into my non-dominant hand, I prepared myself. A flash of black came from the corner of my eye. I pushed a torrent of wind in that direction, hitting the massive dog in the face as it appeared between two mighty burchar trees to my left. Its forward momentum slowed, but it didn't stop. The sound of horses galloping away sounded behind me. I didn't dare look back and kept my full attention on the Cù Sìth.

I'd never encountered anything that could resist such intense wind power.

The beast was exactly as described in the stories, except nothing could have prepared me for the cold, feral look in the animal's eyes or that they were nearly level with mine. The shaggy dog was so massive that it could probably eat Rynn and me and still be hungry.

Step by step, the Cù Sìth edged toward me as the wind buffeted its fur, and its dripping jowls rose to show the pink gums underneath. It was only ten feet away now. I didn't see how my dagger would do any good against the raging beast, so I quickly sheathed it. With the same hand, I concentrated hard to pull my light powers—desperate times called for desperate measures.

But before I could aim, the massive dog leaped. It moved in slow motion as I continued to push torrents of wind with all my might. It was hard to focus on a second magical ability simultaneously. He clamped onto my left arm, sharp fangs digging deep into my flesh as blood poured from the punctures. I screamed as the heavy gale I'd been pushing died, and I transferred all my power into my other hand, focusing it into a single beam of amber light. It cut through the Cù Sìth just behind its front shoulders, cleanly slicing the dog in half.

Loud *cracks* and *crashes* sounded beyond that, but I ignored them.

My gaze met the creature's silver one as I let go of my magic before the rest of the forest came apart. A flash of relief came over its eerie eyes before they dimmed to dull black. The back half of his body fell to the ground with a *thump*. Slowly, his jaws loosened, and the fangs pulled from my arm as his front followed the rest of his body.

I fell to my knees, heaving ragged breaths. My stomach curdled at the sight of the beast cleaved into two parts, with dark blood soaking the earth. I turned my gaze away from it, and I clutched my wounded arm. The look in the massive dog's eyes at the end disturbed me. It was as if I'd freed it from some horrible existence, and it was grateful for what I'd done. Perhaps there was more to the Cù Sìth legend than anyone knew or bothered to learn.

"Aella!" Rynn screamed, leaping off her horse to run toward me.

I'd noted the hoofbeats running away when the dog attacked, but she must have come back as soon as the fight ended. I was grateful she'd listened to me. She wasn't equipped to deal with such a creature, though healers did have offensive measures at their disposal. Those were never taught until they'd mastered their primary talent of helping people. Otherwise, they'd become something else—a dark and twisted version no one wanted to see. She was years from being ready to learn those skills.

"I'm okay," I said, breathing through the pain.

She glared at me with her blue eyes. "No, you're not."

Blood seeped from the fang marks on the top and underside of my forearm, dripping to make a separate puddle from the Cù Sìth's. Each bite wound was as wide as my fingertips. The creature had gouged so deeply that it nearly struck bone, and I grimaced at the sight.

"It could have been worse." I was lucky, very lucky, all things considered. Several of the trees in the woods couldn't say the same, where they lay broken on the ground. The ones near us were massive, and my light power had sliced through them like they were bread. At least they'd fallen away from the path.

"Yes," Rynn agreed, crouching to study my wounds. "And I think I can heal this."

I frowned. "You can?"

She'd been practicing her healing powers for four months now, and Briauna had reported that my cousin was quite powerful and advanced, but it still surprised me. Most people with her gift needed a year before they could do more than repair cuts and scrapes. Not to mention, she was supposed to be specialized in handling incurable diseases, not wounds.

Rynn placed her hands over my arm, brows drawing together in concentration. A tingling sensation came over me where she focused. I gasped. Before my eyes, the puncture wounds began to close. The pain eased at the same rate as my skin knitted together, fang marks vanishing as soon as they healed. It took her all of a few minutes.

"There, done," she said with a weak smile.

It must have taken a lot out of her. "I can't believe you did that."

She shrugged. "Briauna thinks I would have been a healer anyway, which is why I have stronger powers than normal. It's still exhausting. She says it will get easier with practice and as I get older."

"You're amazing." I gripped her shoulder. "Never let anyone tell you different, including our uncle."

Rynn nodded. "He's a chicken arse."

I laughed. That was the term I'd been using for years to avoid using actual curse words in front of her. I'd been so distracted lately that I hadn't used it in a while.

"Absolutely." I pulled us both to a stand. "Let's go home and report the Cù Sìth so they can deal with the body."

No point in some hapless person coming along to find the split carcass.

"Okay," she said.

I took one last look at the creature I'd killed and vowed to research their kind when I had the time. Something told me there was more to the story than anyone knew. Or possibly, no one had cared, but I felt like it should matter.

As I mounted my horse, a sebeska squawked from high above in the flat foliage of a burchar tree. It flew down toward me. I held out my arm to let it land, wondering how long it had perched there. If it had shown up during the Cù Sìth attack, it would have waited until it was safe before revealing its presence. The fact that it had been hanging out somewhere high lent credibility to that theory. They usually flew straight toward their target recipient without delay.

It wrapped its claws around my forearm, surprisingly careful of my bare skin. With my free hand, I took the rolled missive from the bird as it settled its wings. Tension filled me when I recognized Darrow's familiar handwriting. It had been a week and a half since his birthday, but I was still angry with him.

In the note, he gave a succinct apology for our last meeting. It hardly made me feel any better. After that, it requested that I meet him in three days in Porrine at a park using glamour to hide my identity. He knew I was due to visit my sister soon and wanted the use of my skills during the day when I usually couldn't join him. How he'd learned my schedule, I couldn't say. It varied some months, depending on my uncle and training. At the end of the note, he promised it would be worth my while to sacrifice the time.

I looked the bird in the eyes. "He has a lot of nerve asking anything of me right now."

A tilt of its head and a squawk was its only response.

"You can go back to him without a reply," I said in a clipped tone. "He can wait and wonder if I feel like showing up."

Then I lifted my arm, and the sebeska took off in flight. This day just worsened by the hour between my uncle, the Cù Sìth, and then Darrow's message. Did I really want to give up part of my much-needed visit with my sister for my cold, uncaring husband?

Chapter 42

Darrow

Janaseed Park was the largest and most popular park in Porrine, situated west of the royal palace. It was as crowded as I expected during mid-afternoon. Fae of all types strolled along the paths, and vendors were stationed throughout to serve drinks and snacks. Children played games on the blue-green grass in the central open area, kicking balls or chasing each other. Their laughter filled the air. I tried to remember a time when I'd ever been that carefree, but nothing came to mind.

Above me, crabarry trees remained in full bloom under the late summer sun. They regularly shed their numerous dark-red flower petals across the ground and pathways, adding pops of color to the greenery. They would die back in a couple of weeks when autumn arrived, as the thinner and shorter mistarr trees took over with their violet flowers.

The park only had four types. They were equally spread throughout the grounds, each blooming in different seasons. The spring and summer trees lost their mint-green leaves during the colder months, but the fall and winter ones retained their dark green foliage year-round.

A buffryfly fluttered around me and the bench where I sat, waiting for Aella. They were a cousin of the butterfly. Its body was round and small, no bigger than a fingertip, but its wings were large enough to cover my hand. They had a wide variety of colorful designs. This one was bedecked in swirls of blue and red, along with two black antennas that helped guide it toward the sweetest flowers. It wasn't interested in anything other than me right now since it had stayed here the entire time I waited—which was nearly an hour.

Aella was undoubtedly punishing me for the way our last visit went, but I had no doubt she would come despite what she told my sebeska. For now, I waited in one of the lesser-used paths at the rear of the park where foot traffic was light and tree foliage was dense. No one would be able to recognize me at the moment. I'd added glamour to conceal my identity because I didn't want anyone to recognize us together.

Zadrya's capital city was rife with spies. If my plans had any chance of success, we couldn't be recognized together. I emphasized that in the note I sent her.

She was wise enough that she'd surely listen to my instructions no matter her resentment.

My wedding ring suddenly warmed as it sensed its mate nearby. Aella must have just stepped through a portal and begun heading my way. I took out a worn sheet of yellowed parchment containing a map of the kingdom. A green dot on it showed her location, which was Porrine now. I folded it back up, relying on my ring to grow hotter as she came closer. It shouldn't take her more than ten minutes to reach me.

An elf couple, walking arm in arm, passed by the bench. They were so engrossed in their conversation that they didn't look my way, where I continued to sit with the buffryfly. It now rested on the seat next to me, crawling on tiny legs as it inspected the wooden slats.

Almost exactly ten minutes passed when a woman at Aella's height came around the bend in the path. She had golden-red hair, pale skin, and freckles across her cheeks. Her look was certainly different, with nearly all her features altered except her eyes. Their light-green depths fell on me with unrestrained irritation. Despite my disguise, she recognized me as well.

At her approach, the buffryfly flew into the air to sit on her shoulder. She gave it a brief smile before taking a seat at the opposite end of the bench. I said nothing as she smoothed her lavender skirt and avoided my gaze. At least glamour didn't hide her intoxicating floral scent, which I relished.

"What was so important that you needed to interrupt my time with my sister?" she asked, every part of her body tense.

"It's lovely to see you as well, dear wife." I stared at her rigid profile. "As for why you're here...we'll discuss that somewhere more private."

"Then why meet here?"

I turned my gaze toward the place where I suspected Jax now stood. My close friend had the ability to become invisible, but now, he revealed himself and gave me a nod. It had been his job to follow Aella from the portal and ensure her trip here was uneventful. His gesture let me know all was well.

"I had to make certain no one followed you," I replied.

She cast me a furtive glance. "Why would anyone do that?"

I stood and proffered a hand toward her. "I'll tell you more when we reach the townhouse, but first, we must stop at the market."

"For what?" she asked, standing on her own and ignoring my hand.

I sighed and dropped my arm. "You'll see."

Her posture couldn't have been more rigid as we walked side by side out of the park. I'd expected her to have some lingering anger over our last encounter, but not to this degree. My sister had been right that Aella would still be upset.

Before we parted ways again, I needed to return to her good graces, no matter what it took. While I was incapable of having any deep feelings for her, I did regret hurting her, and I could manipulate what little I did feel to aid my cause.

"I know you may choose not to believe it, but I am sorry for how things went the last time we saw each other," I said just before we stepped onto a main street beside the park. "It was my fault for not warning you that it would be dangerous to visit Siggaya again."

She cast me a cold look. "It's no problem. I was the fool who tried to make more of our marriage than what will ever exist, and I should have known better."

I flinched. "It meant something to me that you remembered my birthday."

"I doubt that," she said curtly.

I stopped and waited until she turned to face me. No one was nearby at the moment, so I took advantage of it. Whatever it took today, I would make it up to Aella.

Stepping closer, I cupped her cheek. "Your thoughtful and priceless gifts meant a lot to me and my sister. Considering the history between our lands, it caught me off guard that you would do such a thing. I was also sorry when Faina pointed out that not only did I miss *your* birthday, but I also forced you to aid in an attack on your people that night. If I'd known, I would have chosen another date."

"Why bother?" she asked, brushing off my hand. "I'm your wife in name only, and you hate my family and land. Please don't bother to pretend you care just to make me feel better because you need me for something. I learned my lesson and won't make that mistake again."

I couldn't stand the look of aversion on her face, even in her disguised form. It bothered me in ways I couldn't describe. "You do matter to me, Aella—more than should be possible. We are simply in a precarious situation where we must tread carefully in everything that we do. It doesn't mean I don't want more from this marriage."

"Really?" Her expression turned skeptical. "You can't ever love me, so what does it matter?"

I scrambled to find the right words. "Because a lack of love doesn't preclude me from caring about your well-being, hence why I was so upset that you put yourself in danger. I'd also like to build respect and trust in our relationship—even if there aren't deeper feelings."

Her expression softened a few degrees.

"There is so much..." she began.

Unable to resist another moment, I dipped my head and kissed her. She whimpered. I pressed gently, coaxing her lips to open as she slowly melted against me. One thing the curse did not do was curb my passion for my wife. I wanted her more than I'd ever wanted any woman, and that was enough to spark my need to work through this rift between us.

Those three days I'd had her in my home—even unconscious— made me despise the fact that I didn't have her close anymore. I couldn't protect her when she was far away. Watching the Cù Sìth attack her a few days ago had been one of the hardest things I'd ever done, though I was awed and proud that she defeated a creature most couldn't. Through the sebeska's eyes, I'd seen how she didn't hesitate to fight and protect her younger cousin. Aella was valuable far beyond her channeling abilities for her heart, compassion, and courage.

The heat between us grew, and our tongues danced. She couldn't resist the pull any more than I could. As ruthless as it might be, I would use that to my advantage. While I had her, I would kiss and touch her at every opportunity until she forgot about her previous anger. I would use her desire for me until her heart and soul were bound to me. The urge to make her mine grew stronger with every meeting.

She clutched my shirt, panting heavily by the time I pulled away. Her lips were swollen, and her eyes glazed with pure lust. I felt supreme satisfaction until her expression morphed into horror, and she stumbled back.

Aella scowled at me. "Stop doing that."

"Doing what?" I asked with an amused grin.

"Kissing me."

I ran a thumb over my own lips where I could still taste her. "Admit you enjoy it."

"That's not the point," she said, turning and beginning to walk again. "I shouldn't want to kiss you, so we shouldn't do it anymore."

I easily kept up with her. "Last time you saw me, you indicated otherwise."

She shot me a venomous look. "And you ruined it."

"Why? Because I was more concerned with your safety and put that ahead of our desire for each other?" I asked. I'd turn the tables on her every chance until she looked at that previous encounter differently. It wasn't as if I was lying. That was the reason I'd scolded her and pushed her away.

"If you cared at all, you would have been nicer about it," she retorted.

I winced. Of course, she had a point. "Yes, but you caught me off guard. I've apologized for upsetting you and plan to make it up to you."

"How?" she asked, arching an imperious brow. I wished I could see her in her true form without the glamour. Nothing could be more beautiful than her natural features, especially when she was angry.

I guided her through the vast open market just south of the park, filled with over a hundred specialty shops. Elves, faeries, gnomes, pixies, and more filled the crowded stone paths. The heat wasn't as sweltering as it had been in recent months, making it a nice day to venture out.

"We will start here," I said.

"What do you mean?"

Taking her arm in mine, I led her toward a shop that made beautifully designed receptacles. This particular vendor only came for two days a month, spending the rest of his time crafting his wares. I led her to the most expensive items on the back shelf that were etched with real silver and gold in numerous styles.

"Choose one," I said.

She cast me a wary look. "Why?"

"I owe you a birthday present."

Aella stepped away from me. "You don't *owe* me anything, and I don't want anything from you. Please don't do this out of some sense of guilt."

"You want nothing from me at all?" I asked and gave her a heated look.

She blushed and crossed her arms. "No."

Her denial of our attraction was adorable, but it wouldn't last.

"If you don't choose one, I will," I said, shrugging as if it didn't matter either way. Then I picked up the gaudiest one I could find. It took a special kind of person to appreciate something that resembled vomit in its painting pattern and colors.

She let out an exasperated sigh. "Absolutely not. I'll take that one."

She pointed at a small, plain one.

"Choose more carefully, please."

"This is ridiculous." She uncrossed her arms and threw them up. "I don't need anything from here, so why give me one of these as a gift?"

I lowered my voice and leaned closer. "Because whichever one you decide upon will be filled with holmium. It will be more than enough to last you for a very long time."

Her expression turned to one of shock. "But..." She glanced at the receptacles. "It would cost a fortune with how large these are."

"It still wouldn't equal the value of the gift you gave me, but at least it would be equally useful to you. I will also have it enchanted so only you and I can see it. That will make it easier to conceal." Of course, that would be an added expense, but it would be well worth it.

Aella hesitated for a moment, but finally, her shoulders sagged, and she turned to study each one more carefully. She settled on a pure cream vase with a matching stopper lid and silver filigree vines running from the bottom to the top. It was simple yet elegant.

"That one," she said.

I nodded. "Excellent choice."

We took it to the gnome merchant, who had his wife place the enchantment. After I paid with a bag of coins, we left and headed toward my townhouse. It was a twenty-minute walk from here at our pace, but I was content to spend a little more time alone with my mate before we joined the others. The market teemed with fae, and vendors regularly shouted at passersby, attempting to lure them with their wares.

Aella slowly relaxed next to me as she held the vase, casting appreciative glances at it when she thought I looked elsewhere. It turned out that the woman I'd married enjoyed thoughtful gifts. I would have to remember that and use it to stay in her good graces.

Just before we reached the market exit, a tall elf with long, dark silver hair stepped into our path. The dense foliage from the surrounding trees allowed shadows to swirl around his feet. I stiffened as soon as I recognized his perfectly chiseled face and pale skin. If the nameless ones had any mercy, Vaslav wouldn't recognize me with my glamour, but he was more astute than most.

"Darrow," he said in a cultured voice. "How fortuitous to see you."

There went that hope.

I pulled Aella to a stop beside me, taking her arm. "I doubt fortune has anything to do with it where you're concerned. What are you doing here, darkening our land again, Vas?"

Ten feet separated us, which wasn't nearly enough. The last time we fought two years ago, it ended in a draw that left us both broken and bleeding. While I could move objects with my mind, he could do the same with shadows. We'd faced off in the remote forest of Jolloure Island, or else it would have been catastrophic for a nearby population. Did he mean to curtail my ability to strike back by confronting me in Zadrya's capital, where the fae inhabitants were densest?

He smiled, flashing perfect white teeth. "How I've missed you these last two years. I saw our mother, you know. She was kind enough to host me, and we had a lovely time. Perhaps you could do the same?"

My wife shot an alarmed look at me. "He's Unseelie...and your brother?"

"Yes, though I prefer not to claim him." It was a complicated story that no one in my family enjoyed discussing, and even I had only pieced together bits and pieces, most of which came from Vas. Who knew how much of his word could be trusted?

She glanced at the imposing dark elf who emanated danger like a volcano ready to blow. "I can see that. Was this the one your mother..."

I shot her a look, and she immediately stopped her question. The less we said aloud, the better. I didn't want any Unseelie to realize that Aella was close enough to me that she'd met Zareen.

My brother's silver eyes flashed in the early evening light. "Eight years before Darrow was born, our mother married my father in Faelaria. Ten months later, she gave birth to me and left after I turned two to return to Paxia. I suppose our home world didn't agree with her."

"You made it disagreeable to all Seelie," I said tersely.

It was why we'd had to flee the planet. The fae used to all be one community, but an event long ago divided us. Each individual, regardless of race, had to choose their side and way of life. Elves, gnomes, pixies, and all the rest split down the middle, depending on their preferences.

We didn't interbreed for a long time, so offspring for more than a hundred thousand years were born with the distinctive characteristics of one group or the other. While the Seelie court drew upon their natural environment to harness their magic, the Unseelie court drew upon pain, violence, and other distasteful methods. Without a source for those, they weakened. Other small details allowed us to visually distinguish ourselves from each other, such as the Unseelie being much paler.

My brother shrugged. "It is not so bad, but descending from both courts makes it easier for me to tolerate either location."

What he really meant was that his father's side of the family couldn't handle direct sunlight without it burning their skin. They were fine in the shade or on cloudy days, but they detested how bright our world had been before, so they'd made changes with powerful magic.

Afterward, only the middle third of the planet ever saw the sun, while the rest remained in perpetual darkness due to thick cloud cover. They only allowed that much land to have natural light because most food-producing plants couldn't survive without it. Human slaves worked in that section. Where they'd found the magicless people, I didn't know. It was one of their many secrets.

"I've yet to see you when the sun is high," I pointed out. Many times, I'd fantasized about chaining him to the ground at noon to see how he handled it. Would his skin turn bright red, then begin peeling and flaking? That would be a lovely sight.

Vas gave me an amused look. "It is uncomfortable, but I do not burn as easily as my brethren. I'm certain you're sorry to hear that."

"You have no idea," I replied drolly.

Throughout the conversation, Aella kept glancing between us but wisely kept quiet. Perhaps she sensed the danger we were in with my brother here. I kept a tight leash on my power because I preferred my enemies to underestimate me, but Vas enjoyed intimidating people. His magic flowed in thick waves out of him, much of it swirling shadows, causing passersby to give him a wide berth.

"Who is this woman with you?" he asked, staring curiously at Aella.

I cursed my need to maintain a protective posture over her. "A friend."

He took a few steps forward, nostrils flaring. Unseelie had especially heightened senses. "Hmm, your scent on her is faint. Not a lover?"

The interest growing in his eyes made me wary. Two decades ago, when I first met him, he stole a lover. He took great joy in describing how much she preferred him. I'd never found out what happened to her, but she wasn't on this planet anymore. I'd felt responsible and tried to locate her to no avail.

Aella lifted her chin. "You might be pretty, but I wouldn't touch you with a garden snake."

Vas laughed. "It seems you'll have your hands full with this one—whoever she is with all that glamour covering her."

Of course, he could easily notice that. Any highborn fae would sense it.

"I'm not offering my hospitality, brother, so is there something else you want?" I asked.

He shook his head. "No. I only wanted to see how my little brother was faring since we last saw each other. It seems you stay busy as usual."

"Yes," I agreed.

He looked between Aella and me with a discerning gaze. "Well, I do have other matters to attend, so I will leave you for now."

Vas stepped back into the alley and disappeared into the shadows.

"He's a little creepy," Aella said, then looked at me. "Can you defeat him?"

"Unfortunately, no. We are evenly matched."

She swallowed. "So, if he ever attacks me, I think I'll skip wind and go straight for light power."

I'd seen what her gift could do when she fought the Cù Sìth, but it would be complicated to use against shadows. I wasn't certain if she could cut through them and hoped we'd never need to find out.

"Do not count on anything," I warned, making a mental note that we needed to develop her light magic at some point. The dismembered trees from the other day were proof of that.

"Thanks for the vote of confidence," she grumbled.

I softened my expression. "If it helps, I do believe the two of us could defeat him together. He is excellent at judging a person's magical strength, and I believe that detecting yours was the only reason he chose to remain amiable toward us today."

Some of the tension in her shoulders eased. "Good."

After watching Vas disappear into the main thoroughfare, we headed toward the townhouse. We had a busy evening, and my brother had cut into our precious time.

Chapter 43

Aella

D arrow's townhouse was located on the eastern side of the palace. We passed the spectacular royal gardens along the way. The flowers that bordered the colorful grounds all had delicate pink petals that would lean toward you if you came close, spraying a sweet perfume that could lift anyone's mood.

They made it that much harder to stay upset with my husband as he guided me through the busy street. People innately moved out of his way. His features were perfectly stoic except when he looked at me, and they softened a few degrees. I refused to fall for his act.

Along the garden row to the left we passed now, there were arrecian songbuds. The red and white flowers shaped like a large horn swayed gently and played a soothing song to passersby. I had to give the groundskeepers credit because they were quite high-maintenance, requiring special fertilizers from Southern Alavaar. Years ago, I'd introduced a few to my garden. They annoyed some of my moodier plants and sadly didn't last long. I found them in pieces soon after they were healthy enough to begin singing melodies.

We turned north. On our right was a long row of three-story townhomes constructed with large square-cut stones painted a soft gold to match the nearby palace. Each had expansive windows with hunter-green frames on every floor and a handful of steps leading up to the entrances, with small garden patches on either side of the porches. Alleys ran between them to allow horses and carriages to pass to the back, where the homes had private stables. Only high fae could own the residences in this section of the city.

They all looked the same, down to the types of plants at their front. I preferred nature to run a little wilder, and such deliberate conformity annoyed me, but I had no doubt it was required so that they didn't detract from the beauty of the gardens across the street.

Darrow led me to the fifth townhouse in the row, holding my elbow like a gentleman as we climbed the steps. I clutched my vase tightly. Part of me wanted to jerk away from him, hating that even a mild touch sent a thrill through my body. The other—very annoying—part wanted to sink into his hold and wished I could get him alone.

I was smarter than that. He might be my husband, but he'd always have his own interests ahead of mine. If he cared about my safety, it was more likely because he wanted my portal-opening abilities. Maybe he even took pleasure in ordering around his enemy's niece.

We stepped through the door, and Darrow took the vase from me. "I've got the holmium upstairs. I'll fill it now, but you'll find my sister and the others in the sitting room and kitchen down the way."

"You're just..." I glanced down the hall, able to hear voices coming from there. "Leaving me to deal with them?"

Amusement filled Darrow's eyes. "This is your home as well, so you're welcome to explore instead if you prefer."

I froze. "What do you mean?"

"Don't you remember what I told the king?"

Right. That he was preparing a place in the capital where we could safely live together, regardless of the outcome between our families. I'd put it to the back of my mind. "I don't...it can't really be mine, too."

"The deed is in both of our names, Aella."

I shook my head. "Why would you do that?"

He gave me an intense look. "Like it or not, our marriage is permanent. We may not behave as a true husband and wife right now, but that won't last forever. There will come a time—sooner rather than later—when everyone will know. I am doing all I can to prepare for that day."

Admittedly, I dreaded when that would happen and tried not to think about it. Never mind preparing for the fallout that would come. "Aren't you worried about how your father will take the news?"

"He already knows," Darrow said, quirking his lips.

"What? For how long?"

"Several months. When you spent those three days unconscious in Veronna, the safest place to keep you was in our castle in Darynia. I had to tell my father then, especially when he saw me carrying you."

That was embarrassing. The lord of Veronna—who killed my father—met me in person for the first time while I was unconscious and helpless. I tried to wrap my head around the fact that both of Darrow's parents knew about me, while none of my family had found out yet, aside from Rynn.

"How did he handle it?" I asked.

"He wasn't pleased at first, but I helped him see the wisdom of our marriage," Darrow said. Once again, he seemed so blasé about it while I felt panic rising in my throat. The more people who knew, the more likely it was that the word would get out.

I frowned at him. "How could he possibly be okay with you marrying an enemy of your family?"

"Because you, dear Aella, are the key to retrieving the Naforya Fountain, and he wants it restored as badly as we do," he said.

As I tried to formulate a response, he headed toward a set of stairs with ornate wooden banisters. I watched his broad back disappear up the steps. Why was Darrow dropping all this news on me now? First, he told me the house I just entered for the first time was also mine. Then, he said his father had known about our marriage for months. Ultimately, I played a crucial role in recovering the most significant object in our world, which had been missing for over six centuries. The Andalagar chief had indicated as much, but hearing it from Darrow made it somehow more real.

I rubbed my head. "He's going to drive me insane."

A feminine laugh sounded from down the hall. "Welcome to my world."

"Do you have wine?" I asked, heading toward Faina. "I really need wine."

Darrow's twin sister arched a dark brow. "Will it affect your ability to open a long-distance warded portal?"

She stood there in tight black pants and a matching long-sleeved tunic. It was still summer, yet she'd dressed for a fall weather outing. She also had her brown-black hair pulled back in a braid the way most women did before a battle. It appeared there was a lot more to this visit than I anticipated.

"Um," I stuttered at the random question. "Not if I keep it to only one glass. Why?"

"Because after dinner, we need you to open one."

I drew in a deep breath. "I'm not going back to Alavaar tonight, am I?"

"Nope."

"What's for dinner?" I asked, realizing I'd skipped lunch for a dragon ride with my sister before I had to take the portal to Porrine. My stomach rumbled as I caught the scent of food and moved toward Faina.

"Almornut stew with chippan."

Surprise filled me. "That's my favorite."

"We know, but luckily, everyone here loves it, too," she replied, guiding me into a large sitting room.

Just beyond it was an open dining area with six place settings. Jax and Loden were already sitting at theirs, deep in conversation. Both wore garments similar to Faina's dark tunic and pants. They looked up at our approach and gave me a nod.

I frowned at Darrow's sister. "How did you know what food I liked?"

She shrugged. "Don't you think my brother questioned Cam extensively to learn everything he could about you?"

I stopped in my tracks. "Please tell me he didn't."

"Sorry, he did," Faina said, gesturing toward a chair near the end for me to sit. "I was there, and it was most enlightening."

My husband interrogating my former lover—who happened to be a spy—about me was more than I could handle. "Okay, I can't do this." I spun on my heels and headed back to the front entrance. "You all are too much for me."

Having people who had been enemies for my entire life suddenly start dissecting everything about me was horrifying. I didn't care about their supposed motives since they could have discovered things I'd rather keep private. Camden and I had been together for years, and I'd trusted him. He'd been a great confidant when things were especially difficult in my life. While he didn't know about my uncle's harshest punishments, he did know many other things.

"Aella, please. We're trying to be more upfront and honest with you," she said, rushing to follow.

Was she serious? I glanced back at her as she tried to close the gap between us. "Disrespecting my privacy is not the way to go about it."

Continuing forward, I ran straight into a large, male chest. Darrow had just come around the stairs into my path. I tried pushing past him, but he took hold of my shoulders.

"What's wrong?" he asked.

I gave him a furious look. "First, you dump multiple secrets on me that you should have told me sooner, like that Vas is your brother, and then I find out you've been invading my privacy in the worst possible way. Let me go."

"I need you here, Aella," he said with an intensity that surprised me. "After what happened in Siggaya, I decided we should be more upfront with you. My sister was only doing what I asked."

Faina's footsteps faded as she returned to the other room.

Lifting my chin, I glared at him. "You asked my former lover for personal details about me. Do you know how horrifying that is or how it might feel like a violation? Why not ask *me* those questions?"

"There are time constraints with each of your visits, and speaking with Cam was a faster way to get the information I required before you came tonight," he said, squeezing my arms gently. "After missing your birthday, I realized I had significant gaps in what I knew about you on a personal level."

That would be endearing if I didn't feel certain he had ulterior motives.

"I thought you had plenty of other spies to find out whatever you wanted," I said, unwilling to give him an inch.

His lips quirked up. "Unfortunately, none of them are inside your uncle's castle. They can report your movements in certain locations, but that doesn't help me with your favorite foods or habits out of their view. Trust me when I say your cooperation this evening is vital, and you'll understand once I explain."

I tucked that tidbit about the spies away. "Do you promise to ask me from now on?"

"Yes." Darrow nodded. "I wasn't overly fond of asking Cam about you, and I don't believe he felt very comfortable about the topic of discussion, either."

"I think I'm going to have nightmares about it," I said, grimacing.

He scowled. "That is nothing compared to me having to go to him, knowing he's had you numerous times while I haven't been with you fully. It was all I could do not to stab him in the throat."

"You started it by stipulating we wouldn't have sex when we made our marriage bargain, but I still gave you a chance on your birthday," I pointed out regretfully.

"Under the circumstances, that night shouldn't count against me." Darrow leaned closer and whispered in my ear. "But I hope you will reconsider after our little trip this evening."

"You mean stay the night here?" I asked, shivering as his breath tickled my skin.

He pressed his lips to my neck, trailing kisses to my shoulder. "I'll make it worth your while, Aella. I promise. You will not leave our bed in the morning without feeling fully sated."

It was very hard to resist him, considering how much time had passed since I'd last been intimate with anyone. Not to mention all the late nights I'd spent wondering what it would be like to sleep with my husband. Why did he have to have the most intense looks I'd ever seen on a man? Why did he have to have a seductive voice that could light up all my senses? He was a tempting package, and I desperately wanted to see more. I needed to slap myself.

"We'll see how the rest of this evening goes," I whispered tauntingly. There was little chance I could resist him if I stayed the night here, but I wouldn't make it easy.

"Very well." Darrow pulled away with heat in his eyes. "I'll consider that a challenge."

I took a slow step back while keeping my gaze on his. "Then you better be prepared to work hard for it, and even then, I might deny you."

He gave me an arrogant smile. "Oh, dear wife. I promise you'll be begging for more before the clock strikes midnight, and even then, I might keep playing with your body until you're mindless with need and begging. I do enjoy watching my enemies plea for mercy."

I felt myself growing wet between my thighs at his words. That was only six hours away, and now I'd be doing a mental countdown, anticipating whether he kept his vow.

"Dinner is ready," Jax called from the end of the hallway.

I nearly jumped, having forgotten about everyone else. "Who cooked?"

"Bogdan. He's an expert at quite a few dishes, but especially your favorite," Darrow said, taking my hand to guide me toward the dining area.

His palm was warm and strong in mine. Even that small touch sent my senses into overdrive, and I had a feeling I would spend the whole evening trying to resist him. I was so distracted that it took me a moment to comprehend what he'd said.

"Wait, Bogden? Isn't he supposed to be guarding Jolloure Island or something?" I asked. Not to mention, he was a full dark elf and not supposed to be in Zadrya.

Darrow guided me toward the dining room table. "It's a tedious job, so he's allowed breaks. The king has given permission for him to visit for a few days as a favor to me."

"Another favor?" I asked as he pulled out my chair.

"Trust me when I say that I earn it."

I took my seat, smoothing my skirts. "Will I ever find out what has endeared you to the king so fully?"

"Let's see how tonight goes." He sat at the head of the table in the chair closest to mine. "I think what I have to tell you will be more than enough to overwhelm you for now."

That sounded ominous. "Fine. So, where are we going?"

He waited to reply until Bogdan finished ladling stew into our bowls. Freshly baked bread slices were already on everyone's plates, which were traditionally served with the dish. I took a bite, unable to wait since it looked so good. The taste of the bread was divine.

"The Isle of Penoria," he replied.

I shot him a confused look. Over the years, I'd visited the faeries' island several times and knew it well. "That portal gate isn't warded."

"We're not going to Tinkarous," Faina said, seated at the opposite end of the table. "Our destination is in a remote area on the eastern side of the island that the faeries don't want outsiders visiting."

I only had two rune sequences to the island—one to the city and another along a popular stretch of coastline on the southwest end. Neither were warded. They must have discovered a third that the royal library tome didn't list. How many more was I missing?

Bogdan finished serving everyone and took a seat to my right. He gave me a short nod before digging into his meal. Despite his being a full dark elf, it didn't bother me to be close to him. He had such a quiet and reserved nature that he didn't send any alarm bells ringing like many others of his kind. Even with Darrow only being half, he troubled me more. I was just getting used to it and maybe even learning to enjoy the curl of fear he stirred in me.

I took a spoonful of the stew, blew a few times to cool it, and took a taste. The flavors rolled over my tongue, tantalizing and spicy. "Oh, wow. This is so good."

Bogdan gave me a small smile. "Thank you."

"What is so important that we must go to this remote part of Penoria?" I asked, turning my attention to Darrow.

He wiped his mouth with a cloth napkin. "A world-traveling gate."

"Isn't there already one in Jolloure?"

"Yes." He took a sip of wine. "But that one only leads to locations at our end of the galaxy. This one was designed for more distant travel."

As someone who adored discovering new places, that caught my attention. "Like where?"

"A planet called Earth, where we believe the Naforya Fountain is located," he replied.

I nearly choked on my stew and had to swallow carefully, followed by a sip of my wine. He'd actually named the location, which no one should have known. "How can you be certain?"

"We recently found what your mother sought all those years ago in the Oarwar desert," he said, giving me a sympathetic look.

My chest tightened. Mom had lost her life trying to get that information, and Darrow somehow succeeded. "How did you do it?"

"It took years for my abilities to grow strong enough that I could kill even the largest creatures in the desert who got in my way," he replied, shrugging.

Right. Since he was telekinetic, even giant worms would struggle against his powers. I hadn't considered such a possibility, but clearly, he'd been planning the trip for some time. As I reviewed everything he'd said, I realized why he'd wanted me all along. I'd just given myself to him, having no idea he needed me even more than I needed him.

"That's the real reason you took the deal to save my cousin," I surmised, the ramifications filling my head. I looked at Faina. "Neither of you had any intention of killing me, did you?"

She leaned back in her chair, pasting on that same self-assured smile her brother often gave me. "It was fun watching you squirm, and don't act like you didn't enjoy pinning us to the wall."

"Fine." She had a point. "Maybe I did, but it doesn't excuse manipulating me."

Jax looked up from his half-finished stew. "Maybe they manipulated you a little, but it wasn't like they could come out and say you were useful to retrieve the fountain. Darrow had to see if we could trust you with the information first, though I don't know why he does now."

Among Darrow's friends, he was the only one I didn't like at all. It never took him long to get me upset. "Easy for you to say when you're not the one who is constantly forced to use your powers, including by people who are supposed to care about you and make you do things that go against what you believe is right."

I clenched my hands in my lap.

"If you tried to resist at all, then you wouldn't help your uncle attack our cities and kill our people," he said, glaring at me. "My father is dead because you opened a portal where you shouldn't."

My gaze widened, and now I finally understood why he'd always been hostile. "I'm sorry to hear that."

"What difference does it make to you? He was a simple blacksmith, but that didn't matter to your uncle's army when they ran him through." Jax paused, working his jaw as deep pain filled his brown eyes. "It didn't stop them from raping my mother, either."

My chest tightened. "That's terrible."

"Yeah, it is, but you'll keep opening the portals for him anyway, won't you?" he said accusingly.

Of course, he couldn't know the price I paid every time I resisted, but guilt ate at me to hear his story. Should I have fought harder, no matter the consequences? I pushed my bowl away, no longer hungry, and ducked my head so no one could see the expression on my face. The pain from the many times I'd fought my uncle when I disagreed with him came flooding into my mind. Could I have taken more punishment for the sake of saving civilians?

Jax continued, "Do you even lose sleep for what..."

"Jax, that's enough," Darrow interrupted in a firm voice.

"But..."

A chair scraped across the floor. "I said *that's enough!* Aella didn't attack your family, nor is she afforded many choices about anything. If you can't accept my wife, then get out."

He'd spoken in a loud voice that startled me. The fury in his tone revealed an intense depth of anger that I was surprised he felt on my behalf. Only one other time had he sounded that way, and it was on Jolloure Island months ago.

Silence reigned in the room for a full minute until I finally heard Jax's reply, "You're right. I shouldn't have said those things. I'm sorry, Aella."

I drew on the strength I used when my uncle said horrible things to me at the dinner table. No one had practiced that art more than I, and deep breaths helped. Darrow had defended me, and everyone else at the table appeared embarrassed by Jax's behavior. To be fair, he had a right to his anger. I wouldn't ruin a chance to inspect a ring that might allow us to retrieve the Naforya Fountain. Our planet was getting weaker daily without it, and one argument wasn't worth forsaking that critical fact. I was old enough and mature enough to know where to focus my priorities.

"It's fine." I lifted my head and gave him a weak smile. "You aren't wrong to be upset, and I understand that."

He dipped his chin. "Thank you for acknowledging it."

The tension in the room eased.

Darrow reached under the table and took my hand, unclenching my fist. "I will make it clear to him that it's not an appropriate subject to bring up again."

"Please let it go," I said, giving him a pleading look.

His expression said it wasn't the end of the conversation, but he'd let the subject drop for now. I breathed a sigh of relief when he drew his hand away and settled back into his chair.

"Jax is often an ass," Bogdan said, glancing at me with amusement in his dark gray eyes. "I find keeping a piece of rotten fruit on hand to throw at him makes him less likely to say foolish things."

"Like a *perrun*?" I asked, referring to a dark-red piece of fruit that grew to about the size of a fist. It was sweet and juicy when picked at the perfect time, but turned very mushy once it became overripe.

He let out a deep laugh. "That is my preferred choice. I apologize for being unprepared for it during this visit, but I won't be remiss next time."

Jax rolled his eyes and crossed his arms. "This is why I usually avoid your visits. Last time, I was picking pieces of perrun out of my hair all day because you squashed it on my head while we were on the road, and I had no way to wash it out. I still haven't forgiven you for that."

"I'm sure I'll have trouble sleeping tonight now that I know," Bogdan said wryly.

Faina studied her nails before looking at Jax. "You need to remember that our side has killed Aella's family members, too, so maybe we should remember both lands have lost a lot. If you can't back off, I'll simply put you to sleep until it's time to leave."

"You wouldn't dare." He narrowed his eyes. "You already know what I'll do in return."

"Oh yes, use your invisibility to sneak up and scare me repeatedly." She snorted. "I'll just keep a circle of fire around me so you can't get close."

I'd wondered what her other magic talent might be, and now I knew. Flame-wielding was one of the most common gifts among high fae, with about one in ten having it. Of course, the level of ability to use it varied with each person. I had a feeling she was very strong.

Loden sighed where he sat directly across from me, having not spoken once throughout dinner. "Do you see what I must deal with regularly? Now you know what you'll face when you fully join our circle. I wouldn't blame you if you ran for the Sobaryan Mountains, but I do hope you'll stay and help me keep them in line."

I couldn't imagine how I'd ever be allowed to leave my uncle's home, even once the truth of my marriage came out. He'd want to keep my power for himself or kill me so no one else could have it. That was a chilling thought.

"Please eat, Aella," Darrow said, nudging my bowl back toward me. "It will be a long night, and you'll need your strength."

"Oh, yes, a lot of walking involved," Faina added as she took another bite of her bread.

The twinkle in my husband's eyes implied something more than that. I averted my gaze from him before he made me blush with his obvious thoughts. At least my emotions were calm again, and the knot in my stomach had loosened. I resumed eating my meal, grateful my appetite had returned.

Chapter 44

Aella

Darrow had set up a temporary portal in the yard behind his house so we wouldn't have any observers for where we went. The ring was better constructed than any mobile ones I'd used before—thicker and sturdier. As I began channeling, I found that pushing sufficient power to reach the mysterious Penoria location was nearly the same difficulty as when I'd performed a similar task for the Andalagar chief with the fountain's former site.

Darrow stood waiting, no longer using glamour. Only I would maintain mine as a safeguard while we traveled together. I was no longer in the dress I'd worn when I arrived, though. They had a similar black outfit to Faina's ready for me, so that I could change into something more practical for the journey.

Apparently, we were going to be walking through rough terrain for an hour while trying to avoid faeries. There were likely dangerous creatures along the way as well. Since I'd never been able to explore Penoria beyond the two portals on the southwest end, I was excited to see the opposite side of the island. I only hoped we didn't run into trouble.

The ring popped, and a blue glow appeared. My hands trembled. The wards for this one were considerable and multilayered, so they continued to resist me even after I made the connection. I didn't want to hold it for any longer than necessary.

"Hurry," I urged.

No one hesitated to step inside except Darrow, who insisted on crossing with me. We leaped into the portal that lay flat across the ground, holding hands. My husband used every chance to touch me, and I had no doubt it was part of his plan. He was well aware that I was drawn to him and struggling to resist his seduction efforts. In all my thirty-three years, I'd never felt this level of attraction to anyone. Why did it have to be him, of all people?

We stepped out to the other side, discovering the east Penoria ring was established and upright. A dense forest surrounded it, with only one narrow trail leading away. The others had already moved close to the trees, nearly blending with the dark shadows. We needed to get away from here quickly in case anyone was nearby.

Darrow led the way, silently indicating that I stay directly behind him. The other four followed us as we navigated the trail. While it wasn't ideal to use a well-traveled path, I couldn't see another option. The trees here grew their branches starting from the ground up rather than higher, and between them, all sorts of thick brush grew. Tractvines were plentiful here. I sent out calming magic so they wouldn't attack us because once they caught someone, it was almost impossible to extract them from the plant's clutches.

In all my travels, I'd never seen so much vegetation condensed together. The only gaps were well above our heads. I supposed that made sense because faeries had wings, so they didn't have to travel on the ground much. Still, the soil must have been extra rich to nourish that much life.

We'd only been walking about ten minutes when a swarm of red gornetts swarmed toward us, buzzing loudly. I stopped at the same moment as Darrow. They were my least favorite insects with their five-inch, oblong bodies, sharp stingers, and double sets of wings. I'd never seen fewer than fifty flying together, and tonight, it appeared there were at least that many.

We stood frozen in the hope they would pass. At first, they appeared to be heading in a different direction, but unfortunately, they came close enough to catch our scent. I cursed inwardly. We didn't have them in Therress, as we'd killed them off centuries ago, and we quickly eradicated any that migrated into our land. Most other elf-dominated territories did the same because they had an unnatural love of our blood. The stingers could strike deep and draw as much as possible before flying away. If a swarm attacked one person simultaneously, they usually killed them unless the person had an especially large body.

As soon as they came within ten feet of us, they suddenly froze. I had no doubt Darrow had grabbed them with his mind. In the next moment, their crushed bodies fell to the thick forest floor. He sent them into the brush where no one would notice their carcasses.

In a pinch, I could have blown them away and then run to put as much distance as possible between me and them. I only preferred not to exhaust what little power I had left after opening a difficult portal. While I still had doubts about Darrow on some things, I had complete faith in his ability to protect us. There was no disputing he was one of the most powerful fae in the realm.

We continued down the path, moving painfully slow as we navigated fallen trees, shallow creeks, and other native hazards in the area. The querills became our next close encounter. A family of five grew angry as we passed by their tree and climbed halfway down with their sharp claws. The brown and white stripes made them easy to see when they moved. We had plenty of them in Therress, but it was easier to work around their small territories in open forests.

Their appearance could be deceiving, with their fluffy heads and tails making them look cute, especially since they were no larger than a sebeska. Once they opened their mouths and exposed their long, pointy teeth, it was clear they didn't have friendly intentions.

Darrow used his powers again, holding them still until we were safely out of their territory, which usually ranged about fifty feet. We breathed a sigh of relief when the danger passed. They couldn't have killed us, but their bites would have hurt, and we might have needed to kill them to stop the attack. Ideally, we wouldn't interfere with the wildlife too much while here.

Twice, we also had to stop and hide in the brush while faeries passed overhead. The flutter of their wings was loud enough that even in the dark forest, we could hear them coming well before they came into view. I only worried my thudding heart would give me away.

With all the obstacles, it ended up taking over an hour to reach the ring. It was impressive at a distance, larger than any I'd ever seen, with dark silver metal nearly two feet wide and eight inches thick. Even the algodonite stones were especially big. Unfortunately, a chunk of the portal had broken off on the lower right side, leaving a partial gap. It would never work as it stood now.

After a thorough search of the area, Darrow rubbed his face. "The source we used to locate the ring mentioned there would be damage, but it appears someone not only fractured it but also removed the missing piece. We need to determine what type of metal they used for constructing the ring to replace it."

"At least all the stones and runes are intact," I said, trying to see the bright side.

Loden moved closer to the broken end. "It will take a magic wielder specializing in metalwork to fix it."

My cousin Tadeus could likely manage that. He was powerful enough, but I didn't know that we could trust him with something like this. The others would balk at the idea, anyway. I'd wait and see if they had better alternatives before considering bringing him up.

"Do you know the rune sequence to Earth?" I asked, since he hadn't mentioned it.

Darrow shook his head. "That is yet another task. Having the location's name is a solid first step, but we still need the sequence, and there is a timing issue."

I frowned. "Timing issue?"

"For instance, Faelaria can't always be accessed by a portal. It's close enough, though, that if it doesn't work, you can wait a few hours to try again. With Earth being much farther away, the difficulties will likely be greater for traveling there and back. We'd need precise calculations to avoid being trapped on an alien world for too long," he explained.

I mulled that over. "Like if too many stars are in the way between our point and theirs?"

My portals cut through trees and mountains, but I'd read a book in the royal library that mentioned the sun and certain types of planets could create interference. At the time, I'd wondered why that would matter, but I supposed it made sense when traveling through space.

"Yes, exactly."

"That source of yours gave you more information than I would have expected," I said, surprised he already knew so much. It also hurt to discover how close my mother had been to answers before dying.

Darrow grimaced. "He was a very old seer living in a cave where the Sobaryan Mountains turn to foothills in the Oarwar desert. The troll wasn't pleasant, and it took hours to get the pertinent information out of him. We had to hear random rants about unrelated matters as well."

"Don't forget that awful tea he insisted we drink," Jax said, shuddering.

Faina grinned at him. "It wasn't that bad if you pinched your nose."

"Your humor never fails to delight me," he said dryly.

A rumble of thunder sounded in the distance, and we all looked up to spot a bright flash in the night sky. The wind was picking up as well. All my senses told me it would be storming soon, and it wouldn't be pleasant when it began.

"Let's get the measurements on the ring and then head out," Darrow said, addressing Loden.

The half-elf, half-druid nodded and drew something from his pocket as he headed toward the damaged section. Faina, who carried a small pack, handed out flasks of water. We gratefully drank them down. Loden finished his work and quickly took a swig before Darrow's sister repacked everything.

As we returned to the forest, the air began to cool. Only five minutes into our walk, it started to pour. We stopped worrying about being careful since all living creatures with sense would take cover during the deluge and hurried as fast as we could through mud and puddles.

Chapter 45

Aella

When we stepped through the primary portal for Porrine, mud covered us. It was caked up to our knees and splattered everywhere else. I wished I could have brought us directly to Darrow's house, but temporary rings lacked a unique rune sequence and only worked one way. That left us with no choice except to trudge through the capital city as our boots squished with every step.

Darrow held my hand as we walked past the palace's rear, choosing to cut through the poor section of the city rather than the statelier front. It was nearly ten at night, but people still meandered the streets as they left parties or taverns. We preferred to avoid seeing anyone who might recognize us.

"When the time is right, I could set up a permanent ring at the townhouse if you want," I said, looking up at him.

He lifted his dark brows, mocking amusement in his gaze. "You only saw our home for the first time today, and you're already planning changes?"

I rolled my eyes. "Do you have any idea how much it would cost to hire someone to do it?"

"No. How much?" Darrow asked.

"For a small one that will only allow two people to enter at a time, you can expect to pay at least twenty thousand gold coins," I replied.

Everyone turned to look at me with surprise.

Darrow cleared his throat. "And how much would you charge me?"

"Only the cost of materials, which was about sixteen hundred when I built the one in my garden. Of course, I took my time finding the best deals and had to do it in stages since it was a pain sneaking everything to its final location. I made one for a village in Alavaar that was large enough for four to pass at a time, and I charged them seven thousand since that was all they could afford. The supplies for that one ran me nearly three thousand."

That had been one of the rare times I could earn significant funds for myself without my uncle knowing about it. The village had a portal channeler who could transport them within their kingdom, but he wasn't strong enough to infuse the ring with the power needed to become permanently active. That was how it would naturally generate its unique rune sequence. The moment the magic fused into it, the algodonite stones would flash in the correct order ten times, so one could ensure they recorded it correctly.

The people in the area were so excited that they wouldn't have to travel for two hours on foot to the next closest ring anymore, and I became an honorary member of the town for my efforts. Only seven channelers between the four realms on Paxia could set up a new portal, so we could charge a premium for our work and get away with it. The quote the village received from the only person who could perform the service in Alavaar was for twenty-five thousand gold coins. They were very grateful that I had been willing to settle for less than a third of that.

"Why wouldn't you ask for more?" Darrow asked, curiosity in his gaze.

I gave him an affronted look. "You're my husband, and you said it's *our* home, so that would be ridiculous. Also, I'm probably the only one who will use it. I'd be doing myself a favor."

"Hmm. Good point."

We fell silent for the last few minutes of our squishy trudge through the city that drew a few pairs of eyes. Since we were coming from the north, we had to pass ten townhouses before we reached ours. Everyone pulled off their boots when they reached the door. As soon as I set mine down, Darrow took my hand and pulled me toward the stairs.

"Goodnight, everyone," he said, rushing me away so fast I couldn't even protest before we were on the second floor.

His bedroom was at the front end of the hall, with a view of the royal gardens across the street. I barely had a moment to look around before he shut the door and pressed me against the wall. As I started to say something, his mouth came down on mine. I resisted at first since all I'd thought of after the rain on Penoria began was a hot bath. His fiery kiss made me forget everything except his heat pressed against me.

It wasn't until he withdrew his mouth to rain kisses down my neck that I regained some of my senses. "Darrow, we need to talk about this first."

I'd had time to think about our relationship and how to handle him. No matter how much I tried, I knew I didn't have the strength to resist him, but I could set boundaries. If he respected me, he'd follow them.

He pulled back to look me in the eyes. "What do you wish to discuss?"

"I'm not going to pretend at this point that I don't want you because we both know that would be a lie, but I need to set limits. We can have all the hot sex you want tonight and whenever the opportunity arises, if you promise to stop trying to make me feel things for you. I don't want to fall in love when you can't, and you should respect that," I said, giving him a defiant look.

Darrow ran a hand through his loose, wet hair. "I admit something drives me to want every part of you, including your heart."

"If you care about me at all and want to protect me, like you've insisted, you will keep your distance outside of bed. No more holding me or giving me sweet kisses." Those would be my undoing if he kept them up. I had to make this clear, and to emphasize my point, I dropped my glamour so he had to look at the real me.

He studied my face. "What if I told you that finding the Naforya Fountain is the key to ending my family's curse? Once it's returned to its rightful place, we're free from it."

Shock filled me. It was no wonder they appeared to be pushing harder than anyone to find it, but I didn't understand how the two matters were related. "How is that possible?"

"Because it was two men from my family who were on the guardian rotation when it was taken." He shook his head, sighing. "Whoever stole it rendered them unconscious with no memory of what occurred. Apparently, there was a curse enacted long ago to punish anyone who failed in their duty to protect the fountain and didn't die defending it. The Andalagar and druids told them about it after the fact, but somehow, those details were lost over the centuries, so the current generation of fae didn't know the consequences. I doubt it would have made a difference anyway since both men were honorable and would have stopped it if they could."

"That certainly gives your family line the most incentive to retrieve it," I said, swallowing. I'd wondered what could have been dire and powerful enough to curse them for such a long time.

"Yes," Darrow agreed. "But it means we have a chance to rectify the problem, and then I will be able to feel more deeply for you."

My chest tightened. "You mean it's possible, Dare, but you can't promise it will change anything."

The look he gave me was so intense I could barely hold his gaze. "You're my true mate, Aella. It's why I'm driven by an obsessive need to protect you and keep you to myself. I only learned it after I took you to Darynia for those three days you slept."

"What? How?" He couldn't be serious. Except, some part of me knew it had to be true because it explained the strong connection between us that seemed nearly impossible to resist.

"My father has the ability to sense true mates when they're together. While I held you in my arms to bring you into the castle, he discerned the truth." Darrow said.

I drew in a deep breath. True mates? It was so rare that I'd believed I'd never find mine, let alone it be someone who I'd long considered an enemy until recently. It explained the instant connection I'd felt across the battlefield the first time I saw him and the powerful attraction I felt for my husband every time we were close that I couldn't ignore, no matter how hard I tried.

When we were together, and anger wasn't blinding me, it was like I was whole…complete. His kisses and touches always drove me to want more. If I hadn't spent so much time trying not to develop feelings for him, I might have realized it for myself. True mates always had an overwhelming urge to bond and complete their union, so I'd been fighting an impulse that was never meant to be resisted.

Unfortunately, that made matters more difficult. I wished it could have been wonderful news because it had once been my dream, but now it terrified me. My heart was in more danger now than ever. Why did fate have to play with our lives this way by cursing him?

"Okay, fine." My chest tightened. "We're true mates, and there is a chance we can lift your curse, but until that happens, I still need to keep some emotional distance. There is no guarantee we will reach the fountain and bring it back."

"Aella, I…" he began.

I pressed a finger to his lips. "No arguments. That's the deal—take it or leave it."

He looked away, working his jaw, before returning his gaze. "Very well. I'll take what you're willing to give."

"That also means no sweet, tender sex or anything that resembles making love. If we're true mates, that could be risky as well," I said, blushing. I'd never demanded such a thing from a man before, but I needed to be as careful as possible with him, especially in bed. If he went slow, I'd fall hard, and I knew it.

Darrow's lips quirked, and his gray eyes took on a roguish glint. "That is one point of this bargain where I won't argue. If you want it rough, I'll give you exactly what you're looking for and more. I only hope you can handle it because that will draw out the darker side of me."

"I can handle it." My stomach tightened at the thought. "But first, a bath. We're filthy, wet, and dripping all over your wood floor."

The scent of mud and rain covered us.

"Curse the nameless ones." He let out an ironic chuckle. "That should have been my first thought when we came up here, but seeing you naked in my bed has been on my mind all night."

"Soon," I promised.

He took my hand, pulling me toward the washroom. While he ran the water in the tub, I looked in the mirror, horror filling me at how ragged I appeared. My blonde hair was a mess from the rain, my cheeks were flushed, and my lips were plump from kissing.

Darrow came behind me, meeting my gaze in the reflection. "I've got a robe for you in the closet. I'll get it while you start bathing. Because if I stay in here, neither of us is getting clean."

"You can't be that desperate." Honestly, he was staring at me like a starved man, but I didn't see how that could be true when he could easily get any woman he wanted. Never mind that I looked like a drowned rat at the moment.

He turned me to face him. "I want you to know I haven't touched another woman since I ordered Camden to end it with you."

"Why?" I asked, surprised. Surely, he didn't do it for my sake or out of some sense of fairness since he cut me off. That would go against everything I'd heard about him.

"It hardly seemed fair." His lips quirked. "And other women don't interest me anymore the way you do."

Until true mates had sex, the bond didn't fall into place. We could have still slept with others, though perhaps the connection we'd already formed with kissing and touching still influenced us on some level. After feeling Darrow's lips on mine the first time, I didn't get the same satisfaction with Camden anymore, though I certainly tried during those first months.

I shook my head. This conversation was far too surreal for me to believe. "Please, go get the robe."

"Of course, my lady," he said, sauntering away with a knowing grin.

I quickly got undressed and sank into the deep tub. It was nearly full, so I turned off the water. Darrow had gotten it perfectly hot. For a moment, I let the heat soak into my body and loosen my muscles. Hearing noises in the bed chamber roused me enough to dunk my head and begin washing my hair. He must have taken his time because I almost finished bathing when he returned. I noted he kept his gaze away from the tub as he hung a dark blue robe on a wall hook.

Watching a strong, sexy man fight the urge to look at his naked wife was almost comical. "Give me just a minute, and I'll be out."

"Take your time," he said, turning his back to me. His shoulders were rigid with tension.

I finished quickly, rising to grab a towel from a nearby shelf. Once I'd dried my hair and upper body, I stepped out of the tub. Still, Darrow didn't peek. I ran the towel down my legs to dry them, keeping an eye on him. It felt so incredibly good to be clean again. I crept behind him to hang the towel and grab the robe.

"Your turn," I said once I'd pulled it on and tied the belt. It was impressively soft and covered me to midcalf.

He turned around and looked me up and down. "It looks good on you."

"Hurry and bathe so you can take it off," I replied with a saucy grin.

"Oh, I plan on it."

I left him in the bathing chambers because I was reasonably certain I might not have the willpower to keep my hands off of him once he stripped his clothes. To my surprise, I found he'd lit several candles. They softened the atmosphere and drew attention to the large bed in the middle of the room, which was adorned with a deep red duvet, partially pulled back to reveal black sheets underneath. He'd gone through a lot of trouble for impersonal sex, but I supposed I'd let it go for our first time. A little candlelight wouldn't make me suddenly fall in love, but it would let me see him better.

A silver brush sat on the dresser. I grabbed it and took my time working the tangles out of my hair. Though I'd tried to get some of them loose in the bath, many didn't come free. It took nearly ten minutes to sort them out.

After that, I wandered the room. It was nicely decorated in the same shade as the bed covering, along with splashes of gold and black, but there weren't any personal touches. I wondered how often he'd even stayed here since purchasing the place. It was unnerving how little I knew about my own husband's habits. I supposed that was to be expected under the circumstances, but I wished I had ways to learn more about him the way he did me.

Unable to resist the comfortable bed any longer, I moved over to it and lay across the top. It felt as nice as expected and not as lumpy as the one I had at home. I wondered how he could afford such a place without being a lord or firstborn son. That was another question I'd have to ask when I had the opportunity.

I closed my eyes, promising myself it would only be for a moment, but the next thing I knew, fingers grazed my cheek, waking me. Darrow stared down at my face with hooded lids.

"You look even more beautiful in my bed," he said.

He hadn't put on a robe and stood before me naked. I gulped as I took in his hard, muscular form. With the soft, flickering light, I could hardly make out the scars on his chest, but even those would have added to his savage look right now. He was lethal grace wrapped in an irresistible package.

Darrow ran a hand along my neck and down my chest until he reached the robe's belt. I kept my gaze on him as he slowly opened it, pulling the sides apart to expose my breasts. His hand hovered there for a few seconds before tracing down my stomach to widen it further until nothing covered my front. He'd seen me naked briefly on summer solstice, but this was different. I wasn't trying to hide myself now.

"Something tells me we won't be rising early in the morning," he said as he took me in fully with a savage look in his eyes. It was enough to make me wet. I'd grown so used to resisting him that it was strange to give in to my desire.

I sat up and tugged the robe the rest of the way off, letting it fall to the floor. In the next moment, I was on my back again, and Darrow hovered over me with his hard cock jutting proudly. He stared down at me like a predator that had just caught its prey.

"Are you certain you still want it rough?" he asked, lifting his brows. The scent of sandalwood surrounded me, along with a hint of something else. If there were a way to bottle up ferocity and danger and make a cologne from it, this new aroma he emitted would be it.

I had a feeling I was about to release something animalistic inside him. "Yes."

"Very well, but be aware, there will be nothing soft or gentle once I get started."

I swallowed, because that sounded terrifying and thrilling at the same time. "Good."

My lips parted as he swiftly leaned down and kissed me. It was brutal and demanding without a hint of affection—the way I'd asked. When he pulled away, his mouth trailed slowly down, kissing my neck before reaching my breasts. He sucked on each of my nipples one by one, pulling on them so hard that pricks of pain shot straight through me. My core heated instantly. He nibbled them next, biting hard enough to hurt, but not draw blood. A moan escaped me. I liked it more than expected and couldn't wait to see what else he did.

Darrow smiled and continued a path down my stomach, pausing as he reached the apex of my thighs. Sitting back, he pulled my legs farther apart so I was completely open to him. Then he ran one finger down my aching nub before inserting it inside me.

"So wet already," he said, pulling back.

I made a noise of protest. "Says the man whose dick is hard as a rock."

"Hmm, fair point."

He lifted my right leg and brought my foot to his mouth. One after another, he kissed and sucked on my toes. I'd never known until that moment that such a thing could excite me. Then, he began working his way down my calf. Shots of pleasure flowed from where his mouth bit and licked, forming a trail of pain and seduction. It ended too soon as he stopped at the sensitive underside of my knee to nibble there, but he soon continued his path until he reached my wet center. All he gave was one excruciatingly slow lick before he pulled away and started on my left foot, repeating what he'd done on the other side.

I panted by the time he reached my pussy again. He sucked in the nub and then bit it just hard enough to make me cry out, holding my legs tightly so I couldn't close them. He held it for a long moment while watching my reaction, but I didn't dare protest. It was an erotic kind of pain that I'd never experienced before and only made me hotter. Then, he let go and licked it once to soften the sting.

Darrow stretched my thighs as far apart as they could go. Without warning, he shoved two fingers deep inside of me. I gasped at the sudden invasion but quickly relaxed as he worked me in a rhythmic motion that spun my pleasure higher.

"How rough do you want it, Aella?" he asked, studying my face.

"Enough to make me sore in the morning, Dare."

"Hmm, I like when you say my name properly." He inserted a third finger, stretching me. "I'm going to make you say it many times before the sun rises."

His pace quickened to more forceful thrusts as he watched me closely. I drew in ragged breaths and lifted my hips, needing more. Darrow put my right leg over his shoulder and licked the skin on the underside of my thigh once before biting me hard. A thrill shot through my body at the combined pain of him roughly working my pussy while his teeth bit into my skin. I'd never done anything like this before, but it was shockingly stimulating.

He readjusted to clamp down on another spot as he inserted a fourth finger that he had to thrust forcefully to fit. In and out, in and out, at a punishing pace, with his rough hand working me so hard that he had me gripping the blanket. I began making mewling sounds as the combined sensations of pain and pleasure sent me higher and higher to a precipice. Then, he pushed his fingers as deep as they could go, so it truly hurt, and pressed his thumbnail into my clit, adding a third point of pain.

I was so damn close to exploding. "Darrow, please..."

He unclamped his teeth from my thigh, setting my leg down. He stared intently at me as he worked my throbbing center with his thumb, masterfully creating so much exquisite agony that I could only make incoherent sounds. With his other hand, he reached to take one of my breasts. He squeezed it while simultaneously pinching my nipple so hard I nearly saw stars. I was so close to an orgasm, but he maintained just enough pain that I couldn't quite make it over the edge.

"How do you feel now, Aella?" Darrow asked in a deep, raspy voice.

"Like I'm on fire. I'm not sure how much more I can take."

He switched to my other breast, pinching that nipple hard. "You respond so well to pain. The wild look in your eyes right now is better than anything I could have imagined." He thumbed my clit with his nail, and I jerked. "How much do you want my cock?"

The thought of it replacing his demanding, rough fingers had me moaning again. "More than anything right now."

He stopped his motions inside me, concentrating his efforts with his thumb and the hand on my breast. First, his touch in both places would feel gentle and soothing, but he'd follow a few seconds later with biting pain. Either could have sent me over the edge if he only stayed with one. He was stroking me so raw that I knew once he finally put his cock inside me, it would repeatedly rub against those tender places.

"Dammit, fuck me already, Dare," I pleaded.

He chuckled. "I like having you at my mercy, begging me." He glanced at the clock ticking on the nightstand. "And it's not midnight quite yet."

I started to lunge upward, planning to take matters into my own hands, but his powers clamped me down. "Patience, Aella. It won't be much longer."

"You're using magic," I said, attempting to glare at him as he worked his fingers harder again but stopped touching my clit.

His gray eyes were savage with delight. "Does that bother you?"

"If I said it did, would you stop?" I asked, gasping under the weight of his hold.

The pressure disappeared, along with his hands on my body. He moved to hover over me, leaving mere inches between our faces. "I will always stop if you ask or any time I think you can't take anymore. Otherwise, I'll push you to the very edge of your tolerance. Do you understand?"

"Yes." I nodded, surprised at his change of mood. He'd been so commanding and rough that I hadn't thought he'd end it so easily. "Thank you."

"A woman should never need to thank a man for respecting her body and wishes," Darrow said. He followed that with a kiss that seared me.

Once I was pliant again, he moved his mouth down between my legs to lick and soothe what his rough fingers had done until I was on the verge of coming. He must have sensed the moment I was close because he pulled away quickly.

When he moved over me again, I wrapped my arms around his neck to keep him close.

The corner of his lips quirked. "Are you ready for me to fuck you hard, dear wife?"

"Yes." I drew up my knees and lifted my hips. "I've been ready."

He gave me a pleased smile. "Good, because this is only the beginning."

Darrow surged into me with one swift thrust, and I cried out at the pleasure of him filling me so fully that I was surprised I didn't rip apart. He pulled back a few inches and moved slowly against the places he'd made raw. I dug my heels into his backside, urging him to go deeper again, but he held firm.

"You feel so good, Aella. If you come, you're going to send me over the edge, and I want to enjoy this for a few minutes longer," he said in a gruff voice.

I looked into his eyes and saw the strain in his features. "You're that close?"

"It's been months." He gave me a brief, demanding kiss. "And the way you've responded to me is far better than I could have imagined. I was at the edge well before I shoved my cock inside you."

My breath caught in my throat. Somehow, he was just as turned on as me, and that only built my need higher. We weren't only having sex right now but also learning about each other because this would be something we'd do many times in our marriage. I was with a man with whom there would be no end between us for as long as we both lived.

Darrow began moving again, picking up speed and force with each thrust but never quite going all the way inside. He was building us higher and higher until I was begging him incoherently. He finally slammed fully into me. My orgasm hit with agonizing bliss as I squeezed him so tightly I worried I'd hurt him. He was jerking inside my body, sending his hot cum deep into my core. We both shouted and moaned for long moments until the pleasure finally subsided.

Darrow collapsed beside me, putting a respectful amount of space between us as he gave me a satisfied grin. "Relax and catch your breath while you can. In a few minutes, I'm going to have you on your knees."

"What?" I asked, lifting my head to look at him. "So soon?"

"Oh, dear Aella, I intend to have you in every way possible before the sun rises. Then, you'll take us to Alavaar to research the ring," he said.

I gave him a confused look. "You're coming back with me?"

"Yes, but only for a day. We suspect there may be books there that could be helpful. The trouble is, druids aren't very welcoming when it comes to outsiders accessing their libraries." He idly grabbed a strand of my hair. "I know your sister could assist us with that."

Priyya had spent most of her adult life in Alavaar, and considering she was forty-one now, she'd had plenty of time to form connections. Darrow was right that if we wanted to get into the best libraries, we'd need her help. I was invested now that I'd seen the ring and learned of its tie to Darrow's curse and would do whatever it took to convince her. The only trouble would be explaining why I had a group of Veronnians with me. I'd figure out that obstacle in the morning.

For now, the man raking his fingernails down my stomach had my full attention. I reached down and grabbed his cock in a tight fist, satisfaction filling me when he sucked in a breath and grew harder. The look in his eyes turned absolutely feral.

A moment later, I found myself on my hands and knees with him nudging my thighs apart. A second after that, he plunged all the way inside in a move so forceful my breath left me. Darrow grabbed my hair and yanked my head back.

"Are you ready for more?" he asked in a raspy voice. I'd woken a beast.

"Yes," I gasped.

He began moving with brutal intensity. Now that he'd gotten the long-delayed release after months of us battling our attraction, he didn't have to hold back anymore. While one hand kept hold of my hair, the other gripped my hip tightly.

I couldn't move, only take him deeply inside me again and again. Men had always been gentle with me, but Darrow took me at my word when I said to make it rough, and that's exactly what he did. To my shock, I reveled in the way he handled me. It was wild, hot, and lacked any niceties.

He didn't stop until we were both rubbed raw and panting. Only then did he let go of my hair, wrap an arm around me, and pull my back against his chest. My savage husband dropped one hand to begin rubbing my clit in a hard and vigorous motion. It took no time at all before I exploded. He followed right behind me, not letting me go as he released his hot cum deep inside me for a second time.

Darrow spoke in a gruff voice in my ear. "Was that rough enough for you?"

"Yes," I said, jumping as he flicked my sensitive clit. Not that I could go far with him holding me tightly. "I didn't know you could get this dark, but I like it. In fact, it's perfect."

He raked his teeth across my shoulder, pumping his semi-hard cock a couple of times. "It's all my dark elf side inside you now. It's what I released deep within you twice and will again and again before this night is over. Think you can handle that?"

Darrow pinched my clit hard, and I whimpered. "Yes."

"Then brace yourself, Aella, because you're going to get exactly what you asked for."

I was already sore, but I didn't protest when he nudged me down until my cheek was pressed into the mattress while my ass stayed angled up against him. His dick grew harder inside my pussy, and excitement strummed through my body. I had no idea what my husband would do next, but I had a strong feeling I would enjoy it.

Chapter 46

Aella

Bright sunlight shone into the room, filtering through my eyelids. I lay on my stomach naked and fully relaxed after a long night of hard sex. Darrow had taken me at my word, pushing my body to new heights in the roughest, wildest ways to get us both off. I was entirely sated but also sore—not that I would dream of complaining. It had been good, almost too good to believe.

For a moment, I resisted waking until I noticed the finger tracing my back. It followed one of my many scars that I'd failed to keep glamoured in my sleep. I stiffened and turned my head to find Darrow with a cold, hard expression on his face. This was a conversation I'd hoped to avoid. A part of me had thought his inability to love would include not caring about things like the numerous wounds I'd received over the years.

His gray gaze shifted from my back to my face, softening slightly. "How did you get these?"

I swallowed. "Can we please not talk about it?"

"There are layers of scars from your shoulders to your lower back, some of them must have been quite deep, and they didn't happen all at once." He drew in a deep breath as if he needed to gather himself to stay calm. "Cam said you had them, but he had no idea how they got there and that you never would tell him."

Dammit, I'd forgotten my former lover might have mentioned that during their talk.

"Yes, because it wasn't his business," I replied, twitching when Darrow began tracing another one.

He stared at me intently. "I'm not him and won't accept that as an answer. You're my wife, and someone hurt you. I need to know who did it."

I rolled onto my back and sat up, angling my body so he couldn't look at the scars anymore. "It's not a problem you can fix, Dare. Please let it go."

"No. Tell me," he commanded.

Running a hand through my tousled hair, I glared at him. "This is one subject that is off limits between us, so forget it."

He climbed out of bed, grabbed a robe to pull over his nude body, and began pacing the room. He looked like a caged animal ready to tear free. I watched him with trepidation. At the summer ball, I had wondered how he would have reacted if he'd known about the healing wounds on me. I was right to say nothing about them back then because he wasn't handling it well now. A part of me was relieved by his show of concern, but the other part recognized that it would create a conflict we couldn't easily resolve.

Darrow worked his jaw. "Was it a past lover who did this?"

I kept my mouth shut because I'd almost rather he thought that than the truth.

He glared at me. "Yes or no?"

I shook my head and looked down, letting my hair fall over my face to hide my expression. "It doesn't matter."

"TELL ME WHO DID THIS TO YOU!" he shouted, losing patience.

Now, I was getting angry. I lifted my chin. "Dammit, Dare. You don't get to pry into every part of my life just because we fucked all night." I tugged on the sheet, using it to cover myself as I stood and faced him. "Someday, when I'm ready, I'll answer you. It's not going to be today."

"How do I know that I'm not sending you back to the person who did this?" he asked, voice still raised but a degree lower.

I shook my head in denial at his astute question. "You don't, but that's my problem."

A knock sounded at the door, and a second later, Faina poked her head inside. "Is everything okay?"

"Yes," I said.

"No," Darrow answered.

She lifted a dark brow. "You two sounded like your night went fine, so what's the problem now?"

Before I could stop him, Darrow spun me so my back faced his sister and yanked the sheet down to my waist. The gasp Faina let out let me know she saw everything. I jerked out of his hold and covered myself again. When I turned around, I found she'd opened the door wider so the others in the hall were in view. Their expressions told me everyone had seen my scars.

"Seriously?" I shot Darrow an accusing look. "This is private."

"I would have told them anyway," he replied, anger still in his expression.

Faina came farther into the room, giving me the gentlest look I'd ever seen on her. "Those are whip marks—a lot of them."

"Agreed," Darrow said, and strangely, he looked at Bogdan. The dark elf nodded his head but didn't comment on the matter.

My husband turned his gaze to me. "I'm not going to ask again, Aella. Who did that to you?"

Everyone's attention was on me as I clutched the sheet tightly to my chest, intimidated by their stares. It was clear that I wasn't getting out of this until I gave them an answer, and I might as well get it over with so we could be done with it. "Lord Morgunn and his son, Ulmar."

Audible gasps and curses sounded.

Darrow clenched his fists. "Why?"

"Breaking his rules, defying him, and especially anytime I tried to prevent him from attacking your villages and killing innocent people." I let out an ironic laugh. "You have no idea the price I paid to get him to stop slaughtering Veronnian villagers for all those years."

Jax cursed under his breath, probably remembering what he'd said to me at dinner last night. It wasn't as if he could have known, though. While it wasn't uncommon for fae to punish their offspring or charges like me, they usually didn't resort to the type of violence that I endured with my uncle.

Bogdan took a step into the room, frowning at me. "Whip injuries typically heal without a scar, but yours didn't. Why?"

"They kept an iron cuff on me," I said, shrugging. "Years ago, I fought back with my wind powers, and they decided to avoid that happening again and make me suffer longer afterward."

Darrow stepped closer to me and lifted my chin to meet his gaze. "When was the last time they did this to you?"

I pressed my lips together, but the look in his eyes said he wouldn't let go until I answered him. "The night I met your mother when they couldn't find me in time to attack Veronna," I admitted, taking a deep breath. "I was still healing when you saw me at the ball, but my glamour covered up the marks."

He stared up at the ceiling for a minute as if asking for patience from the gods. "Why didn't you tell me back then when we were alone?"

"It's not as if you could have done anything about it, and maybe..." My voice trailed off.

Darrow let go of my chin, but his focus remained on my face. "Maybe what?"

"I was afraid you wouldn't care what happened. I was in a bad place and couldn't handle it if that was the case," I replied, giving him the truth.

Darrow rubbed his forehead. "I've told you time and again that you matter to me."

"Yes, but why? Is it because I can open portals for you that no one else can? For most of my life, that's all that has mattered to most people—my usefulness." I gestured toward his sister and friends. "Isn't that the only reason they tolerate me?"

Faina opened and closed her mouth before looking away.

Loden stepped forward. "Maybe it was in the beginning, but you're more than that to us now, Aella."

"Why?" I asked, gripping my sheet tighter. "What changed? You all barely know me beyond what your spies have dug up for you. Don't feel sorry for me over a few scars on my back because that isn't why you should suddenly give a damn about someone."

"We know there's more to you than that, whether the information comes from spies or our interactions with you, Aella," Darrow said, frustration written all over his face as he ran a hand through his loose hair. "That must be the other reason Lord Morgunn placed the curse on you, so you can't escape his abuse."

"Which is why this conversation is pointless because *you* can't save me. My sister searched for a way around it, and so did my cousin Tadeus. He hates his father as much as I do," I said, glancing at the others. "That's the reason I avoid discussing it, since there's nothing anyone can do. My uncle could beat me to death, and no one person in the realm can stop him."

The air in the room thickened even more as the others gave each other long looks.

"We'll find a way to free you," Darrow vowed, shoulders tight and rage reflecting in his gray eyes.

Faina nodded. "Yes, we will. He has no right to treat you that way, especially when you came into his care because you lost your parents. It's his duty to protect you, not hurt you."

She truly looked enraged on my behalf when she'd always been standoffish before.

I shook my head. "I think my father knew what kind of man Lord Morgunn was and never left me alone with him," I admitted, recalling those early days when my abilities first appeared. "There were a couple of times that my uncle tried to force me to develop my powers faster, but Dad intervened. I had no one left to protect me after he was killed."

There wasn't anything they could say to that, considering it was Darrow and Faina's sire who murdered mine. On the other hand, my father had taken down their grandfather. We had so much violent history between us that I couldn't fathom why they cared about my scars. They were so insignificant compared to the lives lost over the centuries in a feud that I wasn't sure how it had truly started. I'd yet to find time to investigate the matter further.

Darrow cleared his throat. "I need everyone to leave the room...now."

No one protested, and within a minute, Faina pulled the door shut behind her.

"I should take another bath," I said, heading for the washroom.

"Aella," Darrow said just before I reached it.

I paused. "Yes?"

"It may seem strange that your scars concern us, but you must understand that we're only ruthless to our enemies. Not the innocent, and certainly not family."

I turned and frowned at him. "I'm not family."

"Yes, you are," he said vehemently, fists clenching and unclenching. I could tell he wanted to pull me into his arms, but he held back because I'd asked him to stop touching me for comfort or outside of sex. "Like it or not, you've earned a measure of my trust, which is why I'm sharing my plans. You are not only Veronnian now, but also part of my inner circle. I protect those closest to me, dear wife, and I especially protect what's mine. In case you missed it, that's *you*."

A lump formed in my throat. The sincerity of his words touched something deep within me. Despite everything, including his own curse, I did matter to him. It was there for me to see, written all over his features. I'd spent more of my life alone than not, and certainly never guessed anyone outside of Therress would accept me like that.

"Thank you, Dare."

"There is no need for gratitude." He cocked his head, and his expression changed. "But perhaps you could allow me to help you with that bath if you're feeling generous."

"Without being too soft or gentle? How is that possible?" I asked with a raised brow, grateful for the change of subject. He'd eliminated the tension in the air with a simple suggestion.

My husband smiled wickedly. "I have complete faith in my skills to do as you wish...even then. The real task will be getting us to Alavaar before the morning is gone."

I dropped the sheet, enjoying the sight of his gaze heating up and the anger from before fading away. "Then, what are you waiting for?"

He had me squealing in his arms before I reached the door.

Chapter 47

Aella

The six of us went through the portal in pairs, with Darrow and I going last. It took a dizzying twenty seconds to reach the other end. We stepped into the barren woods, and I noted the deterioration had spread more. I couldn't see any signs of life.

The trees looked like dejected skeletons, no birds chirped, and the magic was down to a tiny trickle that would be gone soon. My body wouldn't be able to recharge until I reached a more fertile area. They would need to relocate the ring soon, or it wouldn't work much longer.

Faina put her hands on her hips. "I didn't realize Alavaar had it this bad."

"The land sickness has been spreading in many places, but this is the worst spot near a portal ring," I said, gesturing for us to begin the trek west along the narrow trail.

It barely stood out against the decayed land. I had to fight the horrible, depressing feeling that threatened to overcome me. By the looks on everyone's faces, they did as well.

Darrow gave me a grim look. "We have eight places in Veronna similar to this."

"At last count, we have four in Therress," I said, sighing. "But we're almost half the size of you all."

We crunched our way over the remnants of dead plant matter for more than ten minutes before crossing into a verdant area with thriving vegetation near the village. A couple of thatched roofs appeared through the tall, grassy pillar trees in the distance. This time last year, I wouldn't have been able to spot homes this far away, which told me the dying forest continued to edge closer despite the druids' best efforts.

As we entered Fionbar, the inhabitants gave us curious glances. I waved at a few of them, and they returned the gesture with hesitant nods. They'd recognize me, but they likely wondered about the rest of my group. We made it to the town center and took the road north. My sister lived at the edge, nearest the path to the dragon hunting grounds.

It was almost lunchtime, so I knew she should be home. With less than six hundred inhabitants in the village—many of them families who lived together—it didn't take long to reach Priyya's two-story thatched cottage. It had a heavy wooden door at the center, single windows on either side, and a covered porch with a swing. In the evenings, we often sat together on it after dinner to enjoy the nature around us. The next nearest neighbor was a few hundred feet away, with numerous mistarr trees in between to lend some privacy.

Drawing a deep breath, I knocked on the door while everyone else hovered behind me. I would have normally walked right inside, but this felt more appropriate considering my company. Priyya appeared a few moments later, frowning at me. She'd pulled her dark-blonde hair into a messy bun, and she wore a loose green tunic with matching pants that almost swallowed her slender frame. Berry stains covered the edge of her right sleeve cuff, probably from mashing poultices for the dragons.

"Why are you knocking? Aella, I was..." she trailed off as she took in the five people behind me.

I cleared my throat. "I didn't think you'd want me barging inside under the circumstances."

As soon as her gaze fell on Darrow and Faina, she stiffened. Most of the realm knew what they looked like with their unique brown-black hair, so it never took long for anyone to identify them. Priyya stepped back before catching herself and pinning me with a horrified look.

"Why do you have Veronnians with you?" she asked in a high-pitched whisper. "Are they holding you hostage? This is the worst place to come because you know I have no money or power to fight them off."

"It's not like that," I said, shaking my head.

Darrow stepped right behind me and wrapped his arms around my waist, causing me to stiffen before I made myself relax. She was going to find out about my marriage soon enough. It would make matters worse if she thought I wasn't a willing participant.

"Your sister and I have been married for over four months, so I assure you, we have not taken her hostage," my husband said in a smooth, compelling voice.

Priyya slammed the door on us.

"That went well," I said wryly, pulling away from him.

Darrow snorted. "She likely needs a few minutes, but I'm sure she'll come around momentarily."

He had more faith in her than I did.

"Did you have to blurt out the news like that?" I asked, turning to look up at him. "Or put your arm around me?"

He arched a brow. "I thought it was best to get the nature of our relationship out of the way, and holding you without any resistance on your part emphasized my point. It was also worth seeing the look on her face before she shut the door."

"I'm going to be lucky if she ever speaks to me again." I sighed. "Do you have a subtle bone in your body, or are you always so domineering?"

Darrow gave me an amused look. "I am not without finesse when the situation calls for it, but you're the one who has demanded the rougher side of me."

"Seriously?" I threw up my hands. "You know she can probably hear us since her windows are open, right?"

"Why do you think I said it?" he asked, wickedness dancing in his gray eyes.

I smacked him in the arm. "Do not make me regret last night."

"Or this morning," Jax said dryly. "We all heard how things went after your argument. No one was the least bit surprised you both came out with big smiles on your faces afterward."

Faina snickered. "It's a wonder Aella is walking normally."

"I think I liked it better when you all were unfriendly," I said, shaking my head at them.

The door suddenly opened, drawing our attention back to the house.

Priyya ran her gaze over everyone else before letting it fall on me. "Have none of you any shame?"

I shrugged. The others answered with various versions of "no" that sounded more proud than embarrassed. I couldn't believe how much things had changed between me and them since yesterday, yet I felt much more comfortable with them than before.

"They're here with me for a good reason, Priyya. We have some information about the Naforya Fountain, but we need your help to follow up on it," I said, knowing that much would trigger her curiosity. After our mother died, she tried to resume the search for a while but didn't get far.

Her gaze sharpened. "Really?"

"Yes." I nodded. "If you'll let us inside, I'll explain everything."

She hesitated. "Are you sure they'll behave?"

"Aella can't give that guarantee," Jax said from near the steps. "But we promise to try."

Darrow put a hand on my shoulder. "I promise if anyone gets out of line, I will send them back outside."

Priyya scrutinized him. "I'll hold you to that."

"As you should."

She chewed her lip for a minute, which I understood since we were throwing a lot at her without time to work through it all. "Alright, you all can come inside, but take your dirty boots off at the door."

No one argued.

***

By the time we explained everything to Priyya and had lunch with her, I'd recharged enough for us to return to the portal gate. She'd agreed to accompany us to the capital city, Tuireen, where the realm had the most comprehensive library. My sister was still unhappy and more than a little skeptical about my secret alliance with the Veronnians, but the importance of the Naforya Fountain helped her put aside her distrust for the moment. We'd made a strong case, though it helped that she trusted my judgment.

It had been years since I'd visited the large druid city, which had over two hundred thousand residents. It sprawled for miles and miles. Some homes and shops were constructed near ground level, although the base floor began six feet above ground level with support beams underneath. They built most structures along the large doak trees that grew everywhere in northern Alavaar. Since they reached two hundred feet in height and up to fifteen feet in diameter, they could easily hold the weight of the houses.

Spring flooding had necessitated their style of living, although much of the area consisted of swamps, which also discouraged living near the ground. The scent of sulfur and decay from the sitting water nearby would have been overwhelming if not for the judicious planting of garsennia flowers. Their stalks rose several feet high, with multiple soft, white blooms sprouting from each plant. They produced a sweet scent popular for making perfume and excellent at covering foul smells.

Priyya led the way through the third-level walkway between trees, guiding us toward the library that rose like a floating edifice ahead due to its massive size. She glanced back at me. "The decay is encroaching near Tuireen as well. It would have already overtaken the city if the residents weren't taking turns daily restoring the afflicted land, but we still lose some ground every month. They estimate we have less than a year before it will reach the outskirts."

"We will do everything we can to retrieve the fountain," Darrow promised.

My sister met his gaze. "If you do that and treat Aella well, you'll have no further problem with me."

"Of course," he said, dipping his chin.

"But..." she paused, stopping and spinning around to face us along the wooden bridge. "If you hurt her in any way, I will bring the wrath of the dragons upon you. I might not be much of a warrior, but *they* won't hesitate to attack on my behalf."

Darrow gave her an amused look. "Your threat is noted."

Considering his level of power, I wasn't certain a dragon was much of a threat to my husband, but if it made my sister feel better to say it, I wouldn't argue the point. She turned around and led us the rest of the way along the catwalk. The extensive library spanned dozens of trees and had three levels, with us entering from the bottom entry point about twenty feet off the ground.

We had to wait outside on the balcony while she went in to get us clearance. I had come here a few times over the years to research various topics, but they limited my access since I wasn't a citizen of the realm. Hopefully, Priyya had higher privileges.

Fifteen minutes later, she finally returned to us. "They have agreed to allow you entry, but you'll have escorts at all times, and you'll only be allowed to look at books and scrolls related to retrieving the fountain."

"That is all we ask," Darrow said.

We followed Priyya into the wide entry with its double doors. I breathed in the familiar musty scent of old parchment, enjoying the comforting smell. We passed multiple rows of bookshelves before reaching a large desk where a stuffy-looking male druid sat. Numerous tables were set up behind him, providing places for people to read and research. Only a few sat at them now.

The central section of the library was open to the top level, aside from a few trees growing within the space and yellow vines winding their way around columns that held up the side floors. Thanks to the numerous windows on every wall, there was plenty of natural light.

"This is Idwal," Priyya said, gesturing at the frail older gentleman who managed to look down his nose at us despite our standing well above him. "He is the head curator here and will be the one to help us."

"You three," the male druid said, pointing at Faina, Jax, and Bogdan. "Will have access to the tomes on metal properties related to portal rings. Someone will be here momentarily to escort you to the appropriate section."

They nodded, seeming to know better than to argue. We were getting more assistance than expected, so everyone had better comply with the rules. Of course, I didn't think they'd risk upsetting library administrators with something this important.

Idwal pointed at the rest of us. "You four will have access to texts on interdimensional and cross-galaxy travel. I will take you to the appropriate section myself, as studying such matters has been my life's work."

"Why interdimensional travel?" I asked, considering Darrow hadn't mentioned anything about that.

He lifted a brow. "Because the thieves originally took the fountain to a hellish dimension where we had no access. That is the unseelie's specialty, not ours, and they knew very well we'd never be able to reach it. If not for a powerful locator spell that required twenty of us to fuel, we wouldn't have known that much."

"But it's not in that dimension anymore?"

The elder druid gave me a disparaging look. "Of course not, or else your search would be for naught—as it was for us when we discovered the problem centuries ago. We continued to follow up with it once we learned the dimension was only temporary. Ten years ago, it merged with our universe and resolved that particular dilemma. Unfortunately, someone took it upon themselves to damage the gate by then. We've had to wait until someone came along who was gifted enough to power it before looking into repairs."

Because, otherwise, the same saboteur might damage it again even worse.

"And that would be me," I said, shocked that they already knew so much, but maybe I shouldn't have been surprised. Getting the fountain back was even more important to druids, considering this was their home world, and they had been here long before the fae arrived.

Idwal looked me up and down with a hint of disdain. "We can hope you are the one, but that remains to be seen." He turned his attention to Darrow, expression every bit as condescending. "Priyya tells me you acquired the name of the planet where the fountain is currently located. Is that true?"

"I did," my husband agreed stiffly.

The elder druid drummed his fingers on his desk in thought. "That was one piece of information we couldn't obtain as our people failed to traverse the Oarwar desert without casualty. What is your power to have made the journey and lived to tell the tale?"

Darrow stared at him. "I'm telekinetic."

"Ah." The elder nodded. "And as a high fae, you could use that ability to stop most anything."

"Yes, most things." Judging by his tone, something told me that he'd found his magic couldn't fix all his problems, such as how to get me out from under my uncle's thumb.

"That should stand you in good stead in your journey. Perhaps your lineage is not such a bad thing if you use your gifts for good rather than all that killing that makes its way into my reports," he said, with no lack of judgment in his tone.

Darrow clenched his fists, so I put a calming hand on his arm. He turned to meet my gaze. I gave him a pleading expression, reminding him how important it was that we tolerate the arrogant druid. He took a deep breath and relaxed a little.

The guide for the other group arrived, taking the three of them away. Ours stood and grabbed his cane before hobbling toward the back of the library. We dutifully followed him. He reached a set of shelves stuffed full of books and stared at the left side briefly before his eyes narrowed on something on the top row. It was far out of our reach. I looked for a ladder nearby, but I didn't see one.

Idwal tapped at a hefty, brown tome with his cane. "Darrow, if you could be so kind as to pull that one and hold it for me."

My husband used his powers to lower the book into his waiting hands. The process continued several more times until we all held at least one heavy book. Then, the druid led us to a nearby table, where he had us spread out our finds. His gaze ran across them before reaching for a dark red tome that was among the largest.

"This one has a list of all the known habitable planets that have been compiled over thousands of years and includes some details about them. Every few centuries, someone is born on Paxia with the ability to open distant rings, and most do some exploration during their lifetime to add to our knowledge."

"I had no idea," I said, giving him a surprised look.

He settled into the nearest chair with a creak and a groan as he opened the book. "Tell me, young lady. Do you often feel the urge to use your gift to visit other places?"

"Yes." I nodded. "Especially once I became strong enough to leave Therress."

"What is the most difficult portal you've opened?" he asked, studying me closely.

"Well, the one to eastern Penoria with the large ring and the one to where the Naforya Fountain should be were both the most difficult." I chose to leave out my trips to Jolloure Island since that wasn't relevant, and it wasn't quite as taxing as the other two locations.

Surprise lit his features. "You successfully opened both of those?"

"Yes."

"Excellent, then perhaps you are the one we need." Idwal turned to Darrow. "Tell me the name of this planet, so that I might look it up."

"The seer called it Earth, but he mentioned they have many languages there, and it might also be known by Terra, Jord, or Erde."

Loden cleared his throat. "There were actually more names, but we stopped writing them down after a while."

The druid grunted. "At least the natives choose nice and simple words. You would be surprised how often planets are called something ridiculous that no one could possibly pronounce, such as Marztepinqtopulandol. I spent months trying to wrap my tongue around that one before succeeding."

"You did it well," I said, thinking it would also take me months.

He shrugged. "It is one of the nearest habitable planets to us and has some fascinating species living there, though nothing of true higher intelligence. Their only humanoid beings have just begun to form written language in the last handful of centuries. As a result, I couldn't fathom why they chose such a ridiculous name for their planet, but of course, they failed to consult me on the matter."

Idwal sighed and returned to his tome, flipping the pages carefully as he searched for the planet we needed. It took him several minutes while we patiently waited. Finally, he found it halfway through the book.

"Here it is," he said, skimming the text. "We've had several channelers visit Earth over time, with the first almost two and a half millennia ago. At that time, dragons and magic were prominent, but the only intelligent, non-bestial races were humans and sorcerers. Hmm, it appears they've never had the fun of fae descending upon their lands and disturbing their way of life. How fortunate for them."

We said nothing to that. I was half-druid and had heard all my life that my mother's people resented giving up two-thirds of their planet so the Seelie could live here. Of course, I could hardly blame them. Our arrival and the subsequent period afterward had been a dark time for everyone involved, but especially those native to Paxia.

"Interesting." Idwal continued skimming the pages. "It appears the dragons on Earth are not nearly as amenable as ours and often attack people. They even eat them, though ours will do that if they go rabid. That's what the slayers are here for, of course."

Within Alavaar, we had a handful of druids who were naturally fireproof and born with the mark of a dragon slayer. They could be quite ruthless and cunning, able to kill even the largest and most threatening of the beasts. We didn't need to call them into service often, so they served as warriors the rest of the time, protecting the realm from other types of enemies.

His eyes rounded when he reached a page near the back. "Over a millennium ago, humans and sorcerers grew tired of the violent dragons. They banished them, along with all magic, to a hellish dimension known as *Kederrawien*. The channeler present at the time barely escaped before the incident occurred. I cannot imagine how the people there could have done such a thing without the assistance of the Unseelie, but as I recall, that period was the last time anyone from Faelaria could open a portal to distant planets."

"So, they could have helped Earth's inhabitants do it?" I asked, surprised.

Darrow frowned. "I wonder if that's where they used to get their human slaves. Except, I am certain they didn't count on not being able to return for so long."

I'd heard there were magicless people on Faelaria, but I'd never considered that they weren't native to the planet. There'd never been a reason to look into the matter.

"If I had to guess, some humans were also swept into Kederrawien when the spell took effect. It would have been easy enough for the Unseelie to take them from there since they have little trouble traveling dimensions." Idwal rubbed his chin. "We know that it ceased to exist a decade ago when it merged with Earth, and they've lost access to their source."

"How do you know all this if you can't go there?" Loden asked, frowning at the druid.

The library curator gave him a disdainful look. "We have a seer whose primary task has been to keep track of the fountain, of course. Thankfully, he has assured us that it remains hidden and currently has guardians watching over its location."

"That's great to hear it's safe for now," Priyya said, leaning forward to look at the tome. "But how do we get there so we can retrieve the fountain?"

Idwal flipped back some pages. "Ah, here we go. This describes the difficulty involved with reaching Earth due to its distant location. It includes a rune sequence, but unfortunately, when that other dimension collided with the planet, it would have nudged it a little out of place. This sequence will no longer be accurate."

If a ring is already powered and active when it is moved, it will flash the new sequence once it settles into the new location. Of course, we weren't there to see that. I had no idea how to discern which runes to use if they were unknown.

Darrow moved closer to the tome so he could skim it for himself. "What does that mean for us?"

"Very complicated math to decipher the new rune order, and I'll need to research further on whether this planet has more than one ring. Obviously, we want to go to the one nearest to the fountain. I'll have the seer help pinpoint the one we need."

Priyya spoke up, "Do we have anyone who is able to do it?"

"Actually, it will require two people to accomplish. One who understands the movement of the celestial bodies, which would be me, and another who handles the calculations. No one in Alavaar can perform the latter, but there is someone in Hisgar," he said, grimacing.

"It's mostly ice giants who live there," Loden pointed out. "But I recall hearing of one who was born with intelligence that far surpasses anyone else in our realm."

"Yes," Idwal agreed. "That is the one I am thinking. We were as surprised as any when a youthful ice giant became so intelligent that the leaders summoned the most learned men and women to teach her. By the time she was twenty years old, she'd surpassed them all. However, we had some difficulty providing writing and reading materials due to her size. Most of our books were no larger than her thumb by the time she was an adolescent."

"We will have to seek her out," Darrow concluded.

The druid shook his head. "Not now. She is due to have a baby in the next week, and we all know how surly ice giants can be while pregnant or soon after birth. If we want her cooperation, we'll have to wait a couple of months."

Priyya's expression turned stricken at his words. "But we're running out of time."

"We have little choice if your sister is going to have any success opening the gate," he said, gesturing at me. "The good news is that the seer and I can begin pinpointing Earth and the ring's current location with a special instrument I recently finished constructing for that purpose. It will take some time due to many factors, but I should have the details you'll need before it's time to visit the ice giant."

"Okay," I agreed. What choice did we have?

"Now, let us see if any of these other books have information that might prove useful," the druid said, gesturing at us to each take one. "Knowledge is power. We certainly don't want anything to go wrong with such a vital quest."

None of us argued the point as we settled into chairs for some in-depth reading.

Chapter 48

Aella

Priyya and I walked along the depressingly dead road toward the portal ring. The morning light did nothing to improve the severe damage done by the blight. It was hard to see it this way and know it would continue to worsen, but at least we had a plan to resolve the problem. That gave us all a measure of hope.

Things had changed between my sister and me over the last two days since she learned about my marriage to Darrow and our quest to retrieve the Naforya Fountain. She still had her doubts, but my husband had been surprisingly charming and convincing. Enough that she even let him stay that first night while the rest of the group returned to Veronna. It had been nice getting a little more time with him, and we'd even gone to see the dragons together. I learned that he had an affinity for animals, and even the large ones responded well to him.

"Last night was a much quieter night," she said, giving me an amused look.

I bumped my shoulder into hers. "We weren't that bad."

"Maybe by your standards, but I was close to fleeing the house to find someone for myself during the middle of the night," she grumbled.

I frowned at her. "You aren't with that one woman anymore? What was her name...Farja, Fennia, Fanta...oh, I can't remember."

"Aella, none of those names are even close." She rolled her eyes and looked away. "It doesn't matter because she wasn't right for me. I guess you're lucky since your search is over now that you're married. You looked comfortable with him, which is still hard to comprehend."

Darrow had left after dinner yesterday, and right after that, Priyya had interrogated me with a thousand questions. We'd talked until late, but she still didn't know every detail. So much had happened in recent months that I'd kept from her. I did tell her about Darrow's curse and why I had to set limits with him until we could lift it.

"We are doing better now, but we didn't start that way. It took a while for us to get over the past and build some trust," I said, a smile pulling at my lips.

I felt truly content for the first time since getting married and maybe even hopeful for the future. The sex certainly exceeded my expectations. As long as we kept love out of the picture for now and maintained mutual respect, I could be comfortable with Darrow.

The ring appeared ahead, but Priyya stopped and turned to face me. "Be careful, Aella. When it comes to the fountain, I believe he does have good intentions. Everyone in all the realms on Paxia wants it back as soon as possible, so there's no doubt about him there. I worry about what comes after that. I hear things about Darrow even all the way here. There is a dark side to fae politics, and his name comes up often enough to be concerned."

I frowned. "Like what?"

"Just that he's seen with the king and his family more often than should be normal as a second son, especially for a half-dark elf. People think he does dangerous things for him, and the fact that His Majesty personally married you two in secret implies they must have a strong alliance," she said, sighing.

I knew what she meant because I'd thought a lot about that, too. "So he helps the king somehow. That has to mean he's loyal to Zadrya, right?"

"Yes," she agreed. "But the question is, what is Darrow doing, and will it somehow affect you?"

"Next time I see him, I'll ask him about it," I promised.

Relief filled her features. "It might be nothing, but it could be everything. I only want my little sister safe."

I knew she felt guilty that she had escaped while our uncle trapped me. Priyya knew about my curse, of course, but she didn't know how he punished me. I'd hidden that from her and ensured Darrow didn't bring it up while he was here, either. There was nothing my sister could do, so there was no point in her worrying. She'd only feel worse.

"You're the best," I told her honestly. She was always there for me in the most important ways, and I was grateful for that.

Priyya pulled me into a hug. I breathed in her floral-scented hair, comforted that it smelled exactly like our mother's. "Take care of yourself, and I'll see you soon."

She pulled away. "You take care, too. Promise?"

I nodded. "Of course."

We parted ways at the portal, and I made myself return to Therress. It was always difficult leaving Alavaar. I found great peace there and thoroughly enjoyed my stay with my sister. It was the only time I could let my worries go and simply be me.

My uncle's servant, Parzival, stood waiting when I stepped through the ring. He had a pocket watch in his hand and glanced at it when I arrived. "Ah, five minutes early for once. Your uncle will be pleased."

From the tone of his voice, he was disappointed that he couldn't get me in trouble.

"My uncle let me have a longer visit with my sister than usual, so of course, I made a point of returning on time," I replied, smiling sweetly at him. It was very rare that I was allowed to stay more than two nights, but for some reason, Lord Morgunn had been the one to insist on longer this time.

"Yes, apparently." He lifted his chin. "Then you should have no problem seeing my lord now in his office, where he is waiting for you."

I considered asking him what it was about, but the stodgy servant would never tell me. "Alright."

Gripping my small travel pack, I headed straight for the castle. He followed behind, managing to keep up with my swift pace. I wanted to get it over with so I could check on my garden. A few days away from my plants always meant plenty of work to do once I returned.

I found my uncle sitting at his desk, staring at a missive in his hand. "Close the door, Aella."

I did as he ordered just before Parzival reached it, getting a small thrill from shutting him out. Then I set my bag by the nearest bookshelf. Turning around, I found my uncle frowning. "The Andalagar tribal leader, Orran, sent me a message today. He regrets to say that he doesn't think you're the right fit for him, and he prefers your friend, Sariyah. The fool even went so far as to tell me he plans to court her."

My jaw dropped open. I hadn't seen Sariyah since her last visit and had no idea they'd progressed further in their relationship. There was a full-time portal channeler at Tradain, so she must have used him to help her get there. If they were developing into something, that was great, but I wished Orran could have waited a little longer to share the news with my uncle.

"I'm sorry, my lord. I honestly tried, and he appeared impressed with my skills, but he didn't seem interested in other ways," I said, putting as much truth into my words as possible.

"That is more or less what his missive says." Lord Morgunn set down the parchment. "But I still expected you to try harder because we need a stronger alliance with him. This is greatly disappointing."

I looked at the floor, knowing that's what he wanted.

"You have so much promise, Aella. I even attempted to find someone you'd appreciate more, but still, you failed to meet expectations." He tapped his quill against the desk in an irritating rhythm. "If not for your channeling abilities, I'd send you to the mines to work."

I'd seen him do that to others before, but never a highborn fae. Still, I said nothing because it was pointless and would only make him angrier if I gave excuses. He loved lecturing and putting me down because it made him feel better.

My uncle sighed. "Luckily for you, I need you to transport my soldiers tonight, so I will have to consider what to do with you later. Don't think about arguing or protesting this because you lost that right when you failed to secure a betrothal agreement with Orran."

My body went cold because I had a sense of where his point led. "What is the destination, my lord?"

"Veronna, of course," he said as I looked up. "You'll find out which village when it's time to leave."

He didn't trust me. First, he sent me away for several days while he undoubtedly prepared for this attack. Then, he refused to give me details. My uncle had probably been preparing this for a long time since I'd failed to be present for his last attack plans. I should have seen it coming.

I curtsied. "As you wish, my lord."

"You may go."

I turned toward the door, but his next words stopped me. "By the way, Ulmar will be with you today. Wherever you go, he will stay close."

Even if I wanted to escape helping my uncle, I couldn't with my cousin following me. I struggled to hide my horror. "Even in my bedroom?"

"Don't be ridiculous." He waved a hand dismissively. "He'll stand out in the hall if you're in there."

That made me feel marginally better. "Very well, uncle."

Lord Morgunn didn't bother to acknowledge me again and merely turned his attention to some paperwork on the desk. I left the office with dread filling my chest. He had to suspect something, but I couldn't think of any way he could know about Darrow. I'd been careful, and no one could follow through my portals. Everyone in my sister's village was a druid and wouldn't spy for him. I never went out in Porrine this last trip without glamour. So what had made him suddenly paranoid?

Chapter 49

Aella

We arrived at Tradain minutes before sunset. Over the last two hours since then, channelers from elsewhere in Therress had sent large groups of soldiers to us. The total number of them now exceeded eight hundred, with more filing through as I watched. If my uncle had been planning this for a while, why didn't he have everyone he needed beforehand?

Ulmar grinned at my confused expression. "Surprised, little cousin?"

"Yes."

"We didn't want Veronna to see the attack coming, so all the soldiers arriving now have come from Reshirk. They've been camped there for the last two days. Even they thought we would invade through that mountain pass," he said, delight in his voice.

Horror filled me, but I kept my expression calm. "You waited until Veronna moved many of its forces to the other side in anticipation of the attack before pulling them back here."

"Yes, smart girl." A pleased expression crossed his face. "I convinced my father of this plan, and he agreed it was a good one."

"Where are we really attacking?" I asked.

"Radoumar."

I stilled. "That's on the west coast by Veronna's gold mines. You think I can open and hold a portal long enough to get that many of our forces there?"

He took a menacing step toward me. "We hadn't planned on that location since we thought you couldn't do it. Then we saw you made it to a heavily warded ring in Penoria a few days ago. It's been a long time since anyone could open it aside from the faeries, but then we realized you've been hiding your true strength from us. We altered our plans accordingly."

The blood drained from my face. "But I..."

"Save it, cousin." His expression turned menacing. "We both know you can't lie your way around the fact you were there, probably looking at that broken ring. The question we can't figure out is who went with you?"

There was only one way he'd know where I'd gone, but not the identity of my traveling companions. They'd somehow been following my movements while I was away. I hadn't sensed any magical tracker on me except Darrow's, but they might have hired someone with the power to do it from afar. Though I'd never met anyone with the ability, I'd heard they existed. I just never thought it would be used on me. There were ways to counteract it, but they were temporary, so I would have needed to suspect they were necessary beforehand.

"I've been trying to find a way to get the Naforya Fountain back," I said, finding words that would only ring as truth. He'd know if I told a single lie, so I had to be careful.

Ulmar narrowed his eyes. "That's not your problem to fix."

"The land is dying, and we can't wait much longer," I argued.

"If my father wanted you to handle it, he would have told you," he said coldly. "I suggest you behave perfectly tonight, or else things won't go well for you when we return. You're already in enough trouble."

His threat was so menacing that it left a chill in the air, making me shiver. Autumn might be only a few days away, but the cool weather coming had nothing on my cousin's ability to drain warmth from his surroundings simply by standing nearby.

Neither of us spoke after that and stood silent as the captains of the various regiments prepared their soldiers. Dread filled me with every moment that passed. They were lining them up, and my final count revealed that there were now over a thousand, with a third of them on horseback. That was a quarter of Radoumar's population, which would be risky, but they'd have the element of surprise. A lot of damage could be done when people were asleep in their beds.

The leadership was organizing the soldiers to ensure they'd get through the ring in the most efficient manner possible. My uncle counted on the fact that I could open a distant warded portal and hold it for a long time to get that many into Veronna. If I failed, he would make me pay in the worst way, but if I did as ordered, they'd lay waste to Radoumar and likely steal any gold stored there. I'd be betraying my husband, even if I had little choice.

My uncle beckoned me forward. I hadn't been allowed to take a horse this time, so I walked through the long lines of troops who stared at me with a varying mixture of stalwartness and anxiety. It started with the foot soldiers, followed by centaurs and satyrs, and finally, the mounted fighters. With trepidation, I reached Lord Morgunn's side by the portal. There was nothing warm or kind in his features. Instead, his ice-blue eyes narrowed on me.

"Get on with it, Aella."

I clenched my fists. "You can't hurt civilians if I do this."

He leaned forward, baring his teeth. "Open the portal, or I'll have you whipped right here in front of my army, and then I'll have Rynn punished next."

My chest tightened because I knew that was no empty threat. How could he be so cruel?

"She has nothing to do with this," I said, trying to hold on to my courage in the face of his malevolence. Of course, he'd back me into a corner.

Lord Morgunn pulled away a little, his features softening slightly. "No, she is innocent. Open the portal, and all will be well. I'll even look the other way at your hiding your full abilities from me, especially since you've become more useful to my plans now than ever."

I only had impossible choices before me. The amount of trouble he'd gone through to set up this attack meant he'd show me no mercy if I refused to help him. If I did what he asked, he'd attack Radoumar and kill innocent people, but their population was large enough to put up a better fight than the places my uncle usually targeted. Maybe it wouldn't be so bad.

Also, Veronna had been gathering its forces in one place in anticipation of Lord Morgunn assaulting the border. Darrow would know we went elsewhere once I crossed onto his land, and he could have his channelers move his already-prepared force to the west to react quickly. I would also do what I could to save his people until he arrived. It was the only way I could see to survive this mess and prevent Rynn from being drawn into it. I'd do anything to protect her.

"Very well. I'll open it," I agreed, still hating myself that I gave in to his demands.

My uncle smiled. "Wise decision, Aella."

I took the small bag of holmium he handed me and a small piece of parchment with the rune sequence drawn on it. Somehow, he knew it. I only memorized the ones I visited often, so I'd hoped I could claim ignorance on how to get there. One little paper destroyed that possibility, but I should have known my uncle would come prepared. I had never volunteered a sequence and always made him provide them, which he did without fail.

Inwardly, I prayed that Darrow would forgive me for this as I began channeling. It was almost as much of a struggle as it had been to reach Jolloure Island, likely to prevent dark elf infiltration, but it didn't take as long as I anticipated. Every time I pushed through a difficult ring, it seemed to get easier the next time as I learned the weave of the wards.

The first regiment of soldiers began moving the moment the air popped, and the blue light appeared, with the cavalry in the lead and followed by troops on foot. I held out my hand, keeping my power flowing as they disappeared inside. They moved so efficiently that the first regiment took just under ten minutes. Directly after them, the second began filing through the ring. It wasn't until near the end of the fourth that I began to feel the drain on my powers. By the time the fifth and last regiment disappeared, my hands shook.

Lord Morgunn grabbed my arm and guided me toward the portal with six soldiers escorting us. No doubt, he'd assign a few to guard me during the battle. I let my powers go two steps before we entered the murky blue. As usual, the portal stayed open long enough for us to enter.

An eternity seemed to pass before we reached the other side, or perhaps it felt like it because I really didn't want to know what I would find once we arrived. Finally, it pushed us out, and we stepped into total chaos. The strikes of swords, *wooshes* of magic, and pained screams filled the air. I'd never visited Radoumar before, but apparently, this was one of the few Veronnian rings positioned within the town. That made it easier to attack quickly, but it also meant I would stand witness to the carnage. My uncle couldn't hide me far away like usual.

Hopefully, Darrow would pick up on my arrival quickly, and he'd bring a large force with him, but that would take time. Lord Morgunn's army could do a lot of damage before my husband arrived.

Furious thoughts raced through my mind. Radoumar appeared to have fought back, based on the dozen dead Therressians I counted on the ground nearby, but the Veronnians must have already been overwhelmed near the ring. Our first soldiers who'd come nearly an hour ago had destroyed everything nearby, and mangled bodies lay everywhere—killed by magic, sword, or fire. My stomach threatened to revolt at the sight.

I took note of my uncle and his two soldiers, including the one who powered an impenetrable shield for him, heading northwest before they disappeared from view. Next, I tried to locate Ulmar but couldn't see him through the dense smoke and blazing buildings. He could have gone anywhere. The four guards my uncle left behind circled me, acting as my wardens and protectors.

They wouldn't be standing for long. My uncle knew I had been traveling places without his permission, and he'd been suspicious enough to keep the details of the attack from me until the last moment. Though I'd certainly pay for it later, I couldn't stand by and watch the massacre without helping. He wouldn't touch Rynn since he made it this far and would need her healing abilities after we returned. The only element slowing me down was having to bide my time for twenty minutes so I could regain a measure of my powers. I'd neared the end of my reserves when I finished channeling.

The waiting while hearing innocent fae die in the distance killed me, but I couldn't help them if I had no magic left. In the meantime, I paced the dais before the portal ring. My guards watched me warily, which made me wonder what my uncle had told them.

Finally, some of the weakness left my body as my strength began to renew. It was time to save as many people as possible. I clenched my fists, lifted my head, and pulled power to me. When it was concentrated enough, I sent it streaming out in every direction with high-velocity winds. It sent the four male elves guarding me flying and also struck down many more of Lord Morgunn's forces within the vicinity. Some hit the ground so hard that they were knocked unconscious, while others struggled to rise.

Not wasting a moment, I grabbed a sword from one of the fallen and raced toward the area with the worst screams. I had to dodge motionless bodies covered in blood and gore, a bleating pack of goats that had gotten loose, a wagon blazing with fire, and much more before I reached an area with active fighting.

"HELP! Please, someone, help me," a terrified woman screamed up ahead.

I squinted through the smoke until I saw a soldier wrestling her to the ground. My vision colored with red. It was bad enough they were killing innocent people, but raping them brought out even greater rage within me. The female elf had tears in her eyes as he yanked up her skirts.

Thrusting out a hand, I sent a focused burst of wind at the soldier. He slammed into the wall of a house directly behind him. I held him there as I ran up to the woman, dropping my sword to help her to her feet. She was trembling, eyes wild, and in shock.

"Get inside your house and hide," I said, catching her gaze. My right hand remained outstretched to keep my wind power going. But I picked up my sword with the other and pressed it into her grip. "Use this on anyone who tries to touch you."

"But..." She turned her head toward the soldier who'd harmed her.

I shook my head. "He'll never touch a woman again. I promise."

Eyes widening, she nodded.

"Now, go!" I urged.

She ran into the next house over from us, disappearing inside with the slam of a door. I was so furious at what this soldier had done that I had no mercy. When I turned to face him, he must have seen my rage because he began to babble incoherently where he lay pressed against the wall.

"You're on our side," he said, voice trembling. "You can't do this."

I pulled the dagger sheathed at my left thigh and stabbed the man in his stomach. My wind power ceased at the same time, leaving the man to collapse face-first on the ground. I kicked him onto his back with my boot.

He choked up blood, but that wasn't good enough. I pulled my dagger back out and stabbed him in the groin next, twisting my blade for maximum damage as the soldier screamed for the same mercy he'd refused to give the woman moments before. Finishing him would have been a kindness, so I pulled the blade and left him to bleed. It wouldn't take long to die, but he'd feel every moment of it until the death god came for him.

I ran through the smoky darkness, saving old men, children, and women as I found them. At first, my powers remained limited from opening the portal. Much of the time, I attacked with blades. As time wore on with endless death and intervening where I could, I knew I needed to conserve my magic for the return trip. None of my uncle's forces would dare harm me anyway since I was their only way back to Therress. I managed to injure some enough that they backed off, a few were too malicious to leave alive, and still more ran the moment I called them out for their behavior. It went on for so long that I lost track of time.

As I ushered a sister and brother—maybe five and six years old—to safety, the pounding of horses' hooves drew my attention. Through the hazy smoke, I caught sight of dozens of troops on horseback. The crest on their armor—two crossed swords with a red snake—proclaimed them to be Veronnian. I breathed a sigh of relief. With any luck, they'd end this battle soon.

Guiding the children to a stone house that didn't have a burning roof, I ushered them inside and told them to bar the door. Only after I heard it slam into place did I turn to watch the soldiers pass, pressing my back into a wall to appear as harmless as possible.

Thankfully, they ignored me. I was dressed in a gray fitted tunic and top with a blade strapped to me, and my blonde hair was pulled into a tight braid, then looped into a bun. It wasn't necessary for me to dress like the rest of the Therressian forces since I usually didn't enter the battle, and our side could all recognize me. That gave me a bit of anonymity in Veronna, but I didn't want to take chances since I was armed.

Once they passed, heading toward the fiercest fighting, I ran southwest toward the Bassaci Sea coastline. I'd seen a group of the Therressian troops go that route ten minutes before. Cutting between burning homes and quieter streets, I reached the edge of a cliff.

The drop-off was maybe fifty feet, and what I saw below chilled me to the bones. Dark elves were streaming out of boats pulled up to the beach. Each could hold about twenty soldiers, with a dozen currently emptying while countless more glided across the shadowy water toward the coast. Their black sails billowed in the wind. Lord Morgunn's forces met the first group to disembark and were undoubtedly discussing their plans. My uncle and cousin were nowhere to be seen, though.

I didn't know how many soldiers Darrow and his father could have mustered on short notice, but it surely couldn't be enough to face down my uncle's army and the coming dark elves. Without hesitation, I gathered power from deep within myself. I'd regained most of my strength since arriving hours ago. I used it to send hurricane-force winds full-scale into the boats. Screaming as the power pulsed through me, I pushed harder than I ever had before to spread the gusts far and wide so that no one on the shoreline would avoid my wrath.

It sent soldiers flying into the sea, capsized boats, and a massive wave formed to crash into the larger ships farther back. Shocked, I took in the damage while I pushed until nothing remained unscathed. I'd never truly let myself go like this. The well of magic had been there for a long time, but I'd never needed to use it on such a vast scale.

I maintained the wind for nearly a minute, ensuring every boat and ship had either overturned or been pushed far back to sea. Most of the soldiers on the beach were submerged in the water, except some who'd made it to a set of stone stairs a few hundred feet away.

My focus on my magic prevented me from seeing the threat until it was nearly too late. From the corner of my eye, I caught the blade's arc a split second before it came down. I shifted to avoid it, but not quickly enough. The tip tore through my tunic and cut into my shoulder. I cried out in pain.

Backing away, I tried to focus my magic to push my attacker away, but the agony made it difficult. The dark elf who'd evaded my attack on the beach had bitter hatred in his eyes. He wore a black leather uniform with countless blades strapped to him, and he had long, dark hair that framed his face.

"You're going to die, girl," he said, raising his sword again.

I pulled my dagger, determined to block him as best I could.

"Not today, she isn't," Darrow said coldly, riding up from my right. He sat on his dapple-gray stallion with blood splatter across his face and uniform. The moonlight revealed features that were fierce and full of wrath.

He lifted his hand, and the dark elf screamed. A moment later, my attacker's body crumpled to the ground in a misshapen heap that shouldn't have been possible for a human body.

"Did you just crush all his bones?" I asked, horrified and relieved at the same time for my husband's timely intervention.

His lips spread with a disturbing smile. "Yes."

"Usually, you settle for breaking their necks," I said, still shocked at his appearance.

Darrow rode his horse closer. "He shouldn't have hurt you."

I gripped the wound on my shoulder, attempting to staunch the blood. "Thank you for stopping him. He caught me off guard."

"I came as soon as I heard the roar of wind, suspecting it had to be you." He nodded toward the sea, where only a few of the dark elves had managed to pull themselves from the water so far. "Thank you for repelling most of them. It would have been difficult to face two forces at once."

"It was the least I could do, considering I brought one of them here."

His gaze narrowed. "Speaking of which, I thought your uncle didn't know you could transport his soldiers this far."

I ran my gaze around us, making sure no one from Therress was nearby to see us. The smoke and darkness made it difficult, but all I could make out were figures fighting between buildings in the distance. No one was close.

"Apparently," I said, returning my attention to Darrow. "He had someone track me while I was supposed to be visiting my sister. He knows I went to Penoria, but he has no idea who came with me. Unfortunately, that trip was enough to prove I've been lying about the scope of my power. It also showed I could bring his troops here. They didn't tell me any of this until it was time to open the portal, so I had no way to warn you, and he threatened Rynn if I didn't do it."

Darrow cursed. "Forcing you to transport him here is likely not all he'll do to you."

It might have been if I had behaved and stayed by the ring for the duration of the battle, but that was a moot point. I'd definitely pay for helping the Veronnians tonight.

"Probably." A lump formed in my throat. "But I have to portal the Therressian army home, and he'll make me return with them. You know there isn't another choice."

His grip on the horse's reins tightened, and the expression on his face was even darker than when he discovered my scars. "I agree you need to get your people out of here, or else this battle won't end until all your soldiers are dead and far too many of my people die with them, but I'm going to find a way to free you. I vow this to you, Aella."

I nodded, a lump forming in my throat. "I know you will, Dare."

With one final intense look filled with frustration and regret, he rode off. He was undoubtedly in charge of his forces and had used precious minutes to save me. We also couldn't afford to be caught speaking to each other. Matters were dire enough already.

I hurried toward the portal. There was so much mayhem and destruction, troops on both sides running back and forth, that it took nearly half an hour to reach the ring. The village only had about four thousand inhabitants, but the homes and shops were spaced widely apart, allowing for personal vegetable gardens enclosed by neat wooden fences. As a result, it turned the town into a large maze with all the fires, smoke, and destruction obfuscating my path.

One of our military healers had already begun work near the ring. He was busy caring for the many wounded, but he handed me a bandage I could wrap around my shoulder until I could receive further treatment. I did my best to wind it tightly so it could help stop the bleeding. One of the guards I'd knocked out with my wind power earlier brought me a canteen of water.

I gave him a surprised look. "Shouldn't you be angry with me?"

"Those two are," he said, gesturing to where his comrades stood about fifty feet away. "Some of us understand why you did it. Attacking enemy soldiers is one thing, but killing innocent people is another. You're one of the only ones who can help them without being charged with treason. You gave us a valid excuse for why we couldn't stop you."

That was the thing about war. There were always good and bad people on both sides, though it was easy to forget that when you were in the midst of too much horror and death. I gave him a weak smile. "Thank you. I managed to save a few lives tonight, so it was worth it."

No need to mention the fleet of boats and ships I'd capsized and the people I'd drowned. I didn't know why the dark elves were here, but it was more than suspicious that they'd arrived soon after my uncle's forces. Of course, he'd worked with them before, so I shouldn't have been surprised even if it would enrage our king.

"You're a good woman, Lady Aella."

Before I could respond, Ulmar appeared in the clearing, passing by the many wounded Therressians. He marched straight for me. "Father is putting out the order to retreat and wants you to open the portal now, but send everyone to Ivory Castle. We need to start moving the injured to where we have healers waiting."

I stood. "Of course."

It was a good thing I'd had enough time to recover from my last use of power, and channeling to locations in my homeland was always much easier. I needed that advantage with my wounded shoulder weakening me.

I pulled my pouch of holmium and began chanting. Within a minute, the blue glow appeared, and all the walking wounded went through first. Therressian soldiers who arrived after that helped carry those who couldn't move on their own, or put them on horses. Before long, they were gone, and I continued to channel as more and more troops staggered from the battlefield. Time seemed to pass slowly as my powers steadily drained to hold open the portal.

Sick relief filled me when my uncle appeared across the clearing, shouting that the last of the surviving troops were following shortly behind him. I estimated I had maybe ten minutes left before I would completely exhaust my magic. Hopefully, they would make it before then.

When Lord Morgunn reached within forty feet of the large ring, Darrow appeared from the smoky ruins to my left with several elves at his side. Hope lifted in my chest at the sight of him and the furious vengeance written all over his chiseled face. He marched forward to intercept my uncle, his hand held out toward him.

My gaze shot to Lord Morgunn, and I found he'd noticed my husband as well. The soldier with the shield had his palms raised already. When I squinted, I could just make out the bubble around him and my uncle. Darrow couldn't get through it to use his powers on them. More fleeing troops arrived and surrounded the front of the ring as an additional layer of protection, while I could do nothing except continue channeling.

My husband and his people, including Loden and a couple of others I didn't recognize, stopped a dozen paces from our group. Darrow's expression turned cold and brutal as he began targeting everyone who didn't have a shield. The sound of breaking necks reverberated around me, and bodies dropped two and three at a time.

Ulmar hid behind me and whispered. "If you stop channeling before we make it through, I swear I'll kill Rynn to punish you."

My chest tightened. The thought of releasing the portal had only begun to form in my mind, but since he was evil, he would have considered that sooner. Now, I had to keep weakening myself while being unable to do anything to help my husband. Meanwhile, Ulmar abandoned me to sneak into my uncle's shield bubble so he could avoid harm. The only good thing about it was that he wouldn't be able to use his pain magic to target Veronnians.

Darrow's companions threw knives at the translucent barrier around Lord Morgunn, but they all bounced off. Then, Loden stepped forward and lifted his hand. A solid beam of red-hot light shot straight at Lord Morgunn. It hit the shield without penetrating, but he continued to feed it, making it glow brighter. My jaw dropped at his impressive control of the ability I had always failed to master.

He might not open portals, but we shared the same light power. It was a common gift among the druids, and since he was half like me, that made sense. I'd never thought to ask what magic he might have. To be fair, I'd never thought to ask much of anything about him, except that Darrow had mentioned once that Loden had never met his father from Alavaar and grew up with his mother in Veronna.

I felt guilty for not showing more interest as I watched him slowly eat away at the shield. Whenever the opportunity arose again, I would have to request his help in improving my skills. The level of focus on his face told me he was giving it all he had so he could reach my uncle.

Finally, a hole formed near the top, about the size of a head. Darrow lifted his hands, ready to grab the occupants inside the shield. My heart thrummed as I waited in anticipation for him to finish my uncle and finally free me.

Ice spears—one after another in rapid succession—flew from that hole and arced through the air. I watched with horror as Darrow, Loden, and the two other Veronnian soldiers attempted to dodge them, but there were too many. My husband deflected many with his power, but they kept coming. In the next minute, all four of them had been struck.

I nearly lost control of my channeling as panic filled me. The men collapsed, and my husband fell to his knees with his stomach impaled. My uncle's magic not only pierced them deeply, but the icy spears began melting and shifting to spread over their bodies with a glaze that hardened as it set. If it penetrated far enough into their bodies, it would freeze and kill them.

That could not happen—not now! Without thinking, I let go of my channeling magic and started to take a step toward them, but I hadn't anticipated how weak I'd grown. My legs buckled. Strong arms grabbed me from behind and hauled me toward the ring a handful of feet away. I tried to struggle, but whoever held me had an iron grip. They rushed us toward it before it closed.

My focus stayed trained on Darrow's face as his furious eyes watched me being dragged away from him. We'd lost our one opportunity to finish my uncle for good. The last I saw was the skin of his neck turning blue and climbing toward his head as I was yanked into the portal.

Chapter 50

Aella

Moments later, I found myself thrust out of the ring and into the Ivory Castle keep. My whole world was falling apart, yet I couldn't do anything to stop it. Could Darrow survive something like that? It had been many years since I'd seen Lord Morgunn use his magic that way, but I remembered it having deadly consequences if healers didn't act fast enough.

Ulmar shoved me to the ground. "You stay there."

"Take her weapon," my uncle ordered, shooting me a cold look. "She drained herself holding the portal open, so we shouldn't need to worry about her powers for a while."

They thought I stopped channeling because of exhaustion, thank the nameless ones.

As my cousin pulled the blade sheathed at my hip, I noted the anticipatory gleam in his eyes. He undoubtedly looked forward to torturing me soon. My only relief was that they assumed my complete drain of magic would mean I couldn't regenerate for nearly a day, negating the need for an iron cuff right now. They had no idea I still had a small measure left, and if I were patient, it would grow. All I needed was time.

Ulmar stood next to me, where I crouched and drew ragged breaths as I fought tears of worry for Darrow, Loden, and the others. I couldn't let them see me cry, or they'd suspect how much I cared about the Veronnians my uncle attacked near the ring. Instead, I made myself focus on my surroundings. Wounded lay everywhere on the staging grounds, with Briauna, Rynn, and other healers tending them. While my shoulder wound hurt, so many soldiers had it much worse. At least I could function and walk.

Lord Morgunn had wandered away to speak with his captains. He'd need to organize the care of the wounded and dead, as well as consider security measures in case Veronna retaliated soon. I hoped that would keep him busy for a while.

A gnome with a kind face brought me some water, and I gulped it down. I hadn't realized how thirsty I was until that moment. Handing the empty cup back to her, I gave her a weak smile. "Thank you."

She dipped her chin. "Of course."

Tadeus worked in the distance, delivering bandages and other supplies. He hadn't gone with us this time. When he came near where I crouched, holding my wounded shoulder, he paused a moment to meet my gaze. The emotion in his eyes...there was terror and worry for me. A chill ran down my spine. I glanced at Ulmar, whose expression curdled my stomach and made me want to run. To test a theory, I slowly rose to my feet.

"You stay right here," he said, grabbing my wounded shoulder and shoving me down again.

Blinding pain tore through me where he squeezed tightly. "Stop!"

"No. I won't allow you to escape the punishment you're due."

His grip was so tight it brought tears to my eyes, and I looked away. After a minute, he released me but stayed so close that he could easily grab me again. More time passed before Lord Morgunn nodded at Ulmar, and he jerked me to my feet. Several guards joined us as they led me toward the castle like a fugitive, and with each step, I had a feeling I was walking to my doom. The look in my uncle's eyes was pure rage.

As soon as we passed the armory, my heart began to thunder in my chest as I noted the direction we headed. "Where are we going?"

Lord Morgunn held up a hand, and we stopped. "I know what you did to the dark elf fleet, Aella, and I also saw Lord Gannon's son save you. As if that wasn't appalling enough, you spoke to him for several minutes. There wasn't a hint of animosity between you."

I swallowed hard. He'd somehow seen us by the cliff, and I'd missed it. I had kept an eye on our surroundings, but with all the chaos and smoke, he might have been far enough back for me to miss him. The only good thing was that he shouldn't have been able to listen to our conversation from that distance. My traveling to Penoria behind my uncle's back to research the fountain might have raised some ire, but consorting with the enemy and helping them was the worst thing I could have done in my uncle's eyes. I really was doomed.

"What are you going to do with me?" I asked, chest tightening.

"You have committed treason, niece, by consorting with the enemy." Lord Morgunn stepped closer with pure malice on his face. "The only thing that will save you is telling us all you know—otherwise, you will be executed."

Panic surged through me, and my mind raced. I refused to tell him anything useful, so what did I do? For all I knew, Darrow wouldn't survive the night after what my uncle did to him. Everything felt hopeless. "Kill me now because you'll get nothing out of me."

He swung his hand so fast I couldn't avoid the open-handed slap. My teeth cut into my cheek, and blood filled my mouth. Ulmar had to hold onto me to keep me from falling.

"Don't be so sure," Lord Morgunn said, leaning close to me. "As you're aware, there are many ways to make someone talk. I will employ most of them before I resort to execution."

My mind flashed to all the previous instances that he'd hurt me in the past, the pain and agony I'd suffered. I hadn't committed nearly as severe offenses those times. He would torture me in ways he'd never dared before, and I didn't know if I could handle it. Not now, not again. My survival instincts surged, and I did the only thing I could under the circumstances.

I pulled in the small measure of power I'd regained since returning to Ivory Castle and pushed wind out in every direction. My uncle, cousin, and the guards flew back twenty feet. I took off running, ignoring how it jarred my wounded shoulder and sent one more strong gust at the guard between me and the direction I wanted to go. He slammed into a side wall of the officer's quarters.

It bought me enough time that I nearly made it to my garden entrance before a knife sank into the right side of my lower back. I cried out, barely keeping from falling to my knees. The sound of pounding footsteps grew closer, urging me to keep moving no matter the pain.

I quickly stumbled into my sanctuary, making it ten feet inside before collapsing onto the cobbled path. The garden was the place I'd always intended to make my last stand if it ever came down to it. Though it was dark, a hint of moonlight cast over my plants.

"Protect me," I begged them in a pained wheeze.

In the next moments, nearly a dozen uprooted themselves from the ground. They moved between me and the entrance like wrathful guards as my cousin Ulmar stopped under the arch. I crawled a little farther away while keeping an eye on him. The blade in my back hurt, but I feared taking it out would make matters worse.

A crunchertrap snapped at my cousin in a warning. He swiped his sword at it, but the plant swayed back to avoid the blade. At the same time, one of the tractvines lashed out and caught Ulmar around the neck and face, sticking its pointed end into his left eye. He screamed as the tip of the tendril gouged into him over and over, with blood and other bits spilling from the wound.

As the plant began to drag him into the garden, a soldier arrived to chop at the vine and free my cousin, but the damage was done. Ulmar backed away, holding a hand to the left side of his mutilated face. I'd just barely caught a glimpse of his empty eye socket and the blackened skin around it where the tractvine must have inserted some of its nasty poison. A healer could stop the spread, but they couldn't repair that kind of damage.

Meanwhile, the hunter-green vereloe to my left sent one of its vine arms toward my back. As the tendril wrapped itself around the protruding blade, another one plucked one of its fleshy leaves, breaking it open to reveal a natural healing gelatin inside.

The brilliant plant quickly pulled the dagger and pressed the leaf to the wound. The relief was almost instant. While the vereloe wasn't mobile, it could tend wounds if someone who'd gained its loyalty came close enough. I'd aimed my collapse precisely. It went after my shoulder next, tucking another opened leaf under the bandage. That gave me more relief.

"You can't hide in there forever, Aella," Lord Morgunn said as he stopped a few feet from the arch with the other soldiers who hesitated to enter after seeing Ulmar. My uncle had a scowl, but his expression transformed into incredulity as he witnessed my flora tending me and the others standing guard, ready to tear him to pieces. "Where did you find all these plants?

It had been a long time since he'd bothered looking in here.

I angled my head to see him better from where I lay on my stomach. "All over the world. When you can access a portal to almost anywhere, you explore and discover all sorts of interesting things."

"So many secrets you kept, Aella. I'd admire you if you weren't undermining my plans." He lifted his hands and shot streams of ice toward the crunchertraps, shocked when his magic didn't touch them. My uncle could only use curses against people, so he'd tried his other gift against my garden. Unlike with Darrow and his people—my heart clenched—nothing in here could be harmed by magic.

I let out an ironic laugh, thankful I'd at least thwarted him on this. "I suspected you might do that someday, so I put protection spells on the whole garden to prevent ice and flames from harming anything in here."

It had been no easy task to develop the right weave of defenses and build them up over the years so that no one could break them easily. He could spend a week trying to crack them, but it would be of no use to him. It would take longer than that. I'd known better than to block him from entering because that would have drawn his attention and made him suspicious. Instead, I'd focused on spells for specific types of attacks. It also made them more impervious to tampering than if I'd created something broader.

Lord Morgunn narrowed his eyes and pulled his sword. My intelligent plants scooted back a couple of feet rather than attack. Every type of defense I had on the place stopped under that arch, and my sweet little beauties knew it. My uncle swung at them, but they avoided his reach.

"You always were too smart for your own good, niece." His gaze returned to me with barely restrained fury. "You know we'll cut down every one of your precious plants if that's what it takes to reach you."

I considered the portal ring at the back of my garden, covered in vines at the moment to hide it. I wished I could use that to get away, but I'd drained myself escaping to the garden. There wasn't enough magic left in me to even channel to the nearest location. Maybe if my plants held them off long enough, but I'd lost a lot of blood, which would slow down my magic regeneration. Even then, I doubted my curse would allow me to channel before putting me to sleep. That could never be my escape as long as my uncle lived.

"You three," Lord Morgunn pointed at several soldiers beyond the archway. "Clear a path so we can reach her."

Unfortunately, I didn't have a spell to protect against blades because that would prevent me from using my trimming shears. My plants would have to defend themselves against swords. I could only pray to the nameless ones that they didn't come to too much harm. That was the trouble with spending all these years tending them—I'd grown attached.

The three troops ran forward, swinging at the crunchertraps in the lead. The massive lavender flowers ducked, so the blades went right over them before lunging forward to take chunks of flesh from two of the elves. Then, the plants flung the men straight into the waiting tractvines. The snake-like flora wrapped themselves around each of the soldiers, squeezing until bones crunched and screams filled the garden.

The sounds cut off abruptly a few seconds later. I didn't dare look, but I knew it meant those elves were no longer breathing. Near the archway, both crunchertraps mauled the third soldier until he was bleeding and missing too much flesh to do more than wail in pain. Someone else darted in quickly to drag him out of there.

"Retrieve more soldiers—as many as you can," Lord Morgunn ordered the remaining female elf.

She dashed away.

My uncle eyed the garden, undoubtedly contemplating how to defeat it. Strategizing against an army of flora was something fae usually didn't have to contemplate. He lifted a hand and once more tried pushing his ice magic toward my large flowers with blood dripping from their petals. One of them sneezed at him, spraying red droplets all over his face.

He scowled in disgust. "How is it that my ice won't even form in there?"

"Oh, Uncle. I wouldn't have wanted them catching frostbite in the winter," I said wryly, though that hadn't been my true motivation. I'd worried he'd try punishing my plants someday instead of only me.

Another soldier arrived, and they moved a short distance from the walled garden, whispering low enough that I couldn't hear them. It would be nice if they could keep planning for another thirty minutes. Maybe I could fool my mind into escaping this place. If I thought about only going a short distance and nowhere out of Therress, would that trick the curse? I had no idea, but it would be worth a try.

My hopes crashed when, less than ten minutes later, the female elf returned with more soldiers than I could count from my position on the cobbled path. I scooted back farther to give my plants room to maneuver. Two of my tractvines were out of the fight since it would take weeks to consume their fresh meals, but I still had a few more that would love to eat something meaty, and one that was only wounded from having a short section of its limb cut off. They mainly subsisted on underground insects and the occasional rodent, so tonight was a real treat for them if they could catch a whole person.

I only felt bad that the soldiers would be seriously harmed or lose their lives because of me. If I didn't know for sure that my uncle was serious about torturing and possibly executing me, I'd surrender to save my plants and the troops. I had to consider the fountain as well. If I died, all hope of retrieving it before our world reached the point of no return would be gone.

The next few minutes passed so quickly that I could hardly keep track. My uncle's military contingent stormed my garden en masse, swinging blades as they moved. The crunchertraps wounded the first handful, tossing a few at the tractvines and other malicious plants before the fae cut them down. A tear fell down my cheek as they dropped to the stones, lifeless and missing many of their petals.

The spittlestalks were out of season, but they managed to spray a little poison when the soldiers passed them. Four elves and goblins choked and coughed, gasping for breath. They fled moments later.

All the remaining soldiers, about a dozen, managed to slice up most of the plants that got in their way. A few fae lost their lives, but the majority managed to keep moving forward. As they approached me, I caught sight of plant pieces littering the path behind them, and I wanted to scream in agony at their loss.

A couple of other deadly varieties remained stationed in front of me as my last line of defense. They sent out tendrils to trip their targets' feet and more to pull off their limbs with ruthless violence that even shocked me. My garden had no mercy for its invaders.

Several troops were torn apart, with high-pitched screams and sprays of blood filling the air. In the end, though, the last of my warrior plants were butchered by blades. There were too many soldiers for them to take on all at once, forcing me to watch their massacre with pain and horror. They suffered and died—for me.

In the end, it turned eerily quiet.

My uncle's remaining soldiers roughly grabbed my arms and dragged me through plant remains and fae body parts toward the archway. My feet scraped against the uneven and blood-soaked stones. Ahead, I could see the anti-magic cuff Lord Morgunn held.

With the vestiges of power I had left, I sent healing magic to my garden. It wouldn't save the ones with too much damage, but it would give some of the others a fighting chance of recovering. I didn't keep a drop of strength for myself, giving them my all. They deserved it.

We made it past the archway, and my uncle took the honor of cuffing me. They callously dragged me along the path toward the front corner of the castle as I tried not to cry out from the pain of my injuries. None of them showed an ounce of mercy after what my garden had done to their comrades. I stumbled down the stairs to the dungeon, twisting my ankle midway. Though I cried out, they didn't seem to care or slow their pace.

Finally, they hauled me into the last cell and shackled me to the wall. Lord Morgunn ordered two of his largest and most vicious soldiers to beat me, but warned them to take care and not maim or kill me. They struck my body everywhere so many times that my screams grew hoarse, and I sagged against the chains. I couldn't say how much time had passed before darkness overtook me.

Chapter 51

Darrow

Every part of me ached as I fought to pull myself from a deep sleep. There was something important I needed to do, but it felt like wading through sludge to try to remember. Little by little, bits and pieces of memories surfaced. I recalled the battle, seeing Aella repel the dark elf forces into the sea, and after that, my facing off with Lord Morgunn. He had struck me with a spear of ice that had felt unbearably cold. The last image I recalled was Aella being dragged into the portal ring, her face filled with fear and horror.

I sat straight up and opened my eyes. The muscles in my body protested loudly, but I didn't care. My sister sat in a chair next to my bed, her feet propped up on the nightstand. A flash of relief crossed her gaze before it turned detached.

"About time you woke up," she said, lowering her feet to the floor and flinging her long, brown-black hair behind her back. "The healer lifted the sleep spell two hours ago."

Two hours? "How long have I been down?"

"About two and a half days."

"Aella is in trouble, and you let me sleep that long?" I asked, furious.

She rolled her eyes. "You were at death's door for most of it. Lord Morgunn does terrifying work with his ice magic, and it took that long for the healers to repair the damage to your skin and organs. At least now we know why we kept finding frozen victims every time we fought Therress."

I lifted the blanket to check myself, realizing I was naked underneath, and noted the top layers of my skin were new and still raw from regrowth. Perhaps it was best I hadn't seen how bad I looked in those early hours after the battle. My stomach still had a dark spot just below my navel from where the spear had impaled me.

If I were this bad... "What about Loden and the other two soldiers?"

"Loden was the least injured since the ice pierced him in the thigh first. He woke last night." She paused and shook her head. "The others were struck higher in the chest and didn't survive the first day."

I closed my eyes, mourning their loss. They'd been good, loyal elves. Once I finished collecting myself, I looked at Faina again. "I need to rescue Aella before it's too late."

She frowned. "What do you mean? Surely, her uncle wouldn't kill her."

I relayed all that I could recall from that night. "He knows she betrayed him, and he's undoubtedly punishing her as we speak."

A deadly, cold calm took over Faina's features. "Then you'll find a way to rescue her."

At that moment, Loden barged through the door. He was still pale like me from his injuries, but otherwise, he appeared fully recovered. "Good, you're awake."

"You know what I need to do." He had been there for much of it, and I'd told him what happened between Aella and the dark elves before we tried to intercept Lord Morgunn.

He nodded. "Our spies reported that Aella was hauled away by her uncle and cousin soon after arriving at Ivory Castle keep, but they were unable to follow and find out what happened to her. Anyone who knows anything isn't talking about it. In anticipation of your waking, I sent one of your sebeskas out at dawn. She should be approaching the castle soon. We can't formulate a plan until we have an idea of what is happening there."

Nameless ones bless him for thinking ahead as always. "Thank you. What is the status of Radoumar?"

"It's a disaster," Faina said, sighing. "After we sent you and the worst of the wounded here to Darynia, we had to track down the remaining dark elves that your frighteningly powerful wife missed. We also had to contain the fires, gather the dead, and set up tents for those who lost their homes, which was nearly two hundred."

She paused, and amusement lit in her gray eyes. "More than once, we heard the story of a beautiful blonde lady in gray who stepped in to protect them from the horde of enemy soldiers. Father isn't happy that Aella opened that portal for her uncle, but he recognizes that she mitigated the damage as much as she could."

"Yes, but she is undoubtedly paying for her selflessness now."

My sister's gaze turned haunted because she had suffered during our yearly trips to Karganoth as well. They usually separated us, and like me, she never talked about her experiences. I had no idea what had happened to her, but I suspected she faced circumstances similar to mine. After seeing the evidence of what Lord Morgunn had done to Aella in the past, we could each imagine how much worse it might get for her.

"That's why I had the healers concentrate more on you and Loden than the other injured," she said, straightening her shoulders as she undoubtedly pushed old memories away. "We needed you back at full strength as soon as possible."

"Thank you."

She shook her head. "No need for that. I only wish I could come with you, but Father has insisted I head back to Radoumar in a few hours. He just returned from there and needs me to take over the cleanup. I only refused to leave until you woke."

I could only imagine how much that task would annoy her, but she'd do as ordered.

Loden stepped closer to the bed. "The sebeska, Tullar, should be at the castle now."

"Good." That was the bird who had the strongest bond with me, which he knew. "I'll mind link with her now."

"Don't use too much energy," Faina warned, narrowing her eyes. "It's going to take another day before you're strong enough to go anywhere, but it will be even longer if you push yourself too hard."

"I'll take care," I promised. There was no way I'd risk becoming too weak to save my wife. Even now, I could feel that I wasn't back to full strength, but a short trip in the bird's mind would only require a small measure of my power.

Lying back down on my large bed, I closed my eyes and focused on the sebeska. A full minute passed before I penetrated the sebeska's mind to see through her eyes and hear through her ears. I allowed Tullar to maintain her autonomy in flight, as she was highly intelligent and understood her mission, but I would guide the bird as needed.

The Ivory Castle keep appeared below with a different range of colors than what my elf vision could discern. It always took a moment to adjust to the change. The walls appeared to have a slight yellow tinge to them through Tullar's vision. I first searched the area near the ring, followed by the training area, and finally Aella's walled garden.

It caught me off guard at what I found there, and shock nearly paralyzed me. Nearly a third of her plants lay in disarray across the central stone path, with some dead and already decaying. Others struggled to recover from a brutality that could only come from sharp blades. A few managed to extend a few roots into the nearby soil for much-needed nourishment, but their dull color wasn't encouraging. Dried violet, yellow, and pink petals lay scattered everywhere with blood and shriveled meat of some sort within some of the damaged bulbs.

Upon closer inspection, I counted five elven bodies with tractvines coiled tightly around them deeper within the garden beds. Their skin was almost black from the toxins the species injected to break down their forms for easier consumption. Lord Morgunn must have chosen to leave his people there because the only way to extract someone from the powerful plant was to hack the victim and vine to pieces.

My wife had a good heart, but she clearly had a dark side, as evidenced by her choice of plants and her ruthless use of them against her own people. That combination was one of her more endearing qualities.

The sebeska I inhabited was especially sensitive to moods within nature, and she sensed the sadness, despair, and worry coming from the surviving plants. As I looked through the bird's eyes, a story began to form.

Aella must have escaped her uncle at some point, soon after returning from the battle, and fled to the garden to make her last stand—already injured. She'd used her plants to help protect her based on the smeared blood that went down the walkway quite a distance and stopped just after the mess. Her guardians had put up a good fight, but they must have become overwhelmed.

If five full bodies remained and various parts of others were strewn about everywhere, how many had Lord Morgunn ordered to invade the walled garden? It could have been two dozen or more. He must have been determined and furious if he were willing to sacrifice that many soldiers to apprehend his niece.

The trail of destruction ended about halfway through the garden from the entry arch. I had to assume that was how far Aella made it before stopping, but why didn't she use the plant distraction to reach the ring in the back? I studied all the evidence, trying to piece together the rest of the story.

Considering the smeared blood leading to a dried pool at the end, she must have been badly injured beyond the shoulder wound I knew about. Holding a portal long enough for all the Therressian soldiers to escape must have been taxing as well. Perhaps she simply didn't have the strength to open another one so soon. Her plants obviously did their best against overwhelming odds, but they couldn't buy her enough time to escape.

Then, it occurred to me that her curse wouldn't have allowed her to flee anyway. She'd likely hoped her uncle wouldn't have gone to such extremes to capture her. Maybe if she'd had more time and fewer attackers, she could have regained enough strength to fight back and even kill Lord Morgunn. Time hadn't been on her side with an uncle who would stop at nothing to retrieve and punish her, though.

The sound of voices nearby drew my bird's attention. I instructed Tullar to fly to a nearby tree and settle on a low branch. Lord Morgunn and Ulmar came into view. The father and son walked side by side, with the younger wearing a large bandage over his left eye. I idly wondered what had happened to him that the healer couldn't have repaired the damage by now. The two stopped at the archway to view the massacre within, disgust on their faces.

"You know I only let her have this place so she'd stay out of the way and not get suspicious of our activities. It was an excellent distraction, but we should destroy all of this except for the snapper berry bushes since I do love the fruit they provide," Aella's uncle said.

Ulmar scowled. "Not all the dangerous plants are dead, and we'll likely lose lives going in there again. I tried tossing poison in there yesterday, but it appears she has a plant in there that can neutralize it. Since she warded against my fire and your ice, the best course of action is to deprive the garden of water and nutrients. Everything will eventually die a slow death without her being able to tend to it."

"She still won't tell us anything, no matter how we torture her, but even if she finally confesses, she'll never be allowed back in here again." Lord Morgunn shook his head. "I lost far too many soldiers, and plenty more are still recovering from their injuries to reach her. Not to mention you losing an eye to those damn vines. I cannot forgive such betrayal, especially after catching her speaking with Lord Gannon's son openly during our battle at Radoumar."

The sebeska and I stilled at those words. He'd seen us together, which would only make the situation worse for Aella. That cold, calculating man would see it as nothing short of treason. I wished I hadn't had to step in to save her from the dark elf, but she would have died if I hadn't intervened. Lord Morgunn must have been hiding somewhere nearby where we couldn't see him. If I'd known, I would have done something differently, though I couldn't say what.

I'd tried attacking him near the portal—the one place I could count on him showing up near the end—but that had gone terribly wrong. For a madman, he was powerful and cunning. If I could have killed him then, Aella would have been safe now.

"It's going to be at least a few hours before she wakes again after her last beating," Ulmar said, rubbing his chin. "The lack of water and food must be wearing on her, along with all the broken bones. Perhaps this evening, she'll rethink her silence if we taunt her about her garden."

As my anger grew, the sebeska shifted nervously in response to my roiling emotions. I had to get a grip on myself, or I'd lose focus. I wished I could kill the two elves now for what they were doing to my wife. They would pay dearly...soon.

"Yes," Aella's uncle agreed. "But I will go to the dungeon to do the questioning. You cannot miss the meeting tonight."

"No, of course not, considering it's my..."

"Shh, we must assume there are ears everywhere. Just be there and make certain the contract is in order beforehand," Lord Morgunn said.

They walked away, voices fading. My fury was so great that I could feel the tension coiling my body in my true form. They'd locked Aella in the dungeon and had been torturing her for all this time. The nameless ones only knew how much she had suffered so far, but the mention of broken bones alone had me seething. I'd known they must have been punishing her while I recovered from my injuries, but hearing the details made it worse. How could they do that to their own family?

I drew a deep breath and concentrated on carefully extracting my mind from Tullar. It was time to speak with my father and form a plan to save Aella before it was too late.

***

Barging into Lord Gannon's office, I found him surrounded by a servant, several military captains, and my older brother, Hagon. They stood at a table covered with maps. My father looked up, gaze softening a degree. "Good to see you up and around, son."

Though it wasn't easy, I did my best to stand straight and hide the weakness in my muscles. According to the healer who saw me right before I came to the office, I'd had frostbite damage deep in my tissues. He'd promised that if I rested for the next twenty-four hours, I'd return to nearly full strength. I was tired, but I had to speak with my father, and then I would consign myself to my bed. Whatever it took to save Aella, that's what I would do.

"I request a force to take Ivory Castle tomorrow night," I said, not bothering with pleasantries.

He gestured at the map on the table. "We are making plans for retaliation, but it will be at least two weeks before we can carry them out. Are you even in any shape to enter a battle right now?"

"I will be in another day, and I can't wait weeks. My wife will be dead by then," I said.

Shock filled everyone's features, aside from my father, because they hadn't known about Aella or our marriage. The time for secrecy was gone. I might not love her, but nameless ones be damned. She was mine, and no one was allowed to hurt her, especially not my enemies.

Hagon frowned. "What wife? Since when have you been married, and why haven't I heard of it?"

He'd been away during the few days Aella spent here unconscious. As the heir to Veronna, I understood his frustration about being kept in the dark, though. One only had to look at him to understand he was born for the role of leading our people. Like me, he could not feel love, but he was wise and sensible, with a rare air of confidence that people followed easily.

He had our father's medium build and warm ivory skin. His brown hair was cut short and styled perfectly neat. Hagon always dressed impeccably as well, currently wearing a golden doublet tailored to fit precisely to his body, a pair of crisp, black pants, and shiny onyx boots. While he wasn't classically handsome, he presented such a strong figure that his presence still drew eyes. I'd always envied him for his clean looks, while everyone saw me as more of a monster than an elf. Then again, I did have more fun playing my darker role.

"I've been married since mid-spring," I said brusquely, stepping farther into the room. "We've kept it a secret due to her identity and other complications."

Strain lined his eyes briefly before he collected himself and put on a stoic mask. "Who?"

"Lady Aella of Therress." I turned to my father. "Her uncle put her in the dungeon soon after they returned from the battle at Radoumar. She fought back, but ultimately, they took her and have been torturing her ever since. Her uncle doesn't know about our marriage yet since she's refusing to talk, but he does know she helped us." I went on to relay all I'd heard from Loden and from spying through my sebeska.

My father moved to the window near his desk, staring out of it in deep thought. "You'll have to kill the Lord of Therress to free her, and without enough justification, the king will have no choice except to imprison you. If you could have managed it at Radoumar, it would have been better, but he is a wily bastard. It doesn't help that he seems to disappear for most of the battle. I suspect he uses some sort of invisibility—the coward."

That was my suspicion as well.

"If we begin spreading the word of my marriage, then I'd have justification to storm Ivory Castle and take Aella from her uncle. If she's harmed, the law will allow me the right to execute him," I replied.

Hagon gave me a quizzical look. "What if Lord Morgunn has that guard with the shields near him?"

I'd already considered that. "I plan to send a couple of men in advance to take that one out while he's not with the lord and wouldn't expect it."

Since one of my closest friends could turn invisible, he'd be able to handle it quietly. Jax could also handle hiding one other person simultaneously. I'd insist on his taking another fae with useful powers, so he wouldn't be alone in enemy territory until I got there.

"Why should any of our people risk their lives for our enemy's niece, even if she's your wife?" my brother asked incredulously.

I understood why he was asking, even if it irritated me that he couldn't simply support me, so I gave him the best reason to motivate him. "She is the first channeler in centuries who is strong enough to open the portal to where the

Naforya Fountain is located. If you ever want to feel love for your wife in your lifetime, you want mine alive and well."

His eyes widened, and he looked at our father. "Is this true?"

"She's passed every test your brother and others have given her with little difficulty. Not even the most heavily warded and distant rings have stopped her," he replied, then his lips twitched. "If that weren't enough, I've never seen anyone with power strong enough to throw a whole fleet of dark elves back the way she did the other night. I heard more than a hundred drowned, and they lost quite a few boats. That should keep them away for a while."

"She did that?" Hagon asked, surprise in his features. It was rare for him to show emotion, but we'd managed to catch him off guard this time.

"It was her," I answered. "You may have also heard the villagers refer to her as the 'lady in gray' who single-handedly saved many of them despite her being identified as Therressian."

Our people might not have known who she was if the soldiers she targeted hadn't kept screaming that they were on her side and begging her not to attack. At least, that was what my sister had told me. I noted my father's captains in the room appeared impressed.

Hagon mulled that over for a moment. "It would be ludicrous to do such things because her uncle would surely find out and consider it treason."

"While that night was the most she's ever pushed her luck, it wasn't the first time she's tried protecting innocents during battle. He has punished her for defending our people before. The numerous whip scars I found on her back prove as much," I replied.

His expression turned stricken. Unlike me, he'd never felt the pain of a lash and couldn't imagine how it felt, but he understood the extremity of it.

"Then, based on everything you've said, we have little time to save her," he surmised, casting a look at our father. "A man like Lord Morgunn will realize he can never trust her again, even for the sake of her powers. It won't be long before he kills her."

Once my brother had all the basic facts, he often came to the wisest conclusion.

Lord Gannon nodded. "I agree. Darrow may take three hundred soldiers with him to storm Ivory Castle, but we must keep the battle contained to that location, so I will lend our most powerful channeler. Take the mountain pass into Therress quietly, and from there, he'll be able to portal you into the keep."

Indescribable relief filled me. "Thank you, Father. That's exactly what I'd hoped you'd say."

"I'm going as well," Hagon announced.

I turned to him, stunned. "Why?"

"We don't always see eye to eye, brother. I recognize that, but my marriage has been cold these past three years since my wife learned of our curse. It isn't even possible to get an heir from her under the current strain. If Aella is the greatest hope we have to end our family's suffering, then my highest priority is to see her safe."

His words surprised me, even if he had ulterior motives. I was more than happy to have him, considering he had two powerful abilities that would increase our chances of success. "Then you are welcome to join."

Hagon nodded. "Good."

"We will plan the battle for tomorrow at dusk and will make certain that by the end of the night, Therress won't trouble us any longer," my father announced.

I joined them at the table as we began to formulate a new battle plan.

Chapter 52

Aella

I lay in a puddle of misery on the floor. My left arm was broken in multiple places, and both my ankles looked like large melons from when they'd thrown me against the wall while I was still chained to the floor. When the swelling became so bad that my feet and left hand changed colors, they'd taken all the shackles off. I was so weak from injuries, dehydration, and blood loss that I couldn't have escaped if they left the cell door wide open.

"I'm running out of patience, Aella. If you don't tell me how you're involved with the Veronnians, I will have no choice except to kill you," he said, glaring down at me.

The horrible image of Darrow freezing to death ran across my mind. Did he survive?

My voice came out in a croak as I returned to the present. "We've been searching...for a way...to get the Naforya Fountain back."

My mind was so hazy from repeated blows to the head, but I stayed with that point no matter what my uncle or others did to me. I was beyond giving clever answers at this point.

"Yes, yes. You've said that already. Do you really think I'm so foolish as to believe that's all you've been doing?" he asked.

I weakly lifted my head to meet his gaze. "Is it really so bad...if some of us are willing...to work together...to get the fountain back?" I asked, wishing for water to soothe my aching throat. "Our world...is dying."

"Have you considered there might be a better solution, and the fountain's return would jeopardize that," he replied.

He was selfish, so damn selfish. How could he condemn the rest of this world for whatever plans only benefited him? Considering his alliance with the dark elves, I had to presume they were part of this as well. If I could think more clearly, I'd try asking him some pointed questions.

Instead, I gave him the most defiant look I could manage. "If you don't want the fountain returned...then we have nothing to discuss."

He crouched and picked up a lock of my matted blonde hair from my face, twisting it between his fingers. "Dear Aella, I must assume Darrow wants your assistance because he believes you are strong enough to channel to its location. Until recently, I hadn't thought you were powerful enough, but now I see why he'd seek you out. Your magic is far beyond my expectations and could easily bring us back to the fae home world. Wouldn't you like that better?"

"Faelaria...is lost to us," I said. Was he delusional? Seelie couldn't even inhabit most of it with all the changes to the planet after we left.

"No." My uncle dropped my hair and brushed my cheek gently with the back of his hand as if he really cared, but I knew he was only employing a new strategy on me. "There is a way back for some of us, but it requires sacrifice. They would certainly love to have someone like you, but only if we can be certain of your loyalty."

"I'm not betraying Darrow," I croaked.

Lord Morgunn snorted. "Do you think his intentions are pure? Someone like him will use and discard you once you've served your purpose. He plays dangerous games. I've done my best to shield you from fae court politics, but he would put you directly in the middle of them."

He paused, giving me a pitying look. "If you tell me what you've been doing with him and what he's told you, I am certain I could resolve the matter so you will be safe from his manipulations."

My uncle must have thought I was gullible. Regardless, if he found out I was married to Darrow, he'd surely kill me. Nothing I said was going to improve my fate.

Drawing a deep breath, I spoke the words that would condemn me. "It doesn't matter...what Darrow was doing...because I will never support you again. You hurt...innocent people."

"You foolish girl," he growled, grabbing my throat to lift me and slam me into the stone wall. "Such powerful, unmatched magic, yet you'd rather die than be loyal to your family."

Stars danced in my vision from the latest blow to my head, and I was unable to breathe.

"If that's how you truly feel, then I'll end you now!" he shouted, mottled rage worse than I'd ever seen before written on his face.

This was it—my time to die. I only wished I could have retrieved the fountain first. Lord Morgunn jerked me forward and slammed me hard into the stone a second time, and agonizing pain exploded as my skull cracked. My vision darkened. Something sticky ran down the back of my neck. I thought for sure one more blow would finish me, and I waited for it with no energy left to resist.

The room suddenly went quiet.

"You are going to gently lower Aella to the floor and let go of her," a familiar voice I hadn't heard in months said. It was so omnipotent and deep that it almost hurt my ears.

"Of course," Lord Morgunn replied.

I wished I could see, but the blows to my head had been too hard. In the next moment, I was carefully deposited on the stone floor. As soon as my uncle let go of my neck, I tried to suck in a breath, but barely any air made it to my lungs. He'd squeezed my throat so hard that it had swelled.

"Now, you are going to leave your niece alone and harm her no more. If anyone asks, you will tell them you're giving her quiet and solitude to consider her choices."

Lord Morgunn didn't reply to that, but I listened to his footsteps as he retreated and shut the cell door behind him. I lay there, unable to rise and barely able to suck in a tiny thread of air.

"Oh, sweet Aella." The nameless god pressed his hand to my cheek. "I'd truly hoped you'd be sensible and string him along with unimportant information until your husband rescued you, but you've really been letting that defiant streak out lately."

Warmth and magic came from his touch. First, the pain in my throat eased, then the back of my head. It only took the powerful being moments to repair the damage. Finally, I could breathe and see again. He stopped after that, though, not touching the rest of my injuries. The swelling around my eyes meant I still had narrower vision than normal, but I would take what I could get. A flask appeared next, which he opened and pressed to my lips. I took small sips for the next few minutes until he removed it from my reach.

"My apologies, but to do more would violate the rules and get me into trouble," he said, pulling away. "I could only help you enough to keep you alive."

Using my good arm, I slowly sat up and leaned against the wall. My numerous broken ribs protested, making me wince and whimper. The nameless god hadn't healed my other injuries, but at least I could think more clearly. That was something.

"How did you make my uncle leave?" I asked.

His silver eyes showed amusement. "I ordered him. He won't remember me or what I said, but he will comply."

"Have you ever done that to me?"

The nameless god cocked his head, and I noted he'd shaven off his black hair since I last saw him. His shiny scalp was the same almond color as the rest of him, contrasting with his pearly-white robe.

"You wouldn't know if I had tampered with your mind, would you?"

I sighed. "Why save me at all?"

"You are important and necessary to the future," he replied as if that wouldn't spark my curiosity. "The rules normally state I can't save any fae's life, but you are an exception."

His vague answers were annoying. "How so?"

"I've told you all I can." He rose to his full height, which had to be several inches more than anyone I knew. "Stay strong, Aella. Your husband will be on his way soon, so your time in this place won't be for much longer."

"Darrow is alive?" I asked, hope filling me for the first time in days.

The god nodded. "With all his parts intact—in case you were worried. He only needed some time to heal before his first thought was of you. I told you he was the better choice."

Then he disappeared, his light vanishing with him. I hadn't realized he'd emitted a glow until he left. My uncle must have taken his lantern with him as well. Now, I was left broken and alone in the dark, but at least my future didn't look quite as grim.

Chapter 53

Darrow

We made it through the mountain pass toward Palbour without incident shortly after sunset. The same tactic we used months ago to nullify the border sentries worked again this time. I'd sent a sebeska to drop a heavy sleeping potion on the two men up there and then had it land nearby while I watched through the bird's eyes to be sure it worked.

No one ever suspected they might be used for such a purpose. It would have been nice if my sister could have done it instead, but she needed to be close, and the guards would see her well before she could reach them. I repeated the drop process with the tower watch near the village.

With my older brother joining us, we took advantage of his ability to create a thick fog that would be impenetrable to the villagers' eyes but thin enough around our forces that we could still see our path. He could spread it far enough to appear natural along the rugged landscape. That allowed us to make it to the ring, located far enough from any homes that the residents wouldn't hear our horses and foot soldiers as they approached.

The channeler we brought with us didn't compare to Aella, but he was the strongest in our land. He could penetrate the Ivory Castle ring's wards now that he was less than two hundred miles from the location and didn't have to push through mountains. I ordered him to begin right away.

My stallion could sense my impatience to reach my wife. I was furious with her family for abusing her and couldn't wait any longer to get her out of there. She was mine. I wanted her close, in my bed, and living in my home.

With her being my true mate, those thoughts had grown especially strong since we'd slept together. I idly wondered how I'd feel if we managed to break my curse. Would my lust and need to protect her grow even stronger, and would I feel love for her right away based on the relationship we'd already developed? We were still too far from recovering the fountain to ponder those thoughts too deeply, but they still crossed my mind.

The portal opened, and I led the way through the soft blue light. My brother would take the rear to organize the forces once they reached the other side. I had

Loden with me, along with five other soldiers who would stay with me as we fought our way to the castle dungeons. Jax and another soldier would meet us at some point. They were already there since they'd had the task of taking down Lord Morgunn's strongest guard with the shields.

Hagon had the mission to neutralize any other threats as well as apprehend the lord and his sons. Since his other gift was being able to blind up to a dozen enemies at once, the assignment was an ideal one for him. Lord Morgunn couldn't hit him with ice if he couldn't see him. We would meet in the great hall once I had Aella. My brother also had a team designated to search for the healers since my wife would need them immediately after I freed her.

The portal sent me and Loden out the other side, followed quickly by the others riding with us. I immediately broke the necks of the two guards at the ring before they could sound an alarm. We raced across the formation area toward the barracks. While I'd never been here in person, I'd seen every nook and cranny through a sebeska's eyes.

All the other incoming troops held positions near the ring to wait for my brother. Only my group followed me, with our first goal being to douse the sleeping soldiers with spells to keep them out of the fight. It was shortly past midnight, so most everyone was already in their bunks. While I would have loved to reduce their forces by attacking and killing them, it would have meant more injuries and losses on our side. We'd had more than enough death lately. Our goal was to move swiftly with as little bloodshed as possible.

One of my men dismounted at the first barracks building and ran inside. He had several potion bottles to throw quickly. It only took him a moment before he was outside again, giving me a nod. The rest of our mounted soldiers hurried to take care of the other barracks buildings. We hurried past the armory, riding parallel to the training field.

Ahead of us, two elves had entered the officer quarters building. They came running outside with several Therressians chasing them. I used my powers to crush all who exited and weren't my people. We needed to keep this quiet for as long as possible to catch Lord Morgunn unaware. I was the only one who could legally kill him in his home because of what he'd done to my wife. Some laws were more than a little frustrating, but we'd make that one work to our advantage.

Just as we reached the unobtrusive dungeon door on the southwest corner of the castle, Jax revealed himself, along with the soldier who'd accompanied him. "I overheard a few guards talking and confirmed she's still down there," my friend said, expression grave. "But they said she's in bad shape, so you need to prepare yourself."

My chest tightened, though I'd expected as much. I'd told Jax not to try getting Aella out before I arrived. Too many things could go wrong with only him and the other soldier attempting to rescue her in an enemy stronghold. I wouldn't risk my wife's life that way.

"How many guards are in there?" I asked.

He glanced at the door with a heavy lock on it. "I estimate three based on who came out during the shift change, but a separate entrance leads inside the castle. If any went that route, I wouldn't have seen them."

"That's fine," I said, dismounting. "I'll take care of them, regardless."

Checking my surroundings, I found our forces already moving toward the front of the castle. The soldier with Jax took control of my mount for me. I stood impatiently before the dungeon door, waiting to break it. It would be loud, so I needed to be sure the others were already sweeping the inside before I did something that would alert the lord and inhabitants. I had to be patient if I wanted the mission to succeed. It wasn't easy.

Finally, I heard shouts and clashing swords at the castle's entrance and drew my powers. Focusing on the black door, I yanked it off its hinges, laying it flat. Then, I raced down the dark, narrow stairs. One guard was already climbing them in a rush. He lifted his sword as soon as he saw me, but that was his last move before I crushed his head and sent him flying back down.

As I reached the bottom, two more came running from the corridor on my right. I lifted my hand, wrapping my magic around their throats, and snapped their necks before they came close. No one down here would feel my mercy.

The lighting was dim, with only one fae lantern illuminating the dank stone floors and walls. It reeked of mold and mildew. I counted six doors, three on each side, but only one was firmly barred. It only took seconds to get through the barrier with my magic, but it was pitch black inside, and impossible to see anything.

Before I stepped forward, I activated two glow stones. I found a crumpled woman on her side in the far corner with her back to me. She still wore the same gray tunic and trousers as the night of the battle, except they were badly torn and soiled with blood and body fluids.

I turned toward Jax, who'd followed close behind me. "Find a blanket." After he took off in a dash, I looked at Loden. "Locate the way to the castle interior and ensure the path is clear."

"Of course," he said, rushing away.

The rest of the soldiers took up guard positions in case anyone else showed up.

Reassured that they had everything else in hand, I moved toward Aella's shivering form. Autumn had just begun, but the air was especially cool down here. She didn't move or acknowledge me in any way. A hot spike of fury coursed through my body at what they'd done to her, and I hated myself for not managing to kill her uncle that night. Aella's torture was the price she'd paid for her selflessness and saving innocent people.

My gaze raked over her, trying to discern where she was hurt. I gently checked over her body, finding a partially healed wound on her lower back that had begun to fester, and the same with her shoulder where the sword had sliced her the night of the battle. She moaned as I turned her onto her back so I could see her front.

Aella's eyes were nearly swollen shut, and there were numerous contusions across her face. Blood caked the back of her head, though no wound appeared there. I found one of her arms bent at multiple wrong angles and countless bruises when I lifted her tunic, indicating broken ribs. Her ankles were also double their normal size.

They'd hardly left a single place on her untouched by violence. My rage knew no bounds, but I forced myself to contain it for her sake. She needed me to stay calm. I also had to get her out of here and straight to a healer.

She partially opened her eyes, pain and anguish within them. "Darrow?"

"I'm here, dear Aella. You are safe now."

"He said you'd come," she rasped.

Had her uncle expected me? They hadn't seemed prepared for my arrival.

I turned toward the doorway. "Someone bring water, now!"

Within seconds, a soldier handed me a silver flask. Using my powers since it would hurt her less, I lifted Aella enough to sit up. Her wince told me it still hurt. I quickly uncapped the flask and poured a dribble into her mouth. She swallowed it down right away. I let her have a few more small drinks before handing the water back.

Jax hurried inside with a large wool blanket. "It was all I could find, but it's clean."

"That's fine. Help me cover her," I said.

Using my powers again, I brought Aella off the ground, and we arranged the blanket underneath her. She cried out as I set her down on top of it. I winced, imagining how much she must hurt. We tucked it around her front until she was covered everywhere except her head. After that, I carefully pulled her into my arms. While I could have used my powers to move her upstairs, I needed to cradle her close. Also, I wasn't familiar with the castle and worried I'd accidentally bump her into objects along the way if she floated separately from me.

She rested her head against my shoulder. "You really...came for me."

"Of course I did," I said as I carried her out of the dungeon cell. Had she doubted me? After everything, I would have thought she'd have had more confidence that I would never leave her to a fate like this.

"I was worried...he froze you."

Ah, yes. That would have been the last thing Aella saw happening to me. "The healers kept me down for a couple of days while they repaired the damage, but I came as soon as I could."

"Thank you."

I leaned down to kiss her forehead. "I'll always come for you, dear wife."

Loden gestured for me to follow him, leading me toward a different set of steps than the ones I'd used to get down here. I moved slowly in an attempt not to jar Aella too much, but she still moaned in pain. My friend pulled the door open when we reached the top.

We made our way through a maze of corridors toward the great hall. I'd never been inside, but we merely had to follow the shouting voices to know where to go. Only alert Veronnian soldiers standing guard and some dead Therressians lying on the corridor floor slowed our pace as we moved through the castle.

The pain on Aella's face grew so great that her features had twisted into a constant grimace. I hated that I was jarring her, but I couldn't avoid it if I wanted to get her help. She'd clenched her eyes and jaw shut, managing to keep quiet despite how her injuries must have been affecting her. I suspected that if she hadn't been abused so many times before, her control would not be as considerable. It sickened me that any man would harm a woman this way, and I couldn't wait to get the anti-magic cuff off. She would recover faster then.

Unfortunately, my powers wouldn't work on the metal band. The person who placed it had to remove it, or their death could also release the magical lock. I needed to determine who had put it there before deciding how to remedy the issue.

We entered the great hall, which also served as the dining area. Over a dozen Therressian soldiers stood lined up, their faces pressed against the wall and their arms bound behind their backs. Lord Morgunn and his two sons stood by the long table with iron shackles on their wrists and a few fresh marks on their faces. Undoubtedly, they resisted at first. Aella's uncle had an outraged expression when his gaze fell upon me.

"Get your hands off my niece, you filthy whoreson."

I narrowed my eyes on him. "She's mine, not yours."

Aella's eyes fluttered open, but she didn't turn her head to look at her family. Her beautiful green irises were glazed with pain as I gently set her on the table. Without needing to say a word, Rynn and Briauna raced forward and began working on the worst injuries, the younger girl crying at the sight of her broken cousin. I stepped back to give them space.

"She may have committed treason by working with you, but she's not yours," Lord Morgunn said, lunging forward. Two guards hauled him back. Apparently, word had not reached him yet of our marriage, but I didn't care at this point. He was dead regardless.

"According to King Worden, who married us four and a half months ago, she is mine. I merely allowed her to remain with you until I could find a way to remove the curse you placed on her. Unfortunately, it appears your idea of taking care of a family member is vastly different from mine," I said.

In truth, I didn't anticipate wanting her at my side when we began this journey. I'd only sought to keep her from falling into enemy hands through marriage, where I would not be able to make use of her abilities. It had suited me to keep her at a distance, able to alert me every time her uncle attacked my land.

Though he couldn't have infiltrated our territory as easily without her, our lands had warred against each other long before she was born. Taking her away wouldn't have stopped the conflict or the deaths.

Lord Morgunn's face contorted. "If you were married, I would have heard about it."

"We kept it a secret, and the king agreed since he knew you were conspiring against him. He simply needed to turn down your betrothal proposals without fully explaining his reasoning. Meanwhile, we have been investigating your recent activities. I wish I could say I'm surprised you're still working with the dark elves despite your reassurances years ago that you cut ties with them, but we suspected that was a lie all along." I stepped closer to him. "It was merely a matter of proving it, and that fleet arriving during your attack on Radoumar was rather damning."

I left out what I knew about the Unseelie. We were keeping that information tightly contained because there was still a lot we didn't know about their plans. The more ignorant we appeared, the more likely they were to make a mistake.

"You can kill me," he said, smugly. "But it will only set off a chain of events you don't want to happen."

I stilled. "Such as?"

Lord Morgunn shook his head. "I'm sworn to secrecy and couldn't say—even if you spent the next week torturing me. You'll have to find out the hard way."

"You speak lies to save yourself," I said, hoping to the nameless ones that I was right.

He gave me a malicious smile. "If you want Aella free of the curse and that cuff, you'll have to kill me, but be prepared to accept the consequences when they come."

I glanced down the table at my wife, where the two healers worked. One focused on her ankles and the other on her chest. They were making progress, but they'd do better with the cuff removed so Aella's body could contribute to the process. I didn't know what the consequences might be, but I had no choice except to kill her uncle. He could not be allowed to live.

I lifted my hand, pulling my power, and aimed it at Lord Morgunn. His collarbone snapped, and he screamed. I waited until he stopped wailing to speak again. "Your death can be quick or very slow. That is the only choice I'll give you."

"No," the stubborn man said, gripping his shoulder.

I broke his right hand, waited five seconds, and then broke his left. I gave him ten seconds to relent, but he remained stubbornly mute. One by one, I snapped each of his ribs as he fell over the table, screaming in pain. It was satisfying to watch him suffer and also amusing to see his eldest son, Ulmar, seethe in rage with his good eye as I tortured his father. Tadeus kept his focus on Aella, concern in his gaze for her and no regard at all for his sire, which was interesting. My sources may have been right that there was no love between the lord and his youngest child.

"Ready to free Aella yet?" I asked Lord Morgunn after giving him a minute to catch his breath.

He snarled at me. "Not for you!"

"Very well."

I flicked my hand and broke his right leg in two places simultaneously. He fell back onto the floor. Then, I similarly broke his other leg. He was screaming and wailing now. I wanted to keep going, but more than ten minutes had passed since we arrived in the great hall, and my wife continued to suffer with the cuff on her. For Aella's sake, I needed to end it.

With one last pulse of power, I crushed Lord Morgunn's skull. His eldest son flinched as blood and brain matter soaked the stone floor, but he said nothing. A cold, calculated look came over his bandaged face that deeply disturbed me.

The metallic clink of metal falling on the table told me killing Aella's uncle had done what I'd hoped. I looked over at her, noting her color was returning, and a faint wisp of smoke trailed from the back of her neck. A sign that her curse had ended as well. Despite her numerous injuries, a faint smile touched her lips. A heavy weight had lifted and would trouble her no more.

I turned to her oldest cousin next, well aware he enjoyed harming my wife.

He fell to his knees immediately and bowed his head. "I humbly surrender and am willing to negotiate a treaty between our lands."

I muttered a few choice words under my breath. I might have gotten away with killing Ulmar as well if he hadn't said those specific words. As long as he cooperated and didn't order his forces to attack me or Veronna in the near future, I couldn't touch him. Fae laws were rather annoying at times. I very much preferred working in the shadows with no one the wiser to what I did.

"I'll deal with him," Hagon said, putting a hand on my shoulder. "You see to your wife."

I nodded. "Thank you. If I look at him much longer, I'm liable to kill him no matter the consequences."

"After seeing what they've done to Aella, I don't blame you. I admire the control you've demonstrated so far, brother." He squeezed my shoulder one more time and headed toward the new Lord of Therress.

I joined the healers. "How is she?"

"We've done what we can for now, but we weren't at full strength since we've been tending the wounded these last few days from the battle at Radoumar," Briauna said, smoothing Aella's brow. "I've put her to sleep, and we'll continue to treat her wounds every four hours until the worst injuries are whole."

"You mean I can't take her home now?" I asked, perplexed.

She shook her head. "There is no channeler currently at the castle who could transport you outside of Therress, and it's best to move her as little as possible until we finish mending the broken bones. Allow Rynn and I to continue working on her while your brother deals with Ulmar."

The channeler I'd brought with me would need several hours before he could open a portal again. Since the return trip wouldn't require him to fight through wards, he could channel all the way to Veronna, but my brother would need him to remain here for our troops. It appeared I had little choice except to spend the night in Ivory Castle.

"Very well. I will carry Aella to her room."

"Good. She will be happier if she wakes to familiar surroundings," Briauna said, giving me a weak smile. I imagined she was horrified by what happened to my wife and not ready to see her leave Therress.

I gathered Aella into my arms and allowed the two healers to lead me upstairs to the tiny room where she'd lived since moving to the castle. It wasn't much larger than servant quarters, but at least it had a window and a fireplace. I laid her limp body down on the coverlet, noting how fragile she appeared. My heart might be cold, but I still felt the fury of what had been done to her. I vowed I'd never let her be harmed like that again.

Chapter 54

Aella

A warm body cradled mine when I woke, and sandalwood filled my senses. I opened my eyes to find I was lying in my bedroom in the castle, but this was the first time anyone had ever been in it with me. Well, not counting a few times when Rynn first came to live here and needed comfort during the night.

I twisted around and found Darrow staring down at me with expressionless eyes. "What..." I sat up, wincing a little at a few aches and pains that lingered. "What are you doing here? My uncle...he..."

"Met a painful end," Darrow replied.

I swallowed, feeling mixed emotions. I hated the man and had wished for his death many times, but it didn't feel real without having seen it for myself. "How?"

"I broke most of the bones in his body one at a time before finally finishing by crushing his head," he replied without a hint of remorse. Not that I'd expect any from him. "Briauna and Rynn were busy healing you and had put you to sleep so you'd be more comfortable. They've come two more times since then."

Taking full stock of my body, I felt much better, with only lingering soreness remaining. "How long was I asleep? Did someone bathe me? I know I wasn't this clean when you found me."

His lips twitched in amusement. "You've slept for about ten hours. After the last healing, they gave you a sponge bath and changed your bedding. We thought you might appreciate not being covered in blood and other things when you woke. You'd been through enough."

The only way I wouldn't have woken for that was if Briauna kept me unconscious for that part, too, because that was certainly something that would have pulled me from my slumber. Despite my discomfort over the idea, I appreciated their thoughtfulness. I had been disgusted by my body and only able to bear it because my pain took precedence. It was a wonder that Darrow had been willing to carry me like that.

My mind turned to another point. "What about my cousins, Ulmar and Tadeus?"

"Tadeus has been confined to his room since last night. Ulmar is in negotiations with my brother, Hagon, for a peace treaty. We aren't open to many concessions, so they should finalize it before long," Darrow replied, studying me closely. "How do you feel?"

"Better, but what do we do now?" I asked, frowning. I could feel that the curse no longer lingered on my neck, but I'd been trapped for so long that I hadn't dared dream of a future where I'd be free of my uncle, even after marrying Darrow. It had seemed hopeless.

"We will go to Porrine first to update the king. He knows I brought a force here to retrieve you and kill your uncle, but he'll want the details. Also, we spread the word of our marriage for the last two days to provide an appropriate excuse for me murdering a lord in his home."

Because that was the only way to justify it by stating that my uncle had harmed me and I was Darrow's wife. Everyone in the great hall last night could corroborate my condition when he found me. "We'll stay a short time at the capital while I smooth any difficulties over before I take you to Darynia."

"Darynia? I didn't think I'd ever be allowed there," I said, surprised. The fact that he bought and renovated a townhouse in Porrine led me to believe that I might never live in Veronna and would always be treated as an outsider.

He traced a finger across my cheek. It was so achingly gentle in contrast to the coldness of his eyes. I should have pulled away and told him to stop being sweet, but I didn't have the strength at the moment. Mentally, I was exhausted and a little broken from everything that had happened. Later, once I pulled myself together, I'd put some distance between us again. Something told me he knew I needed the comfort and gave it freely.

"Despite you portaling an army to Radoumar, you more than proved where your allegiance lays by saving dozens of innocents and sending most of the dark elf army into the sea. My father was impressed, especially once I told him about the price you paid for helping us in the past."

I looked away, memories of every abuse flashing through my mind. "Can we please never talk about that?"

"If that is what you wish," Darrow said, pulling me closer to him and his warmth. "But if you ever change your mind, I will listen."

While I appreciated all he'd done to save me, including storming Ivory Castle, I didn't feel that we were in a place where I could open up to him fully. Would I ever be? Maybe if we lifted his curse so that we could be free to love each other. Not now. Not when he still had too many secrets he kept from me.

"Thank you," I said, finally meeting his gaze.

Darrow nodded. "Perhaps, someday, I'll share stories from my time in Karganoth with you. The level of abuse you have suffered under your uncle is unjust and uncommon in Zadrya, but not as much in the land of the dark elves. I understand what you've endured to some degree, if that is any consolation."

I couldn't imagine what his visits there were like, but I'd appreciate it if he did open up about it because I still hardly knew much about him. "It would be an honor if you did trust me with that."

Darrow's gray eyes darkened with shadows as he eased away from me and off the bed, heading toward the door. "I'll ask the servants to bring some food. Ideally, we should leave in a few hours after your final healing so we don't keep the king waiting. I sent a sebeska last night, but he'll want the full account in person."

"This is happening so fast. I didn't dare hope we'd reach this point, and now we're simply leaving together." A thousand thoughts raced through my mind, making it hard to concentrate. I'd gone from broken and tortured one day to leaving for a new home with my husband the next.

He paused from grabbing the door handle. "Do you need more time?"

It was so hard to breathe. "Sorry. I'm trying to make sense of everything."

I swung my legs off the mattress and tested them by putting weight on my feet. My ankles protested, sharp pain shooting through them, but it was nothing I couldn't handle compared to before. I slowly moved toward the window and looked out, grateful someone had removed the blocking magic on the glass. A gasp escaped me when I took my first good look at my garden. While it usually brought me solace and comfort, it now brought aching horror.

So many of my plants withered away on the stone walkway, having given their lives for me. Just because I nurtured them for that purpose—should I ever need it—didn't mean their deaths didn't tear me up inside. They didn't *have* to help me. I couldn't say I made them swear an oath or threatened them that they'd be punished if they didn't. My most aggressive species had jumped between me and danger without hesitation, fighting until the bitter end in an attempt to save me.

"No," I whispered, knees collapsing.

Somehow, Darrow caught me right before I hit the floor and pulled me close. "I don't think I've ever seen someone whose garden was so loyal to her that they'd defend her like this. They loved you, which I can't believe I'm saying, and that means something, Aella."

"Except they died for nothing in the end. I'd thought they could hold off my uncle and his soldiers until I was strong enough to fight back, but he kept sacrificing more elves until my plants were overwhelmed. Who does that? Willfully sends their people to die painful deaths to take one woman?" I asked, tears streaking down my cheeks.

He pressed my face into his chest. "I wouldn't have believed it either if I hadn't seen the evidence. If it is any consolation, one of your crunchertraps is quite damaged, but somehow it has extended some of its roots and is surviving so far.

I tried to help it earlier this morning, but it snapped at me. Rather than upset it further, I thought it best to wait for your assistance. There are a few other plants that are fighting to survive as well. Rynn has volunteered to help, and I will as well if you want to tend them first before we go."

"Thank you. That would be great," I said, attempting to pull myself together. His mention of my cousin reminded me of another matter. "We can't leave Rynn here. Tadeus would treat her well, but Ulmar can't be trusted. He's always been vile to me and will be to her, too. Could we assume guardianship of her?"

It was only fair that I ask since Fae law dictated that a married couple had to both agree when taking on a ward. Darrow would hold equal responsibility for her, which also meant he'd be agreeing to another Therressian in his home.

"Of course," he replied, tipping up my chin. "Anyone can see her soul is as pure as you promised the day you made that deal with me. My father is already aware of her and won't argue the matter. I will have my brother include it in his negotiations with Ulmar, but we can take her today regardless."

It probably helped that Rynn had their aunt's magic, which made her family adjacent. "Thank you."

He sighed. "There is no need to thank me."

I pulled back, my knees no longer as weak as before. "How can you be so kind and understanding with me? I don't get it."

"You mean because I can't love you?" he asked, arching a brow.

"Yes."

It was his turn to look away, working his jaw as he appeared deep in thought. "My father and brother cannot love, either. It doesn't mean that any of us lack empathy or don't wish for our wives to be happy, but the matter of our hearts seems to always develop into a problem, no matter our efforts. It creates a barrier we cannot overcome. We have often wondered if that is part of our curse—to always fail at marriage."

"As a result, you can't find happiness, either," I surmised.

"Precisely."

I took his hands and squeezed them. "At least we are discussing it and finding ways to work around it. I'll try not to resent you for something that is out of your control."

Most especially after he rescued me and freed me from my curse, I owed him that much.

"Thank you."

My stomach rumbled, providing the perfect distraction. "I think I'm ready for food now."

"I'll get it myself and return soon," he said, leaving the room quickly. Something told me he needed a moment to himself to come to terms with everything. We were both entering uncharted territory.

Rummaging through the chest at the foot of my bed, I found my preferred drab garden clothes. I took them to the bathing chambers down the corridor, quickly washed up and brushed my teeth, and then put them on before returning to my chambers. I wanted a proper bath, but it would have to wait until after I took care of my plants. My desperate need to tend to them took priority, and I'd end up dirty again anyway.

Darrow brought us both a plate, and we ate in silence together. I sat at my window seat, balancing my plate on my lap, and he did the same, sitting on the chest in front of my bed. It was a companionable silence, yet loaded with so many unanswered questions. I would save them until things were more settled.

After finishing, we dropped the plates off in the kitchen before heading to the garden. Rynn already waited for us at the archway. I took a deep breath before entering, telling myself nothing could change what happened before. All I could do was clean up the mess.

I walked inside and took in the chaos that reigned everywhere. Dead, withered plants lay strewn across the stone path, along with a few that struggled to hold on a little longer. The magic surge I'd sent that night had most likely allowed them that much of a chance. I could almost feel them crying out to me for help now, and it broke my heart. They'd had to wait days for me to return.

There was an awful stench of decay and rot, but I tried my best to ignore that.

Clearing my throat, I looked at Darrow and Rynn. "If you two can handle the cleanup, I'll take care of the survivors."

"Anything you need, Aella," Rynn said, blue eyes full of sympathy.

Darrow nodded.

I went to the fallen crunchertrap first. Half the petals with their sharp teeth were missing from the flower and most of its leaves, but it still lifted a little at my approach. The poor thing had fought a good battle. I traced its roots, which extended just beyond the side of the path and found it had dug in there.

"I'm going to get you back into your home, okay?"

It lay still as if that was its way of giving permission.

First, I went and grabbed a trowel and special mulch from the back, carefully stepping around the debris. Next, I went to work at the place where the cruncher trap had been before. They'd always been proud to be guardians of the entrance, and I wouldn't take that away from my remaining one. I loosened the dirt, mixing the rich soil within it. There were plenty of dead and decaying bugs mixed within that it could absorb through its roots until it could eat a proper meal again.

After finishing, I lifted the limp plant, extracting its roots with care. It trusted me completely and didn't fuss. I kneeled and settled it into its preferred home, holding it upright. The plant was too weak to stand tall on its own.

I closed my eyes and began chanting a special spell my mother taught me right after I gained my magic. My power flowed through me into the crunchertrap. With each line I recited, its color returned, and it grew stronger until it didn't need my help anymore. The stalk was thicker and stronger, and the start of new petals peeked from the center. Within a few days, it would likely improve to almost as good as before. The spell had given it a substantial boost to grow faster.

Rising to my feet, I caught Darrow piling fae body parts onto the walkway. There were a shocking number of them. "How many soldiers do you think died in here?"

He dropped a booted foot into the pile like a piece of rubbish. "My estimate so far is ten. The tractvines are still consuming five of them, but your other plants ripped apart at least as many. I wouldn't be surprised if there are quite a few soldiers in the infirmary with missing parts who managed to escape as well."

Rynn was quiet as she gathered the dead flora in a separate location. I appreciated that she took care of each one despite the fact they had no life left in them. The survivors in my garden behaved calmly with me here and gave my helpers no trouble. For that, I was grateful.

I moved on to the others who were struggling and gave them similar treatment to the crunchertrap. Once finished, I watered all the plants and performed any immediate special care they required. It was exhausting, but more than anything, I needed to help them. I could rest and finish healing later.

Darrow used my wheelbarrow to remove the body parts, though I had no idea where he took them. Some questions were best left unasked. I directed Rynn to put her pile in the compost bin I kept just outside the garden entrance. It was situated there so that servants could dispose of various waste that benefited my garden.

It took about three hours before we had accomplished all we could. My body ached, and I struggled to stay upright from still-healing injuries and heavy use of my magic, but it was a small price to pay for my garden. The plants had given their all for me.

I looked at Darrow with tired eyes. "Do you think I'll be able to come back for them sometime soon?"

"Yes." He looked around with a hint of pride, which surprised me. "Once we're settled, we'll find a new location for your garden, but I already told Ulmar that he is not to bother you when you come back to tend the plants or do anything to the garden in the meantime. Still, I'd prefer you come through your private portal and avoid him altogether. I've already put up a ward that prevents anyone other than us from entering."

"Okay," I agreed. He'd thought of everything while I still scrambled to find some semblance of order in the chaos. It was daunting after all I'd been through in recent days.

I swayed on my feet, my exertion catching up to me.

Darrow swung me into his arms. "If I hadn't known you would protest, I would have stopped you from pushing yourself so hard. I'll take you back to your room where you can bathe and change. Briauna will be up shortly to do a final healing and bring you food."

"You can put me down, Dare," I said, wiggling in his hold.

He quirked a brow. "You've worn yourself out. Rest and save your strength because I would like to return to Porrine in two hours if possible."

I sighed and glowered at him even though I knew the trip to my room would be painful if I walked it myself. "Fine, but I want it noted that this is bullying behavior."

"Whatever makes you feel better about me carrying you."

Rynn watched us with amusement. "I'll, uh, go pack."

"Take only what you can carry," Darrow said, turning his attention to her. "We will come back for the rest in a few days."

Neither of us argued with that plan. Despite the unknowns before us, we were ready to leave this place and all the bad memories with it. I only hoped it wouldn't take long before I could remove my plants and put them somewhere they could be happy and safe.

Chapter 55

Aella

We'd packed our bags and stood ready to go when Darrow met us in the great hall. Jax and Loden were joining us, while Hagon would stay behind with the Veronnian troops to finish the treaty negotiations.

I'd spent nearly nineteen years living here, but I didn't feel the least bit nostalgic about leaving. Most of my time had been spent trying to avoid trouble and keeping my head down. I was tired of playing that game. Nothing held me back anymore, so I could find myself and do what was right for me. Either Darrow would appreciate that, or he wouldn't, but that was my plan.

I was sorry I couldn't say goodbye to Sariyah before I left. There was no way we could go to Tradain right now under the circumstances, but I planned to send her a note with a sebeska soon and see if she'd meet me on the Andalagar Tribal land. We'd be safe to talk there. Plus, it would give me a chance to see how things were going between her and Orran.

Kailin wandered into the room and made her way straight toward Rynn and me. For the first time in many years, there was a soft smile on my aunt's face. Her shoulders were straight instead of hunched, and she'd styled her strawberry-blonde hair into ringlets that fell down her back.

Tadeus and Ulmar's mother had even put on a green dress with floral lace that hugged her slender figure, bringing some color to her ivory skin. I was so glad to see her coming out of her shell and choosing a color that didn't indicate mourning despite her husband dying last night.

She took my hands. "Be well, Aella. I'm sorry I couldn't be there for you as much as I should have, but I wish you happiness and a bright future."

"Thank you," I said, pulling her into a tight embrace. "I want the same for you, too. Don't let Ulmar push you around, and keep Tadeus close."

"Oh, I will." Kailin pulled back with misty brown eyes. "It will be much better now."

She hugged Rynn next, wishing her well, too. Darrow was the last to draw her attention. She gave him an enthusiastic hug that shocked all of us, considering he was her husband's killer. He stood stiffly for a moment before gently patting her back. There was a "help me" look on his face when his gaze met mine. I pretended to cough to cover my laugh.

My aunt drew away and smiled at him. "Thank you for freeing me and these two ladies," she said, nodding toward us. "If I can ever be of assistance, let me know."

It was then that I considered Kailin had been born over a century ago in Raumandia—the land north of Therress. Her father had been lord there when he negotiated a treaty with us, marrying his daughter to Morgunn as part of the deal. Prior to that, relations between the two lands had been tense, with many cross-border skirmishes.

A new family ruled now after ousting Kailin's parents over four decades ago, leaving many of her relatives dead from the coup, but Raumandia remained an ally to Therress. I could only guess that she didn't feel much loyalty to either land after all that had happened in her life. Even with her eldest son now in power, she didn't have much of a relationship with him. Ulmar was too much like his father. If she supported him at all, it would likely be for her own ends.

"I appreciate your offer," Darrow answered, amusement in his gaze now. Perhaps he'd come to the same conclusions as me about Kailin.

Rynn and I said goodbye to Briauna next, hating to leave her. The healer insisted this was where she needed to be, especially with so many wounded left to tend after the Veronnians attacked last night. She'd focused most of her energy on me but had to divert it back to the others now.

"Promise to come visit," I said after hugging her.

She winked. "Oh, I will. The men in Veronna have always been kinder on the eyes, in my opinion."

Darrow let out a snort, but I had to agree with her from what I'd seen so far.

Finally, we headed outside. Jax and Loden had our horses waiting. As we mounted, they insisted on taking mine and Rynn's bags, which was good since I needed my hands free to channel. I only kept my holmium vase with me.

As we passed the training area, I noticed it was empty and silent. Usually, soldiers were always out in the late afternoon practicing, but with Veronnian troops still occupying the keep, I supposed they were probably confined to their quarters for now.

When we reached the ring, I pulled the stopper from the cream vase with silver vines that Darrow had gifted me. I'd deactivated the enchantment that hid it while we were riding so that no one was surprised when I took a pinch of holmium from the receptacle. As I began to channel, Darrow took it from me and handed it over to Loden to place in my bag.

Moments later, the air popped, and a blue glow appeared. Since the ring was designed to funnel an army, we had no trouble riding through it together. My last thought was that I would never have to take my uncle's troops through there again, and how much relief I felt with that realization.

Those happy feelings didn't last.

When our horses stepped out the other side of the portal, we found Porrine in chaos. Warning bells rang loudly all around us. Fae of all types were running and shouting, fear written on all their faces. The elf woman who usually manned the capital city ring was nowhere in sight, while she usually stood right by it during the day.

Darrow dismounted and grabbed the first person who came close. "What happened?"

The male goblin's short body shook with terror. "The king and queen are dead, and dark elves invaded the palace! We're afraid they're going to take the rest of Porrine next."

Shocked, we all exchanged horrified looks. How could the king and queen be dead? And how in Paxia did soldiers from Karganoth manage to get here with a force large enough to overtake the royal army? I was glad my husband wore his hair down today, covering his black-tipped ears. Otherwise, he would have stood out.

"I advise you to get inside your home," Darrow said, letting the goblin go.

The fae didn't hesitate to take off running once more.

Jax pulled his sword. "Let's get the ladies to the townhouse, and then we can see about the palace."

"Agreed." Darrow turned to me. "As much as I'd love to keep you with us, you've already drained too much power getting us here, and what you have left should be for defense only. If things are as bad as they look, Rynn will need you to watch over her."

"Isn't the townhouse warded?" I asked, recalling that I'd felt the defenses on the place the last time I'd visited.

"Yes, but we both know those could be broken if someone is determined enough," he said, mounting his horse before giving me a meaningful look. "Protect yourself, Rynn, and our home until I get back. I have complete faith you can do that."

I appreciated his confidence, but it was hard to feel it amid the fear that tainted the air.

"Okay," I agreed.

We urged our horses into a gallop, taking the northern route behind the palace. Our watchful gazes searched for any danger that might lurk along the way as we passed the lower-class tenement housing. It was quieter now that we were away from the shops and other bustling areas. People here had already shut themselves inside, judging by the faces poking around curtains in the windows. We eventually passed them and headed south past a park and small pond, then the royal servants' living quarters.

Finally, we reached the row of townhouses designated only for the highborn fae to reside. There were still people running frantically in this area, some calling for loved ones. Through all this, Rynn was quiet and wide-eyed, taking in her surroundings. I wished her first trip to Porrine could have been under better circumstances, especially since she'd been excited to come here.

Darrow led us to the back area of the townhouse, where we quickly removed saddles and settled the horses into stable stalls. After that, my husband checked the wards before unlocking the back door. I could feel his magic thrumming strongly and planned to add to his protective layers once he left. As husband and wife, our magic would work together.

Rynn, being wise for her age, had a strand of her hair ready when she reached the entrance, handing it over to Darrow. He dissolved it into the magical wall so that she'd be allowed inside without getting burned by the defenses. She was only beginning to learn about wards in her lessons when we left since it wasn't covered until after a fae attained their magic, but I was glad she'd learned that detail already.

She and I entered the kitchen area and turned to face the doorway where Darrow, Jax, and Loden stood. They planned to leave immediately, not wanting to waste time. I worried for the three of them and hoped everything wasn't as bad as it looked. They handed over our bags, which I set on the floor.

"Be careful," I said to Darrow.

He nodded. "I will. You should do the same and trust no one you don't know. We'll return as soon as we can."

With those words, he gave me a quick kiss on the cheek, and then they left. I shut the door firmly behind them and fixed the multiple locks on it. Turning around, I faced Rynn. "How about you go explore while I see what there is to make dinner?"

Darrow had mentioned back in Therress that he'd sent word to the maid yesterday morning to have food delivered to the townhouse in anticipation of bringing me here. There was a cold storage unit in the kitchen powered by magic that would have kept everything fresh. I rarely cooked while at Ivory Castle unless I wanted to bake something special, but I often used the communal kitchen at Tradain. Most meals served by the central dining room left something to be desired.

I was halfway through starting a simple stew when a knock sounded at the front door. Trepidation filled me. Darrow and his friends would have come straight inside since his powers could have undone all the locks. I made my way past the dining area and living room before stopping in the foyer, unsure whether to answer it.

A loud sigh came from the other side. "I know you're in there."

"Who is it?" I asked, vaguely recognizing the voice.

"Vas—your husband's older, better-looking brother," he replied with a hint of amusement in his voice.

I crossed my arms despite the fact he couldn't see me. "That only makes me think I should definitely keep the door shut."

"We could be allies, you know."

I let out a dry laugh. "Not in this lifetime, Unseelie."

"Either you open this door and speak to me face-to-face, or I'll destroy your wards, which will leave you vulnerable after I depart. Believe it or not, I don't wish harm to befall you."

I hesitated, but I didn't doubt the Unseelie prince could take down the wards eventually, and I didn't want to test my powers against him. It would end in destruction no matter which of us won.

"Fine," I said, undoing the locks and pulling the door open to find the tall, silver-haired man standing a few feet away. "What do you want?"

He took me in, likely noting my appearance now that I didn't have glamour covering me. "You've been hurt recently."

I couldn't hide my surprise. "How do you know?"

"Your skin lacks its full color, and your footsteps when you came to the door were uneven." He clucked his tongue. "What happened?"

"What do you care?" I asked, surprised he'd noticed my unsteady gait. Briauna had promised I'd be back to normal once I had more rest, but I remained a little sore even after another healing. The strain of tending my garden had set me back.

"My brother has probably told you some of my brethren don't want you to open that portal to Earth and retrieve the fountain, but I have other thoughts on the matter. Now that I know you're the first one who can get us there in many centuries, I want you alive and healthy," he said, managing to sound genuine.

I narrowed my eyes. "Oh, really? What is your agenda since I can't believe you care about us restoring the fountain?"

"That's my business, but I promise it won't conflict with your goals."

"You know that's difficult to believe, right?" I asked.

He shrugged, then pulled a folded missive from his trouser pocket, holding it out in a way where half of it extended to the other side of the ward where I could safely take it. If it contained anything dangerous inside, it would have burned as it passed through the protective barrier.

I noted the wax seal, which featured a skull surrounded by stars. How odd.

"Give this to Darrow. If he has any sense, he'll read it and consider my offer," Vas said, taking a step back. "In the meantime, stay inside. It's dangerous out here at the moment with dark elves everywhere."

"Like you?" He was double the trouble being a dark elf and Unseelie.

He merely smiled and walked away.

I shut the door, quickly relocking it. I'd thought I had some inkling of how my future might unfold earlier today, but now I was at a complete loss. There were so many questions I needed to ask my husband the moment things were calm enough. I could only hope he'd return safely soon so I could ask him.

***

Thank you so much for reading *Oaths & Vengeance*. I hope you enjoyed this novel and will consider rating and reviewing it. This helps authors so much.

Don't want to miss Susan Illene's next novel? Sign up for her book release alerts here- http://eepurl.com/-pb-L

You can also join her Facebook fan group here- https://www.facebook.com/groups/1657437984566674/

<u>Dragon's Breath Series</u>:
Stalked by Flames
Dancing with Flames
Forged by Flames
Christmas with Dragons
Captured in Flames
Torn in Flames
Cast by Flames
Galadon (spin-off)

<u>Realm of Zadrya</u>:
Oaths & Vengeance
Wrath & Desire

<u>Sensor Series</u>:
Darkness Haunts
Darkness Taunts
Chained by Darkness (novella)
Darkness Divides
Playing with Darkness (novella)
Darkness Clashes
Facing the Darkness (Kerbasi holiday novella)
Darkness Shatters
Darkness Wanes

<u>Dark Destiny Series</u>:
Destined for Shadows
Destined for Dreams
Destined for Eternity

About the author

Susan Illene served in the U.S. Army for eleven years, working first as a human resources specialist and later as an Arabic linguist. She served primarily in Airborne units and did two deployments to Iraq. After leaving the army, she studied history at the University of Oklahoma. She currently lives with her husband and two sons.

For more information, visit: https://susanillene.com/

To subscribe to Susan's newsletter, go here- http://eepurl.com/-pk_f

If you prefer to only receive email alerts when she releases new books, sign up here- http://eepurl.com/-pb-L

You may also find her at:

Facebook page- https://www.facebook.com/SusanIllene1

Goodreads-
https://www.goodreads.com/author/show/6889690.Susan_Illene

Instagram- https://www.instagram.com/susan_illene/

Acknowledgements

There was an indescribable need for me to write this book, with the characters constantly in my head demanding I tell their story. Many people helped me make it shine. I appreciate my father, who is always happy to help critique chapters. My husband for once again helping keep the boys out of the way whenever he was able during the writing of this novel. Also, to my sons for their constant interruptions, though they somehow manage to inspire me to work anyway. My oldest, Adam, helped me pick the character names and loved helping me develop the types of plants in this world. I must give him some credit for that.

A huge thank you to my editor, Victoria Miller, for her hard work on the book and her amazing enthusiasm for it. She worked really hard to get the edits back quickly, so I could give more time for the ARC readers. Also, to my beta readers—Julie, Abra, and Amanda. All of you went above and beyond this time to really help find any weak areas that needed strengthening so this book could be as great as possible, some of you even going over it multiple times. That meant so much to me!

Thank you to my cover artist, Hannah Sternjakob, for the impressively beautiful cover. I still can't stop looking at it in awe. Rob Donovan for your amazing work on the maps where you definitely went above and beyond, and Jesus Da Silva for the stunning character art that has brought Aella and Darrow to life. The list goes on, and I can't possibly thank (or remember) everyone who has contributed in some way. There are so many of you, but that doesn't mean I don't appreciate your help. And last but not least, thanks to all my readers. Your motivation and love for my books are what keep me going while juggling two young boys.